Rebecca Yarros is the No. 1 *Sunday Times*, *New York Times*, *USA Today* and *Wall Street Journal* bestselling author of over fifteen novels including *Fourth Wing* and *Iron Flame*. She loves military heroes and has been blissfully married to hers for over twenty years.

She's the mother of six children and is currently surviving the teenage years with two of her four hockey-playing sons. When she's not writing, you can find her at the hockey rink or sneaking in some guitar time while guzzling coffee. She and her family live in Colorado with their stubborn English bulldogs, two feisty chinchillas and a Maine Coon cat named Artemis, who rules them all.

Having fostered then adopted their youngest daughter, Rebecca is passionate about helping children in the foster system through her nonprofit, One October, which she co-founded with her husband in 2019. To learn more about their mission to better the lives of kids in foster care, visit www.oneoctober.org.

T0349222

Also by Rebecca Yarros

Empyrean
Fourth Wing
Iron Flame

Flight & Glory
Full Measures
Eyes Turned Skyward
Beyond What Is Given
Hallowed Ground
The Reality of Everything

Renegades
Wilder
Nova
Rebel

Legacy
Point of Origin (Novella)
Ignite (Novella)
Reason to Believe

Muses and Melodies

A Little Too Close

NOVA

REBECCA YARROS

NO.1 *SUNDAY TIMES* BESTSELLING AUTHOR

PIATKUS

PIATKUS

First published in the United States in 2017 by Embrace,
an imprint of Entangled Publishing, LLC
First published in Great Britain in 2024 by Piatkus

1 3 5 7 9 10 8 6 4 2

A CIP catalogue record for this book
is available from the British Library.

ISBN: 978-0-349-44247-1

Printed and bound in Great Britain by Clays Ltd, Elcograf S.p.A.

Papers used by Piatkus are from well-managed forests
and other responsible sources.

Piatkus
An imprint of
Little, Brown Book Group
Carmelite House
50 Victoria Embankment
London EC4Y 0DZ

An Hachette UK Company
www.hachette.co.uk

www.littlebrown.co.uk

To Chase—
There is nothing better in this world than hearing you laugh...
Except maybe seeing you smile or squeezing you tight.
You are a gift for which I am eternally grateful.

Chapter One

DUBAI

This place was surreal, a tiny slice of winter inside an eternal summer. Lights shone down, making the man-made snow inside Ski Dubai glitter, and giving me a twinge of longing for the crisp, clear skies over the Colorado Rockies. Aspen would be opening later this month, but we were half a world away in the Middle East and weren't even due back stateside until Christmas.

I caught sight of the cameraman coming down the slope behind me and increased my speed. Most days I had no problem with cameras in my face 24-7, but today it was pissing me off. Maybe it was because we'd just finished our live show a couple of days ago, or maybe it was everything that happened—the incident that had nearly killed one of my best friends and put another one into police custody. Hell, maybe it was the inability to so much as piss without the cameras following me into the bathroom, but I just wanted a few moments to myself.

Shifting my weight, I took the curve along the run, careful to watch the bite against my snowboard as I hit the icy patch just off the edge of the lift track. The entire run took me a matter of seconds, and it sure as hell wasn't going to help me prep for Nepal, but it was better than nothing, especially considering it was ninety degrees outside.

"I almost forgot how fast you are," Paxton said as he skidded to a stop next to me.

"I've practiced a few times this week. I'm not as rusty as I feared." I shrugged. We'd been docked in Dubai with our Study at Sea program for the last five days, and I'd been here almost every day. It had been my only opportunity to use my snowboard since we left Miami three months ago, and there was no chance in hell that I was passing it up.

"Want to go again?" Pax nodded toward the lift as the cameraman finally made it to the bottom of the run. Good thing we'd be doing most of the Nepal filming from the helicopter and GoPros, because this guy was never going to be able to keep up with me.

"How much time do we have?"

He lifted his jacket sleeve and checked his watch. "About an hour. Enough time to get in another run. Leah starts to freak if we're not on board two hours before departure, so this has to be my last one."

"Yeah, well, that's what happens when you're busy making out with your girlfriend in Istanbul and miss the ship."

A slow smile spread across my best friend's face. "Yeah, well, it was more than worth it. What do you say? One more?"

I looked up the hill at the separate runs Ski Dubai offered and nodded. "Yeah, may as well, right? I'm not getting this chance again for a few weeks."

We headed over to the short lift line and waited our turn,

sticking out like sore thumbs in our custom gear against the rented navy and red suits everyone else wore.

I was more than aware of the camera behind us but did my best to ignore it. This whole documentary—*International Waters*—was for Nick, and nine months of having a camera in my face was nothing compared to the rest of his life in that wheelchair. The movie would carry his name with equal billing as the rest of us Originals—those who had started the Renegades—and would put him on the map with his phenomenal ramp designs and stunt setups. So cameras it was.

"Hey, Nova," a girl ahead of us said with a soft sigh in my direction.

"Hey, princess," I answered with a wink. "You having fun?" I ran her face through my mental black book, wondering if I'd ever hooked up with her.

I felt the strength of Paxton's eye roll next to me. He hated my habit—and had no problem voicing that opinion.

"Oh yeah! It's nice to have a little something cold to bundle up for. It's been so hot everywhere else we've been, right?" The blue-eyed girl batted her overly made-up eyes at me.

"It has," I said. *She's on the ship with us.*

"Well, it's good snuggling weather," she said with a bite of her lower lip, then waved as she got on the lift ahead of us.

"Don't start," I warned Paxton when I saw his mouth open.

He shook his head, and we walked forward for our turn.

"I got the confirmations on the Nepal trip," he told me as we sat on the lift chair.

"Yeah? It actually worked out with the school stuff?" We'd been trying to set up a ski trip to get some snow time in preparation, but since we'd been everywhere around the Mediterranean and Africa the last three months, there hadn't been a lot of opportunities for the white, fluffy stuff.

Our trip to Nepal—the one ride I was focused on for the documentary—all hinged on our school schedule, just like everything else this year.

The chair jolted forward, and we were on our way up the man-made incline.

"It comes during the week of the optional shore excursion. So it'll cost us a week in India, but we'll swing it. We have ten days total, and we'll have to write papers on it to make up for the lost cultural excursions."

I shot him some skeptical side eye. "And Leah was okay with this? Your woman is notoriously anal about school stuff."

That lovesick grin appeared on his face again, and I swallowed the irrational flare of jealousy that erupted in my stomach. Pax deserved happiness, love, the whole damn fairy tale. I was just a little bitter that shit wasn't in the cards for me.

I'd fucked up my only shot at love a long time ago.

"She was until I promised we'd stop for a day at the Taj Mahal. Plus, I booked a heli flight up to the Everest base camp."

"So romantic."

"Hey, Leah sure as hell isn't complaining." He stared ahead for a second and then cocked his head to the side. "But yeah…if you have any suggestions for the girls while we're up there, I'm all ears. I don't exactly see Leah heading to the slopes."

"True. We'll find something they'll enjoy. It's going to kill Penna that she can't ski this time."

"Yeah," Paxton said quietly, and we descended into thoughtful silence.

The air was cold on my face, the joyful sounds of those skiing beneath us echoing off the steel walls of the facility. Leave it to Dubai to build a badass indoor ski resort as part of a mall. Penna should be here with us, not hiding away on board the ship. Pax was right—she was going to wither over the next couple months until that cast came off. "I'm worried about her. She's been damn near silent since she got out of the hospital, which is anything but normal."

"She blames herself," he said.

"She shouldn't," I replied without pause. "Her sister lost it. I love Brooke just as much as you do, but you know it's true. None of what happened the last three months—not the accidents, the sabotage, the fucked-up head games—was Penna's fault."

"How are we going to get her to believe that?"

"By making sure she knows she's part of this team," I answered. "It's always been the four of us—you, me, Nick, and Penna. That wheelchair Nick is in might be permanent, but the one Penna's riding in sure as hell is not. She'll be back raising hell in a few months."

"Physically, maybe. But she's going dark, man. I don't know if we'll get her back in the right head space to compete, and you can bet the X Games are off the table for her. She'll barely be out of a cast in time, let alone in competition shape."

I blew my breath out slowly, watching it steam. "Yeah, well, if anyone is going to get there, it will be Penna. She'll be out of that cast in no time and back on her bike before the docs tell her it's a good idea."

"That's our Rebel," Pax said with a grin, giving a little nod to her stage name.

Wilder, Rebel, Nova, and Nitro…the Original Renegades. We might have started in Paxton's backyard and the local skate park, but we were bigger now, with at least twenty Renegades on the ship and more than a few fledglings. No matter how big we got, it would always come back to the four of us. After a decade of risking our lives together, we were a closer family than my biological one. I would give up anything for them.

You already have.

The lift came to an end, and we jumped onto the luscious snow beneath us. God, I missed the crunch, the flow, the way my body was pushed to its limits with only a board beneath my feet. Not that I didn't love skateboarding, but snowboarding was always going to be my number-one love.

"Did you smooth everything out for Gabe and Alex?" I asked as we studied the options beneath us.

"Yeah. The program wasn't too happy about taking them on at second term, but I leaned pretty heavily on the issue."

I snorted. "Since you own the ship and all."

"That may have helped," he admitted. "I know you need them, so it had to be done. They actually flew in this morning, so they'll be ready to start class with us."

"They're the best big-mountain riders of our generation."

"*You're* the best big-mountain rider of our generation," he corrected.

I shrugged. Maybe I was. Maybe I wasn't. But I knew that there was a difference between cocky and confident, and I needed those guys with me in the Himalayas. I needed their judgment and experience to temper my own.

"Hey, let's hit this run," Pax suggested as the cameras caught up to us, nodding toward the black-labeled slope. "It goes right by the place where Leah's watching."

I laughed. "Sure, we'll go show off for your girlfriend." We traversed to where the black run started while I mentally cursed the camera crew. *Try to keep up on this one.* "Speaking of Leah, did her roommate get here? We probably need to include her on the Nepal shit, right?" There were a ton of moving pieces to get that trip perfect, and now I'd need to add one more.

Paxton stiffened next to me. "Yeah, she's here."

"What's wrong?" I asked, slapping his back. "Her friend cramping your solo time with the missus?"

He shook his head. "Nothing like that."

"Hey, Nova," the same sweetly feminine voice called as she skied over to us. The blonde was back. "We have a little time before the ship leaves port. Want to grab a drink at the bottom of the hill?"

Want to fuck me so I have a story to take home? That was what she was really asking. Usually I wouldn't mind, but something about watching Pax and Leah lately was getting to me.

Which really sucked.

"I think we're pretty tight on time here, but maybe if you grab me back at the ship?" I suggested with a smile and hoped I didn't hurt her feelings.

"I'll be on the pool deck." She grinned. "Oh, and I'm Erin," she offered.

"Nice to meet you," I replied. "I'm—"

"Nova," she answered for me, her girlfriend behind her twittering.

Landon. "Right." She wasn't interested in who I really was, just the persona, which was fine. *But it's not.* Besides, it was better than the girls who thought they'd be more than a one-night stand, be the one to reawaken my iced-over heart.

None of them stood a chance.

None of them were *her.*

I shoved the thought back as far as I could get it in my head—and slammed the door shut. The minute I opened it I was useless, barely functional, and I wasn't going back there anytime soon.

"Well, we'll see you on board," Erin said, giving me a pretty obvious once-over before heading back to the easier slope with her friend.

"You didn't seem too interested," Pax said as he pulled down his goggles.

I did the same, the world taking on the sharpened hue that my specialized lenses gave it. "It's because I'm not."

"Ah." He nodded slowly, like he understood.

He didn't understand shit.

"Ah, what?" I asked, briefly checking around us to make sure the camera crew was out of mic range.

"Maybe you're ready to stop fucking around?"

"Hardly," I snapped.

He shrugged. "She was pretty."

Blond hair. Blue eyes. Yeah, she'd been an eight.

Problem was I wanted an eleven, and I only knew of one in the entire fucking world. One with hair blacker than night, a tight, toned body that had fit mine to a T, and almond-shaped chocolate eyes that made me forget my name, but never hers.

"Yeah, well, she isn't what I want." *Let it go.*

He nodded. "Okay."

"What's that supposed to mean?"

"I said, okay."

"That's not what you meant."

"Stop reading into shit. If you don't want the girl, I really don't care. I wish you'd stop self-medicating, because it's eating you up. But that's none of my business, right?"

My jaw locked. "Let's just go."

"You're a pain in my ass," he said, then rocketed down the hill.

I took a deep breath and tried to calm my mind, but once she was in it there was no going back.

I tried to think of the blonde, to fill my head with her face, her offer, the same way I could use her body later to fill the hole in my soul for a good hour or so, but it was no good.

My head swam with *her* face, *her* eyes, *her* incredibly smart mouth. She would have tossed me a kiss and headed down the hill with Pax. She would keep up with me move for move, pushing me farther, faster.

Two and a half years and my chest still felt like it was caving in whenever I thought about her.

Rachel. I let her name roll through me, allowing her in for just a moment. *Just this ride*, I promised myself as I launched down the run. If I gave myself these thirty seconds with her memory, I could shut off the tap once we hit the bottom.

I moved with the run, wondering where she was, what she was doing. Did she still hate me? I hoped so. I deserved it.

Lord knew I hated myself enough for the both of us.

The problem with love was that once it was gone, there was no filling that hole, no substitute for that euphoria. Losing love came with withdrawal symptoms for which there was no known relief.

At least none that I'd found, anyway.

I crouched on the board, gaining speed.

At least sex dulled the pain momentarily, but maybe… Damn, maybe Paxton was right. I was no closer to moving past her than the day I stupidly walked away from her.

Maybe it was time to man up and deal with the shit hand I'd dealt myself.

Just ahead of me, Paxton waved up at the glass, and I looked up, doing the same as I neared where Leah stood watching. She waved to him and then to me as someone came to stand next to her.

Holy shit. It can't be.

Her hair brushed her delicate shoulders, the streaks of purple evident from down here. My head swiveled, trying to keep her in view as I passed.

That pixie face, those angled cheeks, that pert nose, those perfectly curved lips—I'd know them anywhere.

Her hands pressed against the glass—

Wham! My legs were jarred a millisecond before I slammed into the wall. I bounced back, landing on my ass.

"Watch out!" someone yelled in English right before they hit me with their pole.

I'd seriously fallen in the middle of the surface lift—the

only ski lift in the park that pulled the riders up the slope by rope and pommel.

I pushed back, getting the hell out of the way, and looked over to where Leah stood at the window. Alone.

"Are you okay?" she mouthed, her eyes wide with worry.

For fuck's sake, was I hallucinating now? The moment I let my memories rule me for a few seconds, she started appearing?

I nodded to Leah and got to my feet. Was I so far gone that my brain was seeing what it wanted?

"You okay?" a girl asked as she slid by me on the pommel, her skis coming within a foot of my board.

"Yep, thank you," I said, tipping my head. *That's right, ladies, I have four X Games medals, three of which are in snowboarding, and I ran into a goddamned wall.*

Get a grip. I headed down the slope and met up with Pax at the bottom of the slope.

"You take a detour?" he asked.

"Yeah, something like that," I replied, knowing he hadn't seen me make an utter ass out of myself. No doubt he'd see it later when Bobby—the director of our documentary—got his hands on the footage.

Pax didn't question me, just gave me a what-the-hell look. "Time to get back. You game? You look a little pale."

"I'm fine," I said.

They were the only words I spoke while we got out of our gear.

"Landon, are you okay?" Leah asked, racing over to me as we walked out of the frigid air into the dry desert heat.

"What happened?" Pax asked as he wrapped his arm around her.

"Nothing. I'm fine," I answered, giving her a smile. At least, I think I did. I wasn't sure, since I felt numb just about everywhere.

That numbness didn't go away as we were driven back to where our ship was docked. It didn't go away while Pax told me all about our new numbers since he'd just pulled off the first-ever triple front flip on a motocross bike a few days ago during our live exhibition. Our YouTube subscribers were way up and so were Instagram and Snapchat, but our video views were through the roof.

It didn't go away when they scanned my ID card as I boarded the huge cruise ship we'd called home since August. All I saw as I walked into our massive, three-bedroom suite at the back of the ship was the replay my brain wouldn't shut off: the glimpse of the woman I'd seen next to Leah.

"Landon!" Pax shouted, breaking through my brain fog.

My head jerked toward him. "What? Damn, you don't have to yell."

"Apparently I do, since I called your name about three times first."

"I said, I'm fine."

His eyes narrowed. "Right, but I asked if you wanted to go to the pool?"

I blinked. "I need to work out."

"You just finished boarding. Skip the gym for one day and come hang out. I know you're prepping for Nepal, but one day isn't going to kill you."

He was right. I could skip one day. Besides, I was so distracted that I was liable to go flying off the treadmill or some stupid shit that was on par with running into a wall.

"Okay. Pool. The pool is good."

"Hey, maybe you'll find the snow bunny," he teased as he headed up the stairs to his room.

"No snow bunny," I said quietly to myself as I went into my room. Another girl wasn't going to help me in this situation—not when *she* was all I could think about. I'd been through it before; I just needed to clear my head. I stripped out of my clothes and changed into trunks before I met Pax in our living room. Bobby had the camera crew in a meeting at the dining room table. If we hurried we could get some undocumented time.

"Seriously, you're being weird," Pax said while we took the elevator to the pool deck. "Leah said she saw you hit a wall while we were boarding. Do you think we need to get your head checked out? She's already up at the pool saving us some lounges, but we can meet her later."

"I'm fine," I repeated.

"So you keep saying."

Music was blaring on the pool deck as we stepped into the ninety-degree heat. The sun beat down onto my skin, but it did nothing to warm the numbness that I couldn't kick.

Maybe Pax was right and I'd hit my head.

The crowd was thick, and the music was loud—it usually was as we were leaving port—and Pax disappeared to find Leah. I surveyed the gyrating masses and wished I could feel a little of their excitement.

First term was over, there were two more to go, and we were headed toward the Indian Ocean. It was all pretty overwhelming if I stopped to really think about it. Then again, stopping to think about anything was what had gotten me into this situation.

"There you are!" The blonde from the slope bounced over, her tits hanging out of her triangle top.

"Hey." I forced a smile as she looped an arm around my waist.

"Want to get a drink with me?"

Not really.

"You know, I think I'm going to—"

"Oh, come on. The bar is right over here!" she said, turning us around.

Ice hit my bare chest and slid down my abs to my trunks

as I sucked in a lungful of air. Holy shit, that was cold.

"I'm so sorry!"

Her voice hit me with the force of the hurricane that she was, and as she looked up, I lost what breath I'd managed to take in.

Her eyes widened, panic running across her beautiful, so-familiar face.

"Oh God," she whispered.

The purple streaks in her hair rested against the smooth line of her chin, and her lips were parted in a look of shock that I was sure mirrored mine.

My entire world narrowed to the woman standing in front of me. Even my heartbeat stilled in reverence to the moment. How was she here? After all this time, she was close enough to touch, and all I could do was stare at her, like if I blinked she would disappear.

A thousand emotions crashed through me, fast enough to give me whiplash, long enough to sting me with the force of a billion needles, and none were able to steady me. Unadulterated joy and wonder at seeing her after all this time, fear that she was going to toss what was left of those margaritas in my face, and the most overpowering urge to kiss her, to beg her to forgive the mistakes I'd made as a stupid kid and forget the last two years we'd been apart.

But the biggest was sheer and utter relief that I could breathe again, that the numbness I'd felt since the slopes was gone, my skin tingling everywhere as if the blood had finally rushed back into the starving capillaries.

It all came down to one word.

"Rachel?"

Chapter Two

DUBAI

I had thought I was prepared for the inevitability of this moment.

I was so wrong.

Breathe, I told myself—not to calm down, but to push oxygen into my lungs before I passed out. Planning on seeing Landon and coming face-to-face with him were two completely different things. One was purely logical, and the other…well, there wasn't a single nerve in my body that didn't come alive at his nearness.

Now say something—anything.

"Hey, Landon," I said quietly, looking up into shocked hazel eyes. I'd almost forgotten how beautiful they were, how the color changed with his mood or what he was wearing.

Which wasn't a lot at the moment.

Well, he was wearing my margaritas. They were currently

dripping down the insanely hard lines of his abdomen, paying no mind to the myriad of tattoos that colored his skin.

Did he cover up the one he got for me? Not that I could see it under all that bright green muck sliding down his body.

I jerked my eyes back to his, but he was still just standing there...staring. Okay, maybe this wasn't going to be as bad as I thought. "Well, it's good to see you," I said with a shaky smile, taking in every detail of his Hemsworth-worthy face. He'd lost what little softness he'd had since I'd seen him last, leaving the strong lines of his nose and chin, but those lips still looked as soft as ever and just as practiced at smooth lines and smoother exits.

I tried to block out the barrage of memories, but they assaulted me, pelting me with the low timbre of his voice when we would spend hours locked in conversation, the look in his eyes the first time he'd told me he loved me, the feel of his hands on my skin. No matter how hard I'd tried to keep everything locked up tight, it all came rushing back, overloading me with emotions I couldn't afford to explore. Ever.

I'd been on board for a week, known he was here—known the incredibly sneaky lengths Paxton had gone to get me here—and avoided him like the plague he was. I was here for Leah, for me, to touch my own history and find my birthplace, for a hundred different reasons that didn't involve Landon.

"What...how...?" His normally smooth lines were absent.

A thousand times I'd practiced this in my head. How cool I was going to be. How dismissive. How I'd show him that maybe he'd wounded me, but I wasn't broken. My imagination had nothing on this moment, or my physical reaction to seeing him.

Why didn't you tell me you were leaving? Why couldn't you choose me? Why wasn't I enough for you? Every question eighteen-year-old me had cried into my pillow reared its ugly head, and I beat them all back down, swallowing past my suddenly dry throat that had zero to do with the desert heat.

"Um, do you know each other?" the blonde he had his arm wrapped around asked. *I wonder if he even knows her name.*

A wry smile twisted my lips. Different year. Different country. Same Landon. "We used to."

He was still shell-shocked, and I took what little advantage I had. "Well, I guess I'll see you around." I ripped my gaze away from him, my chest aching like he'd left me yesterday instead of two and a half years ago.

I managed to turn and walk away, dropping our margarita cups in the trash. I'd find Leah and explain later, but right now I had to get the hell out of here. The elevator was ahead, maybe only ten feet away when he caught up with me, no blonde in sight.

"Rachel!" he said, his fingers brushing my upper arm like he'd changed his mind midreach.

So close, I thought as the elevator doors closed ahead of me.

I turned slowly, trying to visualize locking up my emotions with a row of dead bolts. He wasn't getting through. "What can I do for you?" I asked his pecs. His chest was safer than those soul-melting eyes.

"Rachel," he whispered.

Inch by inch, I drew my gaze up until I met his over a head above me. Landon's light brown, finger-tousled hair towered above my five-foot-two frame, but the difference had always made me feel protected, like he was a mountain no one could move. Turned out I couldn't really move him, either. "What?"

"I…don't know what to say," he admitted, a look of awe and fear on his face.

Me, either, eighteen-year-old me called out from where I'd locked her away.

"Wow. I have to admit that I expected some smoother lines from you."

He shook his head a little and blinked, like he expected me to disappear, like I was some figment of his imagination. "I wasn't expecting you."

"That's pretty obvious. Look, we don't have to see each other. You stay to your classes, and I'll stay to mine. I'm sure we'll have some overlap with the whole Leah/Paxton thing, but my plan is to generally ignore you." I had to in order to survive.

His eyes narrowed. "Leah/Paxton thing?"

I arched an eyebrow and tried to calm the pounding of my heart. It felt like the damn thing had wings, and it was hammering against my ribs to get out of my chest and back to the one person it had always belonged to. *Hell, no.* "They haven't told you?"

He stepped forward, and I retreated. "Told me what?"

We continued our dance—I backed up and he followed. Each step took me closer to the elevator, closer to getting the hell away from him.

"Rachel, would you stop? I'm not going to stalk you into the elevator."

"Yeah, you're usually a walk-away kind of guy."

He winced. "Really?"

The horn blew, and the ship launched from the dock. "I have some pretty personal experience with that side of you." I looked behind him, where the blonde was staring at us with her arms crossed under her breasts. "And from the looks of things, nothing's changed."

"Rachel…" He reached for me, and I stepped back, turning slightly to hit the down button on the elevator.

"No. You don't get to *Rachel* me. You don't get to *anything* me. You get to be all Nova-y, and I get to stay the hell away from you for the next six months."

"Well, your tactics have worked pretty well, considering this is the first time I'm seeing you and we're three months into the trip."

Did he have to look wounded? Like I'd done something dastardly by hiding away from him? "I only got here last week."

His forehead puckered, and I fought back my urge to smooth those lines with my fingers like I had when we were together. He wasn't mine to touch. He wasn't mine in any form of the word.

"Last week? Funny, that's when Leah's roommate..." His eyes widened to a nearly impossible size.

"Put that together, did you?" The elevator *dinged* open behind me, and I shamelessly retreated into it, seeing the camera crew heading our direction. I needed space, and I needed it *now*.

"Wait." He lunged forward, stopping the elevator door with his arm. "I don't understand."

"Paxton will fill you in," I said and pushed the close-door button.

"Paxton?" He shook his head again.

I blew out a frustrated sigh, realizing there were other students in the elevator. "Paxton Wilder. Your best friend. Come on, Nova—"

"Landon," he snapped. "I've never been Nova to you. Not in that way."

You're like a supernova—an explosion so bright no one can see past you, I'd told him once after he'd won a competition. But like my love, that name had been twisted into something entirely different. Now he was *Casanova*... and no longer mine.

"What we were to each other sure as hell doesn't matter anymore," I countered. "Me being here isn't some act of fate, or God. It's an act of Paxton. If you want answers, go to him.

Once this door shuts, my plan is never to speak to you again."

"You think that's possible? That I'm just going to ignore you?"

"It's worked pretty damn well for the last two and a half years."

Someone behind me coughed to hide a laugh.

Landon glared over my shoulder, and then that arrogant Nova smirk appeared, which twisted my insides in opposite directions—one wanting to smack him and the other inconveniently remembering what this man was capable of doing to my body. "Rachel."

"What?" I shouted. I would pay money to make him stop saying my name like that—like he still knew me, still wanted me, still loved me. Like the last two years had just evaporated and we were still talking about our future in the apartment he'd left me holding the lease for. He didn't get to say my name like he hadn't drastically altered the very fabric of my being—I wasn't that girl anymore.

"We're at sea for the next four days, so it's not like you can leave the ship. This isn't over." He leaned back, removing his arm from the door.

The doors started to slide shut, and he held my gaze, something heating there. Guess the shock of seeing me had worn off.

"This was over a long time ago," I said quietly.

He flinched as the doors shut.

I closed the door to our suite and leaned back against it, letting my head thump on the barrier. *It hurts. God, it hurts so badly.* My hand rested under my heart, praying it would find some semblance of a normal rhythm, but it kept up with my lungs, which worked overtime, bringing giant gasps of air into my chest. Even my throat was on fire from this lump that wouldn't go the hell away. My face scrunched as I fought back tears. God, I hated crying. What was even worse was that it wasn't that I was sad. No, my eyes were prickling from anger, from embarrassment, from the pain in my chest from seeing him, from…the myriad of emotions that my body didn't know how to process.

I drew air into my lungs in a steady stream. *You're stronger than this. You are iron. You are concrete. You are invincible.*

All true, but he was my one stupid weakness.

Somehow in the span of those few minutes, he'd managed to slice open my soul and set me back years. How was this fair? He was the one who'd walked out without a word, leaving me collegeless, with a pissed-off family I had to go crawling back to and a lease I couldn't afford, but from the looks of it, he was *fine*. More than fine, really, and I was the one trying to get over the newly opened fissure in my heart…again.

"Rachel?" Penna's voice came from the living room, and my stomach sank. If there was one person on this ship who hated me more than Wilder, it was Penna. She'd despised me for years—since the moment she'd realized that while I was dating Wilder, I was deeply in love with his best friend.

She'd also become my roommate when Leah moved to Pax's room a couple of days ago. I understood why—Penna needed time to heal out of the public eye, and our suite was off-limits to the rabid camera crew, but man…it was awkward around here at times.

"Yeah, it's me," I answered, walking down the hallway of our suite as I composed myself. The marble floors, double bedrooms, and full amenities were way overboard, but I wasn't complaining. Wilder had gone to a shit ton of trouble to get me here. I just hated that he'd used my best friend to do it.

But he'd fallen in love with her, so I guess it all worked out.

"Hey," Penna said from her wheelchair. Her leg was casted to her thigh and elevated by one support of the chair, and her superlong blond hair was piled onto her head in a knot. Injured or not, she was ridiculously model-worthy beautiful but still rode a motocross bike better than most of the guys.

"Hey," I echoed, sinking into the plush leather sofa and stretching my legs out onto the coffee table.

She turned her attention back to her book, settling us into an awkward quiet.

Nervous energy coursed through me, and I sat up, leaning my elbows on my knees to hold my head. God, this was stupid. This was ridiculous. I had six months here with him. Watching him seduce everything in a skirt. How the hell was I going to handle that? Handle *him*?

"You saw him," Penna said quietly, putting her book into her lap.

I nodded. "I ran into him. Literally. There were margaritas involved."

"Did the alcohol help?"

I looked up. "It ended up all over him."

She snorted, the first laugh I'd heard from her since I got here last week. "Good. Not that he needed it. He's salty enough as it is."

I laughed. "That he is."

"How are you?" Her words were choppy, and I knew how much they cost her.

"Are you honestly asking? Because I'm pretty sure if you weren't in that wheelchair you'd have no issue throwing me overboard."

Her head tilted. "I've considered it."

The last thing I could handle right now was Penna's obvious disgust with my presence, and this was the only place on the ship I was safe from running into Landon. *Fantastic.*

The door flew open, hitting the wall. "Rach?" Leah

yelled down the hall two seconds before she barreled in. "Oh my God! Landon and Pax are going at it right now. What happened?" She plopped on the couch next to me, her legs bare, revealing the parallel scars down the fronts of her legs that she'd kept hidden until this trip—until Paxton had brought out the brave in her. Her whiskey-colored eyes were wide, her brown hair in windblown disarray. Man, I'd missed her every day that she'd been here while I was back in L.A.

"I may have run into Landon."

"Yeah, I got that part," she said. "How are you?"

"I'm fine," I lied.

She laughed but stopped when I glared at her. "I'm sorry, but after he saw you today on the slopes, that's all he kept saying. 'I'm fine.'"

"He saw you on the slopes?" Penna asked, her book forgotten in her lap. This was the longest I'd seen her engaged in any conversation since the accident—since her sister broke her heart.

"He did," I answered with an involuntary smile. "He looked up to wave to Leah, and I'd just gotten there. I had no clue he'd actually see me. But he looked like he'd seen a ghost."

"And then he ran into the wall," Leah said, her laughter rolling through her shoulders.

"No way!" Penna exclaimed, another laugh tumbling out. "Like into the *wall* wall? The side of the slope?"

"Exactly," I said. "And then some girl ran over him on the lift."

I wasn't even near him, and his luck was already turning to shit.

"Oh my God," Penna said, her laughter even louder. "Then what did he do?"

"He looked for you," Leah said to me. "I mean, you were gone by the time he pulled himself out of the lift path, but he looked."

My laughter died as that kaleidoscope of emotion turned in my chest.

"But what was weirder was that he didn't ask about you," Leah continued. "When I saw him, he never asked who was standing next to me."

"He doesn't care," I said out of habit and defense.

"No, it wasn't that. He was shaken. It was almost as if he thought he'd hallucinated you...like it had happened before."

I met my best friend's level stare. "That would imply he ever thought about me to begin with."

"Rachel—"

"No!" I snapped. "He left me without saying good-bye. Left me standing there like an idiot in that ER with five rejected calls, ten unanswered texts, a shredded acceptance letter to Dartmouth, a fractured wrist from falling off our brand-new kitchen counter, and a broken heart—all while the ink on our lease, that I couldn't afford on my own, was still wet. I sat in that apartment for days, knowing he'd gone back to the Renegades but just hoping he would still come home to me, too. Hoping Wilder had reneged on his goddamned ultimatum, or that I would at least get an explanation, or a good-bye. Do you have any idea how that feels—to be ghosted? Abandoned? Treated like you aren't good enough for his love, his time, or even a fucking phone call? Leah, you of all people know what it was like for me to go back to my parents—to grovel and plead for help when I'd thrown my independence in their face. I gave up *everything* for Landon, and it wasn't enough. So please don't imply that he ever gave me a second thought."

"You should let him explain," Penna said softly.

"You can't weigh in on this," I told her. "Not if you want us to have a quasi friendship."

She struggled with keeping quiet. I could tell by the set

lines of her mouth, the way her hands gripped the sides of her book. "Okay," she finally said. "But there are two sides to every story."

Leah glanced between us and clapped her hands. "New subject!" Her eyes lit with excitement. "Pax arranged a trip to Nepal during the optional excursion week in India."

Penna tensed, and my eyes flickered toward hers, which were pointed at her cast.

"Okay?"

"We're all going! Well, if you want to. He found a great spa for Penna and me, and I hear there's some fabulous skiing…"

My eyes narrowed at her. "You're dangling the carrot. You know how much I love to ski."

"I do," she admitted.

"Landon will be there."

"He will…it's actually his trip. He's hung up on boarding some ridgeline up by Everest, and this is his shot. He thinks it would put the documentary over the top."

He couldn't mean… I shut down my train of thought. For God's sake. I'd been in his presence all of one time and I was already concerned about him. I had no business even thinking about him, or wondering if he was actually going to try to hit the Shangri-La spine wall he'd always talked about. It was impossibly high, impossibly steep, and offered a high possibility of death.

"Ugh." I leaned my head on the back of the couch. "I can't escape him, can I?"

"Not if you want all the perks that come with traveling with the Renegades," Penna said. "And if I recall correctly, you were always ready to jump in on anything we were working on. Hell, I think you were more fearless than Landon some days."

She said it softly, without malice. Maybe this roommate stuff would work after all.

"I do love it," I admitted.

"Do you think you can handle being around him so much?" Leah asked. "I'm still willing to leave if you need to. I love Paxton, but I hate what he did—tricking us both to get you on board."

I squeezed her hand. She'd suffered so much in the last few years, and it wasn't fair to take this from her. I could endure six months of hell for her—for the chance to touch a piece of my history after months of research, digging through my parents' papers, looking for the location of that orphanage in South Korea, trying to be as covert as possible so I wouldn't upset Mom... Was I really going to let Landon ruin that?

"I'll be fine. I can handle being around him."

A flicker of relief passed through her eyes, and she loosened her grip on my hand. "Okay. Then how do you want to handle things? Pax wants to include you on the trips."

"Of course he does. He wants me accessible for Landon," I snapped and then grimaced. "Sorry."

"Don't be. You can growl at my boyfriend all you want. He deserves whatever you want to dish at him for this."

"It's fine. I'll only see him on shore excursions. I can duck him the rest of the time."

"Well..." Leah started.

"What now?"

"This might not be the best time to tell you that you're also in two of the same classes this term," Penna answered. "So you'll be around him for those classes, shore excursions, our trips, and any field studies those classes have."

"Fuck my life."

"I figured you would say that," Leah said, squeezing my hand. "Still okay?"

I nodded slowly. "Just like you, I'm a lot stronger than I used to be. Besides, just because I have to be around him doesn't mean I have to talk to him."

"Rachel," Leah cajoled.

"He can be pretty insistent…and convincing," Penna said.

"Yeah, well, I can be as stubborn as he is, and I've had way more practice at ignoring him than he has at seeking me out. There's nothing that guy can do to force me to talk to him."

I didn't miss the glance Penna and Leah shared.

"I'm serious," I said.

"I know," Leah answered. "Your stubbornness has never been up for debate."

"If I have to be stuck in this thing," Penna said, nodding toward her cast with a slow smile, "at least I'll have something entertaining to watch."

How hard could it be to ignore Landon Rhodes?

I had the feeling I was about to find out.

Chapter Three

AT SEA

"What the fuck did you do?" I asked Paxton as I slammed the door behind us, leaving the cameras in the hallway. I didn't give a shit if our producer, Bobby, fined us for banning him from the suite—it was either that or I have this conversation with Pax in the fucking bathroom.

I loved Nick, and for him, I would endure the cameras for stunts, preparation, classes, hell, even at the bar where I scored my hookups. But Rachel? No one got to drag her out and air our shit for a documentary.

"Okay," Pax said, putting his hands up like he was under arrest. "Don't kill me."

"Don't kill you? How the hell can I kill you if I need you to give me answers?" I shouted, uncaring if our neighbors heard us. Given the parade of women I'd had in and out of here, they were used to far worse sounds coming through their walls.

"Let's have a beer," Pax suggested.

I silently seethed while he popped the tops on two Coronas and shoved lime wedges through the bottle openings. Then I chugged half the bottle. Seeing Rachel up close had hit me like a punch to the nuts. She was still so damn beautiful, her frame and face perfect, delicate porcelain, but she had a steel core that I more than admired. She was a tiny piece of dynamite, smooth and pretty but capable of blowing your damn head off.

God, I'd loved that about her.

She was a puzzle I'd never figured out. She'd never bored me, always left me craving her, wanting more, and chasing her down. Given the physical reaction I'd had the minute I'd realized it was really her—the way my heart lurched toward hers like a damned magnet—it was safe to say that hadn't changed.

But the pure hatred shining from those deep brown eyes of hers was definitely different.

"You calm?" Pax asked from behind the bar, using it as a shield, no doubt. Even the bar wouldn't save him from me. He was more built than I was, but I had a good four inches and twenty pounds on him.

"Barely. Explain. Now."

He nodded and took a swig of his beer. "Okay. Remember when we started this idea…"

"A year ago?" I clarified.

"Yeah, once the ship was purchased and UCLA agreed to sign on for the academics, and we knew it was going to work, we were sending out invites to apply, right?"

"Sure," I answered. "That time period was a blur. We were contemplating dropping out of UCLA, prepping for the Winter X Games, so I guess I don't really remember."

He nodded. "Exactly. We needed to fill the ship, so I

sent out thousands of flyers to colleges as well as individual invites to apply. I may have sent that invite to Rachel and her roommate…Leah."

My head snapped up from where I'd been peeling the label on the bottle. "You targeted Rachel?"

He didn't flinch. "I did."

"How could you? *Why* would you? How did you even know where she was?" The questions fired out of me faster than he could answer. Did he want her back after all this time? Now that he was with Leah?

"She went to Dartmouth."

I shook my head. "She declined the acceptance." *Because of me.*

"Her father has a friend in the admissions office. He figured you'd leave her—"

"Be careful what you say here, brother." The warning was more of a growl. "There is a line, and you're about two seconds away from crossing it."

He didn't back down, probably because he knew I'd wronged him way worse than he'd wronged me. "So they left her spot open for an additional month. During that month…"

"I left her." *You proved her father right.*

He nodded, his mouth tightening into a grimace.

We both knew why I had—the ultimatum Pax had thrown down: I could have Rachel or I could have the Renegades, but I couldn't have both. I'd chosen my brain over my heart, and the latter hadn't worked since.

We walked a tightrope, knowing that if we wanted to remain friends, there were things we could never talk about. After all, Rachel had been his girlfriend, but she'd been the love of my life. What I couldn't wrap my head around was that while I'd been blocking every thought of her in my head, he'd been tracking her down.

"And you know this how?"

"Leah. They met at the orthopedist's office the week after you showed up in Vegas. Then they roomed together at Dartmouth and have been best friends ever since."

"How did you know how to send the invite to her?" I asked. "I couldn't find her."

"You didn't look," he said quietly.

"Because of you!" I shouted, slamming my fists into the bar. The sting radiated up my arms, and I welcomed the pain. "I fucked you over. I stole your girl. I know that. You gave the ultimatum, and I came back to the Renegades."

"But you left your heart with her," he said.

"This isn't up for discussion. We agreed on that a long time ago." Emotions were too tangled when it came to Rachel, to what we'd done to Paxton, to what I'd done to Rachel to return to the Renegades. He was prying open the door I'd been leaning against for over two years, and the shit escaping from the blackened area that used to be my heart was ugly. Oh, who the fuck was I kidding? Rachel had blown the roof off that lockbox the moment I looked into those endless brown eyes.

"We have to talk about it. I know you don't want to, but you are my best friend, and I've watched little pieces of you die off since you came back. You've fucked every girl you could get your hands on, and it's not for fun—don't give me that bullshit. And that's not even the worst—the risks you take…you're going to get yourself killed."

"You should be one to talk," I accused.

"Right, only because we haven't been near the slopes for you to kill yourself on that board. I agreed to the Nepal excursion because I know it's what you need for this documentary."

"It's for Nick," I argued. Boarding that ridgeline we'd mapped out would put the documentary over the top and he'd be able to write his own ticket as a consultant in our industry.

Since it was a stunt for our team that put him in a wheelchair, it was our team that would make sure his future was whatever he wanted it to be. That's what family did for each other.

"Bullshit, it's for you. That level of danger…it's like you don't care if you live through it. You're numb, detached, and I'm sick of watching you take recklessness to another level."

"And you thought getting Rachel here would fix that?"

"Yes, since she's what you're looking for, right? I didn't understand it years ago, when you two were sneaking around behind my back, but now that I love Leah, I get it. There's nothing and no one that could have stopped me from going after her. You loved Rachel, and I realize now what it must have cost you to walk away from her."

I braced my hands on the counter, my fingers digging into the wood. "So Leah's scholarship, and all that shit about keeping her close when we first got on board…"

He sighed and rubbed his hand over his black hair. "When Rachel got mono and didn't show up in Miami, I knew I had to keep Leah close and happy. If she left, there was no way Rachel would show up for second term. I also needed Leah to help me with my grades."

"So you used her?" A dark feeling I didn't like rolled through my stomach.

"At first," he admitted softly. "But I fell in love with her, and everything changed."

"And then she found out, right? When Rachel showed up? Jesus. That's why you were such an asshole last week. That was why you altered the trailer for the documentary to be all about you falling for her. So she'd see it at the expo and give you a second chance."

He nodded.

"You're a manipulative asshole."

"I have no regrets," he said. "I brought Rachel here for *you* to get a second chance. I know she blocked you on social media, and I know you haven't gone after her because of us—not just me, but the Renegades. And I know now how wrong it was to ever give you that stupid fucking ultimatum."

For the first time since I'd stolen my best friend's girl, I felt like there was an open, honest line between us, and as pissed as I was at him, I was also blown away that he'd gone through all of this for me, especially since it involved the one person we'd both agreed to never talk about. Him, because I'd hurt him so badly by going behind his back with her. Me, because I couldn't bear to hear her name from his mouth. I didn't care that they'd been together for five months—she had *always* been mine.

"You're seriously pushing me at your ex."

He shrugged. "She was always more of *your* ex. I..." He took a deep breath. "I was never that heartbroken over Rachel. I liked her, but it was what happened between you and me that broke me."

"And now with Rachel here? Everything we've worked for?" Was he risking the Renegades by bringing her here? Our friendship?

"I'm honestly okay. I have Leah, and there is no one on this earth better for me than she is."

"You would walk away from the Renegades for Leah," I said as fact, not question.

"In a heartbeat."

I fidgeted with the label. "I walked away from Rachel. It decimated me, but I did it." And she would never forgive me. I'd seen it in her eyes.

"You had your reasons."

"She doesn't know them."

"Then tell her. It doesn't have to be today, or tomorrow. You've got six months with her living right down the hall."

"She hates me."

"There's a fine line between hate and love, my friend."

I nodded slowly.

"Unless you don't want her anymore?" Paxton asked quietly. "If that's the case, then mend your fences as friends and we just…move past this."

"That's not it," I fired back, my stomach in knots. "I've never stopped wanting Rachel—missing her. There's no one who knows me better than she does. No one challenges me like she does or gives me the peace she can. Hell yes, I want her. But it wasn't like I could really talk about it with you guys."

"I know, and I'm sorry."

I looked up in surprise. Paxton never apologized. Ever.

He met my gaze. "I am sorry that you were hurt, and that I was too selfish and too pissed to realize it. I'm sorry that it took me this long to try to fix things, but you are my best friend, and you deserve to be happy. If Rachel is that happiness, then I'm all for it."

"She won't even talk to me. That ship sailed a long time ago."

"*This* ship is still at sail, and will be for the next six months." He smirked. "You're called Nova for a reason, Casanova. You've wooed every woman who comes within fifteen feet of you."

"Except Leah and Penna," I clarified.

"Penna would punch you in the face," he said with a smile. "And I'd kill you if you went near Leah." All trace of humor was gone for a second.

"Yeah, I know." Not that Leah wasn't beautiful, she just… wasn't Rachel. No one had been Rachel. No matter how hard I'd tried to move on, she was the woman I measured everyone else against. They all came up short.

"My point is, if you want her, woo the fuck out of her."

"And when she shoots me down?"

He grinned. "Woo her even harder."

Woo her. Rachel had never fallen for my crap. She thrived on honesty, passion, and a little danger.

My head was still reeling from seeing her, realizing that she was less than two hundred feet away, but I wasn't stupid. Even if nothing happened between us, if all I could do was make her understand why I left, then it would be worth it.

I just had to start by getting her to talk to me.

Good thing I was a persistent kind of guy.

Chapter Four

RACHEL

AT SEA

"I'm seriously bummed about the beverage situation," I told Leah the next day as I evil-eyed my Pepsi.

"I promise that while we're exploring Sri Lanka, you're not going to be thinking about Cherry Coke." She flipped a page in her economics book and didn't even look up. Her focus was incredible, especially since we sat in a crowded cafeteria with the ocean directly in front of us. Maybe she was immune to the view. After all, she'd been on board for three months already. I was still entranced with…well, everything.

"I'm not sure I'll be exploring with you," I said as I moved my fries over and squeezed a small puddle of ketchup onto my plate.

Leah slammed her book shut. "What do you mean? We planned this whole trip together." Her eyes narrowed. "You don't want to be around Landon."

I dipped my fry, then bit and savored the deliciousness. There was something about having American comfort food when you weren't anywhere near America that had me ready to hug the ship's chef.

"Don't avoid the question by molesting your food," Leah ordered.

"Fine. I don't want to be around Landon. I already have to be with him for two classes, and I don't really want him included in all of my sailing around the world memories."

She narrowed her eyes at me while she chewed thoughtfully.

"Do you want to know what I think?" she finally asked.

"Nope," I said, popping another fry into my mouth. That cheeseburger looked really good, too.

"Well, I'm going to tell you, anyway."

"I figured as much." I sucked down a sip of my Pepsi and waited. The best and worst part of having Leah as a best friend was that she didn't pull punches. She had no problem calling me out on my bullshit.

"I don't think you ever got over him."

My chest heaved, and it took every muscle in my body to keep the soda from flying out of my nose. Somehow I managed to safely swallow. "Seriously?"

"When we met, it was right after Landon left you, and Brian had just died."

"Yeah, we were both wrecks." I loved that she could say Brian's name now without crying. Losing her boyfriend in a horrific car crash had shut her down in every way possible, and I had Wilder to thank for her progress. One more check mark in his pro column.

She reached over and took my hand with a gentle squeeze. "I was a wreck. You were distant, cold to everyone in the world but me, but you held yourself together. You held *me* together for those first months at Dartmouth and then helped me figure out how to live again."

"Leah…" I never had words when she said stuff like that. She'd been so wounded then, barely surviving, and now here she was a hell of a lot more stable than I was.

"You were so busy taking care of me and my grief that you didn't give yourself time to process yours. Between classes and moving and, well…me, you threw all you had into everything *but* dealing with losing Landon."

I crossed my arms in front of my chest like they could fend off her truths.

"Don't get all defensive," she chided. "You're amazing, and stronger than I ever could be. I just think that maybe there's more going on than you're willing to clue me in on — or maybe admit to yourself. You'd never even told me his name, or what happened, and we've lived together for over two years. All I knew was that a guy broke your heart the same day you broke your wrist, and he wasn't up for discussion."

I looked out at the Arabian Sea, watching the waves crest as we cut through the water, and tried to let her words sink in. Was she right? Sure, I'd thrown everything Landon-related into a heartbreak-proof box and shoved it so deep I couldn't even find the thing, but that didn't mean I'd never gotten over him. Did it?

"I probably should have talked to you about him. But you had so much on your shoulders then, you didn't need my issues weighing on you, too. Maybe I used you to hide from my own shit. And maybe I liked that he was blocked out of every aspect of my life at Dartmouth, almost as if another person had loved him," I admitted. Taking a breath to steady my nerves, I chose to rip the scab off and open myself to Leah the way she had done countless times. "What makes this almost unbearable is that I see him, and the memories come crashing back. I hear his voice, and I remember every conversation. But if I think about it, really give myself a moment, then it's just this giant vat of pain and embarrassment."

"Embarrassment?"

I laughed, and it wasn't pretty. "How much has Wilder told you?"

"He just gave me a general overview of what happened, and then told me he forced Landon to choose between you and the Renegades."

My stomach fell. "And Landon chose them. Eventually."

"I'm so sorry."

I waved her off. "Don't be. I learned to depend on myself, to guard my heart, and I met you. Landon and I…well, we're both better off for what he did." My voice trailed off, as if I couldn't tell the lie at full volume.

"You're not, and I know he's not."

"What do you mean?" I abandoned the fry that was halfway to my mouth and looked longingly at the cheeseburger. I was so hungry that I was going to have to talk with my mouth full soon if Leah insisted on keeping this conversation going.

"Pax told me that Landon's been a miserable asshole since he came back. That he was unfocused, and then started to fill the void…" She blushed.

"There's a reason they call me the curse. And don't worry, I know exactly how he filled that *void*." Landon was well known in the extreme sports community, and my father hadn't kept his Casanova reputation from me. He called it "congratulating me on dodging a bullet." I called it rubbing salt in an already gaping wound.

I was apparently easily replaceable by any woman with a heartbeat and two legs.

"They call you a curse?" she asked.

I sneaked a fry and nodded. "Yep," I said after I swallowed. "He fucked up every trick the first six months he was back, and the next thing I know there's a blogger calling it 'the curse of Rachel.' Awesome, right? Even better knowing he'd pulled the quote directly from a Renegade."

"Which one?"

"Penna."

"Penna? But she's so sweet!"

"Until you screw with her family. Then she hates you forever and ever. Anyway, Wilder doesn't know what he's talking about. Landon didn't just get over me, he jumped, hurtled, warp-sped over me."

"That's not what Pax says," she insisted.

"What do I say?" Wilder asked from behind us.

Kill me now. I turned slowly, mentally preparing myself for humiliation. The last thing I needed was Wilder telling me— *Fuck my life.* Landon was coming up behind him.

I spun so fast the ends of my hair smacked me in the face.

"Oh, nothing you need to worry about," Leah insisted as Wilder took the seat next to her, which left the seat next to me open to—

"You have got to be kidding me," I muttered as Landon sat down next to me, an identical cheeseburger on his tray.

I pushed away from the table. This was why I'd eaten in our suite since I'd gotten here. The ship was too damn small to avoid him everywhere. Hell, maybe the earth was too small.

"Rachel, please don't," Landon said softly, his fingers lightly wrapping around my wrist.

That zing of current I only ever felt with him zipped up my arm, and I yanked away.

"Whoa," Leah said as she caught the edge of my tray.

"Sorry." I righted the tray, saving my quickly cooling cheeseburger.

"Rachel, we need you," Wilder said quickly and quietly.

"What? Why?" I asked, locking my gaze onto him. He was safe. He didn't send my hormones skyrocketing or turn me into a puddle of gullible goo.

"Because you haven't signed the media waiver," Landon

answered.

God, even his voice, that deep velvet timbre, sent little chills over me. I crossed my arms so he couldn't see the gooseflesh and kept my eyes on Wilder. "So what?"

"Since you haven't signed it, they won't bother filming us at lunch—they can't use any of the footage you're in until you sign it. We really need to discuss a few things, and unless we want to have the conversation in the bathroom, we can't escape those damn cameras." He motioned behind me.

I pulled my best not-too-obvious turn and saw Bobby with a cameraman shifting his weight from foot to foot across the room. "So you need to use me as a shield."

"I'm getting sick of seeing them everywhere, Pax," Leah whispered.

"I know. Do you want to eat in your suite?" he offered.

"No, I'd like to come down from the ivory tower every once in a while," she said, shuffling her fries on her plate.

Guilt stabbed me in the chest. I'd been so selfishly concerned with running into Landon that I hadn't thought of how this documentary had to be affecting my very shy friend. "I'll stay. For her," I clarified. "Not you."

"Not me?" Landon asked.

"On the condition that *he* doesn't speak to me," I told Wilder. Sitting this close to Landon was hard enough. I wasn't sure I could handle a full conversation without either throwing my food in his face or breaking down completely and begging for an explanation. Neither option appealed to me.

Wilder's gaze swung between mine and Landon's before he rubbed his hand over his head and sighed. "Fine."

"Pax—" Landon protested.

"We have bigger fish to fry at the moment," Wilder snapped. "We've got all of twenty-four hours to figure this stunt out."

I finally dressed my gorgeous cheeseburger, moving my

tomato to the right side of my plate and mourning the fact that I only had three pickle slices, as the guys started talking in low voices that I tried my best to tune out. "There's no salt," I muttered, pushing back from the table. "I'll be right back," I said to Leah before I headed for the condiment table.

"You okay?" Leah asked in a whisper as she caught up with me.

I started to say that I was fine, but the look in her eyes warned me against the lie. As much as I'd kept this part of my life to myself, Leah was in it now. "It's just…really familiar," I answered quietly. "Like really creepy déjà vu."

Except I'd hurt one of them, the other one had broken me, and none of us were dating each other. This took weird to a whole new level.

"I'm so sorry you're in this position."

Looking over her shoulder, I saw the cameras make their way toward the table. "I guess we'd better rescue them."

She squeezed my forearm and gave me an understanding nod. It felt like both sides of my life—both sides of *me*—were colliding, past and present crashing and combining in ways I wasn't ready for.

The cameras backed away as I approached with the saltshaker, one of the crew blatantly rolling his eyes as they retreated. After sprinkling salt on my fries, I finally sank my teeth into lunch, savoring the perfectly cooked burger, the sharp tang of cheddar and twist of pickle.

"You're going to have to ask them to loop back around, or we need to pick a different island," Landon said.

"It's a cruise ship. It doesn't exactly *loop around*," Wilder countered.

"Well, then we wait for a better location."

"No. The timing is perfect, the weather is perfect, and Little John is already there waiting with the boat."

"Well, unless we can figure out how to get back on the

ship, we'll have to cancel it," Landon said with a shrug.

"We're not canceling something this epic."

"Did you ask Penna what she thinks?" Leah asked.

"No," Wilder answered, his voice sharp.

"We tried to, but she won't talk about anything stunt-related," Landon answered. "That's why we didn't want the cameras listening in. She's having a hard enough time with all the shit that just went down; we don't need it replayed for her when the documentary comes out."

That little dead place in my chest I used to call a heart gave a little jolt. Leave it to Landon to say something all sweet and protective.

To keep myself from weighing in on whatever they were discussing, I devoured more of my burger. It was perfection, even with only half the amount of pickles I—

Wait. I slowly put my cheeseburger on my plate and removed the top. I'd eaten half of it and yet there were still three pickles there.

"What exactly are you trying to do?" Leah asked.

And where was my tomato? I'd left it on my plate. The déjà vu feeling hit me twice as hard, and against every ounce of my better judgment, I glanced over to Landon's cheeseburger— and the two tomato slices that peeked out of the side.

Landon had given me his pickles and taken my tomato, just like every other time we'd eaten cheeseburgers together since we'd met. It was achingly familiar, right and wrong all in the same breath.

"We're going to wakeboard behind the boat," Wilder answered Leah.

Had Landon thought about the pickles? Or had it been some subconscious movement, like parts of him had simply readjusted to being next to me?

"What boat?" Leah asked.

"The *Athena*."

Tomatoes immediately forgotten, my attention snapped to Wilder. "As in the cruise ship?" I asked, my mouth slightly agape.

"Yep!" he said with a grin. "It was Leah's idea, actually."

"It was a joke!" she exclaimed.

As the two got into a minor bicker over the outrageous idea, my mind worked overtime. Could it be done? Sure. With major effort, a lot of tries, and some really gifted athletes. But getting them back on the ship?

"You cannot be serious!" Leah hissed.

"Come on, Firecracker. It would be amazing," he countered.

If they got off at the refueling stop, then they'd simply have to get back on while we were moving.

"What are you thinking?" Landon asked me.

I fought the instinct to answer him and looked over at Wilder instead. "Do you have a wakeboard for each of you?"

"Of course," he answered, his eyebrows lowering. "What's on your mind?"

"Do you have a power parasailing winch? Or could Little John get one onboard during the refuel?"

"He could get ours...where are you going with this?" Wilder asked.

"Holy shit, she's brilliant," Landon said, his voice full of the kind of awe I didn't want to hear.

"Rachel?" Leah asked.

"You're right," Landon muttered, grabbing a pen from his pocket and putting it to his napkin. He drew quickly, careful not to tear the paper. "If we mounted it here," he said, pointing to what I assumed was the back of the ship.

"Farther back. Remember the setup when we launched off the back of that ski boat in California? You have to land somewhere, and you have to get it high enough to keep it from rubbing," I said, taking the pen and marking above where he had.

"But how would we get the lines…?"

I kept my eyes on the paper, refusing to look up into the hazel eyes I knew would swallow me whole. "You have to use it as the tow rope. The rider would then have to attach it to his harness."

"We have the chutes on board," Landon said. "But it would be a bitch to keep them dry. The first time we miss the initial rope, they're soaked."

I shrugged. "Wet chutes are prone to sticking and deploying slowly. But if it's open, then you're golden. The hard part would be the initial jolt."

"Are they always like this?" Leah asked.

"Scarily in tune with each other?" Wilder clarified. "Yes."

I snapped my hand back from the napkin like it had been bitten. *Stupid girl.* One mention of a stunt they couldn't work out and I'd jumped right back in, helping plan out details like I'd never left. So much for keeping my distance.

I grabbed my tray with shaky hands and looked over at Wilder. "You two can figure this out from here?"

"Rachel…" Landon pleaded.

"I'll see you later, Leah," I said to my wide-eyed best friend, who looked at me like she'd never seen me before. Then I walked as calmly as I could, when all I wanted to do was run, and dumped my food into the trash can before placing my tray on the pile.

"I know what you're doing," Landon said from behind me when I'd almost made it to the door.

"Oh?" I asked, not pausing in my stride.

"You're trying to ignore me. That's your game plan? When all else fails, avoid the problem?"

I stopped, hating that he knew me so well.

He was so close to my back that I could feel the heat radiating off him through my thin top.

"I'm not going to be easy to avoid, not when I'm putting myself in your path at every possible moment. In fact, I'm going to make it impossible for you to ignore me, Rachel."

His breath ghosted across the shell of my ear, and I barely suppressed a shiver of pure awareness. *Remember what he did to you. Remember watching your phone, packing the boxes, begging Dad. Remember what a broken heart and trampled pride felt like.*

I straightened my shoulders and focused on the exit. "Watch me."

Chapter Five

AT SEA

"Hey, is your head in the game? Because I'm already down Penna, and I can't exactly afford to lose you, too," Pax snapped two days later as our boat hit another wave.

The sun was bright and the weather clear. If this went well, we'd be back on ship in time for this afternoon's classes. That, of course, meant I'd be with Rachel the rest of the afternoon. It was slightly funny to me that the stunt I was about to pull off wouldn't be the most dangerous thing I did all day—trying to get Rachel to talk to me could possibly end in way more bloodshed.

I pulled my focus from the *Athena* sailing ahead of us and, more importantly, *who* was on her. "Yeah, I'm here," I said as I walked the short distance to the back of the ski boat. The sea was relatively calm today, which made this possible.

Rachel made this possible.

When her brain had started cranking away at the problem, and I saw the light come on, realized she'd found a solution, I'd remembered how easily I'd fallen in love with her that first time. How perfectly we'd complemented each other.

"Landon!" Pax yelled.

"I'm here, stop fucking yelling," I said as I buckled my parachute harness on over my life jacket. Little John maneuvered the speeding boat closer to the *Athena*, the hull bouncing as we hit the largest of the wake. I steadied myself on the back of the passenger seat and slipped my feet into the wakeboard boots, fastening the soft closures.

The neoprene was soft against my skin, and I mentally high-fived myself for wetting it before we'd left the small island just north of the Maldives that had served as our refueling stop.

"You sure you want me to go first?" I asked Pax as I lifted my ass to the side of the boat where the tow bar had been positioned.

"You scared?" He grinned.

"Hell no. I'm just wondering if I'm already on that ship, who's going to push you out of the boat when you chicken out."

"You're an asshole." He laughed. "And I'm not an idiot. You're better than me on anything that involves a board. I'll be watching you to see what the hell I'm supposed to do."

The camera came around now that I was buckled in and got all the shots Bobby would need of our equipment.

"You ready for this?" Pax asked.

"Hell yes," I answered. I was about to be the first to do this, which was a bigger rush than the adrenaline alone.

He nodded and slapped my shoulder. "Okay. I'll see you on board. And don't forget to send the rope back down once you're up there," he joked.

"I got this," I assured him, seeing the small flicker of

apprehension in his eyes. That had never been there before Nick's accident. He'd never questioned our gear, our safety, our motives. Now, since the sabotage, was a whole different ball game.

This would be the first stunt we'd completed since the shit with Brooke went down.

"Be careful."

I nodded. "Always."

He stepped back, and I took two deep, steadying breaths. "You know this is pretty fucking insane, right?"

Pax's grin returned. "Our specialty." We passed the *Athena* at a safe distance, and then Little John killed the engine.

"This should do it. You ready?"

"Ready," I said.

A fist bump later, I swung the board over the edge and jumped into the Indian Ocean. The water was warmer than I was expecting, but seeing that we were just north of the Maldives, I shouldn't have been surprised.

Little John maneuvered the ski boat so that the tow rope made it to my hands, and I gripped it tight. We'd moved the tow bar to extend off the side of the boat so it would allow me to wakeboard parallel to the ski boat until I could get hold of the handle on the tow rope that was attached to the *Athena*.

As I bobbed in the water, careful to keep my board flat against the surface, I glanced behind me to see the *Athena* coming up on us. If I didn't know I was about to be yanked out of the water to the exact speed she was going, I might have been a little freaked out.

Okay, there was a giant fucking cruise ship bearing down on me and at least seven cameras catching every angle of my possible demise. I was a tad apprehensive.

"Here we go!" shouted Little John behind the wheel of the boat. I heard the engine kick up as the *Athena* came along beside us. There were maybe fifty feet between me and the hull.

Holy shit, did I feel small.

The ship passed, and I rose and fell with the ski boat beside me as we rode the large waves of her wake, needing the ship to pull ahead before we could launch.

"Now?" Little John asked.

"Go!" I answered.

The engine responded with a roar, and the ski boat leaped forward. Adrenaline flooded my system like a shot of nitrous oxide to a finely tuned engine. Pulling the tow rope to my chest, I kept steady pressure against the water until we were moving fast enough for me to get onto the surface. Then in one smooth motion, I stood, the water gliding beneath my board as we kept pace with the ship. I motioned toward the back of the *Athena*, and Little John obliged, turning us toward the rear of the ship, where another rope dragged through the water about fifty feet behind it.

Don't fuck this up. She's watching.

She'd sworn she wouldn't, that she was pretending I didn't exist for the rest of the trip, according to Leah, who told Pax, who told me like we were back in junior high or some shit, but I knew better.

Rope within reach, I let go of the ski boat's tow rope with one hand and stretched toward it. My weight tipped my board enough to jostle me, and for a split second I was sure I was about to get a face full of the ocean.

Concentrate.

I blocked out the *Athena*, Rachel, Pax, everything that owned any piece of my brain besides the water and my board.

It was go time.

Balancing my weight, I grabbed for the rope…and caught it. The sound of cheers from the boat vaguely registered as I slid the rope through my gloved hands slowly, careful to maintain the speed I needed to stay above the water.

I reached the handle and shouted. Holding tightly to the handle of the ship's tow rope, I let the ski boat rope go. I would have fist pumped in victory if I didn't know it would land me face-first in the water.

Laughing, I whipped my board to the left, then fantailed and shifted back to the right. *Holy shit. I'm wakeboarding behind a fucking cruise ship.*

This part was relatively easy compared to what I was about to do, which was scary as shit but equally epic. Locating the carabiner, I pulled the handle to my chest and clipped it to the corresponding hook on my harness.

"If this doesn't work, it's going to really fucking suck," I muttered to myself. I was locked in, hooked onto the cord that connected to the back of a ship currently going about thirty knots. What could possibly go wrong?

A whole hell of a lot.

Before my brain could go through the hundreds of things that could go wrong—which all included me breaking ankles, legs, a neck—I said a fervent prayer and then pulled the cord for my chute.

A rustle of fabric grew to a roar, and I became the center of a tug-of-war between the *Athena* and my chute. Every muscle in my body strained to stay upright as the chute deployed.

Don't hit the water. Don't hit the water, I begged silently. If my chute took on water, I was fucked. And most likely dead unless I could unsnap fast enough.

I jolted upward as the chute snapped behind me, and air rushed from my lungs in relief. I was airborne. Looking down toward the boat, I saw Pax cheering me on, jumping so high I almost thought he'd go overboard.

"Fuck yes!" I yelled, my arms up in victory.

That was the only moment I gave myself before locating the handles of the parasail as I rose higher, climbing above the height of the *Athena*. A crowd had gathered near the landing site, and I hoped they'd watch as I set this baby down on the deck—instead of seeing a bloody mess in the propellers below.

For the second time during the stunt, I laughed. Now I was *parasailing* behind a fucking cruise ship. Unbelievable.

A minute later, with two of the Renegades manning the winch, I started to descend toward the deck. Rachel had been right—her setup was flawless.

Just like she was.

With nothing to do but watch as they reeled me in, I scanned the crowd, looking for her familiar frame, which finally came into focus when I was about thirty feet from the deck.

She came!

Her arms folded across her chest, she bit her lower lip, her worry apparent in every tense line of her gorgeous face as her gaze flickered between me and the winch team. Not only had she come, but she was worried about me.

Clearing the railing by at least five feet, I concentrated on landing. Gabe and Alex, my snowboarding partners, raced forward as my feet hit the deck and unsnapped the chute behind me, letting it catch on the metal railing so it didn't carry me off the ship again.

Flawless.

I unhooked from the tow rope to the thunderous applause of the crowd. It took all of a minute for Bobby to stick a camera in my face, but I looked past the giant black life sucker and met Rachel's eyes.

At least ten feet and a dozen or more people separated us as she stood on the steps that led to the next deck, but it felt like we were the only two there, maybe the only two in the world.

I vaguely heard the voices calling to me, asking me how I

felt, what the hardest part had been, if I'd been scared, but all I saw was her. For the smallest moment, her eyes weren't full of hatred but something I was scared to call pride.

"Thank you," I mouthed, knowing she couldn't hear me.

A small smile curved her lips, and she nodded once.

A body slammed into me, wrapping its—no, *her*—arms around my neck. "You did it!"

Zoe's voice was like ice water through my veins. Of all the fucking timing. I peeled her arms from my neck and smiled down at her—it wasn't her fault my dick wandered where it shouldn't have. "I did. Will you help them set up for Pax? They have to get the rope back out there so he can get on the ship."

She smiled up at me, oblivious to the fact that our time together, if that's what it was called, was over, and walked away.

When I looked up to Rachel, the cool, closed-off look was back on her face, and I cursed inwardly. She looked away and shook her head, then turned around and walked up the steps.

"Nova, we need you!" Bobby called as he set up an interview station.

I sighed in the direction Rachel had taken, but I wasn't defeated. For just the smallest moment, I'd seen past the walls she'd built against me. For the tiniest millisecond, we'd been connected again, and it sucked to have lost it, but now I knew it was possible.

She could try to ignore me all she wanted, but somewhere under all that hatred and ice, she was still my Rachel—the same girl who'd snowboarded by my side, planned stunts, and pulled a couple of her own. The same girl I'd given up everything for…only to fuck it all up a few weeks later. But she was still under there. I'd seen it at lunch yesterday, and again today.

I just had to find a way to break through to her.

Chapter Six

RACHEL

AT SEA

I tapped my pencil on the desk and looked out over the Laccadive Sea as students filtered into the classroom. The floor-to-ceiling windows were incredible. The whole ship, the experience, was phenomenal.

Except for the six-foot-four Adonis who'd just walked into my classroom. Of course he had a blonde batting her eyelashes up at him as he shut the door on the cameraman who had almost followed him in.

I'd nearly made an utter asshat of myself this morning when he landed on the back deck. For that moment, he'd been Landon and we'd been *us*, and it had all seemed so easy to slip back into that routine. Good thing the leggy brunette latched onto him and broke whatever spell I'd been under.

He had a kind of magnetism that changed the entire atmosphere around him, and I was drawn to him just like before, no different than every other girl on this damn ship. The chemistry between us I could handle, but these memories sucked. I jerked my eyes away from him, but not before I noticed how perfectly his shirt draped over his frame, or the way his cargo shorts hung on his ass. Ugh. How had he managed to get hotter in the last couple of years? He'd lost every trace of the boy he'd been, and all that was left was ridiculously handsome, hard, chiseled man.

"Hi, Nova. Nice stunt today," the girl behind me said with a soft sigh.

Help me, dear sweet Lord.

He gave her a tight smile but bent in front of my desk. "Rachel."

I met those hazel eyes and simply arched one of my eyebrows as my heart accelerated to a gallop. I was not talking to him, not opening any form of dialogue that would make a single part of me vulnerable to him. Hell no, you didn't let the arsonist play with matches.

"Come on," he begged softly.

It felt like ripping off a Band-Aid slowly, but I managed to look away. I was here to learn, not to deal with Landon.

He sighed, and I nearly cheered in victory when he stood, but then he took the desk next to mine and sat down. *Seriously?* The guy hadn't come near me in years and now he had to sit right next to me?

Then he popped the top on a Red Bull and I almost laughed. At least it wasn't a Gremlin. Watching him suck down one of the energy drinks made by the company my dad worked for would have been too ironic—even if it was the reason we originally met.

"It's not going to work," he said, turning in his seat to face me.

I kept my eyes on the professor, who was walking toward the podium.

"I get that you're still trying to ignore me. It's okay, I get it. I fucked up in more ways than I can possibly explain. But I don't need you to talk to me. I just need you to listen."

My entire body tensed. Was he saying he was sorry?

Don't fall for his shit again. You're not that stupid.

Rubbing the wrist I'd broken years ago, I sagged in my chair with relief when the professor started talking.

"Good morning, class," the red-haired woman said. She looked to be in her midthirties and wore a stylish safari dress and cute wedges. "Welcome back to Cultures of the Pacific 310. I hope you enjoyed your brief break. This is your reminder to check your syllabus for due dates and pay particular attention to when your research paper is due. It's on a topic of your choice, but it must be approved by me."

I opened my notebook and then cursed under my breath. I'd forgotten my pen. Nothing like being unprepared.

"What's wrong?" Hugo asked, leaning over slightly from my other side.

"I forgot my pen," I whispered.

"No problem," he answered quickly, reaching into his binder. I'd only known him a week, but I was immensely thankful for him. Being Leah's butler the last three months as part of his work-study, he'd taken care of my best friend when I couldn't. He handed me a pencil with a quick smile.

"Thank you," I said as a pen landed on my desk.

"You hate pencils," Landon whispered.

Every muscle in my body locked as my eyes fixated on the blue Bic. How did he remember that?

"You can ignore the pen all you want, but then you'll just get those giant gray marks along your hand that drive you nuts, and your notes will smudge. Your choice."

God, he didn't just remember that I hated pencils, he remembered *why*.

"It's just a pen, Rach. Not a contract."

Like the one you left me holding when I signed that lease.

I debated shunning the damned pen for all of thirty seconds, but when argued against having smudged notes that I wouldn't be able to read, I gave Hugo back his pencil and picked up the pen.

I focused all of my attention on what Dr. Messina said, taking copious notes, but I felt each and every time Landon's gaze shifted toward me. There was still a palpable connection between us, as if my body remembered his significance, or maybe just what he was capable of doing with it. Ignoring him had to be like when I'd given up processed sugar.

That first day had been torture. That first week? Agony.

But then I got used to it being gone until I'd learned not to miss it.

Yeah, but you've been missing him for the last couple of years.

Years of wondering at what point he'd decided to leave me. Years of wondering if the insane chemistry between us—the undeniable craving to be close to each other—was something I'd imagined. *It's not. Feel that energy between you, that hum that's ready to be cranked up to a million watts? Yeah, it's still right there.*

I steeled myself and concentrated on the lecture until it was time to leave. When she dismissed us, I got out of the classroom so fast it might as well have been on fire.

"Rachel!" Landon called down the crowded hall. I booked it to the elevator and slid inside—

Damn.

He got in just before the doors slid shut, leaving his camera crew on the outside. My timing with elevators on this ship was shit, but at least this wasn't on film. I didn't bother to look at him, just focused on the changing floors as we started to move.

There were at least four other students in here—that had to keep him quiet, right?

"Look, I just need you to listen. Please, Rachel."

Apparently they weren't going to deter him.

Deck seven. Three more to go.

I concentrated on the numbers, and he stepped in front of me, blocking my view with his chest. If I stepped forward, I'd be able to rest my head just under his collarbone, where I could feel his heartbeat. I hated that I remembered that—the feeling of safety, of…love—almost as much as I hated the urge to do it.

"The other people in this elevator aren't going to save you, or me, for that matter. You know I've never given a fuck what anyone else ever thought of me."

I looked to my right, but there were two girls openly ogling Landon and the show he was putting on. *Don't worry, girls. He'll be all yours in a moment.*

Unless they already had been. How many had come and gone since me? *Why do you care?*

"So you can stand there silent. It's okay with me. I'm the one who needs to explain anyway."

Deck eight. Three of the girls got off, leaving me with Landon and one other guy who looked like he'd rather be anywhere else.

"What happened back then…God, Rach. The situation was so fucked-up, and I was such a stupid kid."

I glared at him. He was a stupid kid? That was his excuse for nearly ruining my life? I blatantly looked away. It was going to take something a hell of a lot better than that to get me to listen to him.

"We have six months together."

Don't remind me.

"And I can't help but think that we have a chance to set things straight. To put everything behind us and start fresh. And I know that isn't going to change what happened in the past—"

The elevator opened, and I sidestepped around him,

making a beeline for my room. It was twenty feet. I could make it. I had to.

If I listened, I might pause. If I paused, I might…think. If I gave in to thought, I was already in my handbasket straight to Landon hell.

"But the truth is that I can't change what happened. I can only go from here. Rachel? Please talk to me."

I kept the same pace, refusing to run, but damn if I wasn't going to power walk my way to safety. I took out my key card and swiped it.

Red dot.

Fuck.

"If you'll give me a chance to explain, where we can sit down like the adults we are, there's so much I want to tell you. So much I should have told you then but was too big of a chickenshit to get the words out."

I swiped the card again.

Green.

"I didn't want to leave you," he said, his voice rising in pitch. *But you did.* Hell if I was going to make this easy for him.

I swung the door open and walked in.

"Rachel, please. Say something!"

I threw up my middle finger and slammed the door behind me. My chest deflated as my breath abandoned me, and I leaned back against the door. God, it hurt. Everything hurt. I looked down, half expecting my shirt to be soaked in blood, because it felt like my heart had been ripped out and shredded.

"Well, I mean…I can learn sign language if that's what it takes, but I think I've got that one down already," he said through the door.

I rolled my eyes and fought the urge to let the corners of my mouth drift up. He'd always had that effect on me—the ability to make me laugh when I wanted to throttle him. God, we'd had some of the most outrageous fights. *And phenomenal makeup sex.*

"We're not done, Rachel. I know you're right there. I know you can hear me. And I don't care how long it takes to get through to you, you're going to listen. You might still hate me after, but you have to understand the reasons why."

There was a subtle thud on the door, like he'd banged his head on the surface. "But I'm not going to do it through a goddamned door. You win this round."

Damn skippy I did.

"But I'll win the war."

...

"He's relentless!" I said to Penna two nights later as I sank into the booth she'd claimed at the ship's club, Veritas. "I need a damned drink."

The bass thumped out a rhythm that had dozens of people gyrating on the floor. Maybe if I got drunk enough, I could join them and forget *him* for just a little while.

She looked up from her book. "He being Landon?"

"Yes," I answered. "Really? In a club? What are you reading, anyway?"

"*Love in the Time of Cholera*," she answered. "It's all misery, which is pretty fitting for my mood at the moment. My contract requires that I be down here for filming, but it sure as hell doesn't dictate what I'll be doing." She motioned to the cameras positioned around the club. *Fantastic.*

"Is that for Lit?"

"Nope. Just for me. I figured if I'm stuck in this chair, I might as well catch up on some reading."

"I wish he'd get cholera," I mumbled.

She side eyed me.

"Okay, I don't wish he'd get cholera. I just wish he'd go

back to the neat little box I've had him stashed in. Instead, I go from zero Landon contact to him being everywhere. I'm seriously expecting him to follow me into the bathroom at any moment."

She picked up her book and wiggled her toes at the end of her hot-pink cast. "You could just talk to him. Rip off the Band-Aid, so to speak."

"On the pain scale of my life, ripping off a Band-Aid is probably somewhere around a two. Dealing with Landon? That's off the fucking charts."

"Fair enough." She shrugged, then motioned to our waitress. "Two amaretto sours," she ordered.

"Thank you," I told her, grateful she'd remembered what I liked to drink from last night. I blinked. Was Landon going to turn me into a freaking lush? "I had to basically dive over to Hugo, who sits on the other side of me during Cultures of the Pacific, to be my partner because Landon was already trying to stake a claim!"

"Well…"

"Oh no…no, no, no, no, *no*. His claim-staking days are over. Back then I was like virgin territory—"

She dropped her book and gave me an openly skeptical eyebrow raise.

"What? I was. He was my first. But that's not what I meant."

"Okay," she said, reaching for her book again with a sigh as the song changed and Drake came through the speakers.

"I just mean that back then he could have claimed me all day long. Hell, he did for like half a second. But now, I'm not up for grabs. I'm claimed."

"You have a boyfriend?" she asked, clearly worried.

"No. I've been there, done that a few times since him. I'm in a fully committed long-term relationship with myself."

"Does yourself require batteries?"

"Very funny. I know you're Team Landon."

She put down her book with a longing look and turned to me. "I'm Team Switzerland. I thought it was a stupid idea to bring you here. Don't get pissed—it's just the truth. You are Landon's weak spot, whether or not you're willing to see it, and we're doing some pretty dangerous stuff. We can't afford to have him distracted."

"I didn't come here to screw with the Renegades. I'm here because I wanted to be a part of this program—to travel the world and study abroad. I had no idea Wilder owned the damn ship, or that you guys were using it as your personal worldwide stuntmobile. But you're here, and *he's* here, and leaving isn't an option. I'm not losing the only chance I have to visit the village I was adopted from, and now there's Leah to consider, as well. She's my best friend, and if I leave, she'll leave, too, out of some sense of guilt or obligation, and it will ruin her because she's so damn in love with Wilder."

"I know," she said.

"So, yeah, what I did was shitty. I was dating Wilder, and I fell in love with Landon. We went behind his back. I get it. Put the fucking scarlet letter on my chest, brand me a whore, do whatever it is you need to, Penna. But while I almost broke the Renegades, Landon destroyed me. Annihilated me. I gave up everything for him, and he walked away without a backward glance. So if there's some price you need me to pay, I've already paid it."

She raised her eyebrows.

"What?" I snapped. Damn, my fuse was short.

"I was just waiting for you to finish with the whole self-flagellation routine over there. You're right—you nearly took down my whole family, and I resented you and the lies I told to keep your secret. But I was nineteen and had little to no perspective. I've never been in love; I'm not going to say that I understand why you did it." She leaned forward a little and waited until I looked her in the eyes. "But last week my sister tried to kill Paxton. She blamed him for Nick's paralysis, and in the course of her rather insane plot, she did this to me." She pointed to her cast. "So while I do hate what you did, I can't really hate you. My own family did more to harm the Renegades than you ever could have done. So you and me are going to call a little truce."

"A truce?"

She sighed. "Look. I helped get you on board. I thought Pax was nuts when he orchestrated it all. Trust me, it wasn't easy to convince Leah that her scholarship for tutoring Pax included a full ride for her best friend, too."

"You were in on it?"

"I was. None of us knew if she'd stay when you came down with mono before the ship launched, and none of us could predict that she and Pax would fall in love."

"You never told Landon who she was, or how I figured into it," I accused.

"He would have flipped his lid. You're the one subject he won't discuss, the one person who left a scar, and Paxton thinks you're the only woman Landon's capable of loving. So you're here because Paxton thinks you and Landon are destined or some shit."

Destined? Fuck that. Destiny didn't leave you broken financially, physically, and spiritually. Curses did that. *Fitting, since that's what I am to him.*

"I'm here because Wilder feels guilty about his ultimatum back then," I snapped. "All this did was put two people who have already hurt each other in unspeakable ways together in a confined space. If we're going to have a truce, let's at least agree to be honest."

"Fine. Let's be honest. I helped Pax because the whole situation was fucked-up. You and Landon were dead wrong, but Pax wasn't right to force Landon to break his own heart. Maybe this works, or maybe it doesn't, but you're here now, so we should all just make the best of it."

We didn't shake hands—neither of us was touchy-feely—but an understanding passed between us. "Okay."

She nodded. "Okay."

I shifted in my seat, hating the way my bare thighs stuck to the vinyl. I should have chosen pants, but I'd opted for a short skirt and halter top and was now paying the price.

As I was mid–skirt adjustment, Landon walked in with Wilder. Landon's shirt was rolled at the elbows, showing some of that delicious ink, and his smile was movie star-worthy as they made a beeline for the bar and the gaggle of girls there hitting on the other Renegades. Two of Landon's snowboarding friends had shown up this week, Alex and Gabe, which helped take the contract-clubbing pressure off the newly monogamous Wilder. Leah had been thrilled.

"Shit. Do you want to head back up to the room? I have another half hour down here, but you're under no obligation," Penna offered.

I swallowed and shook my head. "He hasn't noticed me yet. I'm good."

"He will. I swear you two have radar for when the other is near. I know you don't want to hear it, but you guys are kind of inevitable."

A brunette with huge boobs leaned up against Landon's arm, and he gave her his Nova smile, the one that would no doubt lead to her panties on his floor in the next few hours. I took a gulp of my newly delivered drink and let the alcohol slide down my throat, wishing the burn would take away the burn in my heart.

"The only thing inevitable about us is disaster. Landon likes bright, shiny stunts, the impossible…and once I became possible, well, I wasn't so shiny anymore, was I? Nothing has changed in that regard." I nodded toward where the cameras swirled around them and he put on the show he was known for. Why did it hurt so much to see him make that woman laugh? Why did I feel the urge to fly across the floor and tell her to get her manicured hands off his arm? He wasn't mine anymore...not that he'd actually been mine in the first place. He'd always belonged to the Renegades first.

Penna's eyes were soft and understanding but not pitying when I glanced back over. "What he did was horrid. I just think you should give him a chance to talk to you. Maybe it was unforgivable, and maybe it wasn't. Either way, you'd both get some much-needed closure, because listening to you tells me that you're stuck in the same hell he is."

I scoffed. "Yeah, if you count hell as fucking everything that moves."

She glanced in his direction and sighed. "Everyone has their drug of choice. He started self-medicating and hasn't stopped."

"Right, well, while he was busy earning that new nickname of his, I was putting myself back together piece by jagged, ripped, bleeding piece. So you're going to have to forgive me if I'm not ready to let him tear me apart again just so he can feel better about himself. If he thinks I'm a bitch, I'm okay with it. He doesn't get to argue with what he turned me into."

I took another drink and looked over to see him whisper in the girl's ear.

"So then what are you going to do?" Penna asked quietly. "You're stuck on this ship with him for the next six months."

"I'll go to class, get great grades, travel, maybe get to do some fun stunts with you guys," I answered. "Once we get closer to Korea, I'm going to take the hit to my grades, deplete my savings account, and skip a shore excursion to go find the orphanage I was adopted from. Landon isn't in any of those plans."

Penna stared at me quietly, letting moments pass in the beats of the music until she spoke. "Okay. I still hope that you'll talk to him. I get it—I really do. And you have all of my computer skills at your disposal if you need help with the Korea trip."

"Thank you," I said, standing up. "You know what?" I asked, glancing back at where Landon was preoccupied with Big Boobs McGee. "I'm going to go dance. Need anything before I go?"

She shook her head. "Nope, I'm good right here."

"Okay. Just let me know if there's anything I can do for you."

In the past, Penna would have been the first on the dance floor. She got around pretty well in her chair, but I knew she was dying to switch to the weight-bearing cast next week. She'd had it with confinement. "I will," she said. "And Rachel?"

I turned. "What's up?"

Her forehead puckered. "I've thought a lot the last couple days, and if I had the chance to talk to the person who hurt me? The person I loved most in the world? I'd take it. Because all the pain in the world would be worth it for just the tiniest bit of understanding."

My heart ached for her. For Brooke. For everything that had led them to this.

"I'll keep that in mind," I promised as I headed out to the floor.

I moved with the music, away from the reaching hands of the guys around me, until I felt *his* gaze. I looked over to the bar and found him watching me, his eyes hot with undisguised want. Maybe I moved my hips just to see if those eyes would narrow. Maybe I felt a little surge of power when he ran his tongue over his lower lip.

Sex had never been our problem. Trust…that was the deal breaker.

He pushed off the bar and headed toward me, abandoning his latest conquest to the other Renegades. My heart thundered and my breath sped as my fight-or-flight response kicked in.

Flight won.

I spun on my wedges and damn near ran for the door. I wasn't ready to have this conversation, let alone in front of the cameras that would no doubt love to put this into their clubbing sequence. My mangled heart wasn't up for public consumption, thank you.

"Hey, are you leaving?" Leah asked as she stepped out of the elevator I was desperate to get into.

"I have to. I can't be here. Not with him," I explained, almost regretting my choice when her shoulders slumped.

"Okay. I understand. Coffee in the morning?" she asked.

Coffee. Our morning routine since we'd started Dartmouth. The one thing that had kept us both grounded, both ready to face another day. I squeezed her hands and gave her what I hoped was a convincing smile. "Absolutely."

When Landon burst through the crowd, my cowardice got the best of me. "Tomorrow," I promised, then stepped back and hit the button to close the door.

I'd won this elevator battle, but not before I saw the brunette chase after him.

He raked his hands through his hair as the doors shut, and I closed my eyes to the pleading in his.

Even with Penna's words in my head, I still didn't see a way that I could open myself up to Landon enough to even hear what he had to say. I was the opposite of Penna in that regard—I might have pushed the envelope on every stunt, but when it came to my emotions, I chose self-preservation over understanding.

Unfortunately, I also knew that Landon was a persistent guy.

And when it came to self-preservation, he was the most reckless of them all.

Chapter Seven

LANDON

AT SEA

The woman was impossible.

I couldn't remember a time when I'd had less pride than the last two days, trying to track her down. We had two classes together, so I thought it would be easy, but she left as soon as we were dismissed and dodged my every attempt to see her. She'd gone so far as to leave the table in the cafeteria when I sat down to eat, which was almost laughable, because I knew how much that girl loved her food.

It was like she didn't even care that I was on board, yet my every waking moment was consumed with caring that she was. That would have been enough to send me into a tailspin of rejection, but the way she made sure we were never in the same room—except for classes—told me that she cared enough to always know where I was.

Maybe it was grasping at straws, but it was all that I had.

I checked my watch and cursed. Running late for a production meeting was about to get me on Pax's shit list. My mind had wandered to Rachel while I was on the treadmill, and before I knew it another three miles had gone by as I plotted. Not that I was arguing with extra cardio. I had to be in the best shape of my life for Nepal, but now I was definitely not on time.

"Sorry I'm late!" I yelled down the hall as I shut the door to the suite.

"Get your ass in here!" Pax yelled.

"I'm all sweaty, let me shower," I said, coming into the dining room where the staff had gathered around the table.

"I don't care if you're covered in baby oil. Put your ass in the chair," Pax said, pointing to my empty seat.

"Okay, okay, I'm here," I said, taking my chair and trying to focus. Bobby sat at the head of the table, while Pax took the center—he liked to be able to reach every map and picture that lay spread out in front of him. Penna and I took up the other side, while a few of the other Renegades and camera-crew members stood or sat around us.

"I'm really not sure why I'm here," Penna mumbled, folding her hands in her lap.

"Because you're banged up, not fucking dead, Penna," Pax snapped. "You're still a Renegade."

"You sure I should be?"

"Later," he hissed at her.

"Don't fight in front of the kids," I said, leaning forward to see the pictures of Sri Lanka, our next destination. "Where were we?"

Pax ripped his hands over his hair. "Okay. We have three days in Sri Lanka. Day one is taken up by field excursions for class. Who has them?"

A collection of hands went up. The hardest part about filming the documentary while we were on the Study at Sea program was definitely working everything around our class load.

Terms were simple: if we failed, we were off the boat and out of the documentary.

I raised my hand, knowing that I had an excursion to Gal Viharaya, but at least I'd be with Rachel. Whether I could get her to talk to me would be another matter.

"Okay, I think we all have one," Pax muttered, flipping through the folder. "We have permits for the hang gliding stunt off Sigiriya, but I can tell you that it was a very reluctant permit and it's a pretty sacred site. We'll be watched, and since I really don't want to spend any more time in a jail cell this trip, let's mind our p's and q's."

A small hum of laughter went through the group. Pax was right. The shit we'd gone through in Madagascar when Brooke hid the permits needed to be a one-time-only thing. Penna paled next to me, and I put my hand over hers on her lap.

"It was not your fault," I whispered so no one else could hear.

She didn't look up from where she picked at her nail polish.

"The inherent danger here is how we'll be launching. This formation leaves no room for error, not with only a matter of feet between your wing and the person next to you. You have got to be careful and aware of the other Renegades around you. It's not a long flight, but we're packed in like sardines."

"Three point six kilometers," Penna said.

"Rebel?" Bobby prompted.

Penna looked up, but only so far as the pictures on the table. "Sigiriya is about two hundred meters tall. Given the typical rate of descent of eighteen to one, we're looking at three point six kilometers of flight. You'll have to pull the synchronized turns pretty damn fast and really damn accurately."

"You'll?" I asked.

"I'm not going," she said.

Paxton's eyes narrowed. "Another thing we'll talk about later."

"Hang gliding is something you can do with us. One of us will just take you tandem," I said quietly as Pax moved on to the technical turns we'd be making.

She shook her head. "No. Pax should take Leah, and if you're smart, you'll take Rachel as a bribe. You know she loves this stuff, and it might get you a little face time where she acknowledges that you exist."

"Penna, come on. This has always been the four of us."

"Yeah? Well, Nick is paralyzed and I'm in a non-weight-bearing cast, so looks like it's the two of you." She abruptly pulled back from table and wheeled herself out through the sliding glass door to the balcony that crossed the back of the ship.

"I'll take her place," Zoe said, pulling her chair into the vacant spot Penna had left.

"Not necessary," I said, hoping she hadn't listened in.

She shrugged and slid closer while Pax rambled on about the importance of GoPro footage. "You seem really crabby, Landon. Want me to come visit tonight?"

I looked over to her, taking in her brown hair and welcoming smile. There was a reason I'd been "visiting" with her more than I should have the last few months. It was easy to pretend that she was Rachel. But now with Rachel a handful of rooms away, I knew that an imitation wasn't going to do it for me anymore. "Thanks for the offer, Zoe, but I really think I'm good."

"Oh," she said, her eyebrows shooting up in surprise.

We hadn't been an item—she knew better—but damn, it felt like I'd just said, "Thanks for everything, but we're done."

Maybe because I had.

I felt her side eyeing me a few times as we went over the plan again, the gear, who needed what where.

"One more thing...we'd like to do kind of a fun side trip on our last day," Pax said. "There are some natural waterslides in the Nuwara Eliya region, so we've got a totally optional excursion up there to play around, if you guys are interested. It's mostly my way of saying thank you for kicking ass at the Abu Dhabi exhibition."

Everyone cheered, and I pushed back from the table. "Hey, Pax," I said just loud enough to get his attention. "Can you make sure I've got a tandem rig on my hang glider?"

Zoe tensed beside me. Guess it had been loud enough to get hers, too.

"Yeah," Pax said with a grin. "You going to try a little bribery?"

"Penna had the same idea," I admitted.

"Smart girl, that Penna," he said. "I'm all for it. Anything that actually gets you two talking would be great, considering what I went through to get her here."

"Yeah, yeah," I said, waving him off. If I went now, I should be able to track Rachel down in her suite before dinner. "You good here?"

"Go," he ordered. "I need to figure out how to get through to Penna."

"You have to give her time."

"I don't want to lose her," he admitted quietly. "It feels like...like we're falling apart."

"We're not going to lose her. She's still here, Pax. She could have gone home, but she stayed. Penna's stronger than this, she just needs—"

"Time." He sighed.

"Time," I agreed. "I'll talk to her later, but right now I'm going to go find Rachel. Oh, and one more thing—tell

Gremlin I want out. Time for new sponsors."

"You sure you want to play that game with them?" Pax asked.

"Never more so."

"Okay, I'll have Nick deliver the message. Now go get your girl." He motioned toward the balcony, and I headed out.

The warmth of the deck seeped through the thin material of my flip-flops as I stepped onto the veranda. Before I could close the door, Zoe came after me.

"So that's it?" she asked.

Fuck.

"Zoe, you know we weren't a thing."

She put her hands on her hips and glared up at me. "Maybe, but I can't even ride tandem with you?"

I sighed and squinted, the glare from the sun off the glass door hitting me square in the eyes. "You're good enough to fly your own."

"Who is she?" Zoe asked, ignoring my compliment. "What kind of girl does it take to knock Landon Rhodes—the famous Nova—on his ass? Don't think that I haven't noticed that parade of girls in and out of your room has been on pause the last week or so."

"Don't do this."

"Who is she? At least tell me that much."

"Her name is Rachel—"

She sputtered. "Rachel? As in 'curse' Rachel? You can't be serious."

I closed my eyes and took a deep breath. Of course she'd heard about the curse. Hell, I'd just gotten back on top of my game when Zoe'd joined the Renegades. "Rachel's not a curse. She's…" How could I find the words to explain?

"Wow." She dragged the word out. "Does she know about your habits? Because she really should know what she's getting into."

I folded my arms in front of my chest, every sense on high alert. "Stop. Now. I know how much shit you gave Leah, and"—I tilted my head in thought—"well, she dished it back to you pretty well. But you tried to scare her off. You made her life hell because she dared to fall for Wilder."

"So?" Her forehead puckered, but the shame in her eyes didn't match her sharp tone. "Are you getting all protective?"

"I don't need to protect Rachel, which is something I've always loved about her. Leah is one thing. Rachel won't just dish your shit back at you—she'll chew you up and spit you out. Trust me, her teeth are razor sharp."

"So you're going to let this girl back in? Even after she almost ripped the Renegades apart? I know the stories—how she seduced both of you and then fucked your head when she left."

I sucked in a breath and let it out slowly while I counted to ten. "She didn't do anything. I was the one who went after her. I was the one who fell in love with her. Yes, we betrayed Wilder, but I was the one who begged her to stay quiet, not to hurt him, and I was the one stupid enough to leave her for the Renegades when I could have had…" I shook my head, unable to finish the sentence.

"You loved her," she whispered.

"Yes."

Guilt crept in, the taste sour. I'd never promised Zoe anything, but I never should have let it go on for this long. I should have realized she was getting attached. I should have cut it off a long time ago. *Should have, could have, would have. All bullshit.*

"Why?" she demanded, her eyes hardening.

"Because she exists, and it was impossible not to. There's no other way to explain it."

She looked away, toward where the water swirled behind the boat.

I put my hands on her bare shoulders and locked eyes with her. "Zoe, don't do this. You've been with us for a year now. You've earned your place through stunts and ability. You're worth a hell of a lot more than what you think of yourself. Go tell Wilder that you want your own hang glider. Show him your practice times from before we left. You've got this."

"You really think so?" she asked, her voice uncharacteristically small.

"I do."

She didn't say good-bye, just gave me a small smile and a nod, and walked away. God, I wished the woman I wanted was as easy to get through to as Zoe was.

No, you don't. Then she wouldn't be Rachel.

Speaking of Rachel… I took a deep breath and knocked twice before sliding the back door to her suite open.

"She's going to kill you if she sees you in here," Penna said, not looking up from her book.

"Throw me a fucking bone here, Penna. I can't get a word in with the girl. She's purposely torturing me."

"Yeah, well, she has every right to."

"Wait. Since when did you switch sides?" I asked, glancing around the suite. Where the hell was Rachel?

"I have no side. As I told Rachel, I'm Switzerland." She flipped a page. "But I will say that I'm a Renegade first and foremost, and I love you like a brother, but what you did to that girl deserves a good torture."

"Team Rachel," I muttered.

"Team Justice," she said, raising a fist. I sighed. It was the same move she'd pulled when she'd backed Leah in the Paxton-dating-his-tutor debate. "And seriously, if this is only about the sex, you know you could nail just about any other girl on this ship. Leave this one in peace."

I turned my baseball hat backward, tucked my thumbs in my pockets, and rocked back on my heels. "It's not about the sex. The way I loved her…that was beyond anything I'd ever known…or known since. I buried it, moved on with whoever was willing, but I see her and those feelings come rushing back to the surface like we broke up two weeks ago instead of two and a half years ago."

"Right, but those two years…they changed her. She's not the same as she was."

I understood that. "Neither am I."

"She thinks she's bad luck. She joked about it, *the curse of Rachel*, but I could tell that she believes it somewhere deep down."

"She's not bad luck. That curse thing was a bunch of bullshit to excuse my shittiness."

"Well, you might want to explain that to her as you're begging," she suggested.

"Where is she?"

"In the shower."

My eyebrows shot skyward. "Perfect."

"Landon…I'm not responsible for the way she's about to dismember you."

I looked at her pale skin, the bags under her dim eyes, and wished I could take her pain away. "Penna, at this point, her screaming at me would be a welcome change from the apathy I've gotten. Rachel is all fire and passion, and as long as I can tap into that, I have a shot." I squatted down in front of her until she looked at me. "And the same goes for you."

She looked away but nodded, which was more than I'd gotten out of her since the accident.

"Now if you'll excuse me, I have a woman to piss off," I said.

I took a deep breath and went down their hallway until I reached the bathroom door. The water was still running, and I knew from the layout of our suite that she had to come out this one door. But what the hell could I do to keep her in there long enough for me to make my point?

A lightbulb went off in my head. Slowly I opened the bathroom door—and kept my eyes averted from where I knew her sexy, naked body was so very, very wet just a few feet away. God, I'd missed her body, her slight curves, that toned stomach, and her pert breasts. I missed the way she'd felt under me, above me, the fearless abandonment in the way she made love to me.

My chest constricted when I thought about her smile, the one she'd reserved for only me, the sound of her tiny gasps in my ear when I slid inside her tight body for the first time. We'd been so young, so inexperienced, and it had been so fucking perfect.

I snatched her clothes off the toilet seat and quickly tugged away all three towels before escaping, shutting the door behind me.

"Penna?" Rachel called out, obviously having heard me.

She continued her shower, and I went over everything I wanted to say in my head as I put the pile down next to me. *Fuck*, what did I want to say?

The shower stopped, and my heart had the opposite reaction, starting to pound.

"What the hell?"

Even pissed, her voice did things to me, brought back those damn feelings I'd just told Penna about. Hell, I'd always loved when she was pissed off at me—pushing me to be better, expecting nothing but what she knew I was capable of. She'd had enough faith in me for the both of us…until I fucked that all up.

"Penna?" Rachel poked her head out of the door, water dripping from her hair. "What are you doing?" she shouted at me and slammed the door in my face.

Showtime. I braced my hands on either side of the doorframe and attempted to find my balls. Right. Okay.

"Look. This was the only way I could think of to keep you from running away from me. We're on a damn ship, Rachel. At sea. There's literally nowhere to run away to."

"I've done a damn good job so far," she spat back, and I smiled. That was my girl...well, Rachel. I'd lost the ability to call her mine a long time ago.

"You have. I'm pretty impressed, really."

She was silent, so I forged ahead. "I wish I could say that I rehearsed this moment, that I had this eloquent speech prepped, but that would be bullshit. I never imagined this happening, and I never prepped anything because I never thought I'd get the chance to see you again. If I'd known... God, I would have done so many things differently."

I paused, waiting for her to say something, but she stayed silent.

"I know what Pax did to get you here, and I know that you're under no obligation to talk to me, and I'm definitely not stupid enough to think you're even contemplating giving me a second chance."

Wait. Was that even possible? Understanding, maybe, but her actually trusting me again? I shut that thought down before it ran away with me.

She scoffed, pretty much confirming *that* wasn't going to happen. Thank God I kind of had her captive, because none of this was coming out right.

"Right. I'll be quick—you've got to be getting cold. My point is that what happened back then...what I did to you. It was wrong. I was wrong. I did the wrong goddamned thing for what I thought was the right reason, and I'm so damn sorry—"

The door opened, and I stepped back in shock. Maybe I should have led with the sorry in the first place.

Rachel stood there, gloriously nude, water dripping down her petal-soft skin, and it took every ounce of willpower from every man in the world to keep my eyes on her face. She openly glared at me then lifted a single eyebrow, bent to grab her clothes off the floor—*holy shit, her ass could stop traffic*—and walked right past me, her head held high.

My mouth actually watered with every step she took, and I snapped my lips closed to avoid drooling. I barely contained my groan, unsure of what was sexier—Rachel's perfect body that I knew fit mine like a damn puzzle piece, or her I-don't-give-a-fuck confidence as her hips swayed down the hall.

I should have known that a bathroom door was no match for her tenacity.

Point made.

My heart sank when I looked closer at her lower back. There was a vague, silvery mark, but no tattoo. She'd had it removed. Erased it. Erased *us*.

She slammed her bedroom door, and I followed until my head rested against the wood. "Fuck, you are *so* stubborn," I whispered, but it came out as more of a compliment than a measure of my frustration.

I heard a small thud where her head would be if she were in the same position, and some of the fight drained from me. If she didn't want to talk to me, there was nothing I could do to make her.

"Okay. You win. There's nothing I can say to make you talk or give me a chance to explain. The truth is that I don't deserve it, anyway. I fucked up two years ago. Hell, two years, four months, two weeks, and three days ago. I know, because there hasn't been a day that I haven't thought about you. And I know that doesn't count for anything, that it's all just bullshit, but, Rachel, there's nothing I wouldn't do to just have a simple conversation with you. I've missed you so damn much."

There was a sliding sound and another thud.

"So I'm going to stoop to bribery," I said. "I know how much you loved this lifestyle, and I'm going to use it shamelessly. We're doing a hang gliding stunt off the Lion

Rock the day after the Pacific Cultures trip. If you agree to one conversation with me, just to let me explain, I'll take you with me, tandem."

My heart sank a little every second she didn't answer until I was sure that my last-ditch effort wasn't going to amount to anything. Finally, I conceded the battle and started to walk away.

I was halfway down their hallway when her door opened. "Landon?"

I turned so fast I nearly smacked into the wall…again.

She stood there, a white towel wrapped around her, and it was somehow sexier than when she'd challenged me with her nudity. The swells of her breasts rose above her crossed arms, and even without makeup, her face was startlingly beautiful. God, I'd missed her eyes—missed *everything*. The years I'd missed had taken her teen beauty and turned her into a magnificent woman. I tucked my thumbs into my pockets again to keep me from foolishly reaching for her as our eyes locked. That connection between us that a twenty-year-old kid hadn't understood was still there, and now I knew what chemistry was—and how rare the intensity of ours was. "Rachel?"

"I'll do it," she said, brushing a strand of wet purple hair from her eyes and tucking it behind a delicate ear. It had always astonished me how such a fierce attitude could be contained in such a petite package. If her body matched her personality, she would have towered over me in height.

"You will?"

"I just said I would."

"Right." Where the hell was my game? My smooth lines? My ability to charm the panties off any girl?

She's already not wearing them…

"One thing, though. We'll talk in Sri Lanka. I worked really hard to put you behind me, and I'd like a couple days before you go and rip me apart again."

"God, Rach—"

She shook her head. "No. Not yet. There. We're stuck together all day anyway."

I nodded. "Okay. Sri Lanka it is."

She turned to go back into her room but paused just before she entered. "One more thing."

"Anything," I promised. The girl could have my balls in a vise if she wanted them. Hell, they were pretty much there anyway.

"If I'm signing that media release, I want my own hang glider."

A slow smile spread across my face. "Of course you do. When's the last time you were up?"

Her eyes narrowed. "About six months ago. And I bet I'm still better than you are."

Without another word, she shut the door. I'd never been so happy to get so little out of someone.

I couldn't hide my smile as I walked out past Penna. "Thank you for the idea."

She glanced up then back down at her book. "No problem. And funny, I thought you said it wasn't sexual?"

"What?"

She pointed at my shorts without looking up.

Fuck. I was sporting a hard-on that could have knocked on Rachel's door itself. "It's not *only* sexual," I said, covering myself with a pillow so I could get back to my room without getting shit from half the Renegade crew or the cameras in our suite.

"I would hope so. Plenty of girls have had your *only sexual* lately, and if I were you, I'd make sure that shit ended before you even tried to get back with Rachel."

"Who said I'm getting back—?"

Penna's look silenced me. Having lifelong best friends

was annoying as hell sometimes.

"Okay, you're right, but FYI, I haven't fucked anyone since she crashed back into my life."

"Too much info," Penna said, gagging. "Now go before she sees me conspiring with the enemy."

"I thought you said you were Switzerland?"

"Just because they stay neutral doesn't mean they don't have an opinion."

"Traitor," I teased.

"Out," she said, pointing to the door.

Hard-on happily suppressed, I tossed the pillow onto the couch and left. I had two days to figure out what the hell I could say to Rachel to make her understand what had been the hardest choice of my life if I wanted a chance at having any kind of relationship—friendship or otherwise—with the only woman I'd ever loved.

No pressure or anything.

Chapter Eight

RACHEL

SRI LANKA

Was it possible to instantly fall in love with a place? It had taken a two-hour bus ride to get to Gal Viharaya, and even though I'd been aware of Landon watching me from a few rows behind, I couldn't tear my eyes from the countryside. It was lush, green, and, I kid you not, there had been elephants wandering through the streets a while back.

We made our way as a class up the ruins of the Buddhist temple and listened to our teacher explain the details of the weathered structure. Every time I glanced at Landon, I found him watching me, and I ripped my eyes away.

It was like we were sneaking around again, scared that our glances would give us away.

His baseball hat was missing today, his hair in a sexy disarray that my fingers itched to run through. Those hazel eyes pierced straight through me as he headed in my direction once our professor was done and we were dismissed.

He held out his hand, and I glanced at it briefly before looking back up at him.

"Here?" I asked, knowing my stay of execution was over. As much as I'd blocked off my heart, my head, everything that had to do with him, I was about to have to listen to him make stupid fucking excuses for shredding me.

"Maybe somewhere a little more private?" he asked, motioning to a side of the ruins currently unoccupied by our class.

He checked back at least five times to make sure I was following him as we crossed the small distance, passing a giant Buddha, who looked so peaceful. I envied him that.

"Okay," Landon said and took a deep breath. His mouth opened and closed a couple times while we stood there, eyes locked. "God, I had this all planned out, and now it's all just... gone. I'd almost forgotten the effect you have on me."

"Had," I corrected, wrapping my arms around my stomach. "Everything about us is past tense."

"I know I hurt you," he said softly.

"You did," I agreed, trying to block out the imagery those words brought up—the tears, the devastation, the groveling to get some semblance of my life back.

He rested his hands on top of his head, the tattoos on his arms rippling with the motion. For a brief moment I wondered if he still had it, the one token we'd given each other...the one I'd immediately altered. "I don't think there's anything I can say to take back what happened with us."

"There's not." *That sounded strong. Good. Keep it up.*

"For fuck's sake, Rachel. Could you make this just a little easier? I've been trying for a week to get you alone—to get you to listen to me."

"Why?" I asked. That familiar ache rose, a burning acid in my throat—the hurt I'd worked to lock away. Why couldn't he just leave me alone? Why did he have to chip away at the wall I'd struggled to build? Couldn't he see how hard this was for me?

"Because I want you to understand," he pleaded.

"Why is it so important to you? It's been years. *Years*, and you never once tried to contact me to explain. Hell, I'm only here now because Wilder arranged it—not because you had some crisis of conscience or change of heart." Because if he'd come back once—hell, even called or sent a freaking carrier pigeon—I would have melted. But there was zero chance in hell I was going to give him some kind of convenient absolution just because he didn't want things to be awkward.

I could handle awkward. I couldn't deal with heartbroken again.

"You're right. I have a shit ton to apologize for. I left you. I chose the Renegades because if I didn't, they would have lost the sponsors they needed to put on the Renegade Open that day. We were a package deal, and the sponsors threatened to pull out unless I came back. That would have left Pax, Penna, and Nick covering over two million dollars in prize money, plus the vendors that hadn't been paid yet—all because I walked away. I made a split-second decision when Penna called because, though we'd already fucked over Pax's heart, I couldn't do the same to his career—my career, my family. So I tried to do what I thought was the right thing."

"Right for everyone but me." His explanation served up a fresh slice of pain. They'd all been so happy up there on that television screen while my world had slipped out from under me.

Never again. It didn't matter how sincere he sounded, or how much regret shone from those gorgeous eyes of his, my heart couldn't afford to go through that again. I wouldn't survive it intact.

"Yes. I was a stupid fucking kid. I didn't understand that

what we had was something that doesn't come along twice. I didn't know enough about life—about love—to comprehend what I was doing. I. Was. Stupid. And I'm so sorry, Rach. I don't expect you to forgive me—"

"That's seriously the best you have?"

"What?" He blinked.

My chest burned with a tight pressure that made it nearly impossible to breathe. I sucked in a breath slowly while I debated the merits of walking away. No. This was something that had to be said. "You destroyed me, and the best you have is that you're sorry, you were a stupid kid?"

He pressed his lips in a firm line. "What do you want me to say?"

"I don't know. I was hoping for alien abduction. Body snatchers, the donation of a kidney to a dying girl. Something, *anything* that would excuse what you did—that would give me a reason to stand here and listen to your bullshit." How could that be all there was? How pathetic was I for even wanting an excuse that could justify his actions in my eyes? I was already slipping.

"How many times can I say I'm sorry? I'll say it a thousand times."

"Right. Okay. Let me start with the hours I spent in the ER, waiting for you to answer my text. Then we'll move on to tucking my tail between my legs and going back to my parents, who, if you'll remember, pretty much disowned me when I turned down Dartmouth to go live with you in the apartment that…oh, wait, that's right—the apartment I had to liquidate my savings for so I could pay the deposit when you didn't show up to sign the lease. I should have known then, but I was so naive. So stupid."

"God, Rachel." His shoulders fell.

It wasn't enough. Maybe it was wrong, but for just that moment, I wanted to peel myself open and show him the scars he'd left on my heart. I needed him to know.

"Then there was the joy of listening to my father beg his friend in the admissions office to give me my spot back after I'd declared that true love was more worthwhile than an Ivy League education. And you know who was apologizing then? Me. Apologizing for *you*. You didn't just break my heart—you annihilated it. You pulverized me and then went on your merry way like nothing had even happened."

My heart ached with the emotions I'd done my best to lock away since he walked out, but they were now screaming to be acknowledged and set free. But I couldn't let them out. It was like Pandora's box in there, and the minute I let any of them slip, the slivers of me that wanted to believe him—the ones yelling the loudest that this was the man I'd loved—would run amok and then I'd be right back where I was two years ago. Destroyed, angry, and loving the man I desperately needed to hate.

I saw a group of girls from our class come toward us but didn't pause. If I was going to allow myself this one moment to let it go, I wasn't holding back.

"You went back to the Renegades and left me to pick up the pieces you shattered. Maybe I was the whore for cheating on Wilder, for falling in love with you. Maybe I *am* your curse. But I didn't deserve to bear the entire weight of what we'd both done." My throat tightened, and I blinked quickly, fighting back the prickling sensation in my eyes. I would not cry over him. Never again.

"You're right." His fingers tugged at his hair momentarily in obvious frustration. "But I wasn't undamaged. There wasn't a day that I didn't think about you, wonder where you were."

"Hey, Nova," one of the girls said, eye fucking Landon as she waltzed by, swaying her ass.

"Yeah." I laughed. "Good thing you had tons of girls to soothe that hurt, *Nova*."

He put up his hands in surrender. "Okay. Valid point made. I'm a dick, I did dick things, and then I overused said dick in what has been a failed attempt to get over you. Got it. But seeing you again—whether or not it was Wilder's doing—I guess I knew we couldn't start over, but I was hoping that we could at least be friends. You were my best friend, Rachel."

I swallowed. "No. Wilder was. You chose him, and it took me a really long time to accept that as my reality. I waited the first few weeks for you to come back, for an explanation, for you to tell me that those promises we'd made to each other really meant something to you, because our plans, our future, our relationship meant everything to me, and I was so fucking stupid to love you like I did because you moved on like I was nothing to you." My voice broke, and I took a steadying breath, fumbling over my stupid feelings to get a grip. "Yes, we're stuck together for the next six months, but being friends? That's too much. That Rachel—the silly eighteen-year-old you said was your infinity—you killed her. My heart stopped the moment I saw you on that TV screen, and that naive little girl in my soul didn't die…she just ceased to be. So if I'm cold, callous, or unforgiving, then I'm simply what you made me." I shook my head. "No, I'm what I made myself to make sure that I was never fooled again."

"I'm not trying to fool you," he said quietly, his eyes soft and warm—and everything I'd missed about him came rushing back in.

I saw him standing in the rain three years ago, waiting for me the afternoon we'd finally given in to our feelings. I saw the boy he'd been—so passionate, so protective—lying just under the surface of the man before me.

For a second I saw my Landon under Nova…and that was dangerous. My defenses started to shake, a vulnerability I hadn't felt in years, and I scrambled for some kind of ladder to get me out of the pit of emotion he'd dragged me into.

"This is the only time you'll bribe me like this," I said, my tone stronger than I felt. "Thanks to Leah, Wilder has already told me that I can be in on whatever you guys are doing, and I intend to take him up on it. I'll never give up anything for you ever again. So let's just be honest."

His jaw tensed, those eyes a turbulent sea of blue and green. "Okay. Be honest."

"I loved you. You broke me. No matter what connection we still have, I won't ever let you close enough to do it again. That's the place we're at." It was the only place I could afford to be, no matter how loudly my body sang when he was near, or how the deadened little lump of my heart had the nerve to flicker back to life at the sound of his voice.

He stalked forward until my ass hit the stone wall behind me and then caged me with his arms. "You got to be honest. My turn."

"Okay," I said, tilting my chin and hoping I looked unaffected by his nearness. Maybe if I quit breathing, stopped taking in his cedar-and-Landon scent, my body would forget that I knew his intimately.

Instead my own body went traitor and sent heat coursing through my veins, like it remembered every sensation he was capable of producing. The intensity in his eyes stole the air from my lungs and stripped me of my bravado when I needed it the most.

"I loved you," he said, his voice low. "I broke *myself*— whether or not you saw it doesn't change that fact. I'll respect your wishes. I'll keep my distance. But that connection you're talking about? Yeah, it's still there, still humming through my goddamned nervous system every time you walk in the fucking room, so as much as you'd like to, you can't control my thoughts or what I want."

My throat went dry. *No! You're stronger than this.* "What *do* you want?"

He smirked, and my dry throat morphed into drool. Shit.

"Nothing you're ready for. Hell, maybe I'm not, either. But I'm not a kid anymore, and I'm not scared of what we could be—what we already are despite the pain we've caused each other. Six months together, Rachel. You can fight it all you want, but you and I both know we're going to end up here time and again, because if there's one thing our past has proved, it's that you and I are inevitable, no matter who we hurt—even if it's each other. I will never forgive myself for walking away from you. I know you don't believe me, and that's my fault, too, but I'm going to spend the next six months proving it to you. Because what I want is for you to look at me the way you used to, no matter how impossible that seems." He pushed off the wall and walked toward where the teacher was gathering the students.

I looked over to the reclining Buddha, whose face was carved in an expression of utter relaxation and Zen. "Spend some time with Landon Rhodes and we'll see how long you stay at peace," I muttered and headed for the bus to take us back to the ship.

I'd hoped that coming clean with Landon would give me some kind of closure, like tattooing over an old scar so you didn't see it anymore.

Instead it felt like I'd just reopened the whole damn wound.

• • •

"You sure about this?" I asked Leah as I fastened her helmet so she could ride tandem with Wilder. The wind was steady on the ruins of Sigiriya, which was basically a huge plateau that rose out of nowhere. The sun shone perfectly above the lush, forested carpet hundreds of feet beneath us, and it struck me again how lucky I was to be able to get to do something like this. Securing permits to do this near these ruins must have cost Wilder a fortune.

"Absolutely," Leah answered, her eyes clear. "I might not be up to the real Renegade status, but I'm actually learning to enjoy these things as long as I forget that there's always this chance of death lurking."

I laughed. "Yeah, dying would suck."

She joined in, her smile wide and bright. "Totally. Death can be so pesky."

I loved seeing her like this. She'd spent the years after her boyfriend's death like a specter, barely functioning, but now she'd blossomed, and as much as I generally despised Wilder, I was immensely thankful for the unbelievable change in my best friend.

"You okay?" she asked softly, glancing behind her to where the cameras were pointed elsewhere. "Pax told me you and Landon had a showdown yesterday. Why didn't you tell me?"

I forced a smile. "You have enough going on with your life, and for once you're happy. I'm not dragging you down."

"Rachel." Her shoulders sagged.

"Don't *Rachel* me. I'm fine. I was fine before I got here, and I'll be fine after we leave. I just have to keep my defenses up around him."

"Pax said Landon's a mess."

Speak of the devil... Wilder walked over, cutting our conversation short, and checked Leah's helmet. What would normally drive me nuts struck me as sweet. He wasn't taking any chances with her safety, and I respected that.

"I'm glad the weather cleared up," Leah said as he tugged on her straps.

"Yeah, the rain has been ridiculous here this week. I thought we were going to have to cancel," he said to her.

The curse of Rachel. I shook my head, trying to clear it.

Funny how one little line in a blog could hit me so hard. Those first few months I'd read everything I could about Landon, unable to quit him cold turkey, but I'd never expected to be called out publicly as the reason he was off his game. Back then I'd been glad. It was something that told me I still affected him. Now I just wanted to put those days behind me.

Besides, it wasn't like I could change the weather. Even my bad luck wasn't that powerful.

"So, Rachel, do you want to review the hang glider procedure with me?" Wilder asked, all business even though his arm was draped across Leah's shoulders.

"I would honestly rather not," I said with a sweet smile. One day I would forgive him. Today was not that day.

He shrugged. "Okay, I'll send Landon over."

"Oh, hell no. I'd rather jump off this rock sans glider than spend unnecessary time with him."

A snort sounded at my back.

"He's right behind me, isn't he?" I asked.

Leah bit her lip and nodded.

"Well, that doesn't change the truth."

"Yeah, we'll leave you guys to it," Wilder said, pulling Leah away as she mouthed, "Sorry!"

I sighed, steeling myself against the inevitable physical reaction of being near Landon. Then I turned to find him smirking at me. "You'd rather jump off? Really?"

"Yup," I said, no apologies.

"Ouch. Well, let's get you checked out. When was the last time you did this?" he asked as we walked over to my glider.

"Took a hang glider ride off a remote, giant rock in the middle of Sri Lanka?" I asked, trying to ignore the fact that Landon was taking care of me the same way I'd just gone all melty over Wilder and Leah.

"Nice, smart-ass," he replied, setting my helmet on my head and latching it under my chin. His fingers caught one of my strands of dyed hair. "I like the purple."

"I didn't do it for you," I snapped, remembering every time he'd smiled when I'd changed the color of my hair. Dealing with Landon flashbacks was the last thing I needed right now when I was still scraped raw from our fight yesterday. How the hell was he so unaffected, all smiles like we hadn't drawn blood? I backed up a step so he wouldn't touch me. Even just that small brush against my skin had been electric.

He raised an eyebrow. "Can't even take a compliment from me?"

"I'm not taking anything from you," I said, hating the way my body physically warmed at his smile.

"Yeah, okay. What we have here—"

"Is a typical A-frame with control bar and pod harness," I finished.

"God, that's sexy," he said with a groan.

"We need to discuss your turn-on standards."

"Any time, any place," he answered, running his tongue across his lower lip with a slow lick.

Casanova, indeed.

"Just help me into my harness." Crap, was my voice breathless? No. I refused to even acknowledge that possibility, or the effect he had on me.

Landon was all business as he buckled me in, double-checking each line and connection in a way that made me feel protected—cared for. *Don't be so stupid. He doesn't care for you. He just wants to chase you now that you're all shiny and unattainable again.* His fingers lingered, caressing my bare skin where the harness met it, but not long enough for me to snap at him.

Just long enough to wake up every single one of my nerves, which were all pretty much Landon's fangirls screaming that he was back. They fluttered like dancing butterflies in my stomach. No wonder he got laid so often. If he could set me on fire—given the way I felt about him—he must have had the other girls' panties on the ground when he was done buckling them in.

Not that I should care who he was buckling next.

Fuck. I did.

"How do you feel?" he asked, low and serious as he scraped the stubble on his chiseled jaw.

Our eyes locked, his bordering more on the green side of hazel today, and I felt that same awakening ripple through me. Yup, the man was a panty collector.

Mine were *not* joining his trophy case.

"I'm good," I answered honestly, knowing that now wasn't the time to dish shit back at him. This was stunt time. "Wind looks great. I haven't been hang gliding in about six months, but I spent some time with the practice rig Wilder set up yesterday, so I'm feeling really confident. You don't need to worry about me."

"I always worry about you," he said quietly. "You put the insane in extreme."

I scoffed. "There's no *insane* in extreme."

"That's because you haven't been around to add it in lately. I've missed the way you keep me on my toes."

My heart jumped, and I shut up the fangirling butterflies in my stomach with a quick reminder of what it had felt like when he'd walked out on me. I undid the clasp on my helmet, needing to check it myself—to have not depended on him—and the damn thing broke in my hand.

"Seriously?" I asked the butchered plastic like it would answer.

"Did that break? Let me look at it," Landon demanded.

I handed it over. "It's not sabotage, or anything like what you guys just went through. Just my bad luck."

He looked over my helmet, all trace of kidding gone. "You're not bad luck."

"Nova!" one of the Renegade girls called out to my right. "Want to do my double-check?"

"Yeah, Zoe, I'll be right there," he called back. "I'll have a new helmet brought over," he told me. Then he tugged at my rig one more time, nodded to himself, and went to lock in the girl who'd paged him.

God help me, I watched his every movement, analyzing the quick, efficient motions he used on her. There were no lingering caresses, no long gazes...well, from him. She looked like she was ready to eat him.

She probably already has at one time or another.

Ugh. I didn't need to speak the thought aloud to know that it sounded like I was jealous.

I looked up and down the line of Renegades ready to launch. We were definitely guy heavy. Hell, predominantly guy heavy, with Penna out. But as I counted the girls, I couldn't help but wonder how many of them he'd slept with.

My guess? All.

Well, except Leah, of course. I highly doubted Landon would ever make the same mistake twice.

He strapped into the rig next to me.

"What are you doing?" I asked, thankful the wind had calmed just enough to make my rig stop trying to take me backward.

"I figured I'd jump off this whole rock thing. You know, make the cameras happy." He pointed to the camera crew who strategically walked up and down the lines, getting shots.

"Right next to me?"

"Yeah, well, like I said, I always worry about you." He winked and finished strapping in.

My stomach tightened, and I cursed myself and my stupid, girly reactions to him. *Inevitable*, my ass. I was stronger than that.

"Holy shit. Rachel?"

I turned my head since my body was pretty much on lockdown and saw Little John coming toward us, a new helmet in hand. The guy was massive, at least six five, with a belly that far overshot his pants and a shaved-bald head. He was also the one Renegade I adored. My smile was instant and gloriously genuine. "John!"

He ducked under my canopy and enveloped me in a hug. "Damn, I'm glad to see you. What the hell are you doing here?"

"Ask Wilder. Long story."

He nodded slowly. "Well, whatever it was that brought you back, I'm grateful."

"I'm not back," I argued. "I'm just…around."

He glanced between Landon, whose eyes were locked on him, and me. "Well, it looks like not much has changed." He handed me the helmet, and I slipped it on.

"Can you double-check me?" Landon asked as Little John adjusted my straps for a snug fit.

"No prob," he said and went to Landon, doing his safety checks as the two mumbled to each other.

Watching John and Landon reminded me that I hadn't just lost Landon when he'd walked out—I'd lost all the friends I'd made that year.

But I'd gained Leah, who was pretty priceless.

Once we were all locked in, the adrenaline flooded my system, my heart kicking up a beat as Wilder counted us down. This high, this rush…this was life. This was what kept me distracted from Landon in bits and pieces—well, that and taking care of Leah.

At the cue, I raced off the cliff edge, in sync with the others—and went airborne. My heart jumped into my throat as euphoria washed over me. Was there anything better than this? With a few practiced motions, I got my feet into the bottom of the pod harness and, once horizontal, settled into my flight. I tried to take in everything, every sight, feeling, smell, and sound. I wanted to savor this, lock it away in my memory so when I was back home next year, slaving away in the journalism department, I'd have this to remember.

Right now, nothing existed besides the rig and my own ability. I controlled it, careful to watch those around me, and when the signal came, we all pulled the synchronized turns. I checked my distance from the other Renegades, knowing there weren't even inches to spare before we'd collide. From the ground it would look like we were one line of hang gliders maneuvering on a single string as we executed the turns, the dips, and pitch backs. My stomach lurched with every dip, then soared when I pulled up at the last possible second. Once those were complete, we all cheered. That was going to look badass on camera.

Then we were all free. I dipped and turned, laughing with the wind, the way my stomach plummeted only to come back to me when I came out of a dive. There was nothing to distract me. Nothing that labeled me broken or damaged. In those precious moments, there were no parents telling me I was a chronic disappointment, no Landon, no heartbreak, no feeling like I was never good enough for him to choose me.

But the problem with landing was that I knew as soon as I touched down, it would all be there waiting for me.

Especially Landon.

Chapter Nine

LANDON

SRI LANKA

I turned my baseball hat backward and closed our suite's door behind me as I left. An extra hour of working on my paper for Civ meant I'd missed the bus to Nuwara Eliya, but I'd already made arrangements, so I wasn't stressed.

I walked down the hall and knocked on Penna and Rachel's door. Rachel opened the door, her cheeks flushed, a slight panic in her eyes. "What are you doing here?" she asked.

"I could ask you the same thing," I replied, my heart jumping at the sight of her. Hopefully I'd start getting used to seeing her again, but so far it had hit me like a lightning bolt every time.

She rolled her eyes and pivoted, giving me a fantastic view of her ass in tiny board shorts. The neck of her bikini top was knotted just above the tank top she wore. All it would take was one little tug and the fabric would slide so easily—

"Talk some sense into her before we're late!" Rachel yelled back.

Right. I wasn't here to ogle my ex. I walked down the hall to see Penna on the couch, her leg elevated and a book in her lap. "Let's go, Rebel." I threw her stage name at her, hoping it would spark some of the fire she kept banked lately.

"And do what?" she asked. "They changed out the cast into what? Another non-weight-bearing one. What the hell am I supposed to do while you guys are in the jungle doing giant slip-and-slides?"

"Just be with the team?" I suggested. The glare she shot me suggested that I might need to duck if I opened my mouth again.

"You're so right. It's always been in my nature to tag along and watch."

I got down to her level, staring at her until she looked me in the eyes. The normal sparkle in her baby blues had dulled to a defeated matte. "Penna," I whispered. "You have to stop blaming yourself for what happened."

"I can't." The straightforward way she said it sent a lump into my throat.

"I'm not going to be the jackass who tells you to get over it, or that I understand, because I don't. I've never been through what you're enduring. But I know what it is to nearly take this team down, and you did nothing wrong."

She curved her shoulders, hunching in on herself. "I just don't feel like me."

I took her hand and brushed my thumb over her knuckles. "Well, the thing is that we don't feel like *us* without *you*. Take all the time you need, but know that we're here. We're going to be here, knocking on your door, asking you to come with us, leaving your seat vacant."

"Landon…" Her eyes squeezed shut.

"We're going to beg, bribe, and everything short of bully you into getting back out there with us. And that seat will stay vacant, Penna. No one can replace you. But if you're telling me that you're not ready, that you still need to work some shit out, then I'll respect it."

She lifted my hand to her forehead and took a stuttered breath. "Thank you. I'm so sorry."

I leaned forward, kissing her on the temple. "I love you, Pen. We all do. No matter what."

"I love you, too," she said with a sad smile. "Now get out of here before you miss the whole thing."

My stomach sank, knowing that she was saying no. I'd never seen her so down, so unreachable. Brooke had destroyed more than Penna's leg when she'd sabotaged us, and I had no clue what it was going to take to bring her back.

Rachel's eyes were soft as she leaned against the wall in the hallway, watching me. For that second, her guard was down and I simply saw *her*, not the walls she'd hidden behind since I discovered her on board.

She blinked rapidly and cleared her throat. "Yeah, so we should go."

I nodded. "Yeah. Penna, you sure you'll be all right?"

She waved us off, her mask firmly in place. "Absolutely. Take pictures."

I headed for the door, Rachel following. We were silent as we made it to the thankfully empty elevator. The last thing I needed was any more of the girls I'd slept with on this boat getting near us. Oh, yeah, I was reaping what I'd sown, and it tasted rather bitter every time Rachel lifted an eyebrow at me in that knowing way she had.

"You really do love her," she said softly as I hit the fourth deck so we could disembark.

"Of course I do. She's the closest thing I have to a sister."

She adjusted her backpack, the black straps thick above

her swimsuit's halter neckline. "It's just nice to know that you are still the same in some ways."

The numbers lit as we passed through a few floors, and I tried to gather my thoughts. To say something that would give me half a chance of Rachel being real with me at least for the next few hours. "I'm the same in almost every way that matters."

"And those that don't?" she asked as the elevator *dinged*.

"Some better, some worse, all the aftereffects of what happened with us."

She stiffened, but her eyes didn't. "I get that," she said as she walked out in front of me.

We made our way quietly through the disembarkation area, empty since everyone with access to the VIP exit was already gone. Once our IDs were scanned, we headed down the ramp off the *Athena*.

Rachel's shoulders slumped as we looked over the port of Colombo. "We missed the bus." She turned, bumping into me.

My hands steadied her bare shoulders. Shit, her skin was just as soft as I'd remembered. I immediately lifted my hands, knowing our small truce would be over if I touched her when she clearly didn't want me to.

She stepped backward, making my point.

"Yeah, we're about an hour and"—I checked my watch—"twelve minutes late. Don't worry, I had Little John get me a car." A quick search of my pockets and I dangled the keys in front of her.

"You knew?" she asked, her eyes narrowing.

"Knew that I'd miss the bus? Yeah, I had a paper due for Civ. You missing the bus is just an added bonus. Want a lift to the slides?"

She chewed on her lower lip while the gears in her brain turned. The impulsive Rachel I'd loved didn't appear much around me. This one thought through every decision she made if I was involved. "It's a two-hour drive."

"A little over, actually."

She groaned, rolling her neck.

"Hey, no pressure. I'm just a guy asking a girl if she needs a ride."

She arched an eyebrow. "You ask a lot of girls that."

Shots fired. I was going to need a hell of a lot thicker armor if I wanted to get close to her. "Maybe, but you're the only one I know I don't have a shot with."

Something flickered across her eyes. *Was that disappointment? Please be disappointment!*

"Fine. I'll ride with you."

She spun and walked down the ramp, leaving me to follow. Once we hit the pavement, she let me take the lead, finding the Jeep Little John had arranged for us. Top and doors off, it was perfect for the muggy heat.

"How about I drive?" Rachel asked, tossing her backpack in the backseat.

"How about we both live through the drive?" I joked. "See, even the port agrees," I said, pointing to the SAFETY FIRST sign that hung at the gate to the pier.

She huffed but hopped in, fastening her seat belt as I did the same. As soon as I'd entered the GPS coordinates Pax had left me, we rolled out.

The city was busy, but we found the highway easily enough. My stomach wouldn't settle, and my nerves wouldn't calm. It was worse now than it had been the spring I'd fallen for her. Being this close to Rachel was like setting a magnet next to a compass—everything I thought I knew started spinning, and I couldn't tell which way was up.

"Music?" I asked, needing any distraction from the way her smooth legs stretched out from her seat.

"My phone's worthless for everything but iTunes out here," she said, plugging it into the jack that wired to the vehicle's sound system. Fall Out Boy came to life in the speakers, and she pulled her sunglasses over her eyes, then fought to tie her hair back against the wind whipping through the Jeep.

The lush, green hills rose around us as we headed farther inland, and it wasn't long before she pulled out her camera and started snapping pictures.

When Tom Petty came on, I shot her a questioning look.

She shrugged. "It's on random," she said, and went back to focusing her camera through the door space.

My life had been full of moments that burrowed into my soul, the memories crisp and detailed—the smell of the snow as I won X Games medals, the rush of wind skydiving over Madagascar, the taste of her lips the first time I'd ever kissed Rachel. This…sitting next to her halfway across the world as she took pictures, her hair falling from its tie, a smile playing at her lips, the warm morning sun shining through the top, even the music coming through the radio, all imprinted on my memory, and I knew I'd replay it often.

This was what I'd always thought we'd be. Seeing the world together, laughing, fighting, making up, pulling stunts— it was everything we'd talked about, and what I knew we were really meant for.

Hell, sitting next to her, even knowing she'd rather toss me from this Jeep than let me kiss her, was more fulfilling than the last half a dozen girls I'd taken to bed. I just had to find a way to break down her walls somehow and see if there was any part of her heart that could still feel something besides hatred for me.

Because I was still fucking wild over her.

The song switched, Bon Iver's "Skinny Love" coming on, and she immediately tensed. I started to sing, but through quick side glances I saw her fumble for her phone and skip the song. Halsey's "Gasoline" came through the speakers, and though it was pretty much a perfect song for Rachel, I turned it down.

"Why did you skip it?" I asked.

She looked my way briefly before putting her camera back to her eye.

"Rachel," I prompted. "I thought you liked that song."

Hell, I'd always loved that song because—

"It…" She shook her head and gave a self-deprecating laugh. "It reminds me too much of you. Of us. I just never took it off."

Exactly.

My grip tightened on the steering wheel. "Do you do that with everything that reminds you of me? Turn it off? Throw it away?" I asked just loud enough for her to hear me over the road noise.

"Yeah," she answered, but there was no snark to her voice, no sharp bite. "It was the only way I survived." She propped her feet up on the dash. "What about you?"

I passed a slower bus and pulled back into our lane, letting the speed take away some of the sting in her words. "No. If it's on, I let it play. If I see a picture, I look. I learned a long time ago that the only way I could avoid thinking about you would be to shut off my brain or cut out my heart. Since I need both of those to live, I've always just dealt with it." I took a steadying breath. "When did you get it removed? I saw your back in the hallway. I know it's gone."

She sucked in her breath like I'd wounded her when, in this particular case, the opposite was true. "When I finally realized you weren't coming back."

She turned away, focusing on the rising hills around us, and I knew this line of conversation was done for now.

It was pretty apparent that we'd handled our breakup differently—not that I could blame her. What had happened… what I did, well, it was unforgivable. There was a reason I'd never called her, never tracked her down after she'd blocked me on every form of social media. Rachel had always been one to burn the bridge, salt the earth, generally walk away without looking back, and there was nothing I could say or do that would make up for the past.

But she's here now.

I held onto that small flame of hope as we made it another hour and a half toward Kitulgala.

She looked up as the first raindrops hit the windshield. "Well, I didn't see that one coming," she muttered.

"Storms come in fast off the ocean," I said, looking for a place to pull over. The outcropping on the right worked just fine, and I brought us to a standstill. "Remember how to do this?" I asked her.

We locked gazes, and a dozen memories assaulted me of when we'd done the same for the Jeep she'd owned back in L.A.

"Yeah, I think I can handle it." Damn it, her voice was sharp enough to cut again.

We made quick work of pulling the canvas top out of the back and snapping it on. The doors came next.

"I guess it's been the rainiest fall they've had in twenty years or something," I told her as we climbed back in, both splattered with raindrops.

"Really? We're going to talk about the weather?"

"Seems the safest topic," I said as we pulled back onto the road.

Rachel messed around with the defrost until she found a setting that kept the windshield clear. God, I'd missed how well we worked together, how she anticipated every need before it even became one. "That might be true."

We made the turnoff onto the road that led to the slide site. The road cut so sharply into the steep hill that I was sure Rachel could reach out her window and touch the hillside if she tried.

"So, like I said, they've had some pretty torrential rain, so that's why the slides are epic. The rapids are a bitch, but Pax has everyone suiting up in life vests. I guess the pools between the slides are wicked deep."

"As long as he keeps Leah safe, that's all I care about," she said, looking up the hill.

"She's his number-one priority right now."

"I figured that out. Shocked me, honestly, seeing as the Wilder I remembered never saw past his need for an X Games medal." She leaned forward in her seat, staring up through the windshield.

"He's changed. We all have," I said, defensiveness creeping in. "You know, I get it. What happened was horseshit, but we're not the same as we were back then. It's been two and a half years, Rach. Don't you believe in change?"

"Sure. I just think people have to be capable of it. From what I've seen in the media, you've only gone from bad to worse."

"What the hell is that supposed to mean?" I squinted against the driving sheets of rain, trying to focus on the road. The last thing we needed was for me to drive off the edge of the road.

"Want me to take over?" she asked.

"Ha. I've seen you drive. You're far safer with me behind the wheel. So is the entire population of Sri Lanka."

"Weren't you just the one telling me that people change?" She went back to staring up at the hillside through the windshield.

"And you were just telling me that my change didn't live up to your standard." My muscles tightened, and I tried to breathe through my flash of anger. I needed every spare ounce of concentration for the road.

"Live up to my standard? Damn. At least I have

standards."

"What? And you've been a nun since we…"

"Since you left me?" she snapped. "No. I've had boyfriends. I've had sex. Really good sex. I just didn't chase every penis I came in contact with."

Of course she'd had sex with other guys. She was gorgeous, funny, smart, and fully in control of her sexuality, which was hot as hell. But that sure as fuck didn't stop me from wanting to beat the other guys to shit for touching what was mine.

Not yours, moron. You gave up that right.

"You know what? Let's just back out of this line of conversation," I suggested, flicking the windshield wipers on the highest setting. "Apparently we both have some pretty strong feelings—"

"Landon," Rachel whispered.

"No, it's okay that we have strong feelings. We should. That means there's hope. I'd rather you hate me than to not care—"

"Landon!" Rachel screamed. "Look!"

I lurched forward, ducking my head to look up the hillside where she pointed. Wait…was that…?

"Holy shit!" I slammed on the brakes, sending us into a skid as half the mountain came down in front of us.

"Landslide!"

The roar was deafening, and all my powers of speech failed. Rocks, trees, chunks of the earth plummeted, all carried by a deluge of mud. I'd never seen anything so terrifying in my life. The car in front of us by fifty feet or so was in the clear.

My eyes darted to the hillside above us that held steady, and the instinct to flee took over. "We have to get out of here."

There was no chance I was dying on a remote road in the middle of Sri Lanka, or that I was letting anything happen to Rachel.

I slammed the Jeep into reverse, put my hand behind

Rachel's seat, and hit the gas. Thank God there was no one behind us. The rain still pummeled us, but at least the canvas top didn't cover the back portion of the Jeep. I could see out. Barely.

Adrenaline flooded my system, my body familiar with the hormone, and everything became sharp, clear, like I was in the middle of a snowboarding run or a stunt.

I'd just never had Rachel's life in my hands before.

"Oh my God. Landon, go faster!"

I looked forward only long enough to see that the small barricades to keep us from falling off the road were helping to channel the debris flow, and it was headed straight for us.

Thick trees, green branches, and that little white car ahead of us had all been picked up by the raging river of mud.

"Shit! Watch that."

I set all my concentration to the road behind us and prayed that my driving skills were enough to get us out of this alive. There had been a small outcropping right after we'd come through the bend in the road. We just had to get—

"It's gaining on us," Rachel said quietly, the calm in her voice almost eerie.

I skirted around a car that was trying the same maneuver, passing him on the left…the right. Shit, it was all jumbled.

"Tell me if it gets to that car."

"Okay."

The engine protested the high speed in reverse, the whine almost enough to drown out the sound of the landslide approaching. The road was the worst possible place for it to channel—the liquefied soil would carry debris far faster than without pavement.

I sure as hell wasn't telling Rachel that.

"It's picked up the second car."

I chanced a look back and saw it coming at us with only twenty or so feet to spare. *This is so not good.*

Turning my attention back to the road, I saw it. "There!" I yelled. "Hold on tight!"

I spun us into the small outcropping, flipping our direction. Before we came to a stop, I had the clutch in and the car ready for second gear.

"Now!" Rachel instructed.

As I straightened the wheel, I popped the clutch and launched back into the road just as the mud took the outcropping. Then I hit the gas and we sped down the road as quickly as I could safely get us down in the driving rain. Third gear. That was all that was safe on these winding roads, and I had no clue who could be waiting around the bend.

Who might be driving into their worst nightmare.

"It's not going to stop," I told her, knowing we were only halfway down the mountain. "Find another road. We have to get off this one."

The glove box clicked as Rachel opened it, taking out a map. Her fingers flew over the accordion-folded paper. "Where are we…where are we?" she muttered.

I knew better than to answer her.

A quick look in my rearview mirror told me the slide was picking up speed, and we were the next obstacle in the chute.

"Here!" she exclaimed, pointing to the map. "There's a road a half mile on the left. We should be able to get to the highway if this one…isn't available."

She sucked in her breath, and I caught her looking in the rearview as I slammed the car into fourth gear. "Don't look."

"Kind of impossible, seeing as the mountain would like to eat us."

"Yeah, I know."

I cursed, braking through a steep turn, knowing it cost us precious seconds. A glance back confirmed it. I couldn't see the end of the landslide, only the two cars a little farther back in the debris, which meant we were in serious danger of hydroplaning and becoming part of the slide.

"There!" Rachel yelled, pointing to the road on the left.

"Hold on!"

"Never stopped," she whispered.

We locked eyes for a precious millisecond, and then I ripped the car to the left, braking at the last possible second as the car skidded around the ninety-degree turn. I threw it into 4x4 low for the steep incline and tore up the gravel road, the rain forming a creek exactly in the middle of where I wanted to be.

"Landon!" Rachel yelled.

I punched the gas and prayed, thanking God when the tires caught and we lurched up the hill.

I didn't stop until we crested the small hill, leaving at least thirty feet between us and the slide as it rushed by beneath us.

Flinging my door open, I jumped down, immediately drenched by the unforgiving rain. My feet carried me to the back of the Jeep, where I could see the massive river of…fuck, *everything* flowing down the road.

Rachel stumbled around the back, and I grabbed her to me, clutching her tiny frame against my chest. "Tell me you're okay."

She shook violently, and I couldn't tell if she was nodding or not.

"Rachel?" I tilted her chin so I could see those brown eyes.

"I'm…f-f-f-fine," she stammered, raindrops hitting her face.

I sat on the bumper and pulled her with me, cradling her as carefully as I could. "Good. That's good."

As I relaxed my muscles, the adrenaline fled, draining everything from me but the relief that we had somehow miraculously survived. My breath came in great gulps, and I knew that I held on to Rachel more for myself.

I replayed the last minutes, everything that had happened since we saw the ground give way, and my heart pounded against my ribs. "We'll have to take the other road back. There's no way that one will be passable."

She nodded against my chest, her head tucked into that perfect notch just under my collarbone. It might have been years since I'd held her, but she felt exactly the same, her sun-kissed citrus scent still invaded my senses, and for just this moment, she held onto me as if we'd never been apart.

"You're sure you're okay?" I asked, needing to hear it again, needing to know that I hadn't gotten her hurt.

She nodded.

I tilted her chin again so I could see her face. She looked up at me with wide, wild eyes and parted lips that I had the nearly undeniable urge to kiss.

But I didn't. Not like this. Not because we'd almost died.

"Rachel?" I asked. "Say something."

A shaky smile played at her lips. "I'm really glad you didn't let me drive."

We both burst into laughter, washing away some of the terror, and I hugged her close, savoring the contact and the beat of her heart.

Even if this was all we ever had—these few moments where we'd sought comfort from each other—it would be enough. Just having her not hate me for fifteen seconds was a hell of a lot better than the last couple of years.

Okay, that was a lie.

It would never be enough.

Chapter Ten

RACHEL

"Stop looking at me like that," I told Leah as we hunched over our books at the dining room table the next afternoon.

"Like what?" she asked, her gaze still moving over all my exposed parts.

"Like I'm secretly wounded and about to bleed out at any moment." I flipped the page in my notebook. "I told you I'm fine. He's fine. We're…" I shook my head. "Everything is fine."

"You were civil to Landon at lunch," she remarked. "You even let him sit across from you and didn't break into a food fight."

"Yeah?" I uncapped my highlighter and attacked my textbook. *So much for selling this sucker back.*

"Seriously, Rachel, what's going on? Is this about the"—her voice dropped to a whisper—"mudslide?"

"You don't have to whisper, I can still hear you," Penna

called out from the living room, where I was pretty sure her ass was going to leave a permanent indent on the sofa.

"Sorry, Penna. I just didn't want to upset you."

She scoffed. "Upset me? I wasn't the one almost devoured by a piece of Sri Lanka, and I can honestly say that Brooke didn't have anything to do with it."

"Maybe *I* did. After all, I'm the jinx, right? The curse?" I asked.

She tossed her book on the coffee table and staggered to her feet. "I'm not going there. The whole concept of luck went out the window when Brooke flew off the handle."

My highlighter paused in midair as she crutched over to us. Opening up about what her sister had done wasn't really a line we'd crossed before now. Of course I knew what had happened, Leah had filled me in, but this was first time Penna had brought it up herself.

"So you think the weather that almost held up the hang gliding stunt and the mudslide are both…" *The curse of Rachel.* I came back to the Renegades, and all hell was breaking loose. *You're not back in the Renegades*, I reminded myself.

"Shitty coincidences. Well, the rain caused the mudslide, so really it's the weather. Don't be so hard on yourself, Rachel."

I focused back on my textbook, pulling phrases I could cite for my paper proposal. "What I wouldn't give for some good internet."

"Why didn't you say something?" Penna asked. "Grab my laptop."

"You have internet out here? I thought it was impossible."

"Nothing's impossible when you throw enough resources at it," she said. "Seriously, do you need it?"

I looked down at my nearly finished proposal. "I think I'm good, but thank you. I might need it later."

"Just don't tell your mom that you have it," Leah suggested.

Guilt hit me like a Mack truck. "I was supposed to call

from Sri Lanka."

"I think she'll understand," Penna answered.

"You don't know her mother," Leah rebutted.

"True. She's a little…protective."

Leah laughed, then clapped her hand over her mouth. "I'm sorry."

"Don't be. You know how she gets. The only reason they even 'allowed'"—I used air quotes—"me to come on this was because they knew you'd be here, and they hoped you'd keep me in line."

"Yeah, because I have so much control over you," she said, flipping another page in her book.

"Well, I sure as hell didn't tell them you'd hooked up with Wilder. That would have earned me a strict demand to get my ass home. Hell, if they so much as sniffed Landon around me, they'd probably be in India waiting for us to dock."

"They have good reason to hate him," Penna answered. "From the parent point of view, of course."

"That's not going to stop you from coming on the Everest trip, right?" Leah asked.

I groaned. "Leah, as much as I would love to go with you, that's over a week with him. There's a bunch of other optional shore excursions that—"

"Wouldn't be as much fun!" she argued. "Seriously. Pax promised we'd spend one day at the Taj Mahal before flying to Nepal, and that isn't on any shore excursion. You only get that if you come with the Renegades."

"How did you convince him to do that? It's an entire plane ride out of the way."

"I mentioned wanting to do my research paper on it, and he said he'd make it happen if I agreed to freeze my butt off with him in Nepal."

"It's a Renegade-only trip," I argued.

Leah gave me the you're-being-stupid face. "Landon

wants you there."

"Not if he's doing what I think he is. If he's trying to ride that ridgeline for the documentary, he doesn't need me distracting him or just generally cursing him. He's been dreaming of that chance for *years*, ever since I've known him, and I'm not going to be the reason he fucks it up or gets himself killed."

Leah sighed. "I think he'd do better just to show off for you. Seriously. I want you to come, and I know you'd love the trip."

"Coming is optional, of course," Penna added with a snort laugh.

"Nice," I threw in her direction. "That is so not happening."

"Please? We're partially trekking to the Everest base camp, and you know you'll never get that chance again. Not with the way this crazy group does stuff."

Ten straight days with Landon. Nowhere to run or to avoid him…or his effect on me. Ten days of travel and snowboarding and seeing the tallest mountain in the world—a true once-in-a-lifetime experience and one of the things I was on this trip for.

"If I'm going, you're going," Penna ordered.

My head snapped toward her. "You're going?"

She shrugged. "So I've been told. Crutches and all. Fun times."

"We'll have fun," Leah promised. "And we don't have to stay at advanced camp. We can go back down to Lukla and get massages while they're out boarding."

Penna's eyes deadened, and I sliced my hand across my throat, trying to get Leah to stop. Her eyes widened and she mouthed, "What?"

I sighed. Leah might have known them, but she didn't understand Renegades yet—their competitive nature and general hatred of feeling useless. "It's lame," I told Penna. "Fully lame that you can't board. But if what I've been told is correct, you absolutely can ride in that helicopter up to Everest. You're not going to sit that out over a leg, are you?"

"You're not going to miss out on that over a boy, are *you*?" She stared me down.

"Touché. Guess I'm going."

"Yes!" Leah fist pumped.

I glanced up at the clock. "Crap. I have to get to class. I guess this thing is as good as it's going to get."

I said good-bye to the girls and almost ran out the door, a muffin shoved in my mouth and my books trying their best to tumble from my hands. I skidded into the elevator just before the doors closed.

"Bold, running with food in your mouth, given your luck," Zoe said from the corner of the elevator.

My hackles rose as I swallowed the bite of blueberry goodness and punched the button for my floor. "Well, it's better than what you like to keep in your mouth."

"Ooh, you do bite," she said as we started our descent. "Landon warned me."

I stiffened. "He would know."

"So you two aren't…?" She let the question hang.

For the love of God, the last thing I wanted to do was discuss Landon in the elevator with a girl who had clearly slept with him. "We're not."

"Oh…" Her head cocked to the side. "You're the one, though, right? The one who nearly took him out a couple years ago?"

"Is that any of your business?" I snapped at her as she wound her brown hair around her finger.

Three more floors.

"Are you this much of a bitch to everyone? Or just the girls he's slept with?" she asked with false sympathy.

I blew my breath out as I counted to five. "Seeing as I don't exactly have a list of who he's slept with, it would be impossible for me to single you all out."

She snorted, letting that brown curl rest against her breast. She leaned against the wall next to me, her long legs stretched out beneath shorts that barely covered her ass. Yeah, she looked like his type.

I never had been, nor had I ever suffered any insecurity over that fact. I couldn't help but wonder if this girl had—if she'd based her self-worth or her position with the Renegades on whom she was sleeping with. *What a horrible way to treat yourself.*

"Well, it's kind of a crapshoot. If you have ten girls in a room, just start flipping coins."

One floor. This was the slowest elevator in the freaking world. "Like I said, I don't care. But apparently you do," I said softly.

The elevator doors opened, and I turned briefly toward her.

"Personally, were I to ever sleep with Landon…Nova, or whatever you call him, I'd demand the one thing he isn't capable of."

"What's that?"

"Monogamy. I saw you ride. You're good. Don't base your abilities on who you're sleeping with. And for God's sake, don't attack women you don't know in the elevator because you think you need to defend territory you don't have. I'm not your enemy." I shrugged at her with a tight smile. "Sorry if I didn't give you what you're looking for."

Before the doors could shut on me, I ran out—straight into Landon. "God, you're everywhere," I muttered as I regained my balance.

"You seriously don't think I can be monogamous?" he asked, sounding annoyingly wounded. Like I'd pointed out something that wasn't an obvious truth.

"Glad to know you eavesdrop. I'll try to have an interesting conversation after dinner if you'd like to lurk in the corner." I tightened my grip on my books and started down the hallway toward class.

"One, I was waiting for you, not lurking, and two, was that an invitation?"

"Hardly. Besides, if I'm stuck with you for the entire Everest trip, I'm not offering up any more of my free time."

"You're going with us?" He grinned down at me.

His smile does not affect you. Not one bit. Liar.

"Looks like it."

He opened the door to the classroom, and I walked through, trying not to let his small gesture affect me, either. Apparently I was failing at Landon-emotion avoidance today.

"That's fantastic. But you seriously don't think I can do the one-woman thing?"

We took our seats, and I looked over at him. "Why do you care what I think?"

He turned his baseball hat backward, the white of the cap only making his face look more tanned. "Because I don't want you thinking that about me. I could if I wanted to."

"Hey, Nova," the girl behind me greeted him, leaning forward so her breasts nearly fell out of her top. "Wanna study tonight?"

"No, thanks, Amy. Maybe another time?"

I laughed, turning to face forward. "Yeah, you've got a great track record."

He leaned over. "You don't know my track record."

"Yeah, okay, *Nova*." I lowered my voice to a whisper so I didn't hurt the girl's feelings. "Did you not just masterfully turn her down, but leave her with a little hope on that hook of yours so you can reel her in another time?"

His mouth opened and shut. "I didn't want to offend her."

"You're a regular knight in shining armor."

"Just let me know when you're the delicate damsel in

need of saving."

I snorted. "Yeah. Never going to happen. I'm quite capable of saving myself from everything, including you."

"I'm well aware," he said, his voice dropping. "It's one of my favorite things about you. You've always been able to hold your own against me…or with me."

Oh God, there it was—the fluttering in my stomach that led to alarm bells blaring in my head. *Don't believe a word he says. Don't let him in.* The terrifying part was that there was a tiny sliver of me that wanted to, that missed him, and that part was steadily growing louder. At this rate she'd be screaming before we ever got on the plane.

I held his gaze as long as I could before I retreated, shuffling my papers, to take out my paper proposal. We were presenting orally today, and if Dr. Messina accepted, I'd have to type this sucker up all pretty and submit it on eCampus tonight.

"Hey, Rachel," Hugo said as he sat down next to me. Thank God he was my partner and not Landon. Hugo was easy, fun to hang out with, and didn't come with ten tons of my emotional baggage.

"How's it going?" I asked him.

"Can't complain. Happy with your proposal? That rough draft looked pretty tight yesterday."

"It's good, I think. I'm hoping she'll go for the Korean adoption angle."

"Are you digging up your roots?" Landon interjected. "I thought you gave that up years ago."

Sometimes I hated that he remembered so much about the time we'd been together. "I did when my mom asked me to let it go. She's always been touchy about it, like I'd say she wasn't my mom and run the other direction. But she's not here, and I've always been curious. Seemed like a good time."

Look at me, being all civil and open.

"Just curious?" he asked.

I shrugged. My need to explore my beginning wasn't something he needed to understand.

"I'll help you," he offered. "I know I'm not your partner, but I also know what it means to you, so if you need help…"

I swallowed, my throat suddenly thick at the open, pleading look in his eyes. There was no flirtation or suggestion, no hint of Nova looking back at me, just my Landon.

And that was far more dangerous than being pursued by Nova. The warning bells in my head were full-blown wailing now.

"Yeah, I'll let you know," I said.

"Same goes here," Hugo offered, and my head swung in his direction. "Maybe we could talk about it over lunch tomorrow?"

I felt Landon's stare burning holes in my back. I liked Hugo. He was nice, kind, quick with a smile or a joke. He's just what I would have gone for last year.

But as much as I hated myself, I had to be honest, up front, and not lead him on. "That would be great. It would be nice to have a friend to talk it over with."

His smile fell slightly, but he nodded as he absorbed how I'd just labeled our relationship. "Sounds good."

I didn't turn back to Landon as our professor started the lecture. I didn't want to see his face or that cocky smile. I didn't want him to gloat over my realization or to find a way to use it against me.

As much as it would have been fun to start up a relationship on the cruise and make memories with someone, to flex the walls of my heart and see if they'd budge, I also knew the truth: Hugo wasn't Landon.

And sitting between them, that made all the difference.

Chapter Eleven

THE TAJ MAHAL

It amazed me, the difference three days made in my life. Seventy-two hours ago, I'd been on board, barely agreeing to come on this insane trip. Then I'd given up the school-sponsored excursion to Delhi and thrown in my luggage with the Renegades.

Never thought I'd see the Renegades touring the Taj Mahal, but in all honesty, I never thought I'd see the day where Paxton Wilder was willing to take a six-hundred-mile detour from his planned adventure in order to appease a woman. Add in the fact that said woman was my best friend, and it was even more bizarre. But I was thankful, not just for the chartered plane and the opportunity to experience this, but for the way he treated Leah. Maybe he really had changed.

Maybe it was possible for a Renegade to truly love someone more than the sport.

Not Landon, though. He'd chosen the Renegades over love, or at least *my* love, which I was reminded of nearly every time I saw him. At least he'd kept his distance. *We're less than a day into this trip, so I probably shouldn't get my hopes up.*

"I can be monogamous," Landon said from above me as I crouched down to get a better picture of the Taj Mahal.

So much for keeping his distance.

"Are you still hung up on that?" I asked, adjusting the focus of my lens to get a better angle. Had the guy been reading my mind?

"You seriously think I can't be?"

I sighed, blowing a lone strand of black hair from my face as I stood. I'd tied it up, most of the purple highlights hidden in the updo. "It's been three days since I said that. Isn't there anything else on your mind? Like, oh, I don't know, the giant monument in front of you?"

"I can't believe you don't think I can be a one-woman guy."

I gave up on avoiding the question. The guy was freaking determined. "I think you don't want to be. Maybe you can. Maybe it really doesn't matter to me."

I stood and sent a longing look in Leah's direction where she walked hand in hand with Wilder. Stopping to grab pictures hadn't been my best idea, but being the third wheel in that lovefest was uncomfortable as hell. But at least the camera crews were following the lovebirds and leaving me the hell alone for the moment.

"It should matter," he said.

"To me?" I craned my neck to look up at him and took a step back so we weren't so close.

"Well, yeah." He tucked his thumbs in his pockets.

"I can think of about a hundred things off the top of my head that matter more to me than the frequency of women through that revolving door you call a bed." Okay, maybe that was a lie. But just a little one.

"Well, that's a shame, because there's nothing I can think of that matters more to me than who sleeps in your bed."

Well, shit, I was speechless. Luckily, I recovered quickly.

"Does this matter right now? Because we are standing in front of one of the most beautiful tributes to love in the world, and I'd honestly like to enjoy it without arguing with you."

"I never said I wanted to argue," he, ironically, argued as we walked the path toward the giant marble mausoleum. The afternoon sun softened the white glow of the structure, giving it an ethereal glow.

"Yet here you are, arguing with me." Could he be any more frustrating?

He grinned like he'd followed my exact train of thought.

"What?" I snapped.

"Just enjoying our progress." He shrugged, his eyes dancing.

"Progress?"

"A week ago you weren't speaking to me. Now I've gotten you to go away with me and we're bickering like we used to. Progress."

"I did not go away with you!"

"Well, by definition, we are *away*, and you are standing with me."

"Oh my God, I'm not talking about this anymore."

"Fine. Change of subject. How is it you can find a grave to be a monument to love?"

Every step we took brought us closer to the structure, the details appearing and consuming my vision. "Just look at it," I said as we paused outside the entrance. "Look at the beauty, the symmetry of the inscriptions, the hue of the marble. It's perfect. He loved his wife so much that he built her a monument to be unrivaled."

I felt his eyes on me but couldn't tear mine away from

the intricate carvings along the arches. My attention was constantly shifting, drawn by a new element. "It's exquisite."

"I never thought you were a romantic."

I shrugged. "I'm not. But when you're shown a love like this, what other choice do you have?"

"It's a beautiful building," he said as we started up the steps.

"No," I told him softly, taken in by every nuance of the monument. "It's perfection. The symmetry is perfect, the art is perfect, the setting is perfect. Everything is taken into account."

I glanced over to see him observing the architecture as we made our way around the space. "They're both buried here?" he asked.

"They're in the crypt below," I answered. "And the only imperfection lies where the marble was broken when Shah Jahan was laid to rest with his beloved."

"How beloved could she have been if he had other wives?"

"You're one to preach on monogamy," I drawled.

"There you go again," he muttered. "I've done it before. It's possible. With the right person."

I looked up at him, skepticism crinkling my forehead. "Right. And how did that work for you?"

He stepped in front of me and turned, forcing me to stop. After a tense moment of silence, I finally brought my eyes up the wide expanse of his chest, over the lips I knew were impossibly soft, and to those eyes that currently looked incredibly wounded by my sharp tongue. "I didn't say I didn't fuck it up. I said it was possible for me to be with one woman. Love one woman."

My stomach clenched, and my grip on my camera tightened. I tried to ignore the slamming of my heart and the way that tiny little flame of hope I'd tried to snuff out flared up just a bit. Maybe he meant it. Maybe he meant *me*.

Do not go there. He left you. Destroyed you. He only wants you because you're unattainable, and once he has you, he'll mark the notch and move on like last time.

"One woman like me?" I asked, my voice a hell of a lot stronger than I felt.

"Maybe *only* you," he said softly.

Don't let him weaken you. I gathered the bricks of my crumbling defenses and shoved them back into place. "What is it about me? Is it the chase? Are the other girls on board too easy for you, Nova? Am I a convenient game?"

His mouth dropped slightly. "You are *anything* but convenient. I've had parachute malfunctions more convenient than you. You're the most frustrating, complicated, utterly addictive woman I have ever been around, but you are sure as hell not *convenient*."

"So it's the challenge. Nice to know." Why did he have to do this here? Why couldn't he let shit go and leave me in peace? I took one last look around and walked outside the mausoleum, leaving him behind.

I took a breath of the stifling, hot air and wiped the small line of sweat from my forehead. Breathing acid would have been easier than trying to breathe around him.

"Stop walking away from me," he said as he came out behind me.

"Stop trying to convince me that you could be some devoted…" Lover? Boyfriend? "…guy."

I kept moving until I reached the edge of the reflection pool and saw Bobby crossing the distance with a cameraman. Perfect fucking timing.

For the thousandth time, I cursed myself for signing that stupid release.

"No, Bobby. Not this," Landon said, putting his hand over the lens. "I'll give you whatever the hell you want later, but get this thing out of my fucking face."

"Landon, it's part of the experience," Bobby argued, his safari hat ridiculously out of place.

"It's my life right now."

Bobby groaned. "You agreed, and we have every right—"

"And I've been pretty damn cooperative up until this moment, but that can stop."

The two waged a silent war for a minute, then two. Finally Bobby glanced over at me before letting out a dramatic sigh. "You owe me," he told Landon.

"Whatever you want," Landon agreed.

Bobby retreated with the camera guy, leaving me with a visibly angry Landon. His frame was tense, his jaw locked, and his eyes narrowed on me. "I never cheated on you. Even the time between, when you were dating Wilder, I never cheated on you. Can you say the same?"

I shook my head. "Nope. I was awful. I dated him and loved you because I was too young and stupid to understand at the time that it was all going to crumble anyway. Our fate was sealed that first time you kissed me." *In the rain.* He'd kissed me so thoroughly, our mouths so intertwined, sealed so tight that not even a single drop of water had slipped past our lips.

"Not the first time," he whispered. "You weren't his yet then. But he doesn't know that, does he? I never told him."

I shook my head. "No. It didn't seem relevant at the time."

"It was. Everything was."

I stepped back, needing space. "It wasn't. It didn't matter that we'd met months before, that I had no clue you'd show up at Wilder's, that you were the same Landon he talked about. It didn't matter, because what we did was wrong, and we paid for it, right? We all did."

"I loved you. The entire time we were together, there was no one else. I didn't want anyone else—just the possibility of you was enough for me." His voice was clear with the kind of truth I couldn't bear to hear.

"Stop," I begged, clutching my camera to my chest.

"I don't want to."

But I needed him to. Every time he said something like that—every time he reminded me of what we'd had and how very much I'd stupidly loved him—it shook my resolve, and that wasn't something I could afford.

Fire heating my blood, I looked up at him, at the eyes that were more blue than hazel today against his collared, rolled-sleeve button-down. "What do you want from me?"

He swallowed. "I want you not to hate me. I want you not to think that I'm some heartless bastard who didn't love you. I want—"

I couldn't take another word. What did he understand of love? Love didn't walk away without a word. It didn't leave the person who shared its very space writhing in agony and confusion.

"Stop. Look around you. Look at that grave, that crypt. He spent twenty-one years building a place that he thought would be good enough to bury her. Twenty-one years, Landon. You couldn't even make it two months with me before you ran back to Wilder."

"Rachel—"

"No. Enough. Look at the towers. Do you see them?"

He sighed, the sound rushed and angry. "What about them?"

"He had them angled away from the mausoleum, just in case there was an earthquake. He made sure that there was no chance they'd fall into her resting place, that they'd hurt her. Even after her death, he protected her. *That* is love, or at least the kind of love I want. The kind that takes every precaution to protect the person your heart belongs to. The kind that's an equal partnership, and devotion, and passion, and trust. Sure,

I can do without the seventeenth-century polygamy, but the rest…that's golden. *That* is love. Love isn't abandoning the woman you say you love without a word."

"God…" His eyes squeezed shut tight, and something shifted in me. I didn't want to hurt him. We'd done enough of that to each other for two lifetimes. I just needed him to understand—needed him to stop inadvertently hurting *me*.

Reaching for him, I laid my hand against his warm, solid forearm. "I don't hate you. Sure, I did once, but I grew up and moved on. If that's all you're looking for, you have it. *I don't hate you.* What happened between us sucked, but I think we can agree that we were both at fault at different points."

His eyes opened, pleading with me for something he wouldn't name, and I was grateful for the silence.

"I think we can be friends, but you have to stop pushing me."

"I can't. After everything, you're here, and I can't stop pushing. Believe me, I've tried. I can't stay away. I go for a walk and end up at your door. I grab lunch, and I find a Cherry Coke in my hand when you know I can't stand that stuff."

"Landon—"

"I am incapable of not pushing, because you're *here*. The simple fact that you're near throws every logical thought out the window."

The slight plea in his voice slid through me, sent chills up my arms. *He left you and didn't bother to even come looking to explain.* If I wasn't here, he'd be chasing his next conquest, because that's what he was doing now. I just happened to be the one he was pursuing for the moment.

Leah waved to me across the courtyard, and I took the coward's way out. "Just pretend I'm not here. You were doing fine before I showed up."

He caught my hand as I moved to leave, but I didn't look back. Not when he was so close to burrowing through the very defenses he'd caused me to build. "I can't. Didn't you hear anything I just said? Every thought I've had since you came on board has revolved around you."

I tensed, and for that second I wished it was enough. *Since you came on board...* But I couldn't remember a day I hadn't thought about him in some way over the last couple years. I licked my dry lips and swallowed past the growing knot in my throat. "Don't worry. That will go away again as soon as I leave. Out of sight, out of mind, right?"

He let my arm go, and I walked away as calmly as possible, concentrating on putting one foot in front of the other as I made my way to Leah.

The truth hurt him, but it hurt me more.

He might have had me on the brain since I got here, but he'd been in my head since the day I met him. Even now, with the hatred and the spite draining away, the need to defend myself against him screamed at me.

It didn't matter how sweet he was here, how caring, how...*Landon*; my subconscious wasn't ever going to let me forget that he'd been the hot stove I'd held my hand to at one point. I still had the scars, and if they weren't warning enough, the way he'd invaded every aspect of my life since coming aboard should have done the trick. He was everywhere—my classes, the halls, the cafeteria, even my thoughts weren't safe. If I wasn't thinking about him, I was fighting back memories, thinking about how to avoid him, how to build stronger defenses against him.

I nearly hit my knees but somehow stayed on my feet as the realization drove itself home. Leah was right.

I'd never stopped thinking about him because I'd never gotten over him.

Fuck. My. Life.

Chapter Twelve

LANDON

The late-morning sun shone through my hotel room as I pulled myself up on the bathroom doorframe for the twenty-eighth time. I'd done my best to sleep on the plane last night when we'd flown from Agra, but I still felt twinges of exhaustion as I pulled up for number twenty-nine.

There was a knock at my door. "Come in," I said, proud that my breathing wasn't heavy as I hit number thirty. I'd busted my ass to stay in shape this trip. While Wilder had been hitting on Leah, I'd been hitting the gym.

All for this trip.

"Hey, did you want some lunch…?" Rachel's voice trailed off, and my smile lit right up. She might not *want* to want me, but that didn't change the fact that we still had some undeniable chemistry.

I dropped to the floor and grabbed the towel I'd left on

my chair, wiping the sweat from my face and neck. She stood with her arms crossed under her breasts, looking anywhere but at my bare chest.

Her cargo pants hung on her hips like a wet dream, and her long-sleeve henley and Patagonia vest hugged her perfect torso. Rachel did the impossible—made expedition gear sexy.

"So, lunch?" I asked.

"So, shirt?" she responded, glancing up and then right back down.

I shook my head and grabbed the shirt I'd left on the bed with my pack. "Not like you haven't seen it before."

She snorted. "Yeah, well…that doesn't…whatever."

Rachel is flustered. The revelation brought a bigger grin to my face, until I was pretty sure I was reaching clown proportions.

"Let's go," I said after pulling on the shirt. I grabbed my wallet off the dresser and locked the door behind us as we walked down the hallway. "Where is everyone?"

"At the café across the street," she answered as we took the stairs down from the third floor.

"And you came to get me? How thoughtful!"

"Wilder sent me. He's still hung up on throwing us together at every possible opportunity." She made it to the ground floor first, but only because I really liked to sneak peeks at her ass when she didn't notice.

Yes, I was going to hell.

"And you agreed?" I asked as we walked into the lobby.

"He said no one was going to get you if I didn't, and I figured you'd eventually get hungry." She shrugged.

Damn, that sweet, swelling feeling was back in my chest.

"So you decided to give in so I didn't go hungry?"

She spun in the middle of the lobby, blowing a strand of her purple highlights out of her face as she stared me down. "Look. Just because I don't want you weak before we head up to twenty thousand feet doesn't mean that I have gushy feelings about you. Don't read into it."

"Gushy? Pretty sure you killed every gushy feeling yesterday." God knew she'd effectively removed my heart and stomped on it. I was getting used to it when it came to her.

Her face scrunched. "It needed to be said, and I'm not sorry."

"Well, you made your point." I yanked my beanie out of my left cargo pocket and tugged it over my hair, already missing my baseball cap.

She shifted her weight and recrossed her arms. "So… friends?"

I laughed, the urge to kiss the frown off her face stronger than almost anything. "Rachel, we will never be just friends. But we can fake it for as long as you like. I owe you at least that much."

She sighed, and when I gestured toward the door, she led us out. From the lobby, I'd barely noticed that we were in Nepal, but once we walked outside, there was no denying it.

My eyes were drawn everywhere at once. The bright flags hanging on streamers stood out against the crystal-blue sky. Sounds of traffic, people, and bells from passing bicycles rang out on the crowded street.

"Is that…?" Rachel asked, looking toward the awning of the next building over.

"That's a monkey!" I told her.

The smile that curved her lips was breathtaking, breaking through the prickly barrier she kept up.

"Does it ever hit you how amazing this all is, how lucky we are?" she asked, stepping into the street to cross.

I yanked her back just before a bicycle could take her out. She fell into my arms, and I held onto her for a second longer than was necessary. "Every day since you showed up."

She looked up at me. "Lunch," she whispered.

I nodded and let her go. We picked our way across the street to the café where the others waited.

"You made it!" Pax called out from the circular table. Leah, Little John, Alex, and Gabe were there, Penna holding down the opposite side of the table with her leg elevated on an empty chair. "We already ordered for you guys."

"We would have waited, but the plane leaves in three hours," Leah explained with a sympathetic look.

"No problem. Thanks for taking care of us," I said, pulling out a chair for Rachel. She eyed me with a healthy dose of skepticism but took her seat before I did mine.

"So, I know your name is Rachel…" Alex started, his eyes locked on her.

This was not going to go well.

The guy was grunge to his core, shoulder-length hair and a permanent half-baked look. He was also one of the only Renegades who might be able to snowboard that ridge with me and not get himself killed.

"Yep," Rachel answered, playing with her fork.

"We're dying to know, are you…*the* Rachel?" Gabe questioned, leaning forward. He was cleaner cut, but I was going to punch his pretty little face if he looked at her like that for one more second.

Damn it, why didn't I cover this with them?

Rachel sighed and rolled her neck. "That's me, the curse," she said sarcastically.

"Seriously?" Now Alex's eyes were ready to pop out.

"Absolutely. I have no idea why the hell you guys even let me come along. I'll probably call down lightning before we get to the airport."

"How can you think that?" I asked her, unable to sit there and listen to that shit.

"Oh, for fuck's sake," Penna snapped at the guys. "She's not a curse. I was stupid when I said it."

"You're not," I told Rachel. I hated that she'd let that into her head. It wasn't her fault that I'd been majorly distracted after I left her. Hell, it was less than what I deserved for what I'd done to her.

Our lunch arrived before I could take it any further. I gulped down rice, vegetables, and some kind of curried chicken, knowing it would probably be my last good meal for the next few days. I was going to need some serious carb loading for the week ahead.

"So you ready for this, Nova?" Alex asked. "I only know of two other big-mountain free riders who have done that ridge."

Rachel paused with her fork halfway to her mouth.

"I'm in the best shape of my life. What can you say for yourself?" I ragged on Alex.

He pulled his shirt up, exposing six-pack abs. "I think I'll be okay."

"Yeah, well, let me know how those treat you at twenty-one thousand feet."

"Twenty-one thousand feet?" Rachel asked, her voice weaker than usual.

With one glance at her, I could tell that she knew, and she wasn't amused. *Or impressed.*

"You want to board like a god, then you have to get closer to them," Gabe answered, high-fiving Alex.

"Wait, I thought we were just going to see the Everest base camp," Leah said, her eyes narrowing on Wilder.

He leaned forward and kissed her forehead. "Don't worry. I'm not going up there with them to board, just to watch from the advanced camp."

"You're not?" she asked, clearly relieved.

"He's not good enough," Rachel said quietly. "Not for what they have planned."

"Rachel!" Leah exclaimed.

Part of me wanted to crow that she knew I was better than Pax, but the look in her eyes told me she wasn't in the mood.

"No, she's right," Wilder said. "Sure, I can snowboard, but this big-mountain free-riding stuff is way beyond me. Even I know my limits."

"How dangerous is it?" Leah asked.

"It's up there," I admitted.

"Leah told me you wanted to board up here, but I was hoping my first hunch was wrong," Rachel begged me. "Tell me you're not going for the Shangri-La spine wall?"

"I promised I'd never lie to you again," I answered. I wouldn't. No matter how painful the truth was, that was all Rachel was getting from me.

"We can't even get your body down if something happens to you," she whispered.

She was right. If anything went wrong up there, it was twice as dangerous to try to bring a casualty down, but I had zero intention of dying.

"I always did love the mountains," I said with a lopsided smile. "I'll be fine."

"You don't know that."

The blatant fear in Rachel's voice got to me like nothing else could. The snarky, prickly shell she wore never intimidated me, because I'd always known what was underneath. Hell, the sharper her tongue, the harder my dick got. But seeing a glimpse of this Rachel, the soft vulnerability she kept so closely guarded—this was the Rachel I loved, the one who could break me down with a look or a touch.

"I've spent the last year training for it. I've done Denali, the Alps, even headed down to South America to make sure I'm ready for this," I assured her. "I just need a few days at altitude and then it will be manageable."

Sure, being at sea level for three months hadn't done me

any favors, but—

"I'm not going to advanced camp. I'll come back down with Leah and Penna."

Oh, hell no. "What? No. You'd kill to be in on something like this, even if it's navigating from camp. I know you can't board it, but this is the stuff you thrive on." I needed her there, watching, supporting, keeping my ass in check.

"The last thing you need is me up there distracting you. One stroke of bad luck—"

"No." I cradled her face, needing contact even though I knew she was likely to shove me away. "You are *not* bad luck, and no matter the shit we've been through—I want you there."

"Landon." She closed her eyes and shut me out.

I stroked her cheeks with my thumbs until our gazes met. "Besides, I'll do better if I'm showing off for a pretty girl. I can't exactly let myself fall on my ass in front of you."

She let her breath go on a ragged exhale. Her shoulders fell, but I knew better than to think she was defeated. "Fine."

The battle was won—for now. No doubt we'd have the same argument up until the moment I hiked up that ridge. "Good."

Alex cleared his throat, and I became more than aware that we were having a private moment in public. I released her soft skin at the same second she pulled away.

"Okay, final mission brief?" Pax asked, sliding over the file I'd spent the last six months compiling. "This is your show now."

Damn straight, it was.

This ridgeline was everything I'd been training for, and it was finally time for the plan to fall into place. Sure, there were ten thousand things that could go wrong. But I had Rachel with me, and that was one hell of a right.

Chapter Thirteen

RACHEL

LUKLA, NEPAL

"Switch with me?" Landon asked Little John after we'd gained our cruising altitude, which, when I thought about it, was going to be our normal altitude day after tomorrow.

Little John shot me a look, and though I rolled my eyes, I nodded. The plane was only big enough for the ten of us, one on each side down the length, and with Pax and Leah at the front, all the way to Bobby and another cameraman at the back, we were full.

"Sure thing," Little John answered, vacating the precious territory.

So much for peace.

Landon sat down and buckled in. I turned toward the window and looked over the scenery below. Nepal was heading into winter, but the fields at this altitude were still green, terraced in places and thick vegetation in others. Where we were headed, vegetation couldn't survive.

Then again, humans weren't meant to, either.

"Are you seriously going to try to ignore me?" he asked.

Exactly when was my heart going to stop stuttering in response to his voice? "Just taking in the view. You should, too. It's not something you see every day."

"Neither are you."

Ugh. Like *that* response. The one where my chest tightened and those stupid, naive butterflies danced in my stomach. I tried to kill the butterflies and turned to Landon. "It's Nepal. How often do you plan on coming back?"

He shrugged. "I can fly here any time, grab another flight, and watch the ground roll by underneath us. You…well, I have no control over where you are or when I get to see you. So I choose you."

But you didn't. I shut down the thought. It wasn't going to do us any good to hash out the same stuff again and again.

"You know how impossible this is, right?" I asked him across the aisle.

"What? Me talking to you?"

I almost snorted. "No. You trying to ride this ridge. We have, what? A week?"

"Six days left," he answered. His eyes looked blue against the gray beanie he wore, and there wasn't a trace of worry to be found.

"Right. We lucked out that the visibility was good enough for us to make this flight. What are we going to do when we can't get up to base camp the day after tomorrow?"

"Take another day to acclimate to altitude. Lukla is at nine thousand feet—the extra day won't hurt."

"Right, and what happens when the helicopters can't make it to Pangboche? When they can't make the flight to base camp? Then to advanced camp? What happens when we can't see the ridge and the weather rolls in?"

"Rach, I can't solve a problem that doesn't exist yet."

I shook my head. "You have too many variables, and on a trip like this, you can't afford them."

"I can't afford not to try. We're here. The timing coincided with the week the program gave us for optional excursions. What would you have rather I done?" He looked so relaxed, so at ease with the fact that he was putting his life on the line.

"Oh, I don't know…maybe come back when you could have devoted all the time you needed to a trip like this, instead of working it in while we happen to be docked in India? This isn't something to take lightly."

Twenty-one thousand feet meant that one bad choice, one slip, one second would end him—and any chance, no matter how slim, of us healing the rift in our past. Twenty-one thousand feet meant help couldn't come, and I couldn't even deliver his body to his mother…if she so much as knew who I was.

He reached across the aisle and unfisted my hand, stroking his thumb across the line of indentations my fingernails had made in my palm. "This documentary we're making—we're each going after one thing. This is mine. I've planned for this, trained for this, and am prepared for this."

"How can you possibly be prepared for this when you've been on a cruise for the last three months?"

"In the last year I've spent time in the Denali, the Tetons, and the Alps. I'm not a stranger to free riding. You of all people know that."

My eyes dropped from his, and I pulled my hand away, remembering why he hadn't been around when I'd initially met Wilder. So many things would have been different if he'd been there to begin with. But I wasn't thinking about that, because if I couldn't move on from the past, it was going to kill any chance I had at the present.

That's what I'd told myself the last two years, and it had

worked well.

"You're in shape?" I asked.

"Would you like to see?" he teased, his eyes taking on that mischievous glint that I'd always loved. *Liked. No love.*

"I'll pass, but thanks."

"I'll just have to keep offering."

"Can you please take this seriously?" I asked.

"I take everything about you seriously."

"Not what I meant. Alex? Gabe? They're good enough to go with you? You found a pilot willing to get you that high?"

The corner of his mouth tilted up. "Be careful. You keep asking those questions and I'm going to start to think that you care."

God help me, I do care.

He sighed. "Yes, yes, and yes. If there were an issue about any of this, I wouldn't do it. I might be a little reckless, but I'm not stupid."

"That remains to be seen."

"God, I've missed you." The yearning in his voice echoed the little voice in my soul that I couldn't keep gagged.

The aisle between us was too much space and not enough.

We were told to prepare for landing, our quick, half hour flight at an end. I shifted my attention to the ground below. The mountains rose above us, beautiful and just as ominous as the tiny runway carved into the side of the rock.

"Holy shit, is that the runway?" I asked, seeing a small strip of pavement beneath us. It was the shortest one I'd ever seen.

"That thing is wicked!" Gabe yelled from the row ahead of us.

"Fuck me," Paxton said.

"I totally forgot you weren't a fan of flying," I called up toward Wilder.

"It's actually one of the most dangerous runways in the

world," Landon told Gabe. "It's not just the altitude, but the runway runs right into the mountain if we don't stop in time."

"Not helping!" Leah barked at Landon.

He just laughed.

I looked forward and saw Leah taking Wilder's hand. Landon offered his, and I rolled my eyes. "It takes more than a landing to scare me."

He shook his head with a grin, and I clutched my armrests until we landed.

"Welcome to Lukla," the captain said as we taxied to a stop.

"Nine thousand feet," Landon said.

"Twelve more to go," I answered.

"That's my girl, always looking up." He paled the second it was out of his mouth, and his eyes flew wide.

I needed to get away from him. Now. Grabbing my backpack, I stood, thankful the aisle had cleared and it was my turn to get off the plane. "Yeah, well, that girl learned that you have to look down. It does you no good to keep your eye on the sky if no one is waiting for you when you fall."

"Rachel…"

I didn't answer. Instead, I retreated—ran away.

Checking in to our little hotel, I chose the room farthest from his.

At dinner, I sat at the other end of the table.

At night, I locked my door.

But how was I supposed to lock my heart?

• • •

"Do I need to find you a teapot?" Leah asked the next morning, sitting down next to me in a small courtyard outside our hotel. The morning was clear and crisp, in the low fifties. It would only get colder as we headed up to today's higher elevations. Base camp ran around freezing this time of year. I leaned against my pack, mentally preparing myself for the day. The pavement beneath our feet was made of broken cobblestones, and the colored flags waving above our heads had the same vibrancy as the blanket we rested on, the same as the temple we'd visited yesterday. I'd taken hundreds of pictures, tried to absorb every detail about the small village that was the gateway to Everest.

"I do not need a teapot," I promised. "Besides, we agreed that those were for after we got through hot water. I'm still steeping in mine."

She tucked a strand of hair behind her ear and curled her legs under her. "I bought you one in Istanbul. Figured it would be for having to stay behind when you got sick. But I think this might be more appropriate."

I really looked at my best friend, the healthy color to her cheeks, the smile she was quick to show, the fact that she only had her legs covered because it was fifty degrees up here and not because she was scared of what anyone thought of her scars. It had taken a lot of teapots to get her here—too many times I wasn't sure she was going to pull free of the depression that had held her under when her high school boyfriend died.

"I'm glad you're happy," I told her. "Really and truly. What you and Wilder have…" I shook my head. "It's precious."

She reached over and squeezed my hand. "I want you to be happy, too. I can't imagine what it's like to be here around Landon, but I can tell that you're not happy."

"Happy is a relative term," I said with a forced smile. I could put up with Landon—with the rending of my heart—if it meant Leah stayed here with Wilder.

"Stop. Stop faking it. Stop telling me you're fine and agreeing to stuff you don't want to do because you think it's what I need. You don't have to take care of me anymore. I'm okay. I need you to focus on you. Be honest with me."

As if they were a physical thing, I felt my defenses slide away. Leah and I were too close for me to lie. "I think you were right. I'm not sure I ever got over him."

"I know," she said softly. "You were so busy taking care of me that I don't think you ever really stopped to process what happened. He left, and within weeks we were at Dartmouth and you went from full-time heartbreak to full-time caregiver." Her forehead puckered. "That was a lot to ask of you."

"Never." I covered her hand with my own. "You are my best friend, and the only good thing to come out of what happened with Landon. Maybe it was all supposed to be this way. Maybe he was supposed to leave me so I could find you and you could find Wilder. Maybe it's all part of some big cosmic plan."

"Or maybe…" She looked away.

"Maybe what?"

Her nose crinkled. "Don't kill me, okay? Maybe you're supposed to be here—with Landon. I'm not saying you have to be with him, or have to give him another chance. I just think that this guy really hurt you, and I hate him for it, but I've also gotten to know him over the last few months, and the same things that are broken in you are broken in him, too."

"His dick seems to work just fine."

"Yeah, well, I think that's just a form of self-medication."

I raised my eyebrows at her.

"I didn't say I agreed with it. Look, you have five days with him—no class and no distractions. Maybe you stop letting him leave, stop running away, stop protecting yourself. Maybe you use this time to either put him in your past…" She shrugged.

My eyes narrowed. "Or…"

"Or maybe see if there's a future."

"Leah," I growled. She of all people knew what he'd done, the condition I'd been in when we met.

"Oh, look, there's Pax!" she said in overexcitement as Wilder appeared.

"Coward," I whispered.

"Just pushing you the way you pushed me," she said as she stood. "Whether or not you are willing to admit it, this is what you need."

I pouted as my best friend walked off with the love of her life, no doubt to go have another of the extended make-out sessions they were always caught in the middle of.

Okay, maybe I envied that—not Wilder, of course, but the connection. The ability to touch someone you loved, hold them, know that you were more than a physical gratification.

I looked up at the bright blue sky and wished it wasn't Landon's face, Landon's body, Landon's touch that came to mind when I pictured that feeling. I knew Leah was right just as certainly as I knew that I'd never gotten over Landon.

But letting him in was easier said than done.

My instincts warred with each other the moment I saw him, my fight-or-flight response kicking in. But maybe it really was time to see what emotions were under those instincts, if I could manage to shut them down long enough to see.

"You ready to go, Rachel?" Little John asked from the doorway.

"I think I am," I answered, gaining my feet.

He wrapped his arm around my shoulder as we walked toward where the others had gathered. Penna stood between Gabe and Alex, her crutches bracing her weight. Bobby directed the camera guy, who I'd learned last night was named Mike, while Wilder, Leah, and Landon talked to a group of Sherpas.

"How you doing with that one? No bullshitting."

"Do you believe in the curse?" I couldn't help but ask.

He stopped before we got to the group and looked down at me. "The one about you?"

"Yeah."

"No. I was there. When he came back…" He glanced over to where Landon stood. "He was destroyed, like one of those Jenga towers. Too many of his pieces were missing. He wasn't stable, he wasn't focused, and he wasn't safe. It wasn't because of you, Rachel. It was because of what he *did* to you, the parts of himself that he left behind. I don't think any of us realized the extent of what he felt about you until he turned into this shell. You are not a curse. You were his compass, his North Star, his constant. And then you were gone."

"And now?"

"Now that's up to you two."

I sighed. "Let's just get him through Nepal alive, shall we?"

"You're here. I'm the least worried I've ever been about him. Well, not for his safety, since I'm pretty sure he should hide sharp objects around you, but he's more himself. Plus, I haven't seen any girls—"

"You're blushing," I said, laughing. There was something about a six-foot-five, three-hundred-pound guy turning red like a schoolgirl that had me in stitches.

"Yeah, yeah. Shut up."

Landon turned as I approached, a soft smile playing across his face. "Good morning. Did you get enough to eat?"

"I'm good, thank you for asking."

His eyes narrowed slightly. "Feeling okay?"

I almost laughed again at his skepticism. Maybe burying the anger hatchet would be more fun than I initially thought. "Just peachy. We ready for a little hike?"

He nodded slowly. "Do you have everything you need? This is the last place to pick anything up."

I tugged on the straps of my framed pack, thankful Mom had suggested I take it, and the sturdy hiking boots, and my thick Patagonia cold gear. Okay, I was just grateful my mother was a ten on the worrywart scale.

Damn, I was going to have to admit that to her at some point.

I'd purchased the rest of my gear in Kathmandu.

"I'm good to go. It's a six-hour hike today, right?"

"Yes, miss," one of the Sherpas answered. "We will take you to Namche Bazaar."

"Rachel, this is Tashi, one of our guides," Landon introduced us, stepping closer to my side.

I met the others in turn, instantly enchanted by their easy smiles. We said our good-byes to Penna, Little John, and Bobby, who took a helicopter to our next destination. Wilder asked Leah if she wanted to go with them, but she insisted she could make the hike.

What a hike it was—six miles of some of the most gorgeous scenery I'd ever been privileged to capture. My camera clicked so often that I high-fived myself for remembering two extra batteries and data cards. I knew we were doing it for the exercise and acclimation to altitude, but I loved it all the same.

We passed through valleys where we crossed flag-adorned rope bridges over rushing rivers, the blue of the water standing out like a beacon through the greenery.

"Want to wiggle?" Landon asked, moving his eyebrows as both his hands closed around the ropes.

"Don't even think about it," I told him sternly but couldn't hide my smile.

He laughed, threatening to rock the bridge as I walked toward him. For every step I took, he backed up one.

"Seriously? You know I can take you, right?" I asked.

"I can handle a little thing like you," he countered.

"Knock your shit off. If anything happens to Leah on this thing because you're goofing off, I'll destroy you," Wilder threatened from behind me.

"Joy killer!" Landon called back. One more grin and he

turned around to follow our guides, leaving me laughing and staring at his incredible ass. What was it about those cargo pants that showcased him perfectly?

Look all you want now—soon he'll be covered up in snow gear.

The trail was worn but still rugged, and when I struggled over a boulder, my lack of height getting in the way, Landon lifted me, his touch lingering for the smallest second after. Some areas were like hiking through any other forest, but the higher we climbed, the more the vegetation spread out and the landscape was revealed. The trail switched back half a dozen times, and when we crossed the highest bridge, it was empowering to look down a thousand feet at the one we'd crossed this morning.

As we stopped for lunch, Landon made sure we were under shade to get me out of the sun. I shared one of my very rationed strawberry Pop-Tarts with him.

"Really?" he asked, taking the overpreserved pastry from my hand. "You love these things."

"Yeah, I do," I answered with a smile.

"In that case…" He leaned over me, reaching for the other Pop-Tart, and knocked me backward onto the leaf-covered ground.

"Hell no!" I said, laughing as I rolled away.

He sat up and took a bite of the Pop-Tart as I brushed the dirt off my shirt. "See if I share with you again."

"I just wanted to make sure you were still Rachel and hadn't been taken by body snatchers."

Then he winked.

No, no, no… That sweetness that had invaded my chest all day slipped farther down, igniting an ache that I knew only Landon could fully sate. Trying to shake it off, I half smiled and then devoured my Pop-Tart.

The problem with burying the anger hatchet with Landon

was it only left the insane attraction I had toward him. There was a reason we'd always collided, a force that had drawn us together stronger than sex or love...it was something intangible that I could never describe—or find in another person.

Only Landon.

Anger was safe. It kept me protected. Dropping that weapon from my arsenal left me vulnerable, and I knew that warmth rushing through me wasn't from the sun shining overhead.

We made it to Namche Bazaar in time for dinner. The small village was high in the mountains but beneath the tree line and populated enough to have several lodges along the wide, winding dirt streets. The buildings were all stone, most of the color supplied by the flags that draped across streets and the tourists there to stock up before pushing the rest of the way to Everest. The air had turned sharp; I'd have to get my winter gear out tonight for the trip tomorrow.

"We have to leave first thing in the morning if you want to see the Everest base camp," Landon said after dinner, walking me along the outside of the inn to the room I shared with Penna.

"Sounds good," I responded as we approached my door. My hand lingered on the rustic handle, and for the first time since I'd found out he was on board, I wasn't using every possible excuse to get away from him—because I didn't want to.

"Rachel..." he said softly, putting his hand just above mine.

I turned my head but didn't speak, afraid of what I would say. Afraid that I would tell him how hurt I still was over what he'd done, but terrified I'd tell him that I wanted him anyway.

Stupid girl.

"I'm really glad you came. I never dreamed I'd get the

chance to have you here for this, but now that you are, I can't imagine doing this without you."

I did what I did best when it came to Landon—forced a smile, tucked, and ran.

. . .

Using Everest base camp as our launching point, we took helicopters the rest of the way up to advanced camp the next day. I wished we'd had the extra day to acclimatize and hike the rest of the way, but it just wasn't in the schedule. Landon was shoving a monthlong trip into just shy of ten days.

This place had been called the throne room of the gods, and now, being here, I understood it perfectly. No mortal was meant to survive here for long. Jagged peaks rose above us, Everest being the most daunting of all.

There was a thin layer of snow on the ground here, the harbinger of an approaching winter, but I knew it would only be deeper farther up the ridge.

I hid out while the Sherpas showed Landon the camp. Watched from a distance as he explored the base of the snowy ridgeline.

I sighed with relief when the tents were set up and I could duck beneath the cool exterior of my bright orange North Face shield.

"You're hiding," Leah accused as she came in next to me, arranging her sleeping bag in what we'd dubbed the girls' tent.

"Am not," I objected. "I'm acclimatizing in private."

"You're hiding," she said again.

"How's it going out there?" I asked, playing with the zipper on my parka. The temp was a balmy twenty-two, but I knew it would dip once the sun set.

"Weather's moving in. They say it's supposed to be a quick storm, though."

If there was one thing that didn't give me warm fuzzies, it was hearing the term "storm" sitting at eighteen thousand feet in the Himalayas.

As if he needed to confirm my worst fear, Wilder invaded our tent. When he didn't bother making goo-goo eyes at Leah, I knew something was wrong.

"What is it?" she asked.

"It's going to be bad," he said, his face hardening. "I need to send the chopper back down. It can't take this beating, and I want you on it."

"No," she answered. "Penna needs to go. Her leg will swell at this altitude. Get her down."

His jaw flexed. "Fine, but you go with."

"No," she said again, surprising me with the force behind her voice. "Penna will need help. You have to send Little John."

"I…" He shook his head. "With the weight limit on the bird, he's two people."

"Okay, then you send Penna, Little John, and Little John," she answered.

Wilder swung his gaze at me with a plea in his eyes.

"Don't look at me. You're the one who made her all mouthy. She was docile as a lamb when I sent her to you."

He took a deep breath and let it out slowly. "Fine. But you're bunking with me."

"But Rachel will be all alone!" Leah protested.

"Trust me, I'm happily alone. Very alone. Solo. Single. Glad to have some me time," I responded.

Leah pouted and swore but finally agreed.

I didn't know how badly I would regret that decision until the snow started to fall and the temperature dropped.

Then I was really alone.

Really solo. Single.

And super fucking cold.

Chapter Fourteen

Advanced Camp, Nepal

Cold like I'd never known invaded every cell of my body until I couldn't remember the last time I'd been warm.

The storm had raged for hours, and though I no longer heard the crackling of snow hitting the tent, the roar of the wind was impossible to ignore. I slid deeper into my sleeping bag, covering my nose with the nylon fabric and using my breath for warmth.

The tent rustled, and I sat up, staring at the door as it unzipped, snow falling into the tent as a huge figure tumbled in. The flash of fear I felt died in the second it took me to recognize Landon's jacket as he closed the tent.

"Sorry," he muttered after he ripped the gaiter down that covered his nose and mouth. "Why didn't you tell me you were alone in here? I had to hear it from Pax when he came to our tent for extra supplies." He took off his hat and gaiter, tossing them on the floor where Leah's bag had been.

"It d-d-d-didn't matter," I stuttered through the shivers.

"It sure as hell does," he barked, stripping off his coat. "You're shaking like a leaf and probably freezing. How the hell would anyone know?"

"I'm f-f-f-fi-fine," I managed.

"Yeah, seems like it." A moment later his snow pants joined the jacket on the floor, leaving him in the breathable light track pants he wore underneath and a long-sleeved henley. "Move," he ordered as he knelt next to my bag.

I was too cold to argue.

He unzipped my bag, and I gasped as the colder air hit me. But then he slid in with me and zipped the bag behind him.

Warmth—sweet, wonderful warmth—hit my face first as he wrapped his arms around me, holding me against his chest. My cheek rested along his neck, and I breathed in his cedar scent. He maneuvered one of his legs over mine until I was completely surrounded by him.

"Fuck, Rachel. You're a block of ice."

"It's cold up here." My stammering stopped.

"I noticed while I was digging through the snow to get to you." His arms tightened, and it felt so damn good to be held by him.

"You shouldn't be here," I said, voicing the last defense of my brain while my heart told it to shut up. Every nerve ending agreed, savoring his warmth.

"Well, Gabe and Alex both volunteered," he admitted.

I tensed. "But you risked the storm and fell on the knife, eh?"

His chin rubbed against the top of my head. "I wanted to be the bigger man and give you some space, but the idea of one of them holding you…" He swallowed. "I just couldn't do it. I'm sorry, I know this isn't really what you want."

I relaxed completely, my muscles abandoning the war they'd never wanted to wage. He was wrong—so very wrong. There was no one in the world I'd rather have holding me than Landon.

But that wasn't something I was capable of admitting, not when it was the equivalent of letting down the drawbridge for him to walk straight into my heart and trample around.

He stretched the bag so he could look into my eyes. "What are you thinking?"

"Nothing I can say," I whispered.

His hand came up, stroking my hair back from my face, his thumb caressing my cheek. "Okay. Then let's just get you warm. Tomorrow we can go back to whatever stalemate we seem to be at."

"Deal," I agreed. "Besides, you have bigger things to worry about."

"Not sure I'd agree with you," he said, tucking me under his chin again to give me as much skin-to-skin contact as we could get without removing clothes.

Remove the clothes! All the clothes! my sex-starved inner demon demanded.

I told her to keep her horny pants on and settle for this, which was better—and more dangerous—than anything I thought I'd ever have again. Landon was breathtaking to look at, but being held in his arms was a whole new torture. He was intoxicating, and if I didn't keep a tight rein on my self-control, reckless, wonderful, *regrettable* things would happen.

"There's a twenty-one-thousand-foot-high ridgeline behind me just waiting for your board. I consider that bigger."

His hand tunneled through my hair, holding me to him. "I don't. Damn, I'd almost forgotten how perfectly you fit against me. Shit. Distract me. Talk about anything."

"Like the giant snowstorm going on out there?" I teased, careful not to move against him.

"It's a rather small one, I promise. The last guys who did this had a ten-day one to compete with. I think we can handle an overnight."

"Speak for yourself."

"Tell me about your paper. Are you really looking for your orphanage? Or is it more than that?"

I rubbed my nose along his throat, unable to help myself. "I'm not sure? I want to see it, to know where I came from. I'm not on some delusional quest for my birth parents, I promise."

"I never thought that."

"I just want to understand the need...what makes those mothers give their babies up. Hopelessness? Poverty? Culture? A hope for a better life?"

"Yes to all?" Landon suggested, his voice deep and comforting on a level that soothed the cracks in my soul. "And what happens if you don't find an answer that satisfies you? If you don't like what you find? Have you left room for those possibilities, too?"

I nodded. "I think so. I don't have any expectations other than to see it, to feel connected somehow. There's always been this part of me that's felt untethered, and maybe I'm hoping finding it will ground me in a way."

We were silent for a moment, the only sound the gusts of wind or static tapping of snow hitting our tent.

"Okay. I'll take you."

"What?" I asked, pulling back again. "You don't have to do that."

A half smile lifted his beautiful lips. "If you'll let me, I'd like to be there for you. I kind of fucked that up a long time ago."

He did. I knew it, and so did he. But wrapped in his arms like I was something precious, it suddenly seemed like a lifetime ago...and yet like we'd never been apart.

Everything was familiar and yet new. His scent was the

same, the undertones of his skin unchanged by whatever cologne still managed to cling to his clothing. His voice still slid over my nerves like silk, his eyes the same ever-changing hazel that held me captive. His hands cupped my face with the same tenderness while the strength in his arms had only grown.

He was my Landon underneath all that Nova, only ten times more…everything.

"Rachel," he whispered. "Don't look at me like that."

"Like what?" I asked, knowing damn well what he meant.

"Like you used to."

Like there weren't two years of betrayal, heartache, and struggle between us.

I couldn't make my voice work, couldn't find words to express the jumble of emotions crashing through me. Our eyes met, unspoken emotions sailing between us.

In that moment, I knew that it didn't matter who had wronged whom. Who had walked out, or who had paid the price. It didn't matter how many years had passed or how many *would* pass. This intense connection that strung us together would always be there. Buried, burned, or frayed, but never destroyed.

Landon was always going to call to me.

His gaze dropped to my lips. "Tell me no," he said.

"Landon," I said softly, my hands coming between us to push against his chest.

"Tell. Me. No."

My mouth opened, but nothing came out, and even though I'd commanded my hands to push him away, they were gently stroking the lines of his chest.

"Rachel," he begged, but I wouldn't answer him because I couldn't.

His thumbs stroked my cheeks, and I saw the moment his eyes changed from conflicted to determined.

His mouth found mine, and I was home.

His kiss was soft, and he groaned as he shifted, sinking his hands into my hair as his lips caressed mine. Slow, sipping kisses assaulted my senses, made me forget where we were... or what year it was.

His tongue flirted with the lower line of my mouth, and I opened for him. He slipped inside like he'd never left, his taste and touch overwhelming as he filled the cracks in my soul he'd put there in the first place. He made me feel whole for the first time in more than two years.

"Rachel." He sighed, saying my name again before tilting my head so I could take him deeper. Our tongues slid and rubbed, and everything that had been forgotten came back with startling clarity.

This...there were no words for what he did to me, the way every nerve ending sparked to life as our bodies came into contact in the compact space. As my hands slid over his chest to grasp the back of his neck, one of his skimmed my spine until he cupped my hip.

God, this was what I'd missed. The few guys I'd let kiss me had been good, but they'd never had this effect on me, never turned me molten with a single kiss, never blocked out the world around us with the simple glide of his tongue.

Only Landon.

Heat flushed my skin, raced through my veins, waking up even the most dormant parts of me—those that screamed for him, begged for me to loop my leg over his hips—the parts I'd tried my best to kill off.

He was an amazing kisser.

Because he's had a hell of a lot of practice.

Because he'd left.

Because I wasn't enough for him.

His name was Nova now, due to the revolving door that had become his bed. His mouth. His hands were practiced at giving pleasure, and his heart had already schooled me in the art of heartbreak.

I ripped my mouth from his. "No."

"Rach?" he asked, immediately pulling back.

"We can't. I can't. I…" I looked up into those hazel eyes, already greenish with want, and I did the one thing I swore I never would and let fear rule me. "I won't."

He flinched, and a spike of anger flashed over the need that had control of my body. Who the hell was he to look hurt?

"Okay," he said softly with a tiny nod. "Do you want me to go?"

Did I? I didn't have the immature need to stomp away, to run like the child I had been when he'd walked out, but I wasn't capable of more. "No," I answered. "I just…I can't."

"I understand."

"Do you?" My hands withdrew, but with the confines of the bag, they only made it to rest between us.

"I don't want to. I want to kiss you until you forget what I did and what I've done since then, but I gave up that right a long time ago. So if this is where I have to start with you, I'll take it. It's a hell of a lot better than I ever thought I'd get."

I cracked a huge yawn, exhaustion reminding me that it was still an issue. Warmth finally infused every part of me after hours of bone-chilling cold, and my body was ready to shut down.

"Get some sleep. I promise I'll be a perfect gentleman."

I snorted.

"I mean it. Just sleep and let me hold you."

My choices were to shiver myself to sleep or choose the nuclear reactor that had climbed into bed with me. "Okay. But just tonight."

"Just tonight," he agreed, but I swore I heard him mutter, "for now." Then he sucked in a breath as I tried to get comfortable. "Don't wiggle, okay? Things are hard enough as it is."

My eyes popped open as I realized he was rock hard against me. "I'm sorry," I mumbled as I executed the most awkward roll in history in the tight space to give him my back.

"Not helping," he groaned as my ass pressed against him.

"Want me to move?" I offered, knowing there had to be an extra bag somewhere.

"No, I want you to *stop* moving."

A small smile spread across my face. At least I still had the power to move him. Then again, probably half the girls on the ship had *moved* him. "Okay," I said through another yawn, sleep reaching for me.

"Get some sleep," he ordered again.

My eyelids agreed. "It didn't mean anything," I said, my words heavy and slow as my breathing evened out. "The kiss," I added, in case he didn't understand what I was saying.

"Maybe to you," he said quietly, pressing a kiss into my hair as his arm wrapped around my waist.

"To you?" I asked as the world darkened and I slipped into sleep.

"Everything," he said in my dreams.

Chapter Fifteen

LANDON

HIMALAYAS

"You're a lucky SOB," Pax said as he eyeballed the ridgeline. We stood side by side in full gear, my snowboard strapped to my back. But I had crampons for ice climbing clipped on my boots, and Pax definitely did not.

"In what way?" I asked, my thoughts trailing to how Rachel had looked this morning, curled into me like she was meant to be. I'd kissed her, and for those rare, precious moments, she'd let me — and kissed me back.

God, she'd tasted like summer days in the middle of January, like hope, and home, and everything I'd been searching for since the last time I'd kissed her. But then she'd pulled back, and I couldn't blame her.

I wouldn't trust me, either.

"In the you-have-one-good-day-of-weather-and-a-new-foot-of-powder-up-there way," Pax clarified.

"Yeah, that," I said, nodding.

"Don't do that," he lectured, crossing his arms over his chest in a crinkle of cold-weather gear.

"Do what?"

"Get distracted. Not today. I'm well aware of where you spent last night, and I get it. Leah drove me out of my damned mind. But you and Rachel…" He shook his head.

"I'm fine."

"She wasn't the curse. You know that, right?" he asked.

I looked over to where Rachel stood with Leah, the short black strands of her hair peeking out from her Jones snowboarding cap. "I was," I answered quietly.

"You were," he agreed. "I brought her here, and hell, I'm glad you survived a night next to her without claw marks of the nonsexual variety. But you cannot be distracted, not today. Not with twenty-one thousand feet trying to kill you. Understand?"

I clapped him on the back in understanding. "I love you, too, brother. I've trained for this, I'm as acclimatized as I'm going to get, and I wish you were headed up with me. I've got this."

He took a deep breath, exhaling in a burst of steam. "Okay, then fire up the helicopter and get up that ridgeline. Today is the only day you get."

"Then today is my day."

We made the last preparations while the pilot preflighted the chopper. It was eleven a.m. and the sky was crystal blue, but I knew tomorrow wouldn't be the same story.

And if we stayed any longer, we'd miss the ship's departure, so today was my only opportunity. Bobby checked out the GoPros, clumsy with heavily gloved fingers, and told us to make sure we didn't go until the small biplane they'd rented was passing the ridge.

"You know the chopper can't hold that altitude, so get

the hell off it the moment it touches the ridgeline," Bobby warned us.

"We got it," I assured him when I saw the same fear Pax wore flicker across his face. It seemed like everyone was on edge except Gabe, Alex, and me. But maybe my adrenaline was masking it.

The human body was spectacular.

As we started to make our way toward the helicopter, Rachel called my name. "Go ahead," I told the guys, and they continued to the chopper.

"What's up?" I asked her once she was close enough to kiss.

She tugged her lower lip between her teeth momentarily. "The powder actually makes it more dangerous. Easier for traction than ice, of course, but—"

"More prone to avalanche," I finished.

"Right. Just watch your lines, make sure you're keeping an eye on the slough. That one line on the left looks to be the safest, but I know you'll shoot for its big brother on the right."

"I could kiss you right now," I said, my smile so wide I nearly cracked my lips where the altitude had already ravaged them. The slough—the loose snow that I'd bring with me on the ride down—was always a concern, but more so after a snowstorm piled powder onto an icy spine like that ridge.

"What? You will not."

"I didn't say I would, I said I could." It took every ounce of willpower in my body to leave my hands hanging at my sides and not reach for her.

"That kiss didn't mean anything." She lifted up her sunglasses, like the way her eyebrows arched could convince me that she meant it.

"Okay," I teased.

"Landon," she warned.

"Hey, at least if I die it will be with your kiss on my lips."

Her eyes widened, and she sputtered. "That's…that's not funny!"

I laughed. "Relax, Rachel. Nothing's going to happen, not when I've got this to look forward to."

"Hey, Casanova, you want to hop this bird or what?" Alex called into my radio.

Her eyes hardened, and I could have kicked that asshole for reminding her what I'd turned into. "You'd better go, Nova," she said quietly.

"Do me a favor and man the radio? I know Little John came back this morning, but you always were the best at picking out a clean line."

She blinked, her defenses softening the tiniest bit, but I'd take it.

"Okay."

"See you in a few, Rach."

As I turned to walk to where the chopper threw up a small snowstorm, she called out, "It didn't mean anything!"

"Who you trying to convince? Me or you?" I yelled back over the hum of the rotors.

I wore a smile as we lifted off a few moments later, launching into the sky despite the thin air. We'd hired the only company in Nepal stupid enough to risk a flight for fun at this altitude, but even they wouldn't take us to the summit of the ridge.

The world below fell away as the ridgeline came closer, and my adrenaline cranked a notch. There was no room for fear up here, only precision, instinct, and guts. Fear and indecision got you killed.

"Right there," the pilot said in heavily accented English as we approached the landing spot at the highest point on the ridgeline he could manage. "You must exit quickly. I cannot maintain a hover at this altitude."

"Roger," I said.

We opened the doors and unbuckled, readying ourselves.

"Now," he instructed.

We bailed out.

The jump was only a couple of feet, and I dug my boots in as I caught my balance. Within seconds the chopper headed down the opposite side of the ridgeline to thicker air.

"Everyone okay?" I asked as the guys stood.

"Here," Alex answered.

"Yup." Gabe nodded, then looked down at the same time I did at the perfect forty-five-degree angle that sloped both sides. One misstep and we weren't boarding this ridge. We'd be tumbling.

"Well, looks like there's only one way down now," Alex joked.

"Second thoughts?" I asked, pulling down my goggles to keep the wind from attacking my eyes. We'd only climbed an additional three thousand feet in the helicopter, but I felt it in the burn of my lungs.

"Nawh. Wouldn't matter anyway," he joked. "Kind of committed here."

But what a place to be committed. We took the moment to look around us, and the sight stole whatever breath the altitude didn't. Frosted in new white snow, the Himalayas spread out before us in a display of mind-blowing perfection.

"Throne room of the gods," Alex muttered.

I nodded in agreement, too overcome to say anything. How could I when Everest rose in my line of sight? This was the stuff of dreams—of legends.

My hand rose to the radio that hung between my left shoulder and neck, pressing the button with my thick gloves. "Rachel?"

A few moments of static followed before she answered.

"I'm here. You guys okay?"

"Yeah. I just wish you could see this."

"Is it everything you dreamed?" Her voice sounded miles away and yet had never felt closer.

"It's perfect." *Because you're here, too.*

Maybe it was the thin air that brought clarity to my mind, but I was filled with the kind of certainty I'd only ever felt about stunts.

I was going to win her back. Not just her friendship. Her heart. Her love.

Maybe I wasn't worthy of any of it now, but I could be. I could earn her.

"I'm glad to hear it," she said, and I wished she'd heard my thoughts, my resolve, but I knew she wasn't ready for it. I'd scare her away if I said anything.

Pax's voice came across the radio. "You guys better get a move on."

I could have laughed. Twenty thousand feet in the air, another thousand feet to climb, and I still had Rachel on the brain. "Going now," I said. "You guys ready?"

"Lead the way," Alex said, motioning up the ridgeline. He passed the rope, and Gabe hooked on, then me. If one went down, we could catch him. If two…well…probably not.

I tucked my gaiter around the lower portion of my face to keep the wind at bay and started the long, cold, deep trek up the ridgeline. We sank to our knees in snow in places, to our ankles in others as we made our way, our breathing ragged.

Maybe I wasn't as acclimatized as I thought.

Knowing what to watch for, I did a quick self-assessment. I wasn't dizzy, no headaches, no vision issues—just fighting for air that wasn't there.

Two hours later we made the summit.

"Holy. Shit," I said, breathing between words as I hit my ass on the only bare piece of rock I found. We took out our waters, hydrating the best we could for the next half hour while we caught our breath and prepared, discussing the lines.

"I'm not sure about this one," Alex said. "I saw a cherry line a little farther back."

"Ride whatever you're most comfortable with," I said as I took off my crampons and stored them in my pack, ready to strap on my board. Then I looked down over the line I'd come here for. "I might need a belay over this first part."

"I can do that," Alex offered. "Gabe?"

He looked down and cringed. "What do you think that is? Sixty degrees?"

"Sixty-five," I answered.

"*Fuuuuuck,*" he drawled. "Well, it looks epic."

"Epic is as epic does," I answered.

"I'll go with you. Alex, you okay solo?"

"Yeah, I got this," he answered, already readying ropes through his harness.

I hit the button on the radio. "Rach?"

"Here," she answered, her voice better than a hit of oxygen. "You holding up?"

"Yeah. We're rested and I think about ready to drop in to the line. I'm feeling the one on rider's left."

Her laughter came through the radio. "Of course you are. Okay, rider's left it is. Watch that secondary chute and steer clear, there's a cliff midway that will hang you up."

"Roger. We're hooking up belay now. The first forty feet or so look sketchy."

"Agreed," Pax said from the other set. "Only you would choose a line that you have to pretty much rappel down."

"Yeah, well, that's what the real men do," I teased.

"Shut the fuck up. And be careful," he finished on a serious note.

"Roger."

I strapped my board on as Gabe did the same, threaded the rope through the harness, and said a prayer as I waited for Alex to be ready.

We watched for the small plane that held the camera crew, and as it neared, I nodded to the guys.

Then I went.

My turns were as tight as possible, covering little to no horizontal distance as I made my way down the steepest part of the slope, blocking everything from my mind except the snow beneath me and the rock above me. Every time I jumped into the air, pivoting my board, my heart slammed, knowing I might not find purchase when I hit.

"Nearing the end," Alex said through the radio as the rope tightened.

I found the small, flattened spot where the steepest angle ended, and hit my radio. "Going off belay."

Then I unclipped and stood there as Gabe made his way down the same path. My breath came in gulps, my lungs desperate for oxygen that wasn't there. Sweat ran in a cold river down my spine, my torso feeling like a fucking oven. I knew better than to unzip my coat, but that didn't mean I didn't long for a way to cool down that wouldn't kill me.

Gabe skidded a few too many times for my liking, sending more than his share of slough down the mountainside.

"Come on, come on," I urged in a whisper, holding my breath when his last skid was close to a fall.

This whole damn ridge was a no-fall zone.

Finally he made it to my level. "Going off belay," he said over the radio.

The rope snaked past where I could see on its way back up to Alex.

"Good luck, you two. I'll see you at the bottom," Alex said through the radio.

"Be careful on your line," I told him.

Gabe's chest heaved as he rested. "Fuck. Me. That. Was. Intense."

"Just getting started," I said with a smile. "Sun is shining, powder is good, and I'm ready to drop in when you are."

He nodded. "Just. Give. Me. A minute."

"No problem." I hit the button on my radio. "We're almost ready to drop in. Everything okay down there?"

"We're good," Pax answered after a moment. "Just packing up camp so we can get the hell out of here when you're done."

"Good plan," I answered. "We'll wait for the plane to come back around and then drop in."

"Roger that."

"Rach, is that line still looking the best?" I knew it hadn't changed in the hour it had taken us to drop this far, but I just wanted to hear her voice again.

"You're still in the clear," she answered. "Be careful."

"Always," I replied. "Ready?" I asked Gabe.

"As I'll ever be. Fuck, I miss air."

"Amen, brother."

Funny thing about altitude—all the training I'd done in the Tetons, the Alps…none of it rivaled this. The only true training for the Himalayas was the Himalayas.

"Dropping in," I said over the radio.

Gabe and I fist bumped, and I mentally prepared myself for the toughest line of my life.

It didn't disappoint. Each turn had to be perfect, thought out, and it tortured my lungs in a way I'd never realized possible.

Then I hit the chute, traversing below Gabe, and felt the adrenaline give way to the sweet feeling of victory.

I was doing it. Boarding the Shangri-La spine wall.

A stream of slough hit my board, and I got out of the way, watching above me to see that the river of snow came to an end before going again.

Another stream fell, and I skidded.

"Landon, watch out!" Rachel cried into the radio.

It was already too late.

I felt the roar more than heard it as snow slammed into my legs, buckling my knees. "Fuck. Fuck. *Fuck!*" I yelled, trying to get a grip on the earth that moved as a river beneath me.

Then something hard slammed into me from behind.

Gabe.

I lost all traction, and suddenly I was no longer boarding down the spine—I was carried away by a raging current of snow.

I tumbled headfirst once. Twice. Then I lost count. I flexed, catching the board enough to stop my tumble, but Gabe was long gone.

The snow covered me—devoured me, but our fall didn't stop, a torrent of ice and snow. I closed my mouth, trying to breathe, but the snow was everywhere as we plummeted.

God. God. God. Don't let her see me die.

Chapter Sixteen

Rachel

Logically, I knew the rotors of the helicopter weren't beating with the rhythm of my heart. They were faster, almost a whirl, but everything around me slowed as we flew across the snowy ground toward the base of the ridgeline.

It's taking too long.

I fumbled with the seat belt clasp, my hands shaking.

"Here," Pax said, his voice calm as he undid the buckle. We touched down, and I flung the door open, jumping to the ground below.

Wilder shouted something to Little John and tucked me under his arm as we cleared out from underneath the chopper. As soon as the bird was in the air—headed back to advanced camp to get more searchers—he grasped my upper arms.

My gaze swung in every direction. There was so much snow. More than I'd ever seen in my life. Landon was under it.

Somewhere.

Oh my God. Oh my God. Oh my God. The chant began in my head and wouldn't stop, drowning out every other thought as my eyes grew wider and my chest tightened. Was that altitude? Oxygen?

The whole chute had come down, and I'd only been able to keep my eye on the tiny speck that was Landon for milliseconds before he'd been swept away.

"Rachel."

I looked up to meet his gaze.

"You're panicking," he said softly.

"No, I'm not," I fired back. "I don't panic. Landon doesn't have time for me to freak out." I shoved my gloved hand into my side pocket and retrieved the small handheld device.

"Right," he said, calm and steady as always. "You got this?"

"I got this." I could lose my shit later.

We spread out over the avalanche field. Alex arrived and took the far side. Then Pax, Little John, and I walked a silent, steady line up the snow path, our avalanche beacons all held in front of us like we were searching for buried treasure.

Landon was so much more precious than gold.

Every minute felt like an hour as we carefully picked our way over the snow.

Please, God. Please. I'll go back to church. I'll focus more on charity work. I'll give up anything if you just give him back.

I'll forgive him.

I bit back the panic that clawed at my insides, telling me what logic dictated—that any normal man couldn't survive under the snow.

But Landon wasn't a normal man. He'd grown up on a board and spent every spare second riding big mountains. He knew how to handle this—how to form an air pocket. I just had to find him.

The helicopter arrived as we were halfway through the field, bringing Leah, Bobby, and one of the cameramen. As more searchers fanned out, we hit a signal.

"I've got one!" I yelled.

Please be Landon.

My heart leaped, pulsing in time with the flashing light that pointed me in the direction of one of the beacons. I held the little device steady, keeping my eyes locked on that light as I made my way higher up the field. The ridgeline loomed above me, and though we'd traveled up a good distance, it was nothing compared to the thousands of feet of sheer spine that Landon had tumbled down.

"Got one!" Alex called out.

With both beacons found, the team split, and I found myself surrounded by Little John, Leah, and Bobby while Pax headed to help Alex with the cameraman.

The beeps grew closer together, and the distance shortened on the beacon until we hit the single digits.

"Hit the snow," Little John ordered, and I hunched as we walked slowly, looking for the smallest number on the beacon.

"Seven," Leah read.

"Six," I said next. We were so close.

"Five. Four. Three," Little John said, my throat too clogged to speak. We were going to find him. It was the only possibility.

"Four. Five…" Leah said.

"Back up, slowly," I told them, and we inched our way back until we hit the three-feet mark. "Dig!"

Little John took out a long pole and gently pushed it through the snow until he found resistance. "Got something."

Someone.

Pulling out small, collapsible shovels, we started to dig. My chest heaved, tight and burning, and my vision started to haze the harder we labored.

"Miss, can you give me that?" one of the Sherpas asked, reaching for the shovel. I handed it over and stumbled backward as another did the same with Leah. I told my inner feminist to shut the hell up. They were acclimatized, stronger, more capable, and there were men's lives at stake.

When had the helicopter brought another load of searchers?

I looked over to see the bird parked on the snowfield, waiting to airlift the boarders.

"I've got him!" Little John said from inside the pit they'd dug.

Leah's arms surrounded me. *Please be alive.*

"He's breathing! It's faint, but he's alive!"

"Thank you, God," I said, sagging in relief as my face pointed heavenward.

"Gabe is alive!" Little John called louder to Pax across the field.

Gabe. Not Landon. It was Gabe.

Which means… My head swung in Wilder's direction, and I broke from Leah's hug to run across the avalanche field where Wilder was digging in the same kind of pit.

My legs dragged like lead, unwilling to move as fast as my mind begged them to. It might have only been fifty yards, but it felt like fifty miles. The altitude was draining me of every last ounce of energy.

We hadn't acclimatized nearly long enough.

"Wilder?" I asked in a desperate cry as I made it to the small huddle.

"Less than a foot," he called up to me, now digging with his hands.

I heard a gut-wrenching sob, the sound so miserable that it ripped my soul, the pain excruciating.

"It'll be okay," Leah promised as she caught up, looping her arm around me.

I heard the sound again and realized I was the one making it.

"Here!" Wilder yelled, and I saw the tip of Landon's Jones hat before he was surrounded by guys digging just as furiously.

"Wilder?" I begged, ready to crawl out of my skin. Had it been a half hour? Had he exhausted an air pocket if he'd managed to make one? Were we too late?

"Wilder?" I called again as they dug. It took everything I had not to shove my way through the sea of men and dig him out myself, not to get my hands down there and do something. Anything.

"Just a sec…" He grunted.

"Paxton!" I shouted, unable to take another second of not knowing. God, if he wasn't breathing, if I'd lost my only chance—

"He's alive," Wilder said.

The Sherpas split, and as Landon's face came into view, I hit my knees.

"Rachel," Wilder said softly, taking a second to look up at me. "He's alive. He's breathing."

Thank you. Thank you. Thank—

The snow was red along his upper body as they dug farther.

"Where is he bleeding from?" I asked, my fists clenching and unclenching with the need to act.

"I can't tell yet," Wilder answered. "Ready?" he asked Bobby.

"Let's get him."

As they struggled, Leah and I unfolded and snapped into place the stretcher that Little John handed to us.

"Gabe is loaded," he said quietly. "Need a hand?" he asked louder, toward Wilder.

"We're in position," Wilder said.

It took a few of them, but they lifted Landon to the surface and laid him flat on the stretcher.

"His arm," I whispered, seeing the blood seep from the fabric of his coat.

"We've got to move!" Wilder yelled.

I got one heart-stopping look at Landon's pale face before they carried him off. A flood of adrenaline swept through me, bringing me the energy to run after them—terror beating back exhaustion.

"There's only room for two more," the pilot said. "One up front with me, and there's a *very* small space between them back there."

"I'm going," I told Wilder, daring him to challenge me.

His eyes flickered toward Leah, and I saw the battle rage there.

"I'm fine," she said, putting her hand on his chest. "Pax, go. You've got to get help for them."

"I can't leave you on this mountain," he said, grimacing.

She cupped his face. "You can and you will. Landon needs you. Gabe needs you. Rachel needs you. I'll take the next flight out."

His face contorted, but he nodded. "Get another chopper up here," he ordered the pilot.

"It'll be another ten grand," the pilot said.

"I don't give a fuck, just get it done." He kissed Leah quickly and turned to me, but there was no anger or judgment that I'd just taken Leah's seat. "You'll have to take care of them until we can get down."

I nodded.

Leah hugged me. "Go."

"I'm so sorry," I said, squeezing her tight. "I just took your seat."

"No. If Pax were hurt, that would be different. Landon is hurt and that is *your* seat. I would have done the same. Now go."

I hugged her again, then let go to climb into the helicopter, careful as I scrambled over Gabe to sit between the two stretchers.

Wilder passed me the medic bag and headphones, and we were airborne before I could question what the hell I'd just gotten myself into.

After slipping the headphones over my ears so I could hear him on comms, I opened the bag and then looked down at my two patients. "Get pressure on Landon's arm," Wilder ordered.

I grabbed a pair of scissors and silently begged Landon to forgive me as I cut off the right arm of his favorite boarding jacket. The cut was long and jagged down the inside of his arm, but it wasn't pulsing in time with his heartbeat, so it wasn't arterial. I put the dressing against the wound and pressed.

I kept my eyes far away from his face. The moment I let myself actually realize that this was Landon, that we'd come a hairsbreadth from losing him and still might, I knew I'd be useless.

"Good," Wilder said, turning around to watch me. "Little John says most of the bones are broken in Gabe's legs, and at least one in his arm. Not sure about his ribs."

"Can you reach?" I gestured to Landon.

He contorted his position, twisting to keep pressure on Landon's arm as I looked Gabe over.

"He's a mess."

"Check his stomach."

I removed the solar blanket, unzipped his jacket, and then lifted his shirt over his belly. Then I spread my hands and lightly pushed. "He's warm, but it's a little hard, Wilder," I said softly.

"Fuck," he swore. "Okay. There's nothing we can do from here. We just have to pray he makes it to Kathmandu."

I turned back to Landon and took over compression on his arm. Finally, my eyes drifted over the material of his jacket to the stubble on his face, to his closed eyes.

My fingers traced the line of his jaw, and then I laid my hand flat against his face, trying to absorb some of his chill. I leaned forward and brushed my lips against his stubbled cheek. "Just live through this, and I'll think about us, okay? I'm not guaranteeing anything, but I'll…I'll think. But I can't do anything if you don't live."

"He loves you," Wilder said, looking down over us. "I don't think he ever stopped."

My eyes squeezed shut against the emotions that assaulted me at those words. The hope, the sweet feeling of home, all of it that I couldn't let in, couldn't remember how good they felt, because it would be so much harder when he left me again.

"All the girls—" Wilder started.

I locked gazes with the only man I'd ever cheated on. "Don't."

"They were substitutes. You have to know that. I knew it. He knew it, and I think every single one of those girls knew it. He never got over you, Rachel. Never. He never stopped loving you."

"Love was never our problem."

"Love is the best place to start."

"Listen to you. You spend three months with my best friend and already you're an expert on love and how to make it work."

He flinched. "You spent three months with my best friend and it's lasted years without being near each other. Why the fuck do you think I went to all this trouble to bring you out here?"

"Can we just not do this?" I asked.

"Hell no. I have you trapped for another half hour, and he's out cold. I'm taking full advantage of this."

I snorted. "If she didn't love you so much…"

"Yeah, yeah," he said, but I saw the nervousness in his eyes, the set of his jaw as he looked over our friends. "I'm just saying that everything happens for a reason, Rachel. You're here. He's here. Life is showing you what it could be like with him"—his gaze flickered to Landon—"or without him."

I didn't want to think about that—a life without Landon. Not that I wanted him *in* my life, wrecking what peace I'd managed to attain, but I couldn't imagine a world where he didn't exist.

I checked over both of them as the flight continued. Landon's pulse was strong, the warmth returning to his face, but Gabe's was weakening.

Through the comms, I heard the pilot making arrangements in Nepali and assumed it was with the hospital. As we approached the small landing pad, I knew I had to have been right.

"They are expecting us," he said.

My nerves fired back to life as we touched down on the pad, and the doors were opened by medical personnel waiting with gurneys. They took Gabe out first.

"Do you speak English?" Wilder yelled over the noise of the rotor blades to one of the doctors.

"Yes!" he shouted back.

"Avalanche. Broken bones, we think internal bleeding, and his pulse is thready. His name is Gabe Darro."

They nodded and sped away.

I tossed my headphones on the seat and climbed out after the medics took Landon on the gurney. God, they were going to take him. What if he never woke up? They didn't have his medical records here; they knew nothing of him.

He was just another tourist to them, another idiot who'd nearly gotten himself killed because he couldn't respect the mountains they knew to fear.

We followed them into the hospital.

"You speak English?" I asked one of the doctors.

"I do," he answered.

"His name is Landon Rhodes. He's twenty-two years old. It was an avalanche, and he has a two-inch laceration inside his upper right arm. His pulse is strong, but he hasn't woken up yet."

We reached the swinging doors that had a universal sign for no entrance.

"Okay, we have him from here. You can stay in the waiting room down that hall," the doctor said, pointing toward the well-lit hallway.

"No, I'm not done," I nearly shouted, my chest tightening. That damn lump was in my throat again.

"Rachel…" Wilder warned.

"He's O positive for blood. If you need to transfuse him, come get me. I'm the same. He had his ACL repaired when he was sixteen. Tonsils out when he was seven, and he's allergic to penicillin."

The doctor's eyes softened. "Thank you."

I nodded, my teeth slicing into my bottom lip as they wheeled him away. The doors swung shut, and as if they closed on my adrenaline, too, my body crashed, exhaustion and fear overwhelming me.

"Rachel," Wilder whispered and gathered me into his arms as I started to sob. The cries were loud and ugly, giving voice to the wild emotions that had been penned up inside me.

If it hadn't been for the avalanche, for Landon, for the blood, for the thought of almost losing him, I wouldn't have been so weak. I would have stood on my own, walked away with my head high.

But that ridgeline had taken more than just my breath.

For the first time in years, I let the man I'd betrayed hold me.

Because he was in love with my best friend…and I wasn't sure I'd ever stopped loving his.

I watched the seconds tick by on the face of the clock in the waiting room. They'd had him back there a half hour.

"He's got to be waking up, right?" I asked Wilder as he handed me a steaming cup of coffee. "Thank you."

"I know you're a bigger tea fan, but I couldn't find any."

I blinked. "You remember that?"

He shrugged. "Leah said something about teapots."

I smiled and sipped at the hot liquid, hoping that it would warm where my chest felt numb. "She's amazing."

"She is," he agreed. "And…" He sighed. "And I know I have you to thank for that. After the accident, when she was hurt and her boyfriend died, I know you're the one who pulled her through. Thank you."

"I didn't do it for you," I said softly.

"I know."

"You don't. When Landon left…when he went back to you, she was all I had. If I pulled her through, it was only because she held me together, gave me something to do so I didn't lose my mind."

He unzipped his jacket and did a little juggling with his coffee to get it off. "Crazy how everything interweaves, right?"

"Yeah. If I'd never met Landon…never met you, I wouldn't have been standing on that counter, trying to change a lightbulb in our brand-new apartment. I wouldn't have fallen and broken my wrist and met Leah in the ortho office. Maybe we would have met at Dartmouth or not, but we were both so damaged that we kind of filled in each other's cracks."

His forehead puckered, and he tilted his head. "If you'd

never met Landon…"

I sipped my coffee, cringing a little at the bitterness. "Right?"

"You said that first."

I looked over at him and narrowed my eyes. "He never told you."

"Told me…?" He shook his head.

I laughed softly. "I met Landon when I was seventeen. My dad was working on a Gremlin-sponsored event, he'd just taken over that division, and Landon was boarding—competing. I wasn't good enough, of course, but I met him in Aspen over Christmas while we were on the slopes at a Gremlin competition."

"But you met me in February at the skate park."

I smiled. "Put it together, Wilder."

His mouth dropped slightly. "You knew him first."

I nodded. "Yes. I knew him first. We had that whole week together, but I wouldn't give him my number. My dad was way against extreme athletes, given what he does, and Landon…"

"He's the most extreme of us all."

"Exactly."

"And your dad is fucking scary," he said.

"It's that I-control-the-Gremlin-sponsorship-money thing."

"It's the I-know-how-to-use-a-gun-because-I-used-to-be-in-the-military thing."

"Okay, I'll give you that. So I returned home, and I met you…"

"Landon was gone most of that spring for competitions," he said, filling in the gaps to himself. "Even then he was dreaming about getting to the Himalayas."

"And when he walked into your house when he got back and I saw him…well…the rest is history. We never meant for it to happen. I swear. I know I've said it before, but it's

the truth. We talked a lot about our feelings, your feelings…
but…"

He rubbed his hand over his forehead. "I get it. I don't
want to get it, but I do. If Leah had been with someone else,
nothing would have stopped me. That kind of need is a force
of nature. Why didn't he tell me that he knew you?"

"Then? Because you were happy. He thought if he told
you, you'd see right through us…and that was before anything
had happened yet. It's exactly what you said, a need. Animal,
primal, and something neither of us could ever ignore."

"Why not after? Why would he carry that?"

"My guess is that he refused to lessen his burden. He
broke you, broke the team, and then broke me. Landon's
always been good at torturing himself. I'm just… I'm so
sorry about what we did to you. It wasn't right, and we hurt
everyone in the process."

That sharp look in his eyes he'd had since the day we
were found out faded. "It was nothing compared to what I
did to you guys. Everything he's become…it's because of me,
because I made him choose between you and our team. If I
had to walk away from Leah, I'd be the same kind of hollow
shell, but I'd never—" He paled.

"It's okay," I said. "You'd never walk away from Leah.
She's good and honest and brings out the best in people. I'm
not Leah, and Landon walked away. I think he always will."

That's what it came down to. Knowing that it didn't
matter what he'd done, my soul would always reach for his,
my body would always crave what I knew only he could give
me. I knew that all with the certainty that if he were forced to
choose between the Renegades and me, he'd walk again.

"Rachel, that's not—"

"Rachel Dawson?" a young nurse asked.

"That's me!" I said, standing up and sloshing coffee on
the floor. "Shit," I mumbled.

"Go, I got it," Wilder said.

"You'll be okay?"

"I'm fine. Leah should be here soon."

We locked eyes for a second, and it was easy to see why I'd been with Wilder in the first place. It was such a weird dynamic between us all with our history. But even as beautiful as Wilder was, he had nothing on Landon's hazel eyes, the way he turned me on with just a raised eyebrow, or how he'd set my body on fire with a touch. It wasn't just Landon's body or face that made him spectacular—it was the effect he had on me. I'd liked Wilder, but I'd loved Landon.

Because Wilder wasn't meant to be mine, and I was never really his. But Landon…

"Go," he said softly, like he could read my mind. "Go to Landon."

I gave him a smile and then followed the nurse, nearly running to get to Landon. She led me down a series of hallways.

"How is he?" I asked.

"Awake," she answered with kind eyes. "Your other friend is in surgery."

Relief sang through me, letting precious air fill my lungs fully for the first time since I watched the mountain consume him.

"He is here," the nurse said, opening the door for me.

"Landon?" I asked, coming into the sterile hospital room. The dying afternoon light was soft on his face.

"Hey, Rach," he said, holding out his unbandaged arm.

I flew around the other side of his bed and hugged him tight, burying my nose in his neck.

"I'm okay," he promised as I started to shake. "Rach… baby, don't," he whispered, but I couldn't stop the tremors.

It felt like every ounce of adrenaline, bravery, whatever had kept me going all simply drained away, leaving my body unable to cope.

His hand swept down my back until he got a good grip on my ass, and before I could lecture him, he lifted me onto the bed, tucking me in next to him.

"Landon, you'll hurt yourself," I protested.

"Shut up and let me hold you."

I did.

He lazily traced patterns on my arm, my back, my waist as I lay there, my head on his chest, listening to the utter perfection of his heartbeat. The shaking stopped, and a wave of sheer exhaustion swept over me.

"Gabe is in surgery," I told him. "He had some internal bleeding."

He nodded. "They told me."

"But you're okay?"

"Cut on my arm was pretty nasty, and I have a lovely concussion, but that's it." He tensed. "My board?"

I shook my head. "I don't know. It wasn't with you."

His arm tightened around me. "Okay. It doesn't matter. I'll get another one sent to the next port."

"I'm sorry you lost your ridge."

He took a deep breath. "Yeah. Me, too. We can't make it now, can we?"

I shook my head. "We have to leave first thing in the morning to get back to port or we'll miss the ship." Gently pushing off him, I raised to see his face. "You okay?"

He stared up at the ceiling. "As long as Gabe is, then yeah."

"That's not what I mean."

"I know. I never imagined I would train all this time, work my ass off in planning, and then have that happen. I know it happens, I'm well aware of the statistics, but I never imagined it would happen to me."

"I'm so sorry," I whispered, resting my chin on the scratchy material of his hospital gown. He brushed my hair back from my face, and I scrunched my nose. "I'm in desperate need of a shower."

He huffed a small laugh, but it was big enough to tell me he'd really be all right. "You are beautiful, always have been. And you have nothing to be sorry for."

Didn't I? I was turning out to be the curse Penna had named me.

"I feel like there are things to say," I whispered.

"Do you want to say them?"

Every ounce of self-preservation in my body told me to shut the hell up. But I'd never gotten far in my life by taking the safe road. "I promised God that if you lived, I'd think about us."

His eyes widened. "And?"

"And I'm thinking."

A slow, incredibly sexy smile spread across his face. "Okay."

"Are you thinking?" I asked.

"Nawh. I already know."

I raised an eyebrow. "Know what?"

"I know that I want you to stay with me tonight. The rest we can figure out tomorrow."

I should have said no. He needed rest—well, what rest he'd get being woken up every few hours by the nurses. But the idea of leaving him so close to almost losing him was unthinkable.

"Okay. I'll stay. Just tonight. But no kissing. Don't even think about it."

He grinned. "That's a start."

Maybe it was.

Chapter Seventeen

LANDON

AT SEA

"You're looking at another five days at least," the on-ship doc told me, putting another bandage over the seventeen neat stitches in my arm.

"And other than that?" I asked, already doing the math for the Jakarta stunt.

He typed into his computer and then looked over the screen at me. "Other than that, Mr. Rhodes, you have a clean bill of health. How did Mr. Darro fare?"

Every muscle in my body locked, including my jaw. I took a deep breath to loosen up. "He won't be coming back with us. Too many broken bones, and he's still recovering from surgery. But we have friends with him, and his parents are on the way to Kathmandu."

"Well, I'm sorry you boys got into trouble. Ever think about avoiding the trouble to begin with?" he asked without looking up.

"That never did suit me," I answered and glanced up at the clock. "If that's all, I really need to get to class."

"Off you go. Come back in five days and we'll look at your arm again."

"Four days?" I pushed.

He looked up over his glasses at me and sighed. "Four days."

"Thanks, Doc."

I said my good-byes and ran out of the infirmary, clutching my Civ books with my good arm. Not that the right one hurt too much, but I figured if I gave it some time off, I might get those stitches out before the next stunt.

Especially since I'd just blown the one I'd been planning for a year. It wasn't just an accident, it was an epic failure that was no doubt going to be a great teaser for the documentary—where I would get to watch myself fail over and over again... with an audience. *Unacceptable.* What the hell was I going to do? I couldn't get back to Nepal until after we finished the program, and by then it would be too late to put it into the documentary. It was bad enough that I'd failed myself, but to fuck up the one thing we'd been doing for Nick was incomprehensible. I was going to have to get ahead in all my classes and then pray I could find a couple days somewhere to get back up on that ridgeline. That was the only acceptable option.

Of course the cameras had been waiting for me outside the infirmary, but at least Bobby was quick with the questions about how I was healing.

An elevator ride later, I hit the eighth deck and headed for class. *Five minutes early. Even Rachel will be impressed.*

"Hey, Nova," a girl's voice called from behind me.

I turned to see a pretty brunette catching up to me with a sly grin, and the cameras still following me. Shit. What the hell was her name? Sandy? Sarah? It came to me with the memory of having her in my cabin one of the first nights on board.

"Hey, Sabrina, how's it going?" I asked, more than aware that we were being filmed. Shit, I was going to have to talk to Bobby about the image he wanted me to play.

She looped her arm through mine, and I felt an odd twinge of unease. She wasn't doing anything she hadn't done before, but now it felt wrong. "I was wondering if you were going out tonight? I haven't seen you at the club in forever."

Because I hadn't been there. Since Rachel had come on board, I hadn't gone in search of a woman, which meant I hadn't gone to the club, much to the chagrin of Bobby, who was dying for more footage.

"Yeah, it's been a while. I spent break in Nepal. How about you?" I asked as we approached the door to Civ, which was propped open. Just a few more feet and I could slam the door in the camera crew's face.

"I did the Mumbai excursion," she answered. "So I was wondering if you'd be at the club tonight."

"Actually, I will." Mostly for work stuff. I'd promised Bobby a couple shots. I'd give him what he wanted one last time, but we were going to have to come to a new agreement.

"Then I'll see you later," she said with a bright smile, then headed down the hall to her next class.

"My God. Do you even realize the effect you had on that poor girl?" Rachel asked, leaning against the wall near the door to our class.

"Well, good afternoon. What are you doing out here?" I asked as she pushed off the wall. She had part of her hair pulled up today, but there were strands that framed her face, drawing all of my attention to those warm brown eyes that were currently narrowed at me.

"I was waiting for you, but I see you were otherwise occupied."

Wait. Had I been flirting and not even realized it? *Huh. If I didn't know better I'd think she was…*

"Jealous?" I asked as I followed her into class.

"Hardly," she shot over her shoulder as she sought her seat.

Oh, this was too good. I couldn't remember the last time Rachel had been worked into a tizzy over me.

I slid into the one next to hers and turned my baseball hat backward. "Really? Not even a little?" My tone was joking, but damn if I wasn't curious. I was jealous of anyone who had the right to breathe in her general direction.

She shook her head as she opened her book. "Not one bit. Jealousy implies that I'd have a reason to be."

She trusts me!

"And since I have no claim on you, or vice versa, and we're not together, then there's really no reason for me to give a hot damn who's snuggled up on you. Right?" She gave me a smile that I couldn't read.

Well. Shit. That backfired.

"So you—"

"Welcome back from fall break. I hope you all had fantastic trips and chose to spend your time to its best advantage," Dr. Messina said, cutting me off as she took the podium. "Anyone want to tell me how you spent your break? Diving into Indian culture? Hopping a flight to the Maldives? What about you, Mr. Rhodes?"

I gave her a smile. "Took a little trip to the Taj Mahal with Miss Dawson, and then hit up Nepal, where I climbed to twenty-one thousand feet and had my ass handed to me by an avalanche."

Her eyebrows rose. "Well. Not quite what I was expecting."

"I can say exactly the same. What about you, Dr. Messina?"

She smiled with a look of appreciation. I'd learned early that women didn't just like to be heard, they needed to know you were listening. "Well, I was actually ship's faculty during this break, so I mostly saw the port. Thank you for asking."

As she launched into our lecture today, this time focusing on the seven indigenous Indonesian tribes, I took careful notes, knowing we'd have a paper assigned after our shore excursion next week.

"I've arranged for us to visit an isolated tribe, so make sure that your schedules are clear for the second day in port. This will count as class credit and you are expected to attend. This is quite an honor," Dr. Messina told us. "Also, don't forget that your outlines for your term research papers are due to me by the Sydney port, which is only ten days away. If your outline is approved, then you can begin your rough drafts. If not, it's back to the drawing board."

"How is yours coming?" I whispered at Rachel.

She shrugged. "I'll let you know if I can open that line of communication with my mother without her sobbing hysterically that she's not enough for me."

I cringed, remembering just how protective her mom was. "She loves you."

"She does," she agreed.

"That's all I have for you today. Make sure you're caught up on your reading, and I posted an interesting article on eCampus that I'd like you to read before class on Wednesday. You're dismissed."

Rachel gathered her books, and I did the same, getting to the door before she did and waiting for her.

"Does it ever feel like we have two lives?" I asked as we walked down the hall. Thank God there were no cameras.

"What do you mean?"

"Like in one life we're college students, going to class, doing our homework, writing papers, and the other is out there on a limb somewhere snowboarding the Himalayas?"

She glanced up at me briefly. "Yeah. I get that. At least for you. It's like you're two different people."

I hit the elevator button, and we waited with a group of students. "Like student Landon and extreme Landon?" I asked, side nudging her.

She kept her eyes on the elevator doors. "Like Landon and Nova," she said quietly.

"Nova!" another girl called my name from the left.

"Hey, Mandy," I answered with a wave and polite smile to my physics partner.

"Did you want to work on that project later?" she asked with a smile that said studying wasn't all she had in mind.

The elevator *dinged*, and Rachel got on, shooting me a look that said she'd heard Mandy's implication, too.

"You know, I have plans later, but maybe tomorrow?" I told the redhead as the crowd passed me to pile into the elevator.

She twirled her hair as her gaze darted between me and Rachel. "Right, but it's due in two days and we're barely drafted. Not sure about you, but I can't afford a bad grade on this."

Neither could I if I wanted to find some sliver of time to get back to Nepal.

I sighed and looked into the elevator where Rachel stood, a single eyebrow arched.

"Rachel…"

"See you later, Nova."

Alarms blared in my head. *Fuck. She called me Nova.*

The door closed.

Never thought I'd wish to be back in that Himalayan blizzard, but she'd been warmer at eighteen thousand feet than she was at sea level.

The music thrummed through my body, the base line moving the ginger ale in my glass. Usually I had something a little stronger, but the waves in the Indian Ocean were hellacious tonight, and I wasn't risking my much-needed faculties for dealing with Rachel. She was still irritated, if her icy demeanor at dinner was any indication.

"Could you at least pretend to have a good time?" Bobby asked after pointing out where the cameras were around the room. "With Wilder going monogamous and shit, you're all I've got on the other aspect of this show."

"The man-whore aspect?" I asked.

He scoffed. "Since when do you object to being a ladies' man?"

Since I realized there's only one woman I want.

"Look, Bobby. We're going to have to sit down later and talk this out, because I'm not comfortable with this. Not with…" *Rachel.*

He ripped his hand over his thinning hair. "Seriously? You, too? Your contract says—"

"That I'll let you film just about every facet of my life for these nine months except when I take a piss. It says nothing about scoring chicks in a bar. I know you want the party part of this trip to play a role in the documentary, and I get it, but I'm drawing the line."

"Un-fucking-believable. Half the reason you're gods to your followers is the extreme way you take on every part of your life, and you're just going to turn it off? Penna's sitting on the sidelines, and Wilder's…well, what does that leave me with?"

"Every other Renegade," I said as Alex made his way across the club to join me. "I'll do your shots, come to your parties, but don't expect any action. I'm not leaving with anyone." Nick, of all people, would understand the line I was drawing. What Bobby was about to miss out on with my social life, I'd make up in stunts.

"Just give me a few good frames, and I don't care what the fuck you do with your night," he said by way of farewell.

"What's up his ass?" Alex asked as he leaned against the bar.

"We fucked up in Nepal, and now he's feeling short of shots. He's got the dramatic failure, but no comeback and triumph to follow it up."

"We didn't fuck up; Mother Nature took our asses out."

"Yeah, well, either way, that was supposed to be the money shot for this term. We didn't get it, and we lost Gabe."

"What do you expect?" he asked. "We're on a hellacious schedule. The shit you guys have us doing would need an entire year of planning, and we're pulling this stuff off at least once a week. Not everything is going to go perfectly. We needed more time up there."

Time was the one thing we didn't have on this trip. Already we'd turned our attention to the Jakarta stunt, always looking forward. I was the only one even thinking about going back.

As Alex turned around to order a drink, Sabrina walked up with another girl. Thank God I hadn't slept with this one yet. With Rachel on board, I was beginning to feel more than a little dirty over what I'd been doing while we were apart.

"Hey, Nova," Sabrina said, leaning against the bar so that her breasts pushed up out of her low-cut top.

Funny, it didn't bother me when she called me Nova, when any other girl reminded me of how I got to be called Casanova, really, but Rachel saying it always felt like a kick to the balls.

"Hey, ladies," I said with a practiced smile. "How are you tonight?"

"Better now that you're here," she answered with a sly grin. "I was beginning to think I'd never get you alone again."

Shit. She wanted a repeat performance.

"It's been a busy term," I said, then slammed my hand on Alex's back as he choked on his drink. "How was your excursion week?"

"Oh, I took the Mumbai trip, and then we headed down to the Taj Mahal." She batted her eyes up at me. "You know, it's a huge monument to love."

"Yeah, we made a stop there before flying to Nepal." *Even after her death, he protected her. That is love, or at least the kind of love I want.* Rachel's words came back to me, and everything finally clicked. She might have wanted the space she asked for, but she needed me to fight for her. Not just to sit back and wait for her to make a choice, but to show her that I'd protect her heart the way I should have the last time I held it.

I had to get out of this damn bar and find her.

"It really has been a busy term. You need some stress relief?" she asked, her eyes making clear what her offer really was.

This was the shit that was going to lose me any chance of being with Rachel.

"I need some stress relief," Alex muttered.

"I actually need to g—" My words failed as I caught sight of Rachel across the bar. She had on some kind of getup that must have qualified as a dress, and it gave her super-petite frame million-mile legs.

Fuck me.

Her hair was down, sleekly brushing just under her chin, the purple highlights caught in the club's lights. She looked like every man's untouchable dream, the girl you knew would either give you the best sex of your life or the fastest ass kicking you'd ever receive.

To me, she'd always been an intoxicating combination of both.

She smiled at some overgrown meathead who leaned

on the table next to her, openly ogling her breasts between comments that made her laugh.

My Rachel, laughing. Smiling. Did she just touch his arm? Look up at him through her lashes? Holy shit, was she flirting with him?

He brushed her hair back behind her ear.

Oh, hell no.

I was halfway across the club before I realized I'd taken a single step. Rachel did a double take when she saw me, her eyes raking up and down my body. Even though she arched that damn eyebrow at me, her lips parted.

That's what my Rachel looked like when she was interested.

Not this smiley, flirty version this guy thought he was getting.

I didn't stop until I was within kissing distance of her. She tilted her head at me, her lips curving at the edges.

"Can I help you?" Meathead asked, puffing out his chest like I gave a fuck who he was.

"Nope," I answered without looking away from Rachel.

She shifted her weight and held my gaze. *So damn beautiful.*

"Is this guy bothering you?" Meathead asked Rachel.

"Every day of my life," she answered.

"Look, I don't know who the hell you think you are," Meathead started.

"Hers. I'm hers," I finished. There. Line drawn in the fucking sand. I was here to fight.

Her eyes widened, and all trace of playing left her face. "Landon…"

"Rachel."

She looked over to Meathead. "Can you give us a second, Thomas?"

He looked between us and then swore under his breath. "Yeah. Sure." He grabbed his beer bottle and left.

"Seriously?" I asked her.

"What? He's in my geography class, and he asked me out this afternoon."

"And you said yes?"

"Apparently," she answered. "Just like you said yes and ran off with physics girl this afternoon."

"She's my lab partner."

"Sure, that's all," she said sarcastically and took a sip of her cider before putting it on the table next to us.

Why the fuck didn't she believe me? *Because you haven't given her a reason to.*

"It is all. And what is this? Payback?"

"This is me living." She shrugged.

I tucked my thumbs into the front pockets of my jeans to keep my hands off her. I wasn't sure if I wanted to kiss her or throttle her, and neither was a good option. "I thought you were thinking about us?"

"Thinking means weighing my options."

"And he's an option?"

"Everything and nothing is an option," she answered, sipping from a bottle of hard cider. "And if I marched over every time a girl had the nerve to touch you, I'd live plastered to your side." She peered around me. "As a matter of fact, I think you're being missed right now."

"I don't give a fuck."

"You'd hate to miss an opportunity to uphold your name, wouldn't you?"

I would have fired back if that little comment hadn't been accompanied by a flash of pain in her eyes. "I'm exactly where I want to be."

"Sure. For this five minutes, because I'm shiny and fun to chase. Every girl has fallen in your lap the last couple of years, right? I must be an intriguing little challenge."

"Damn it, Rachel. I thought we made some progress in

Nepal. Is it always going to be one step forward and two steps back with you?"

"In Nepal it was easy to remember why I fell for you. Here on the ship, it's so much easier to see what you've become. How many have there been, Landon? How many memories are in your bed nowadays?" She forged on ahead, her eyes glossing over with a layer of what I was hesitant to call tears. "Can you remember them all?"

Heat rushed through my veins, a nauseating mixture of anger, shame, and the bitter taste of regret. My brain screamed at me to retreat and lick my wounds, to try again with her when she wasn't on offense.

My heart reminded me that I was going to have to fight for this woman with every weapon in my arsenal if I wanted her.

And damn, I wanted her. Craved her. Needed her.

She was the only one I'd ever felt connected to—the only one my heart woke up and shook off the ice for. The only woman who challenged me and took me down in the process.

I stepped forward and clamped both of my hands on the table, boxing her between my arms. She craned her head to keep my gaze, unwilling to back down. It was the quality that both frustrated the hell out of me and turned me on faster than anything—her constant refusal to yield for just a fucking second.

"Can I remember them all? Probably not."

She snorted.

"You want to know why?" I didn't wait for her to answer. "Because blonde, redhead, brunette—I saw their features for a millisecond. The moment I had one of them in my bed, they all had eyes the color of dark chocolate and hair so black it was almost blue…" I glanced at her hair. "Or purple. I never needed to remember them, because they were always *you*."

"Don't say things like that," she begged. As if I could

physically see her walls start to crumble, she softened. "You don't get to say things like that to me. Not anymore. Not when everywhere I go on this ship there's a bevy of girls you've fucked, Landon."

"Yeah, well, I was a stupid asshole. And the worst part is that I used every single one of them to try to forget you, only to turn them into you in my mind. I have no excuse."

"What do you want me to do with that?"

"Forgive me. I want you to forgive me. Not just say it, but mean it. Do it. I want another chance with you, because I promise I won't fuck it up. Not this time."

She swallowed, and my breath caught as I saw her—my Rachel—the side she protected and hid away from the world. The one she'd been before I'd destroyed her.

"Did you ever stop to think that there's a difference between me forgiving you and me trusting you? I do forgive you for what happened with us years ago. We were kids. I don't need to forgive you for becoming Casanova, because you didn't do anything wrong. But that doesn't mean I can trust you now."

"You can," I urged. "I lost you once. I'm never going through that again."

"So what? You're going to promise me forever? We've been breathing the same air for three weeks, Landon."

"I didn't need three minutes. The minute I saw you on that deck I knew I wasn't letting you get away. Fate brought us—"

"Wilder brought us together!" she shouted. The music kept its driving beat, and it struck me as almost hilarious that I was having the most important conversation of my life in a damn club.

"Yeah, he pulled the strings—"

"You don't get it, do you?" she cried, her hands fisting in the front of my shirt. "I loved you. I gave up *everything* for you, and you chose him. You don't get to just jump in and get me back because Paxton Wilder snapped his fingers and offered me to you. I'm not his to offer, or yours to take."

I blinked. "That's what you think? That I only want you now because Pax says it's okay?"

"Isn't that the truth? Two years of silence from you, and then he serves me up on a platter for your dinner, so now it's okay. Do you seriously not understand how badly I want you? How much I want to trust you? To try with you? Being with you again isn't just a rush, it's intoxicating. It's like coming home—that's how well you know me—but you burned that home down, and while I've accepted the past, that doesn't mean I'm going to hand you the gasoline to torch my future."

Out of the corner of my eyes, I saw a flash, the reflection of the light on the camera lens. "Damn it. Let's go somewhere more private."

"No," she refused, letting go of my shirt. "The minute that happens, you'll kiss me, and I can't think when you do that."

"Doesn't that tell you something? That one kiss and we're both lost?" I challenged. There was nothing compared to touching Rachel, to finding myself while I was exploring her.

"That we've still got some insane chemistry? That we're still really attracted to each other and had some mind-blowing sex?" she threw back. "You've had sex with easily a dozen girls on this ship, Landon. What the hell makes you think I'm signing up to be added to that number?"

"You are the number!" I yelled, my temper finally snapping. "I can't change what I've done. But I can tell you that there's been no one since I saw you again. I haven't touched, kissed, or even thought about sleeping with anyone else."

She wavered, her shoulders slumping. "And how long could that possibly last?"

"Forever." I answered instantly, and knew it to be true. "You're it. You've always been it, and I don't care if I have to prove it to you over the rest of this damn year—you're the only girl I'm going to touch."

She stared up at me silently, and I saw the war raging within her, hating myself for having put her in the position in the first place. Hating that I'd left her, thinking that it would be better for both of us in the long run, and yet wishing I could go back and tell the world to fuck off, to quit being Nova and just be Rachel's Landon.

"If you'll let me prove it to you, I swear that I will keep a personal bubble around me big enough for only you to fit into. And you're pretty tiny."

She glared up at me, that fire sparking back in her eyes at me calling her tiny.

That's my girl.

"I'll show you," I promised. "I'll wear you down, I'll get past all those goddamned walls you can't stop building, and I'll earn your trust…and your heart."

Her lips parted, and her eyes went liquid.

I lifted one hand to her cheek and stroked the softness of her skin, resolve filling every single one of the holes I'd felt since I'd left her. I felt whole, determined, and strong enough to be whatever she needed.

"I'm still considering my options," she whispered, letting me know that I might have gotten close to her defenses, but she wasn't tearing them down yet.

Then I conquered my own desire, and instead of kissing her lips, I brushed mine against her cheek. "Consider, if that's what you need to realize that there's nothing in the world like what we can have together. Have a nice rest of your date."

Then I walked away, but I felt her eyes follow me past the other girls and out the door.

She'd better remember what I'd just told her, because I meant every word.

And I was ready to prove it.

Chapter Eighteen

RACHEL

AT SEA

I wanted to die. Hell, I'd already sent up a few prayers with that request. The tile of the bathroom floor was cool against my cheek, and I tried to concentrate on that sensation instead of the hell that was going on in my stomach.

"Rachel?" Penna asked through the door. "Is there anything I can get you?"

"No," I grumbled. "But thank you."

"Are you sure? I have to head to class, but I don't want to leave you here."

Class? What time was it? The nausea had struck as I'd left the club not long after Landon professed his intentions, and the puking had started soon after.

"I'm okay," I promised, watching the contents of the glass of water I'd poured myself rise and fall with every freaking wave. "Can you make the boat stop rocking?"

"I wish. Hold on, someone's here."

I heard her shuffle away, finally in a weight-bearing cast. A minute of muffled voices later, she was back at the door.

"Rachel, Landon's here."

"Great. Tell him to go away." There was no chance I was letting him in here. Not when I could barely move, and I was pretty sure there was vomit in my hair.

"Not happening," Landon said through the door.

"Trust me, you don't want to come in here."

He juggled the door handle. "Unlock it, Rach."

"No. Trust me, I'm saving you."

"How long has she been like this?" he asked.

"Since last night," Penna answered. "So about fourteen hours, give or take?"

"For fuck's sake," he growled. The handle moved again, then the door popped open. "Rachel…" Landon sighed as he hit his knees in front of me, gently lifting me into his lap.

"How did you get in?"

"It's a bathroom door. Not Fort Knox." His hand swept across my forehead. "You're all clammy. Is it something you ate?"

"I don't think so," I said as my stomach rolled again. "I just…I need the boat…" *Oh God. No.* My mouth filled with saliva and I bolted off Landon's lap, lunging for the toilet. "Get. Out," I told him, my voice echoing strangely in the bowl.

"I'm not leaving you."

He rubbed my back, and within seconds, I was heaving, acid burning my throat as my stomach emptied itself of bile. Not like I'd eaten anything… At just the thought of food, my belly rebelled again, my abs tensing with every dry heave.

"You're seasick," he said as I flushed the toilet.

"Bingo." I struggled to my feet and then swished with the water, spitting out the vileness that had taken up residence in my mouth. I braced my hands on the edge of the sink and glanced quickly at the mirror before looking away.

I looked like I'd been run over by the freaking cruise ship that was causing my misery.

"It's just because we're on the open ocean. The waves are a lot bigger," Landon explained, reaching around me to wet a washcloth.

"Not helping," I muttered.

He wrung out the blue terry cloth and then wiped my face. The cool water against my flushed skin was heaven sent. "How about you go lie down on the couch? I'll open the sliding glass door and let some fresh air in."

"I don't want to move."

"It smells like someone died in here, and then someone ate that something before throwing it up." He crinkled his nose. "I think I know just what you need."

Without giving me a chance to protest, he lifted me in his arms. My head fell to that magical spot on his chest, where I tucked in perfectly under his collarbone. "You shouldn't be carrying me."

"Why not?" We headed down the hallway, Landon pausing to brace himself as we hit a bigger wave.

"Because I smell."

"Yes."

We passed the bar and the dining room table.

"I have puke in my hair."

"Yes." He gently laid me down on the leather sofa, propping a pillow under my head. "I'll still carry you."

My stomach pitched, and I drew my knees to my chest. "Stop being nice. It's easier to stay away from you when you're cocky."

He laughed, moving loose strands of hair from my face. "I'll keep that in mind. Okay, you wait here. I'll be back as soon as possible, okay?"

I nodded, taking a deep breath. I hated that he was right,

that the fresh air felt fantastic. I hated when he was right about anything.

I loved that he'd just taken care of me even though I told him not to.

Ugh. It was complicated.

The glass door opened and shut behind me, and I spent the next few minutes trying not to heave up anything else. I felt empty, my throat raw, my stomach weak from what felt like ten thousand sit-ups. And the damn boat would not stop rocking.

In through my nose...out through my mouth. I took measured breaths, and questioned each of my life choices that led me to this moment.

The door slid open about five minutes later. "Sorry it took me so long," Landon said, coming around the sofa and crouching to my level. "Give me your arm."

"What?"

"Trust me," he said, turning those eyes on me.

"Only because I'm near death," I teased, and thrust out my arm.

He slipped a black band onto my wrist and tightened the watch-like clasp until a small, hard disk pressed into my wrist. Then he did the same with the other. "They're Psi bands. They should help take away the nausea."

"Really?" I asked, looking at the little bracelets.

"Absolutely. And if you'd told Penna you were seasick, she would have told me sooner," he chastised. "She thought you ate something bad. Guess she figured you were too much of a badass to get seasick."

"I just didn't realize," I said. "We've been on board for weeks."

"Yeah, well, you didn't do the Atlantic, so this is your first ocean crossing. Don't worry." He stood and walked over to the bar, pulling a glass down from the cabinet. A pop and fizz later, he handed me a glass of soda. "Ginger ale," he told me.

I sat up. "I'm not drinking anything. It'll come right back up."

"Well, we've got to get some liquid into you, and this is better than nothing. Just give it a few minutes for the Psi bands to kick in."

"How did you know I was sick?" I asked.

"You missed class this morning, and I knew you couldn't be that desperate to avoid me," he said with a tiny smile.

"I'm not avoiding you. You really came to check on me?" Okay, maybe that melted me just a little.

"Yeah, it's what boyfriends do, right?" he asked with a tiny, really stupidly sexy smirk.

"You're not my boyfriend."

He shrugged. "I was always taught to dress for the job I want. I figure this is no different. I'm not opposed to wearing you down by sheer force of will."

"As I recall, you always wanted to be Batman," I teased, the nausea in my belly easing.

His eyes lit up. "Remember that, do you? Cool toys, code names, worldwide notoriety—I think I got as close as possible."

"And so humble."

"It's all worth nothing if I can't have the only thing I need."

"And what's that?" I asked, my chest tight for reasons that had nothing to do with being sick.

"You."

The way he looked at me when he said it would have knocked me to the ground if I hadn't been sitting. There was no flirtation in his eyes, no manipulation or charm—just honesty.

The ginger ale was sweet as it slid down my throat, and I realized the nausea really had subsided. It was there, but manageable. "I think I need a shower."

"You do have puke in your hair," he agreed.

I rolled my eyes. "Do I leave these things on?"

"If you'd like to shower without vomiting on your toes. Want some help in there?" He drew his tongue over his lower lip.

There was the charm.

"I just spent over twelve hours puking and you're still trying to get into my pants?" I would have laughed if I didn't still feel so weak.

"Hey, I'll take you however I can get you."

I shook my head and stood, still a little wobbly on my feet, and thrust out my hand when he tried to help. "No. I'm good. I've got this."

Keeping my hand on the wall for balance, I made my way to the bathroom as swells kept the boat rocking. It probably wasn't the best weather for me to be showering in, but there was zero chance I was going to sleep this off with puke in my hair. A girl had her standards, and puke was definitely crossing the line.

I washed as quickly as possible, and even though I felt better for being clean and puke-free, I was exhausted by the time I got out of the shower.

Wrapped in a fluffy blue towel, I tiptoed down the hallway to my room, figuring Landon was still here. Sure, I'd dropped towel to prove a point when I'd first gotten here, but I wasn't ready for a repeat performance.

A pair of fuzzy pants and a tank top later, I found Landon leaning against the wall in the hallway, holding a rolled-up paper.

"What's that?" I asked.

"Get in bed and I'll show you."

"Where have I heard *that* one before?"

He laughed, and my heart skipped. "Come on. I'll grab

the ginger ale and some saltines and meet you in there."

My eyes narrowed.

He stuck up two fingers. "Scout's honor. I will do nothing of a sexual nature. Nada. Zilch."

"Fine," I answered, more than aware that he really was wearing my armor down to nonexistent. I climbed into bed and had the covers pulled over me by the time he walked in, balancing the glass of ginger ale, the paper, and a sleeve of saltines.

My stomach rumbled, and I took everything but the paper as he climbed into bed next to me, staying on top of the covers.

"I took notes for you this morning, and I figured I'd read to you so you're caught up for tomorrow," he said as he unrolled the paper.

"You're going to read me my homework?" I repeated, not sure I'd heard correctly.

"I am."

I raised both my eyebrows at him.

"What? I'm just showing off my boyfriend moves."

"Landon, we're not—"

"Yeah, yeah." He waved me off. "I know. Now, don't you want to hear all about the Korowai? They live in badass houses in the trees."

I guess if I had to spend a day in bed with Landon, reading to me was the least harmful thing he could be doing. Turning on my side, I let myself watch him, since his eyes were glued to the printed article. His voice was low and soothing, and I couldn't look away from the movement of his lips, the way his tongue would run across the lower one when he flipped the page.

When he finished with the Korowai tribes, he moved on to the Dani and the Lani, and I couldn't remember a time I'd loved listening to an article more. At one point he began stroking my hair with his free hand, and I leaned into his touch, too tired to do much else.

By the time he'd finished, my nausea was gone, thanks to the magic bands he'd brought me. He stared vacantly for a moment, the paper forgotten in his lap.

"Where are you?" I asked.

His hand paused on my head. "Wondering how Gabe is."

"Understandable." At least Little John was with him, and his parents had flown in. It had killed Landon to leave him there, but if Pax had missed the boat, he would have been kicked out of the program. They had a one-and-done policy around here, and he'd used his get-out-of-jail-free card a couple months ago when he'd been left behind with Leah in Istanbul.

"Is it?" he asked, still staring at the wall. "Because while one part of me is praying that he's okay, the other part is wondering when I can get back up there. Trying to work out in my mind if I have the time to acclimatize and still get it into the documentary."

I tensed as a cold fear ran chills down my spine. But as much as Landon had changed over these last couple of years, I knew that underneath it all, he hadn't. "You can't stand thinking you failed."

"I did fail, and not just me. I failed Gabe by choosing the chute with the biggest risk. He trusted me, and I got him hospitalized. I failed Nick, too. We needed that stunt for the documentary. He needs it."

"Mother Nature took your chance," I argued. "That fresh snow on top of the ice…it was a recipe for disaster, and you can't feel guilty about that."

"I should have known. I should have chosen the lesser chute—the one Alex took. I never should have pushed the summit."

"That's who you are," I said. "You would have seen

anything less than the summit as failure."

"Yeah, well, my ego cost Gabe months of recovery. It almost cost us our lives."

"No. Your way of life did that. You *both* chose it. You weren't up there dragging him around—he went of his own free will. You're not to blame."

He shook his head slowly, letting his breath out at the same pace. "I don't know. Maybe if I'd chosen a lesser chute. If we'd gotten there two days earlier—"

"Maybe if I hadn't been with you," I said softly.

He slid until he was lying across from me, his head propped on his arm to mirror mine. "What do you mean by that?"

"You haven't once thought about it?" I asked. "You haven't once had the curse cross your mind."

"There's no damn curse."

I scoffed. "Landon, since you've seen me on board, you've run into a wall, had torrential rains almost take out the Sri Lanka stunt, nearly washed away in a mudslide, been buried alive in an avalanche after a freak snowstorm came in, and now the ocean looks like we're in a bad remake of *The Poseidon Adventure*."

"Okay?" he asked, tucking my hair behind my ear like he couldn't not touch me.

"Seriously?" I asked, a slight twinge of sadness creeping into my voice.

"You're not a curse. I don't know how many times I need to tell you that. Look at everything that's gone right since you got here. Pax nailed his triple front—"

"Because I didn't go to the exhibition," I argued. "I knew my reputation."

"You were avoiding me."

"That, too," I admitted.

His thumb caressed my cheekbone, and the look he

gave me was so tender, I couldn't help but slip a little down the Landon-wanting slope. "Since you've been here, I have survived a mudslide that I might not have if you hadn't been in the car. I spent a night with a beautiful woman in my arms in a Himalayan snowstorm, and I cheated death in an avalanche. Maybe you're more of a lucky charm than you realize."

He leaned forward and pressed his lips to my forehead in a sweet kiss. Cocky Landon I could fight. Player Landon I could ignore. Nova I could despise.

But this was my Landon, and I was helpless.

"Don't worry, I won't kiss your mouth," he whispered.

"Okay."

"But it's not because I don't want to," he said, pulling back to look in my eyes.

"Oh?"

A corner of his mouth tilted up. "First, I want you to realize that this isn't just sexual for me. I meant what I said last night. I'm not touching any other woman, and that includes you, until you realize that it's not about the score."

The look I gave him must have been skeptical, because he grinned at me.

"I'm dead serious." He gestured down his body. "All this is closed until you believe that I'm in this to win it. The long haul. Your heart. All of it."

God, I wanted to believe him. My heart was practically banging at my ribs to get out and launch at him. But I knew better, didn't I? I wasn't some starry-eyed girl who thought she could change Landon Rhodes. I was the girl he'd left standing in an empty apartment with no savings, no college, and no family.

But there was this tiny part of me that was growing steadily stronger, begging to give him a chance. To put those claims to the test. But I also knew that was the last part of me that had never gotten over him, and with one misstep, he'd kill off that chance for good.

"And what's the other reason you won't kiss me?"

How long could he hold out if I really pushed? If I frayed the edges of his nonexistent control? How long would it take to prove that he just wanted to score the one girl he thought he couldn't have? Wasn't it safer in the long run to break my heart at the size it was now as opposed to letting it grow bigger for him again?

He crinkled his nose. "Your breath smells like puke."

I couldn't help it; I burst into laughter.

Testing him was going to be so much fun.

Chapter Nineteen

JAKARTA

"Stop scratching at it," Penna snapped as we stared out over the calm waters of the crane park. The water was glassy within the sectioned-off area of the bay, no waves lapping against the various ramps, air cushions, or docks that held the huge cranes that would soon catapult us across the water.

"I'm serious," Penna warned.

I lowered my hand from its exploration of the waterproof plastic covering my stitches. Sure, I needed the protection, but damn if I didn't feel like a set of leftovers in cling wrap ready for the microwave.

"You're one to talk," I told her as she shifted next to me. "Or was that not a coat hanger I saw you shoving down your cast this morning?"

She pointed her finger at me. "You have no clue what it's like to be in a full freaking cast in this heat and humidity.

None."

"Touché," I agreed, tipping my baseball hat in her direction.

She rolled her eyes, and I grinned. Damn, I was just glad she was out here with us. It had taken every weapon in our arsenal to get her to the stunt site, and even though she insisted on sitting in the shade with a book, I'd take it.

It felt like the first step to bringing her back.

"So what's up with you and Rachel?" she asked, picking her nail polish off and flicking it onto the wooden deck, just to watch it fall between the cracks to the water.

"That, my friend, is the million-dollar question," I said. I turned my hat around backward, then leaned over the railing to see Paxton fifteen feet below on the lower deck, making the final arrangements for the stunt.

I should have been with him, but I needed Leah to get here and sit with Penna so she wouldn't try to run away.

"I'm just glad you two aren't pulling each other's hair anymore," Penna said as she leaned against the railing with me. "You'd better not fuck this up."

"Doing my best not to. She doesn't trust me."

"Can you blame her? You left that girl high and dry and then went on to become a superstar. Add that to your propensity for fucking anything in a skirt—"

"I'm done with that," I cut her off.

"Just like that?" She tilted her head. "You, who I'm not sure has even gone a day without sex in the last two years, are going to give up your little addiction cold turkey?"

"Already have," I told her as I spotted Rachel walking toward us with Leah. She had on board shorts and a tank top, and her hair was pulled partway up, leaving the line of her chin bare.

"Seriously?"

"I haven't breathed in the direction of another girl since I saw Rachel in Dubai. That's over three weeks."

"Wow. That's almost thirty days sober. I applaud you." She saw Rachel and Leah coming and whispered, "Does that include your lucky charm over there?"

I grinned. Rachel really was my lucky charm, even if she was convinced that she was cursed. "Especially her," I told her in low tones. "I have to convince her that I'm after more than her body."

She snorted, threading her long blond hair through a ponytail holder, but before she could say anything, the girls had reached us.

"Pax says he's ready for you," Leah told me from under her giant, floppy sun hat.

"You going to join us?" I asked.

She glanced at Penna. "Nope. I think I'm just fine shore bound today. You guys have fun. Rach, did you want to leave your stuff in my bag?"

Rachel looked over the railing at the setup and then nodded. "Yeah, that might be easiest. You don't mind?"

"No problem." Leah opened her massive beach bag and took out a few of her schoolbooks. "Slip it in."

"Awesome," Rachel said. Then she crossed her arms in front of her, grasped the bottom of her bright green tank top and pulled it up…and off.

Fuuuuuck. A buzzing sound hit my brain, and every thought went out the window as she tossed her shirt in the bag. The top of her bikini was modest. Hell, there were only a few inches of that very toned, very soft stomach showing, but it was enough to make my tongue stick to the roof of my mouth.

Add that to her breasts pushed up against the stretched material, and I was in trouble.

"You okay?" Penna asked in an overly concerned tone.

"Yep," I said with a cough.

Then Rachel dropped the board shorts, leaving her in a pair of boy-cut bikini bottoms that hugged every curve of her ass.

I was still trying to form a thought when she threw the shorts in Leah's bag and smiled up at me. "Ready?"

Hell yes, I was. Right here. There was a little office building about thirty feet away that had to have a lock on the door.

"Landon?" Rachel asked, her forehead puckered.

"Yeah, let's go. Leah?" I asked, motioning to the bag.

"Yep." She nodded, holding it open for me.

I peeled off my shirt, happy to be rid of it in the nearly ninety degrees and humidity. It landed in the bag with my hat. I was ready to roll.

Rachel's eyes went wide and raced over my chest and abs, no doubt cataloging the tattoos I'd added. Then she swallowed and ran her tongue over her lower lip before shaking her head. "Yeah, let's go. Now."

I could have crowed knowing that I still had an effect on her, but then she walked away and I was too busy staring at the sway of her hips to care what she'd thought about me.

"Yeah, good luck on that no-sex thing." Penna laughed. "I give it a week."

I didn't bother correcting her.

We met up with the Renegades on the lower deck and prepared for the stunt. Everyone clasped their life jackets. I pulled the side straps tight and made sure I was secure, then headed over to where Rachel stood on the deck.

"You got it?" I asked.

She looked up at me under impossibly long lashes. "Not sure. Want to pull me tight?" she asked with a little bite to her lower lip.

Danger, Will Robinson. She was up to something, but hell if I cared at the moment. I cupped one side of her rib cage with one hand and pulled the side straps snug on the other side, then flipped and did the same on the other.

"Better?" I asked, my voice low. I needed to back the hell away from her before my body had a bigger reaction than my swim trunks could disguise.

"Much. Need any help?" Her fingers traced the small strip of skin that my life vest didn't cover.

Damn, I'd almost forgotten what it was like to have her full attention—the power she held in those deep brown eyes. I tried to chill the want that lit up my nerve endings like the Fourth of July, all hungry for her touch, but it was pointless.

Pissed-off Rachel was a sight to behold.

Worried Rachel made me want to solve her every problem.

Open, honest, defenseless Rachel stole my every heartbeat.

But flirtatious Rachel? Fuck, I was screwed.

"I'm okay," I told her.

She rose up on tiptoes and ran her lips along the line of my chin, barely able to reach. "You could be better than okay."

My hands clenched to keep from reaching for her. I'd been so accustomed to the gluttony of taking what I wanted these last couple of years that restraint was something I was going to have to work for.

But she was worth it.

And with that tiny little smile and devilish bite of her lower lip, I knew she was testing me. She assumed I'd fail and give in to my nearly painful need for her before she was ready for everything I wanted on the emotional level.

Not that I could blame her—I hadn't shown her much else yet.

But she had no idea how determined I was.

"Better than okay?" I asked her with a little smirk. *Playing with fire*, my subconscious warned me.

"Much better," she promised.

"You guys ready?" Pax called.

"Not sure. Are you ready?" Rachel asked me in open challenge.

"I can handle everything you've got, Rachel."

She shrugged. "We'll see about that."

We quieted as Pax ran through the plan. First runs would consist of those of us on wakeboards. We'd be pulled by the cranes, the centrifugal force propelling us at dizzying speeds toward the ramps.

Snowboards, skateboards, wakeboards—whatever. I was at home.

Like someone had flipped a switch in my brain, my concentration shifted to the stunt. I examined every angle of those ramps, the speed I could attain, which tricks I could pull off.

One by one, the Renegades strapped up and hooked on. Pax went first, and I shamelessly used him as my guinea pig, watching where he hit the fastest, which angles he got wrong.

Then I turned my attention to where they'd set up the human bowling lane.

I made sure the giant foam barrels were placed correctly in the water, stacked in a pyramid in the direct middle of the crane park, just waiting for the first Renegade to come sailing along and knock them over. The barrels were as tall as Rachel, three times as wide, and stacked on each other in a pyramid in the middle of the park.

"So what's the objective here?" Bobby asked as a camera appeared.

I put on my game face. "Knock down as many of those barrels as possible."

"With what?"

"Your body." I grinned, pointing to the nearest crane. "You have to swing out on the wakeboard, hit the ramp, and aim for the stack."

"Are you feeling focused after what happened last week?" Bobby asked.

I kept the smile plastered to my face. Hell yes, I was focused. "Absolutely. You can't afford to do what we do and not be focused. That's how…"

"People get hurt," Bobby supplied.

"Right."

As Pax walked up the dock, the cameras took mercy on me and headed toward him.

But although I was fully focused on the stunt at hand, Rachel was never far from my mind. How could she be when she was never more than twenty feet away? Her smile was electric as she watched the others ride, and I wasn't the only one who noticed.

The newer Renegades—the ones who didn't know our history—were lining up to get a couple of minutes with her. Of course they were attracted to her. She was gorgeous, smart, and capable of keeping up with our insane lifestyle. She thrived on this just like I thrived on *her*. A wave of possessiveness washed over me, but I didn't need to act on it. She had their attentions firmly under control.

I strapped on my wakeboard, checked my GoPro, and took my position on the dock, ready to jump-start my run before the bowling started. Two deep breaths later, I'd blocked out the avalanche and every voice in my head that screamed this wasn't a good idea.

Of course it wasn't a good idea. That was why we were doing it.

I signaled the crane operator and gripped the rope handle, ready for the yank I knew was coming. It didn't disappoint. The speed with which the crane instantly pulled me gave the needed velocity to start from dry land instead of the water, and I hit the smooth surface with a measured impact, heading for the first jump. I adjusted my grip, bent my knees, and took the ramp, pulling an immediate airborne 360.

It felt glorious.

Next ramp I hit a flip, my body falling back into effortless rhythm. The angle of the rope from the crane gave me better lift, higher jumps, and the speed didn't hurt on the air time for inverts and grabs. Somewhere in my head I recognized that the speed was dangerous, that if I hit the dock I'd end up with more than a few stitches in my arm. But I was in complete control, and it was exactly what I needed.

I'd had one disastrous, shitty stunt, but I was still a Renegade, still capable of pushing my body to the very limit in the name of epic stunts. Just for fun, I hit the next ramp— the highest one in the park—at the fastest speed I could pull and then flipped my body once, and then again, my board smacking against the water just after I brought myself back vertical. Even Pax couldn't pull that one off.

I went through the gamut on my run, savoring the movement, the speed, the adrenaline rush. As I cruised to a stop, I mock bowed to the applause. Once I hauled myself up onto the dock and unstrapped my board, I looked up to see Rachel grinning down at me.

"Super?" I asked after the cameraman scored his shot and went to his next location.

Her grin faltered momentarily before she shrugged. "Almost."

"What's it going to take?"

"Not sure this time. I'll let you know when I see it."

"Yeah, yeah. Get your butt down here. You're up first for bowling."

I finished inspecting the tow rope attached to the crane and then double-checked the boot sizing on Rachel's wakeboard. Once that was done, I tested out the latches and nodded to myself. It was safe for her to ride.

I gave her the nod, and she disengaged from the four guys

who had flanked her, none of them realizing they didn't have a chance in hell with her. I almost felt bad for them. Almost.

"All safe?" she asked.

I gave the cable another tug. "You'll be okay."

"So the idea is that I knock over those foam barrels," she clarified.

"You got it. The more you take out, the more points you get."

She looped her arms around my neck. "What do I get if I win?"

I glanced over her shoulder, where Bobby was smacking the cameraman on the shoulder. "Anything you want," I promised her.

"Oh yeah?" She came up on her tiptoes, and I backed off.

"Cameras," I explained. "Look, I'll go public with you any second you want, but I'm not going to push you there."

Her arms slid from around my neck. "Yeah. Cameras. Of course. What was I thinking?"

"That this was easier the first time we tried it?"

She laughed. "Ha. Then we were just sneaking around from Wilder. Now we're hiding it from an entire documentary."

"Hiding what?" I prompted her.

She rolled her eyes. "See you on the flip side."

I retreated as she strapped on her wakeboard. Once she gave the signal, she was off without another glance back. It was one of the things I'd always loved about her—she had the same drive, the identical need for the adrenaline rush that I did. I never had to explain myself or the stupid shit I pulled, because she was right there with me.

I held my breath when she hit the ramp. Knowing she was more than capable didn't mean my stomach didn't clench when she went airborne, or when she let go of the rope from the crane and spun in midair, flinging out her arms to topple as many barrels as possible. She brought them all tumbling down and then came back to the surface laughing.

Once the scores were tallied between the newer Renegades, I wasn't surprised in the least to see who topped the leaderboard.

One by one the guys fell away, and even Zoe shook her head.

Rachel just looked at the list with a shit-eating grin and then blew me a kiss.

Damn, that woman was irresistible.

And mine.

I rolled my neck, stretching the sore muscles as I leaned on my deck railing. This was one of my favorite parts of the ship, and the only place that was only mine. Not that I was against sharing, but in the last four months that we'd been on board, private space was the only luxury the ship didn't really provide.

There was a knock on my door, and I sighed. *No alone time for you.*

"Come in," I said from the deck, turning to lean against the sturdy metal rail.

"Hey," Bobby said, putting his head inside the door. "I just wanted to tell you that we got some great footage of you today. You were really back on your game."

Tension filled my muscles. "You were worried?"

"After Nepal? You bet your ass. A lot of guys can't come back from something like that, and you just bounced right back. Says a lot about your professionalism. How is Gabe?"

"Good," I answered. "His parents flew him home today, so I'll check on him in a few weeks when I get home for Christmas."

"I'm glad to hear it." His forehead puckered. "Look, we

got some other footage today…"

"Don't use it. What's going on with Rachel and me isn't for public consumption."

"It's a hell of a story between you guys, from what I hear. You two…well, the history between you three has been the talk since she showed up." He had that speculative look in his eyes, but I didn't give a fuck. Rachel wasn't some trick for ratings.

"No. If she wants to go public, that's one thing, but you're not pressuring her into anything for this goddamned movie. That's where I draw the line, Bobby." I would do anything for Nick, who was the primary reason we were making the documentary in the first place, and I knew he'd back me on this choice.

Rachel came first.

"Fine, fine," Bobby said, putting up his hand. "I'll kill the footage. Just let me know if that changes."

"I have a feeling Rachel will make her feelings pretty well-known."

"Fair enough. She looks like she's always belonged with you guys."

"She has. She's always belonged with *me*."

"Man, what I wouldn't give to have footage of some of that drama going down back then. You're sure you don't want to include any of that history…"

"No, Bobby."

He sighed. "Okay. Anyway. Good stunt today."

"Yeah, the crew really pulled it off."

"You all did. Later."

I gave him a nod as way of good-bye, and he shut the door behind him. Could I trust that he wouldn't put the footage in the documentary? Not entirely. Bobby would do whatever he thought was in the best interest of the film, but I'd be damned if I'd let him ruin my only chance with Rachel.

After the shit run of luck we'd had, it had been a huge relief to have everything go off without a hitch. It was a great stunt, something fun to balance the seriousness, but it didn't make up for Nepal. Luckily I'd already talked to Nick today—the time difference was a bitch—and he was on it.

A quick glance at the clock told me that I had another half hour before I was supposed to meet up with the crew for dinner. That meant I had an entire thirty minutes alone to—

Knock. Knock.

I sighed in frustration and walked over to the door, yanking it harder than I needed to. "What?" I snapped, then immediately regretted it as Rachel quirked an eyebrow at me. "Hey. Sorry."

"Would you like me to come back at another time?" she asked.

"No. My room is open to you at any hour of the day. Use it any time you feel like it." *Or use me.* I opened the door fully, and she walked in.

She'd showered since the stunt, smelling like that unique combination of peppermint and lavender, her hair hanging in silky locks just past her chin. I swear, my body remembered that scent and was immediately revved from zero to redline. She'd changed clothes, too, and was now choosing to torture me in a pair of blue shorts that landed a few inches beneath her sweet ass and a white halter top.

Her eyes darted around my cabin, no doubt taking in every detail. The thing about Rachel was that she noticed way more than most people realized. She picked up the two-year-old picture of the X Games on my desk and smiled faintly. "How is Nick?" she asked as her thumb stroked over his face.

"He's good. Keeps mostly behind the scenes now, but we're trying to change that. He's actually working on mapping out a time I can get back to Nepal to finish up that ridgeline."

She shook her head with a sad smile. "I should have

known you'd never walk away from that ridge."

"You're not going to yell?" I came up behind her, gently taking the picture from her hands and putting it back on the desk. I wanted her hands empty because I needed them on me, even if just for a few moments.

"No point in yelling. You're always going to push whatever line you can, and I learned a long time ago that trying to change you was futile."

Ouch.

Her eyes shot up to mine. "That wasn't a dig or anything, just something I've always known about you. I called you Supernova for a reason. Sometimes all I could do was sit back and watch you go."

A smile played at the corners of my mouth. "You kept up with me move for move."

She shrugged and turned, walking out onto my private balcony. "I'm a little out of practice, but sometimes it feels like I never left."

I followed her out, glad that the partitions gave us complete privacy. The humid breeze licked at me as the sun set behind her, illuminating her skin in a warm glow. "I get that," I said, standing next to her. "There are moments when it feels like nothing's changed, like we're on some altered timeline."

She turned toward me, bracing her back and hands on the railing before hoisting herself to sit on the thick metal barrier. My heart caught even as she wrapped her ankles in the framework to steady herself. It was a long way straight down. "And the others?" she asked.

I stepped between her spaced thighs and put my hands on her hips. Just the simple pleasure of having her under my fingertips sent my heart into irregular beats. God, I'd missed the feel of this woman. "The other moments it feels like I've been drowning for years, and I can just now breathe again."

"Landon," she whispered, her hands tightening on the rails even though I was right here to hold on to.

"I'm not going anywhere. If I have to tell you that a million times before you'll believe me, then I'll do just that. You and me—we're our own little infinity. Our forever is wrapped up in everything that's between us."

She let go of the railing and ran her hands up over her hair in frustration. My fingers dug into her hips to keep her safe.

Her head tilted, and her eyes danced in playfulness. "Why, Landon…does it scare you that I'm up on this big railing?" she asked, looking over her shoulder at the water ten stories below.

Of course it bothered me. One move and she'd break her damn neck. But that was never going to happen while I had her.

"Not when I've got you. You can let go any time you like; I'll never let you fall."

A quick flash in her eyes told me more than her lips ever could have—*you did once*—but she quickly forced it back. She was struggling, and I couldn't blame her, couldn't get angry, couldn't expect her to open her arms wide and trust me. I had to repair every crack I'd put into her and pray her faith in me would return.

"You've got me?" she whispered, leaning slightly backward.

I swallowed the urge to yell at her not to do that, and instead moved my hands slightly to slip my thumbs through her belt loops and gain a more secure grip on her ass. "You always have to push that line, don't you?" I asked, throwing her earlier words back at her.

"I learned from the best," she said with a smirk.

Damn it, I wanted her. There was a sharp edge to Rachel that I'd searched the world over for, just to realize it only existed in her. That edge turned me on, pushed me further, held me tighter, drove me insane with the need to tame the one woman I'd never been able to fully claim.

If she needed to dangle over the edge of danger, I was more than happy to hold her there. She stretched her arms above her head and smiled, but kept her ankles locked around the railing. I'd take semitrust any day.

She slowly lowered her arms until her hands ran through my hair, her nails gently scraping my scalp in the way she knew I loved. Then her gaze dropped to my lips and hers parted.

Make the move, Rachel. It's your turn.

She stared at me so long, so hot, that I was ready to combust, but I wasn't going to cross the line—not when she thought sex was all I wanted.

Then she pounced.

Thank God.

Her mouth slanted over mine, and I was done for. The rest of the world could have been on fire and I wouldn't have noticed, not when I had Rachel in my arms.

I let her control it, gave her the power I knew she wanted as she gently sucked my lower lip between hers. Her hair fell around us, hiding us from the world and enveloping us in the scent I knew would always trigger me for sex.

She slipped her tongue into my mouth, rubbing against mine, and that was the end of her control. A sound like a growl erupted from me, and I pulled her down off the railing just so I could press her against it. One of my hands tunneled in her hair while the other flexed on her hip. She was so damn tiny, but my body curled around hers as if it remembered exactly what to do—exactly how she needed to be kissed.

She opened fully under me, and I sank into her, stroking the roof of her mouth, savoring every tiny sound she made and returning to whatever would have her make it again.

She kissed me back as if she'd been just as starved for it as

I was, arching against me, pressing her soft breasts against my chest, and I was instantly as hard as the railing behind her. I kissed her like she was the oxygen I'd been missing, breathing in everything about her until my heartbeat finally steadied, then slammed.

The world didn't tilt off its axis—it finally came back to normal, as if everything had been out of whack until this very moment.

I didn't hold myself back like I did with those small kisses in Nepal. I let her know exactly how badly I wanted her. She gasped when my hand slid north, skimming the soft skin under her halter top. Her stomach quivered with her shaky inhale of breath, but she never stopped, only tightened her grip in my hair.

Fuck, I could kiss this woman every minute for the rest of my life. Kissing her didn't only involve my mouth; she awakened every nerve in my body, not just the ones she touched.

My thumb stroked higher, coming just under her bra, and she pushed forward. I rode the line between absolute pleasure and supreme need, my body remembering all too well how perfect it felt to be inside her, the way she came apart under my hands and dragged me with her.

"Landon," she whispered, straining against me to stand taller.

I grasped her ass with both my hands and lifted her until her legs wrapped around my waist, and then I moved us to lean her against the partition so the railing didn't dig into her back.

She rocked against me, and I groaned, realizing how close she was and how very little fabric separated us. Our kiss deepened, and it took every ounce of concentration I had not to take her farther, to move my hands the few inches it would take to slip my finger under her shorts.

So instead, I kissed her like there was nothing beyond that, relearned every curve of her mouth, and breathed every gasp, tasted every sigh.

"Rach? You in here?" Leah's voice hit me like a bucket of ice water, and I broke our kiss.

"Yeah?" Rachel asked, resting her forehead against mine as her heartbeat hammered, echoing mine.

"Oh. Oh!" Leah said as she walked onto the deck. "Okay. Well, your mom is on Skype." The last sentence sounded farther away. She must have gone back inside after catching us.

"Shit," Rachel swore.

At her first wiggle, I let her down, every inch of her body scalding its imprint into my hands before she hit the ground. I couldn't speak—too tied into knots that I knew only she could undo.

"We'll talk later?" Rachel asked, and a surge of pride went through me that she was a little wobbly on her feet.

"Yeah," I said, my voice gravelly and almost unrecognizable.

She nodded and ran out to the take her mother's call.

I turned and grasped the railing, looking out over the skyline of Jakarta. One fucking kiss and I was damn near destroyed. It had taught me two things: the first was that our chemistry was still powerful enough to destroy all reason.

The second: one crook of her finger and I would still go running. She owned me.

Chapter Twenty

RACHEL

JAKARTA

"I don't understand why it took you this long, or why I had to call *you*," Mom said, her blue eyes wide with hurt.

For that moment, I wished our connection was a little shittier.

"Mom, I told you. We only have good internet in port, and I've been a little busy. Our port days are our busiest because we have shore excursions, and I still have to study and stuff." I tried my best to appease her.

She sighed, her shoulders brushing her dark brown hair that was streaked with silver. "I just worry."

"I know," I said softly. "But I'm okay. I'm better than okay. I've already done so many amazing things."

Her eyes lit up as I told her about the safer things: the hang gliding in Sri Lanka, the elephants I'd seen there, the majesty of the Taj Mahal, and the trek through Nepal.

Her eyebrows furrowed. "I didn't realize you were going into Nepal."

"It was a last-minute trip I couldn't say no to. Seriously, Mom, I can't believe half the things I'm seeing. In a couple of days we're headed to see a tribe in New Guinea."

She smiled. "It all sounds amazing."

"It really is." In that moment, I wished my heart could reach through the screen. She was always overprotective— they both were—but I knew how hard it had been for them to adopt me, how tedious the process had been, and how badly they'd wanted a child of their own.

Of course she was going to worry.

"How is Leah?"

"She's..." *In love with someone you despise.* "She's great."

"Well, she looked great when she popped in. Who was the blonde who answered?"

"Penna. She's my roommate, too."

"Oh, I thought it was just you and Leah..." The door opened behind her, and she clapped her hands. "Stan! Look who's online."

At least that saved me from telling her that Leah had moved in with Pax. I wasn't sure what she'd hate more—the implication of premarital sex or that I was on a ship with Wilder.

My father dropped his briefcase in the hall and ran over to the computer, hunching down next to Mom. "There's my girl! How are you, sweet pea?"

"I'm good," I promised. "How is everything there?"

They didn't even look at each other, which struck me as odd.

"Good," Dad answered.

"Fine," Mom added in.

"Uh, okay," I said, my eyes narrowing as I leaned my elbows on our dining room table. "Did something happen?"

"No, not at all," Dad promised, loosening his tie. "We just miss you. When do you get home for Christmas?"

"I fly in the fifteenth, and then I have about two weeks."

"Good. We can't wait to see you," Mom said.

"Oh, I need a favor, if you guys get a second?"

"Absolutely, what's up?" Dad asked.

"Will you peek through my records? I'm looking for my adoption stuff for a class paper."

He stiffened, and Mom's eyes widened. "Why would you want those? What kind of class paper is this?" Mom asked.

I took a deep breath and kept my voice off the defensive. My adoption was such a sore spot for them, like they were ashamed that they couldn't conceive on their own—ashamed that they'd needed a baby to solve the problems in their marriage back then.

Maybe they didn't realize I knew that, but my aunts had big mouths.

But hey, they were still together, so I guess I did my job well.

"I'm taking this Cultures of the Pacific class, and we're doing research papers. I want to do mine on adoptions in Korea. I figured since that's the country with the second highest number of adoptions, it would be good."

"Why not do China?" Mom asked.

I blinked. "Because I wasn't adopted from China."

"Right. Of course," Dad said. "The papers should be filed in storage. We haven't had them out since the year of your adoption. I'll dig around."

"Thanks, Dad," I said, my heart panging with missing them. I loved being here and would never second-guess that choice, but I missed my parents, too. It was one thing to be across the country from them and another to be across the world.

"No problem," he said as the sliding glass door opened

behind me.

"Hey, is Leah in here?" Pax asked. "Oh, you're—"

I cringed. "Talking to my parents."

He nodded slowly, and then gave them the wave, clearly in their line of sight. "Mr. Dawson. Mrs. Dawson," he said with a tight smile. "I'll…uh…just look for her somewhere else. Anywhere else."

I rubbed my forehead. "I think she said she was going up top with Penna to watch the departure."

"Yeah. Okay. Thanks. You good?" Wilder asked, knowing the shit was about to hit the fan.

"Yep," I answered, offering him a smile.

"I'll make sure you have some privacy…" he said, backing out of the door and shutting it.

"Rachel Christine Dawson," my mother snapped.

"Mom." I turned in my chair with a false smile. "What's up?"

"Who was that?"

"Leah's boyfriend," I said, hoping they hadn't seen him clearly.

"That was Paxton Wilder," Dad said. "Damn it. I knew they were off making a documentary, but I didn't realize it was on your ship."

"It is on our ship, and he's dating Leah."

"After what happened with you?" Mom exclaimed.

"Mom, I hurt Wilder, not the other way around. They're really good together, and she's happy. It's not complicating things at all. They were together before I even got here."

"And what about the other one?" Dad growled.

I swallowed. "Landon is here, too."

Mom's indrawn breath was the shot heard around the world.

"He'd better not come near you," Dad hissed.

Too late.

"Landon is fine. Don't worry about me. A lot has changed in the last two years."

"That boy wrecked you!" Dad was turning a mottled shade of red, something that only arguing over Landon had ever accomplished.

"And I rebuilt. Dad, I know you're worried, but I'm fine. Landon is…" I sighed.

Dad cursed.

"I'm fine," I promised. "He's not getting in the way of my academics, and everything is fine. Sure, it was awkward at first" —*like when he stole my clothes out of the bathroom*— "but we're both older now, more mature. Less likely to pull stupid stunts."

"Like leaving you high and dry and breaking your heart?" Dad asked.

"Yeah, like that," I said weakly, mostly because I didn't know. Like Skype had a sense of mercy, I got the poor-signal warning as we pulled out of port. "Look, we're about to lose signal. We'll be in New Guinea in a couple days and I'll try to call again, okay?"

Mom nodded, her face tight. "Just…just be careful, Rachel. You only have one heart."

And Landon already owns it.

"I know, Mom. I love you guys, and I'll see you soon, okay?"

Our good-byes were tense but over quickly, and my shoulders sagged in relief as I closed my laptop.

Dad's job—handling sponsorships at Gremlin—had made it possible for him to make the Renegades' life way more than difficult after Landon left me, but he'd taken the high road and let them keep their funding. Besides, this trip was fully sponsored by Wilder Enterprises, so it wasn't like he could hurt them.

I scoffed and rested my head in my hands. A few weeks

around Landon and I was already defending him to Dad, who had basically fixed my life when Landon had walked away.

The two sides of me warred, my heart telling me that Landon was the only one I could ever willingly give it to, and my brain warning that there was too much pain in our past for us to ever really work.

I told them both to shut up and concentrated on my stomach. It wanted ice cream, which was the safest of all the options.

. . .

"Now this is really quite a privilege," Dr. Messina told us as we lined up against the back of a dark hut in the middle of Papua New Guinea three days later. "This isn't something average tourists see, so be quiet, be invisible, and be respectful."

"She sounds like my mother," Hugo said from next to me.

I smothered a laugh.

Landon rubbed against my right shoulder, no doubt to remind me that he was here. Not that I needed any reminding. He was everywhere—class, Renegade stuff, my suite. Trying to give myself a little space was nearly impossible.

"You've been quiet all day. For the last couple days, really," Landon noted quietly as Dr. Messina walked away.

"I'm speaking to you," I said without looking up at him.

"If you had tried to get any farther away, you would have had to go to the moon," he responded.

I shrugged. "I'm fine." *My parents just served me up a hot reminder of what you cost me the first time, and I'm wondering if I've lost my mind.* Like I was ever going to say *that* to him.

"You're not fine. I'm not sure if it was the kiss or talking to your mother—"

"Shh!" I hissed. "That's not something we're talking about in…you know…public," I said, pointing to the camera that had surprisingly been let in.

"Well, if you'd talk to me alone, I wouldn't have to try in public."

I finally looked over at where he sat next to me, his elbows casually braced on his knees. The small fire in the middle of the hut threw shadows across his face. He was hot as hell, like bottled sex, and I was the one with the cap.

"I'm not avoiding you or anything."

"Going to class, minimal conversations revolving around only stunts and homework, and showing up for the excursion doesn't count. Your mom spooked you," he guessed.

"My dad made some memorable comments," I answered. "They didn't change anything, I just…needed a few minutes."

"You had a few days," he retorted. "I'm not in a rush. I'll wait forever for you to figure out that I'm in this, but I'd rather you come to me when you're spooked. I can't stop that little mental fight you're already in with me if I don't know it's going on—if you can't let me in your head."

He was completely right. It chafed me to admit it, but he really was. "Okay. You're right."

His mouth dropped open.

"What?" I asked.

"I'm just watching hell freeze over."

"Shut up," I said, leaning into him. "Talking to my parents was hard. They put me back together when you…" I trailed off. It wasn't fair to keep shoving our past at him. If I was going to actually be with him, then I couldn't drag him through that mud over and over.

"When I left you," he finished. "Look, I fucked that up. It changed us both, and we have to be able to talk about it. Your parents rightfully hate me because they saw the aftermath. If I saw that, I'm sure I'd hate myself a hell of a lot more than I already do."

I blinked at him, trying to organize my thoughts. "In a

million years, I never imagined you saying that. You hate my dad."

"I hate that he hated me, and then I went and gave him a damn good reason to." He shrugged. "When we get back to L.A., I'm going to grovel, and I'm really not looking forward to it, but I'm honestly just hoping that I've at least won you over by that point—"

"What?" I asked a little too loudly. Dr. Messina shushed me from her seat across the hut.

"—because I can't fight a war on two fronts. What do you mean, *what*?"

"When we get back to L.A.?" I asked. "You mean… you've thought about that?" *About what would happen once you actually caught me.*

"Well, yeah. We're not going to be on this ship forever, right? Unless you have some lifelong plans that I'm not aware of?"

He'd thought about more than the chase, the pursuit. He'd looked ahead to when real life was going to hit us again. God, I hated the damn cameras, because I wanted to kiss him, to show him what I couldn't find the words to say. Instead I leaned my forehead against his shoulder and breathed in, knowing he'd just knocked loose one of the last bricks in my defense against him.

He pressed his lips to my hair and rested there for a second.

It wasn't enough for a moment like this, and yet it meant everything.

I don't know how long we sat there, but the next thing I heard were the chants of the incoming Dani men. As they entered the hut, in ceremonial clothing and faces painted with bright colors, I lifted my head and reveled in the beauty of a different culture.

"Amazing to think they've never met before," Landon

whispered as the women entered, their faces painted with the same bright colors. I knew from class that they only married outside their own villages, but that both parties had to consent before the matchmaker would agree to their union.

I looped my arm through Landon's and drew my knees tighter to my chest to give the men room to circulate. They chanted and sang what I knew were tribal songs about marriage, rotating between the women in their official ritual of courtship. Around and around they moved, the excitement palpable in the air as one by one, they sat next to the woman they intended to court.

"Imagine that," I whispered. "No dating, just finding your person and saying yes to the rest of your life."

Finally they were all seated, cross-legged, hands intertwined as they sang.

"That's a huge decision for a split-second meeting," he noted.

"Not as much for the men," I added. "They can take more than one wife, but the women can't." I looked over and watched him as he studied the ceremony. "Would you want that? More than one wife?"

He looked down at me, a smile tugging at the corners of his mouth. "I can barely keep up trying to chase you. So that's a no."

Softly laughing, I looked back to the men and women who sat next to the person they would marry. The hope in their eyes was enough to overflow into me.

"But I would have sat next to you," Landon whispered into my ear. "I would have fought off any man who thought he was a better fit and paid whatever price your father demanded, and then some."

Chills raced over my skin, prickling and warming me all in the same breath.

"No price would have been high enough, no challenge big

enough. But I would have won."

"So sure of yourself?" I asked, just loud enough for him to hear me over the singing.

"Yeah. I am. Because I know you would have fought for me, too."

My chest filled with the sweetest pressure, and I pushed it down, knowing exactly where it led—knowing that I wasn't ready. "In an alternate timeline," I said, remembering our earlier conversation.

He tipped my chin up but didn't kiss me, simply looked deeply into my eyes until I was sure that I would melt into his. "In every timeline."

I looked away when I couldn't take it anymore, when the force of our connection threatened to override my common sense.

His words stayed with me long after the ceremony, and I couldn't help but realize that we'd sat there in the same position as the newly intendeds—arms intertwined, ankles crossed.

In every timeline, indeed.

"It's like you're twelve and back at Camp Sunnyville," I muttered to myself as I walked down the path of bungalows our class had taken over for the night. Of course Camp Sunnyville hadn't been in the middle of a rain forest or had its accompanying humidity.

Between the ceremony and the hike back to our residence, it had to be at least midnight. If we were in the States, I would have texted Landon. Or Facebooked him. Hell, Twitter might have been an option.

The minute my temporary roommate's boyfriend showed up in our little thatched cabin, I got the hell out of there. No chance I wanted to hear whatever was going to happen on the other side of our room.

I wasn't even that close with Leah, nor did I ever want to be.

With the full moon above me, all the bungalows looked the same. Crap. Which one was he in?

"Rachel?"

I spun in the darkness toward Hugo's figure. "Hey. What are you doing out here?"

"I could ask you the same." He laughed.

"I'm looking for Landon's room. My roommate needed to put a sock on the door handle."

"Ah," he said with a deep head nod. "I understand. I'd say that you're welcome to come back to my room, but I have a feeling you're not just looking for an escape."

"Yeah…" I sighed. "Sorry."

"Don't apologize. You two have some weird magnetic pull that I'm not stupid enough to get between. I have a feeling whoever does gets crushed."

Like Wilder.

"Yeah, we're…us," I said, failing to find a better word.

He laughed. "You and Leah and those Renegades. I think he's in the last one on the right. I remember him being alone, too."

"Thank you!"

"Want me to walk you down?"

"No worries, but thank you for offering."

"Okay, but I'll wait here until you get inside."

With a wave, I was off. I tightened my hands on the straps of my day pack and walked the distance to Landon's bungalow.

As I walked up the steps, I turned to see Hugo watching, and I waved in thanks.

A soft light shone from under the door, and I paused,

my hand raised to knock. What was I doing here? Other than avoiding the sexcapade in my own room? Maybe I was looking for the same thing. I rested my forehead against the smooth wood of the doorframe and took a deep breath.

I'd already let him get so close. Despite my best intentions, he was right there, close enough to my heart to break it again, and I was a breath away from surrendering everything to him. But Landon had always been about the chase, and that's still where we were—he was still chasing me. What happened if he caught me?

You won't be so bright and shiny, and he'll move on.

The thought rocked me, because the more time I spent with him, the more I knew I didn't want him to move on.

But how much worse would it be in a few weeks? Months? Wasn't it better to get the breaking done now, when I was only losing the possibility of Landon?

Oh my God, how long was I going to stand out here debating?

Don't be a chicken.

I knocked.

"Come in," Landon called out, and I sighed in relief. At least I wasn't knocking on some stranger's door in the middle of the night. Even worse, it could have been Dr. Messina.

I opened the door and found him lounged on his double bed, mouthwateringly shirtless with a book perched in his hands.

"Rachel?" He sat up fully, putting the book down next to him.

"What are you reading?" I asked.

"*A Moveable Feast*," he answered. "What are you doing here? Are you okay?"

"I'm fine. My roommate is currently getting some, which isn't anything I wanted to be around for, and it was either Hugo's room or yours. I chose yours."

"Good choice," he said.

"So, Hemingway? Is that on your reading list for Lit?" I dropped my bag and sat on the corner of the bed, since there was nowhere else to sit.

"No," he answered.

That simple word told me that part of him—the book lover—hadn't faded in time. "How is it?"

"Good," he answered. "Kind of makes me feel a little like a voyeur, though."

"Because he never meant to publish it?" I asked.

Landon smiled. "Ah, the journalism major knows her Hemingway."

I shrugged.

"God, I've missed you."

My eyes shot to his, and I held them there, refusing to look at the yards of inked skin that he had on display. One look at those swirls of color and I'd ache to trace them with my fingers—my tongue.

"I have," he reiterated. "Not just the sex—though it's the best I've ever had—just being around you. Not feeling the pressure to live up to some hype."

"You weren't as big of a deal when we first met," I reminded him.

He didn't deny his current status or feign being humble. "I'd trade it all," he said, ripping his hand over his hair with a self-deprecating laugh. "God, Rach. Looking back, I would trade everything to have you in that apartment. I know I don't get to complain, not after what I did, but it's been so empty. Nothing filled the void you left. No amount of tricks or medals or mountains or girls touched it. If anything, it grew until I was one giant pit of empty."

I squeezed my eyes shut. "Don't say things like that."

"Like what? The truth?" I felt the bed move as he did.

I covered my face with my hands. "Things that make

me…feel things I'm not ready to."

"Okay," he said softly as he pulled my hands from my face. "What are you ready to feel? Just tell me that."

He sat a breath away from me, his eyes luminous and so very green in the lamplight. My chest felt like it would explode or I was going to fly; one way or another, things were changing…but one thing had stayed the same.

I hadn't fallen for Landon—I'd never recovered, never unfallen, never gotten over him—and that spark in my heart told me there were much bigger words and emotions at play. Emotions that would crush me with their weight if I let him in and he repeated our past.

"Rachel?" he asked softly.

Without letting myself examine it too much, I moved, straddling him easily with one knee on either side of his hips. His eyes were wide, but I saw the barely leashed hunger there as I cupped the back of his neck.

"You. I'm ready to feel you."

Chapter Twenty-One

RACHEL

I kissed him with a hunger I hadn't known I was capable of. There was no sweet preamble or soft intro. No, there was tongue, heat, and the sweetest groan I'd ever heard out of him.

"Rachel, baby," he said against my mouth.

"Touch me."

His hands ran up and down the back of my tank top, like he was relearning the line of my spine. Then he filled his hands with my ass and squeezed. "I am touching you."

My tongue traced the line of his ear. "I want more. Don't make me beg."

Faster than I could blink, Landon spun us, moving so I was on my back in the middle of the bed. *God, yes.*

I'd almost forgotten what he looked like above me, his hair falling rakishly near his eyes, the need in him palpable. "You're beautiful," I told him.

He grinned. "Nothing compared to you." He ran his finger across my collarbone. "This skin, so soft." His hands traced the outsides of my breasts. "This body, so fucking perfect."

Both of his hands skimmed my curves until he cupped my face. "But this face…the stuff of dreams. I would know, since you've haunted mine." His mouth crashed into mine, and I met him, kissing him back with everything I had.

To think I'd almost never had this again.

I was going to enjoy every second of him, because even as I lay there beneath him, I knew my allure would fade the moment he'd caught what he'd been so diligent in chasing. In that moment, I didn't care. I was doing this for me, and if this was the only time I'd hold him, then I was going to relish it.

He abandoned my mouth, raining kisses down my jaw to my neck, where he licked and sucked his way toward my collarbone. I moved restlessly beneath him, running my hands down the smooth, inked skin of his back.

He looked up at me and reached for the bottom of my tank top.

I nodded, and he took it off, slipping it over my head before throwing it somewhere. His breath left in a quiet hiss, and then he set his mouth to my stomach, kissing every curve and hollow with a soft nip or soothing stroke of his tongue.

His hands ran up my back, and I arched to accommodate him so he could get his fingers to the strap of my bra. I nodded again when he wordlessly asked permission, and with a snap of his fingers, my bra disappeared.

"Damn. You're just as exquisite as I remembered," he said as he carefully cupped both of my breasts. "You fill my hands exactly, like they were made only for holding you."

I looked down at the erotic contrast between my pale skin and the colorful tattoos that decorated his, and a wave of desire washed over me, warming me from head to toe.

How had I almost forgotten the way my body called for

him? I hadn't been abstinent. I'd had two lovers since Landon, but neither of them made me feel this primal, screaming need. Only Landon.

His lips replaced his hand, licking and finally drawing my nipple into his mouth. My back arched off the bed as every nerve begged for more. Pleasure swept over me at the feel of his tongue, the caresses of his fingers, the scratchy material of his shorts on my freshly shaved thighs. Even his weight on top of me was inflaming me.

I wanted to flip him over, to run my mouth along the carved lines of his chest, to worship him as I'd dreamed for an embarrassingly long time now. But I could do that later. For now, I'd let him do whatever he wanted to with me.

He knew I loved everything he did.

I whimpered when he ran his tongue over my nipple, the feeling good, but I needed so much more. Every wave of desire he brought was washing over me, crashing and pooling right between my thighs. "Landon," I pleaded.

"What do you need?" he asked as one hand stroked the skin of my stomach to the button of my shorts. "Here?"

"Yes," I said when he flicked open the button.

"This?" He unzipped the fly.

"Yes," I said through a gasp of breath as he rolled my nipple with his other hand.

"What about here?" he asked as he braced his weight and slid his hand into my shorts, running his finger along the edge of my panties.

"Yes!" I cried, my hips rocking up.

His breath caught, and I looked into his eyes. If I wasn't already aching for him, the open, ravenous look of need on his face would have gotten me there. As it was, the way he ran his tongue over his lower lip had me squirming.

Eyes still locked, his fingers *finally* slipped under the silk fabric and found my center. He groaned at the same time I did.

"Fuck…Rachel. You're…God, you're so wet."

My hips bucked as he swirled his fingers over my clit. Sparks raced through me, pleasure spinning my senses until there was only Landon above me, his fingers on me…inside me.

"Take them off," I ordered. I needed him — needed to feel him inside me, filling the emptiness that no one else could.

His jaw locked, like he was steeling himself. *For what? And did…?* Yeah, his hands shook as he drew both my shorts and my underwear down my legs. Seeing him so lost for me only revved me up another notch, until my body was humming, need coiling in my stomach.

He closed his eyes for a second, and two deep breaths later, he opened them, looking over me like I was everything he needed — like I was the ridgeline he was desperate to ride, the trick he'd spent every minute prepping for.

In one simple look, he made me feel like I was beautiful, precious, and so very desired.

He rose over me and then kissed me, his movements leisurely. He only pulled back when his hand stroked down my body, watching my every expression as he returned to my core.

Then his fingers… Oh. My. God. His fingers found me.

"Yes," I whimpered. "Landon!"

He pressed kisses to my jaw, my cheeks, my lips as he stroked me, pressing and swirling in rhythm. My hips rose for his touch, and my hands threaded through his hair to hold his mouth to mine.

My breaths stuttered, gasping as my heart pounded. He groaned as he sank one finger inside me. "So. Fucking. Perfect."

The pressure in my belly wound tighter and tighter as he worked me over, using his fingers to stroke just right inside me as he rubbed over my clit with his thumb. He played me like an instrument, knowing every note he could wring from me, exactly how I liked it.

"I can't wait to taste you again," he said against my lips, and I began to quiver. "Not this time, because I'm saving it. But soon. I can't wait to feel you shuddering around me, coming apart under my tongue."

His words pushed me over the edge and I flew, the tension within me bursting into radiant stars with an intense orgasm. He covered my mouth with his when I screamed his name, then kissed me back down until I was shuddering with aftershocks beneath him.

"That was…I don't…there's no words." I couldn't even string a sentence together as I floated inside my own body.

I ran my hands down his torso toward where he strained against the material of his shorts, and he caught my hand. "God, no."

"What?" I asked, not understanding.

"That's it. Only you." His voice was strained, his breathing labored with mine.

"You want me," I said defensively, feeling the sting of rejection.

"More than I want to breathe right now. Yes. I'm dying to bury myself inside you."

"Then why?" I asked, wrapping one of my legs over his hips.

He groaned, his hand running along the curve of my thigh. "Do you love me?"

"What?" I dropped my leg and sat up, scurrying back until I reached his headboard and drawing my knees to my chest. *He did not just say that.*

"Do. You. Love. Me?"

"Why? What does any of that matter?"

"It matters." He sat back on his heels, the delicious lines

of his abs tightening with each breath as his erection distorted his shorts in a way that firmly disagreed with what he was saying.

"What? It never matters to you. Why should it now?" He would sleep with every girl he came into contact with but me? What the hell was this?

He closed his eyes as his jaw flexed—the classic Landon getting his shit under control look. His eyes were just as fierce when he opened them. "You're it for me, Rachel. You are the only woman who matters to me. No one mattered before you, and no one has mattered since. Only you."

"But you won't sleep with me." God, I wanted to believe him. But he'd said it all before, and that hadn't exactly gone well for me.

He shook his head. "No. Because I want to make love to you, not sleep with you. I want to look into your eyes and tell you that I love you with my words, not just my body."

The orgasm had made me boneless, but his words melted me. "Landon…"

"You can't say them yet. I'm okay with that. I'm okay with waiting, because the first time I slide inside you, you'll love me. You'll know that I'm not going anywhere, that you're my choice and my first priority. And until you know that, I'm not doing this, no matter how badly I want to."

"Seriously?"

"Very seriously. Besides, I know our pull—our chemistry—but you can't tell me that part of this wasn't to see if I'd lose interest after I got you back under me, and that's not how *this* is going to happen."

My mouth snapped shut. "How…?"

His smile made him even more beautiful, even as pained as it was. "I think I know you pretty well by now. I tell you I'm done fucking around, you spook and take off your clothes to test me."

"*You* took off my clothes," I grumbled.

"Semantics."

"It wasn't all a test," I admitted.

"I know that, too, which is what makes it that much harder to tell you no."

"So you're not going to touch me until I can say…that?" God, I couldn't even think those words. Those words—whether or not they lurked in my heart—opened the door and handed him the match to burn me down.

His grin turned wicked. "I'll touch you whenever you like. I'll make you come thirteen different ways every single day if that's what you want. But I'm not making love to you until it's that. I've waited too long to get you back in my bed to just have sex with you, Rach."

I looped my arms around my knees, simultaneously frustrated, turned on, and stupidly moved by his words. The Landon I knew would have taken me any way he could get me. Nova would have done it without blinking and walked away in the morning. This patient, determined guy…hell if I knew what to do with him.

"So what now?" I asked.

"Now we sleep," he said, pulling back the covers and sliding underneath. "Unless you want a second round?"

My mouth opened and shut like a fish out of water. Of course I wanted a second round. But I wanted him inside me, with me, not just orchestrating my pleasure. I wanted his, too.

I had two possible courses of action.

I could crawl in next to him, curl into his arms, and sleep…

Or I could slide on top of him and test just how firm his resolve was.

But that slight pleading in his eye told me more than his words. So did the tiny dots of perspiration on his forehead. If he was willing to put himself through this in order to prove himself to me, then I could at least not make it hell on him.

I cursed as I found my panties, then slid them and my tank top on before sliding under the covers with him.

"Sleep," I said.

"Sleep," he repeated, pulling me into the curve of his body.

For every inch I gave him, every part of me that relaxed into him, there was a part of me banging even harder against the bars to flee.

I just wish I knew which one would be stronger.

Chapter Twenty-Two

LANDON

AT SEA

She was going to be the death of me. I'd never been this turned on for this long since...ever. I hadn't planned that night in the bungalow. Not that I regretted it. Hell no.

How the hell could I regret any moment that I had my hands on Rachel, her breath in my ear, her tight body under mine, my name on her lips?

And shit, now I was hard again.

It was like a permanent fucking condition lately—especially the last three days since we left Papua.

She walked into class? Hard.

Sat next to me? Hard.

Looked my way? Bit her damn lip? Brushed against me in the hallway? Hard.

Said my name? Answered a question in class? Took a swim in the pool?

Fuck my life. It was like I was fifteen again.

I relished every second of it, except maybe the cold-ass showers.

I wasn't stupid—I was well aware that she was scared, testing the hell out of me, waiting to see if I'd finally give in and sleep with her, or if I'd fuck someone else. I saw it in the way she constantly watched my reactions, the way she pressed against me, kissed me, gave me every out in the book for this relationship.

She didn't trust me—didn't trust herself.

Part of her wanted me to fail.

The other girls who hung around weren't an issue. I'd lost the desire to touch anyone else the moment Rachel appeared on board. Everything else felt shallow, cheap, and I was more than willing to wait for her as long as she needed.

"Hey, Nova," Zoe said as I walked into my suite. She was stretched out on our couch with two other girls in string bikinis, and from the look of those Solo cups and rum bottles, they'd been drinking awhile.

"Hey, Zoe," I said, heading to my room to drop my bag.

Of course she followed me. I turned to find her lounging on the doorframe, her long, lithe figure draped to showcase its best attributes. "Long day?" she asked.

I shrugged. "Not really. A good workout, a couple classes. What about you?"

"Oh, the same. I actually helped Pax out with some stuff for Nick, then I grabbed lunch up on deck twelve…"

"Okay?" I knew she was leading into something.

"Oh, it's probably nothing, but I saw your girlfriend eating with someone." Her sweet smile didn't fool me. I also didn't bother to correct her. I was perfectly fine with everyone in the world calling Rachel my girlfriend. It was Rachel who objected.

"Yeah? I'm glad she got lunch," I said, putting my books

onto my desk.

Zoe's eyes narrowed. "It was that Hugo guy. The cute one with the dark hair?"

"That doesn't surprise me. They're friends."

She walked over and sat on my bed, crossing her legs. "It doesn't bother you? I mean, they looked *really* friendly. I just don't want you to get hurt."

I did my best to swallow back my annoyance at both. I knew Hugo wanted more. Hell, I'd been there when he'd asked her out. But I'd also been there when she said no, and when she came to my bungalow. I wasn't going to play into Zoe's need to incite a riot.

"No, it doesn't bother me that she had lunch with a friend. And thank you for the concern, but Rachel and I aren't up for discussion, Zoe."

She squirmed under my stare. "Fine. I just care about you."

"You want to get out here and—" Pax startled when he saw Zoe draped over my bed like a damn porn star. "Uh. Hi, Zoe."

"What's up?" I asked, sending him a little telepathic *save me* message.

"Bobby needs you in the dining room."

"On it," I said, walking out of my room without a backward glance. "Thank you," I told Pax as we walked past the bar and the other girls in the living room.

"You didn't...?"

"Hell no!" The girls all turned to look, and I lowered my voice. "I haven't touched anyone but Rachel since she showed up."

The relief on his face was almost palpable. "Oh, thank God. Because the last thing I need is Leah hating you. She's already had a hard enough time accepting you were the one who hurt Rachel in the first place."

I slapped him on the back, admiring the change in his priorities these last couple of months. I'd stupidly worried that Leah would distract him, but she'd focused him, given him a purpose that turned into an even more intense drive. "No worries."

Penna came in through the sliding glass door, moving surprisingly well considering the giant boot she wore. "What did you guys need?"

"Originals production meeting," Pax said, and we pulled out chairs at the dining room table while Penna stood. At least a production meeting meant there weren't any cameras.

"I don't really have anything I need to be here for," she said.

Pax's eyes shot fire. "I'm done with this shit. Your leg is healing, and you're coming back. It's been us three since the start. If we made it through almost losing Nick, we can handle this, too."

"Nick didn't almost destroy us," she said quietly, her eyes flickering to where the girls were discussing some reality TV bullshit.

"Neither did you!" Pax shouted, uncaring about the audience.

Penna crossed her arms over her chest.

"Pax…" I warned.

"What? She didn't." His gaze swung back to Penna. "I get it. You feel guilty. Guilt that you didn't know, that you didn't catch on, that she is your sister. I get it. She's your family, but you know what? We are, too. So sit your ass down and help us figure out this scheduling mess, Penelope!"

She arched a single eyebrow at his tirade.

He sighed and pulled out her chair. "Please."

She looked at me.

"We have always needed you, and that's not going to change," I said softly.

Her sigh was audible, but she sat.

Bobby came over from where he'd leaned against the wall while waiting for us to get our shit together and laid out the calendar in a series of papers along the table.

"I talked to Nick. Your timeline is fucked," he said, not mincing words.

"Well, that sounds promising," I said as the sliding door opened again. Leah and Rachel walked in.

Rachel had on a little green sundress that had to have been specially designed to bring me to my knees. There was no other explanation for the immediate need that clawed at me to strip it off her.

"Hey, Firecracker, come on in," Pax said to Leah.

"I thought it was an Originals-only meeting," Zoe said as she came out of my bedroom. *Shit.*

In my fucking Led Zeppelin T-shirt.

Fuck. My. Life.

Rachel's eyes widened as she looked at Zoe, then swung to me in question.

I held her shocked gaze and shook my head.

No, I didn't touch her.

To my utter relief, she didn't freak. "Nice shirt," she said to Zoe.

"Yeah, it's his favorite," Zoe replied.

"We don't have fucking time for this," Pax hissed under his breath.

"I know. I was with him when he bought it," Rachel said with a sweet smile, and firmly put Zoe in her place.

Fuck, I adored her.

She walked straight over to me, and as I turned to pull out the chair next to me, she sat in my lap instead. *Even better.*

Once Leah was seated, Bobby started again. "Okay, here's the deal. You've got Sydney tomorrow, then New Zealand, then midterms in Fiji, then home for Christmas."

"Where's the issue?" Pax asked.

"Well, your boy here wants to go back to Nepal," he said, pointing at me.

Rachel turned. "You're serious?"

"We all had one thing that we wanted to nail during this documentary. That ridgeline is mine. I'm not okay with what happened. I'm not okay walking away having failed. The documentary needs it. Nick needs it. *I* need it."

I awaited her judgment with held breath and watched emotions cross over her face in waves. Surprise, worry, and finally resignation.

"Okay."

"You're okay with it?" I asked.

She shrugged. "I can't remember the last time you let anyone tell you what to do when it came to free riding. And honestly, if it's going to eat at you that you didn't complete the summit run, then it's worth it. This trip is all about taking chances and avoiding the *what-if*s. Right?"

Uncaring that we were in the middle of the suite, I kissed her. "Thank you."

Pax cleared his throat. "Okay, well, now that you're committed to trying to kill yourself, when would you like to go back?"

"Christmas?" I asked. "That's the only two-week time frame, right?"

"You won't be ready for the X Games if you don't spend Christmas practicing," Penna answered, leaning forward to look at the calendar. "You're in decent shape, but when's the last time you were on a half-pipe?"

"Fair point," I said.

"What about invitations?" Leah asked quietly.

"Our medals from last year serve as our invitation," Pax answered. "Plus, it's us, so as long as we're there a few days early for qualifying runs, we can pretty much enter whatever event we feel like we're ready for."

"It wouldn't hurt to butter up your sponsors, seeing as you've dropped off the face of the earth this year," Penna added.

"Your sponsors, too," I reminded her, tensing slightly. Gremlin was still a major sponsor, and Rachel's dad, who was in charge of that contract, pretty much hated my guts. I was going to have to follow up with Pax about that situation.

She snorted. "Yeah, okay. I can go be a pretty statue, but considering this thing doesn't come off for another month, I highly doubt I'll be ready to hit anything."

"You can still compete in snowmobile," I said. "Your leg should be good enough by Christmas to practice. That's two weeks in Aspen, then you're back on board for three weeks before we head to the Games."

She shrugged. "Not sure."

Rachel gently squeezed my thigh, and I heeded her warning. Penna was at some kind of crossroads right now. I just wished that I knew which way she was headed.

"Okay, well, we can talk about that later," I acquiesced.

"So the question is when we can get you back to Nepal," Pax said to himself, looking at our schedule.

"If I can't do it over Christmas break, I'm not sure when we can make it happen." This was why a ton of the guys on the circuit were shocked we were even trying to finish up college. It was fucking with our careers.

"We need the footage for the documentary and, honestly, we're kind of already on this side of the world. I don't know when you'll get the time to come back between classes," Bobby added.

I rubbed the skin between my eyes. When did this all get so fucking complicated? Everything was precisely timed with our ports, our finals, our classes, and with one moment, I'd fucked everything up.

"There's one week here." Bobby pointed to the January calendar. "It's the Great Wall stunt, but if we split the crew, you could go back to Nepal. You'd just have to leave early, and you'd risk missing the ship on the return."

"What do you think?" I asked Rachel.

She sighed, looking at the calendar. "I think you're taking a huge risk without really acclimatizing, and you can run into the same exact issue. You get one chance, and that's it."

"She's right," Pax said. "I don't mind financing another expedition. Especially since it would be badass to get into the documentary, really kind of tie it together with the struggle, but one thing goes wrong and you're out of time…again."

"But what if I don't have those issues? Isn't it worth the risk?"

The table quieted.

"If you think it is," Rachel answered.

"We'll back you," Paxton agreed.

"Will you come with me?" I asked Rachel. "I know it's a lot to ask."

She took a deep breath. "Can I think about it?"

"Of course. There's no pressure." I wanted her with me, but after the hell I'd put her through last time, I couldn't blame her if she wanted to say no. My feelings on the subject probably would have been way different if I'd had to dig her out of an avalanche.

"Okay, then we'll start planning that and splitting the crew," Bobby said. "Do we have the X Games handled?"

Pax cringed. "Nick is in talks with our sponsors right now. I have a meeting with the dean tomorrow. We'll see what he says. We'd have to miss at least a week, if not ten days. Between travel, qualifying, and the actual games, we'll miss all of the Japan stop."

"Has anyone thought about skipping this year?" Leah asked. "It's not like you guys are sitting around doing nothing."

Pax shook his head. "We'll lose our sponsors and our titles."

Her nose crinkled.

"Say it," Pax ordered.

"Are you even in shape for that? I mean, not that you're not in shape, but *that* level of shape?" She covered her face with her hands.

Pax laughed and pulled her hands away to sneak a kiss. "Yeah, we're fine. We have all of Christmas in Aspen, and that's only a few weeks before."

"Then it's decided. Nova is back to Nepal in January, and Wilder will work on the X Games," Bobby said, snapping his folder shut. "Go team."

"Now on to more important things," Pax said with a grin.

"Like?" Rachel asked.

"Like turkey," I said enthusiastically.

She laughed, and it was the sweetest sound I'd ever heard.

· · ·

"I'm fine, Mom," I said into the laptop the next day as I buttoned my shirt. Leah had threatened us all within an inch of our lives if we didn't dress up for Thanksgiving.

"Are you sure? I mean, we heard about the avalanche, Landon. The least you could have done was called." Mom gave me *the* look, and I sighed.

"I didn't think you'd ever find out. Promise. Never thought that Gabe's mom would call you, and I'm sorry. You're right. I should have called. But I'm fine."

"How are your grades?" She moved on with her typical finesse.

"Good. Holding my four point oh with no problem."

"Well, at least you haven't let your silly little activities derail you on that. Any thoughts on which law schools you'll be applying to next year? I know you're a semester behind because you thought it would be more fun to go snowboard some godforsaken mountain, but this is important."

I swallowed, my tongue thick in my throat. "Well—"

"Get off the boy, Hazel." Dad's voice came in as his face appeared next to hers in front of the screen. "How's it going, Lando?"

"Good, Dad. I was just calling to say happy Thanksgiving."

"It's not even Thanksgiving here," Mom said.

"It's Thanksgiving *there*," Dad told her with a shake of his head. "Meet any girls yet?"

"He's concentrating on his studies," Mom argued.

"He's twenty-two, almost twenty-three, and he's trapped on a boat where at least half the population is female. I hardly think he's spending all his free time at the library."

"No, he's busy trying to get himself killed. Think about that avalanche, Art!" she snapped.

If there was one thing I didn't miss about being home, it was the constant bickering between these two. I knew they loved each other to distraction, but sometimes I failed to see the connective tissue.

"He's fine. Landon, how did the new avalanche beacons work out?"

"Great," I answered truthfully. "Rachel was the first to get a hit, and they had Gabe dug out in record time."

Mom blinked, and Dad's mouth dropped open. "Dear…" Mom started. "When you say Rachel…"

I laughed, loving the ability to shock her every once in a while. "I mean *the* Rachel. She's here."

"How?"

"Are you two together?"

"I need details!"

My laughter nearly overpowered their demands. Nearly. "You guys. Okay, look. I'll be home for Christmas, and I'll bring her by, okay? But you have to swear not to scare her off. Promise."

"Scout's honor," Dad said.

"Well, I mean, I've always wanted to meet her. Where

does she go to college when you're not sailing around the world? And what's her last name again?" Mom asked, no doubt ready to demand a background check on her.

"She goes to Dartmouth, and she's a journalism major. And Mom…no. Don't do it."

"What? Don't look out for the best interest of my only son?"

Dad rolled his eyes. "Landon, we love you. Go have a great Thanksgiving, and we can't wait to see you once you're home in a few weeks. Be safe, okay?"

"Always, Dad. Mom, I love you."

"I want her last name, Landon!"

"What was that? I can't hear you. We're breaking up or something…must be pulling away from port… Love you! 'Bye!" I slammed the laptop shut.

I quickly tied my tie and then ran my hands through my hair. This was as good as I was going to get…as soon as I adjusted this knot.

"How is it possible to be so incredibly sexy?" Rachel asked from my doorway.

I winked at her in the mirror as I finished with the tie and caught my breath. My fingers tangled in the knot as she walked in. Her black dress wrapped around her body, hugging each line, and was secured by a single tie.

One little pull.

Her hair was swept up, and she looked different somehow…

"Need some help there?" she asked with a smile.

"You have makeup on," I noticed, appreciating the way her eyes stood out.

"Well, we're not in a mudslide or stuck in a Himalayan snowstorm, so I thought it seemed appropriate."

"You're gorgeous either way," I told her honestly as she adjusted my tie. "I happen to adore every side of you. Makeup, no makeup…clothes, no clothes."

She smiled up at me, and my heart clenched, then flew. How easily this could be our normal life. We could be getting ready for any event, a graduation, a date…an anniversary.

"Thank you," she said simply. "You make me feel beautiful."

A longing took hold in my soul. I'd always told her that she was it for me—my own little piece of infinity, but here, I saw it. Felt it. Longed for it. I wanted her boarding next to me on the slopes in Colorado. I wanted her coming home to me in L.A. after a long day. I wanted her arms around me when shit went wrong, and I wanted to celebrate with her when it all went right.

She smiled, patted my chest, and headed out. "It's going to be cold if you don't hurry up."

God, she really was everything I wanted for my entire life wrapped in one petite package that packed a hell of a punch.

I stood in my doorway as she hugged Leah, then grabbed a bottle of wine for the table. Every movement was graceful, just like she was. My mind took flight and imagined another Thanksgiving in a few years, where maybe there would be smaller versions of ourselves running around, and for once, the prospect of true adulthood didn't terrify the shit out of me.

Because I couldn't fail if Rachel was with me. We balanced each other out, traded off times when we each needed help. We were strong, but together we were invincible.

"Holy shit, I'm in love with her," I whispered.

"Just now figure that out, Captain Obvious?" Penna said as she walked by.

I stood there speechless until she turned around.

Penna stopped. "Wait, are you seriously just figuring that out? Because we've all known for a good three years or so."

My mouth hung slightly open as I shook my head. "No. I mean, yes. I mean… Hell, I don't know."

"Words typically help," she said, hobbling back to me.

"I knew I never stopped loving her, not really. But…I'm *in* love with her. Completely, heart-shatteringly, madly in love with her."

Penna grinned. "Good. Now keep her."

"How can she possibly love me back after everything I put her through? I abandoned her without a word for reasons that no longer seem anywhere near good enough."

Penna took my hand and squeezed. "You make it up to her in every way possible. You earn her trust back, and then you never break it again. You deserve happiness, Landon. You both do. Whether or not she loves you is up to her. All you can do is be the best version of you." She looked back over to where Rachel stood with the other Renegades, our dining room table extended to fill the living room. "Something tells me it will be more than enough."

I walked Penna to the table and pulled out her chair so she could sit. Then I found my seat next to Rachel and kissed her soundly, uncaring that I smeared her glossy lips or that the entire Renegade family was watching.

She smiled and kissed me back. "Good thing the cameras aren't in here, huh?" she joked as everyone gave a little hoot.

But I wanted the cameras. I wanted the entire world to know that I was hers and she was mine, and that the only person I'd ever be using those Casanova moves on was Rachel. But she wasn't ready, because she didn't trust me yet.

As we sat to Thanksgiving dinner, which Pax had no doubt paid a fortune to have delivered to our suite, we all took turns saying what we were thankful for.

Finally, it got to me.

"I'm thankful for our families, both biological and chosen," I said. Then I turned to Rachel. "And second chances."

I wouldn't need a third.

Chapter Twenty-Three

RACHEL

"We're going to be late if you keep that up," I said to Landon, exposing more of my neck for his mouth. The man was going to have me in a giant puddle, and I wasn't sure I cared.

"We could stay in today," he countered, backing me against the wall of our hotel room.

"We could," I agreed, running my fingers through his hair. Every muscle in my body clenched with the unbelievable pleasure he sent spiraling through me. It was like my neck had a direct line to my core, and Landon was taking complete advantage. I moaned when he set his teeth to the delicate area where my neck met my shoulder.

"Yes, let's do that," he said as his hand slipped under my halter top and underlying bikini to cup my breast. His thumb found my nipple, and I arched, wrapping one leg around his waist.

For not having sex, we were certainly pros at the hottest make-out sessions ever.

Hard against me, he strained against the material of his cargo shorts, and I grasped him through the layers of material. He was hot and heavy in my palm, and the moan he gave me when I gently squeezed him sent a fresh wave of need through me.

"Fuck," he said, leaning his forehead against mine as I stroked his length.

"We could, you know," I suggested. It had been two weeks since his self-imposed celibacy, and he'd not backed down even an inch.

He grasped both my hands in his and held them against the wall above my head. "Stop trying to rob me of my virtue, Ms. Dawson."

"Stop driving me out of my mind, Mr. Rhodes," I complained.

He kissed me long and hot, his tongue twisting around mine, drawing every ounce of pleasure he could between our mouths. With my hands pinned, I could only accept his kiss, but I leveraged my lower body and wrapped leg to rock against him. How long could this madness continue?

Three loud slams at our door were followed by Little John's voice.

"The van is waiting on you two. Let's go."

"We're not going," Landon called, his mouth hovering just above mine.

"Like hell you're not. Unwrap yourself from your girlfriend and get your ass in the van now, Nova."

Landon's eyes raked down me. "What do you want to do?"

"I want to put you on that bed and ride you until my sexual frustration is a distant memory," I said, nipping at his lower lip.

He growled.

"But I guess we really should go, seeing as we flew all the way down here last night, don't you think?" I asked.

"I'm not kidding, guys!" Little John called through the door.

"Fucking fine! We need a minute." He backed away from me and glanced down at his erection. "We need a couple minutes."

I stalked him, and he retreated. "Don't even think about it," he said.

"Think about what?" I asked innocently, laughing at the absurdity of this six-foot-plus guy backing away from a five-foot-two girl.

"No," he said, stopping and pointing a finger at me. "You touch me, and I know I'll fucking lose it. You'll be on your back on that bed, against the wall, in the shower, on the damned bathroom counter in less time than it would take you to count to three, and I don't even know where to buy condoms here."

"You didn't bring condoms?" I asked, folding my arms across my chest. "What kind of sex god are you?"

"One trying to convince the girl of his dreams that he means serious business!"

"Well, I seriously could go for some sex!"

"I could go for you two getting your asses into the goddamned van!" Little John called out.

Laughter bubbled up through my lips, and I covered my mouth as I tried to get myself under control. "Oh my God, he must think I'm the horniest girl *ever*."

Landon joined in, pulling me to his chest and kissing the top of my head. "Yeah, well, apparently I'm the prude here."

"And I'm getting sick of asking you guys to get out here!"

We grabbed our bags and headed out the door. Little John stood with his arms folded in the hallway. "It's about damn time."

Landon didn't make any excuses, just shrugged his shoulders and held his hand out for mine. I slipped mine into his, and we made our way to the van.

"For fuck's sake, you two," Pax called out. "We have an appointment."

"You know what? Until one of us misses the boat, you have no room to talk about tardiness," Landon answered with a grin as we pulled into traffic, the camera crew following in the van behind us.

"Fuck off," Pax answered and put his arm around Leah's shoulder.

"Later," Landon promised in a whisper as I leaned against him, buckling my seat belt.

"Later what?" I asked.

He moved his lips next to my ear. "Later I'm going to strip you out of these shorts and bury my tongue inside you. I can't have my girl walking around all sexually frustrated."

I turned so fast that our lips brushed. "How about this? You get to put your mouth on me when I get to return the favor."

"You play hardball, Ms. Dawson."

I grinned. "Learned from the best, Mr. Rhodes."

"I can't remember ever wanting someone as bad as I do you, Rachel," he whispered.

The van was crowded, but it felt like we were the only ones on the planet.

"I might know how that feels," I told him.

He ran his thumb over my lower lip before kissing me. It was soft, lingering, and full of the barely restrained passion I knew lurked just beneath his surface.

"There's only one thing to do when I'm this damned turned on and can't have you."

"And what's that?"

"Go jump off shit."

"Sex is comparable to cliff swinging?" I asked.

"Hell no. Sex with you blows everything out of the water. But I'll take what I can get."

"You can have it all," I told him in all seriousness.

"Yeah, I know," he said, kissing me again softly. "That's why I'm waiting on the sex."

Damn it. He was good.

A hot Kiwi strapped me into my harness as Landon watched. "Are you ready for this?" the guy asked with a sexy little smile.

A couple of months ago, I might have gone for him.

Now the tall guy brooding behind him was all I could handle—or want.

"Tallest cliff swing in the world? Bring it on," I said, carefully examining the latches on my harness.

"A girl after my own heart," he said, pulling the strap tight. The metal platform we stood on hung over 350 feet in the air, and I could already feel my body readying itself to take the plunge. I freaking loved this stuff.

"Mind if I look?" Landon asked.

The guide knew the Renegades by reputation and backed away with his hands in the air. "Feel free, Nova. I strapped your girl in tight, I promise."

Landon went over every strap and latch, pulling the one around my waist a little more snug before he was satisfied. "You sure you don't want to go tandem with me?"

I rolled my eyes. "I think you'll be safe on your own, honey."

His eyes lit up at the endearment. "What will I do without my lucky charm?"

"Vomit," Pax said from behind him. "Rach, you strapped in?"

"Yeah, I'm good to go," I told him, my eyes still locked on Landon. His eyes looked blue today against the fabric of his shirt, and they were looking at me in a way that said he'd rather be watching me naked.

Well, that makes two of us.

"I saw you at the X Games last year, Nova. You're pretty badass on that board of yours," the guide said as Landon gave his final approval on my harness.

It was completely overbearing and a little primal but hot as hell to watch his concern for me.

"Thanks, I love what we do," he told the guide.

Leah walked out onto the metal walkway until she reached us.

"Firecracker, what are you doing out here? I'll take you with me," Pax promised.

"I'm going to ride tandem with Rachel," she said. "You have stunts you need to do. There's no chance I'm holding you back from that."

"No. No way. I'll take you. I'll just come back up—"

"Hell yes!" I said. "A girl jump!"

Leah smiled and pulled away from Paxton, her harness already in place and no doubt examined like she was launching into space. If I thought Landon was obsessed with my safety, well, Paxton was ten times worse with Leah.

"This okay with you, mate?" the guide asked, not knowing which guy to ask.

"Well, since she said it's okay with her, *mate*, it doesn't matter what the boys say," I sang sweetly.

Leah echoed my smile. "I'm quite capable of making my own choices."

"Fuck my life," Paxton muttered. "Fine. Rachel—"

"Save it, Wilder. She was my best friend long before she was anything to you," I said with a grin. "Strap up, Leah!"

"Guys, I'm going to have to ask you to wait off the

platform," the guide said. "We already have a camera out here, and you're in my way." He showed them the way off while they sputtered about safety and harnesses.

"Well, girls, what do you want to do? The drop slide? The backward fall? The cutaway?"

Leah blinked up at me, realizing what she'd signed on for. She had been petrified of heights when we were at Dartmouth, but Wilder had helped her work through a ton of it. But having gone through the accident she did a few years ago, it didn't surprise me to realize some of that fear would linger.

"Cutaway?" I asked Leah. "Instead of rushing off, we hang there for a second, and then they cut the rope."

"Yeah, that sounds better than just falling off," she agreed.

They latched us onto the cord and walked us through the procedure once the ride was over. Then they hoisted us until we hung suspended over the platform. We were jostled as we attached to the line that would swing us down the canyon.

"Oh my God, this sucks," Leah said, gripping her rope. "Talk to me."

"About what?" I asked, watching the river raging in the canyon beneath us.

"Anything!" she snapped. Then she took a deep breath. "I can't let him think I'm upset. He'll freak out."

"Ready, girls?" the guide asked.

"No!" Leah yelled.

"It's not bad," I promised her. "You just let yourself go. The cord does all the work."

"Not. Ready."

"She needs a second. Is that okay?" I asked the guide.

The guide looked behind him, where Pax and Landon stood on land, their arms crossed. "You can have as long as you need."

"Thanks," I said, shifting us so that I could slip my arm

around her. "Are you okay? You don't have to do this."

"No. I do. I'm good. I just… Ugh. Distract me for a second. How are things with Landon?"

I blinked at the change of topic. "Great. We're connecting again, and I'm happy."

"Do you love him?" she asked.

"What? We're not talking about this right now."

"For fuck's sake, Rachel. I'm dangling three hundred and fifty feet over a river, getting ready to tell this guy that he can cut the rope that's holding us here. The least you can do is tell me if you're in love with Landon so I can die peacefully."

My mouth opened and shut. "Uh. Well. I mean…"

I looked over to where he stood, shifting his weight back and forth in nervousness. He did this kind of thing all the time, so I knew it was worry for me. Ugh, that melty feeling in my heart was back.

"Are you?" she asked, gripping our harnesses like her life depended on her hand positioning.

I would have rather swung down the canyon wall than discuss my freaking feelings.

"Yes," I finally admitted. "Yes, I'm in love with him. I'm sure it makes me the stupidest woman on the planet, seeing what he did last time we were together, but I honestly can't stop my traitor of a heart. Are you happy now?"

"You're not stupid," she said softly. "He loves you. I know it."

"Well, love didn't help us last time."

"But it will this time. You'll see," she said with all the faith in the world. "You just have to let go and trust. I know that's the hardest part for you—the trust—but you two are more meant to be together than anyone I've ever seen."

I sighed at my sappy, trusting, perfect best friend and wished I saw the world through her eyes. "Letting go is the hard part."

"Not really. You just fall." She used my earlier words against me.

"Are you ladies ready?" the guide asked.

"I am," Leah said, her smile a touch devious.

"You did it on purpose," I said. "You wanted my confession."

She shrugged. "Maybe. Now let's fly, shall we?"

I laughed and hugged her. "I'm so glad I have you."

"Ditto," she said. "Cut us loose!"

The guide took out an actual knife and started to saw through the white rope that kept us tethered to the base. In a second we'd be swinging by only the cord.

I looked up at Landon and realized that Leah was right. I just had to trust. Maybe it would get me burned. Maybe it would hurt so much this time that I wouldn't survive it. Or maybe we'd fly. Whether or not I wanted to deny it, my heart knew the truth—I was his, so in love with him that my heart fluttered with the sweetness of the emotion.

I was done fighting it.

The knife cut through the rope, and in one instant, I hung above the canyon.

The next…I let go and fell.

When the ride was over, and we were all gathered at the vans, waiting to return to the ship, I made sure the cameras were on and then walked straight up to Landon, wrapped my arms around his neck, and kissed the hell out of him.

His surprise lasted all of two seconds before he lifted me off my feet and robbed me of every thought. We ignored the catcalls around us as our kiss lasted way longer than publicly acceptable, both reveling in what I'd just done.

Whether we flew or failed, we were public now.

Chapter Twenty-Four

RACHEL

FIJI

Crystal-clear water stretched out as far as I could see as we walked the white sand beach. This was truly paradise.

Now if only I could get my thoughts on the same page. Since I'd come to the revelation that I was in this relationship to the hilt, that there was nothing I could do about being in love with Landon, I'd been a freak show. My emotions were all over the place, scrambling to think of a way to tell him, or a way to keep it to myself in case he fucked something up and left me again.

"How did your other midterms go?" Landon asked as a wave gently lapped over our feet. I lifted the hem of my purple maxi dress so it didn't get uncomfortably soaked for the skiff back to the *Athena*. He looked like he belonged here in Fiji, his white button-up shirt rolled at the elbows over his blue shorts and tanned skin.

"Good, I think. I turned in my outline for my research paper, and I'm still waiting on my grade from Marine Life. What about you?"

"All A's," he said with a little grin.

"Of course."

"Don't hate me because I'm smart," he said, lifting me from the sand for a kiss.

Our lips met, sending a torrent of flutters to my stomach.

"Are you all packed?" he asked against my mouth.

"For the most part. I figured I'd finish tomorrow while we're on our way into port. We should head back, right? The charter boat will be leaving in about an hour." The day had been perfect. No classes, no stunts, no stress. Just us.

"We have time. Want to explore with me for a second?" His eyes lit up as he lowered me to the sand.

"Sure, but if you make us miss that boat, I'm going to flip," I warned.

"Don't you worry. I'll have you exactly where you want to be."

His smile was enough to stop my heart as he took my hand, leading me down the beach to where a wide wooden path began. It stretched out over the crystalline water, supporting bungalows on either side.

"Are we supposed to be here?"

He shrugged. "We're just exploring. Let's take a peek and see if it's somewhere you'd want to come back for vacation after you graduate."

I slipped my flip-flops on so the wood didn't burn my feet and followed him onto the boardwalk. "How about I just say yes now?" The bungalows were everything I'd ever imagined about a vacation—serene, beautiful, and somehow sensual with the waves gently reaching them.

But saying yes meant I saw a future for us. Of course I did—I wanted to—but the real world wasn't anything like what we'd been living the last seven weeks.

"So what do we do over Christmas?" I asked as we passed several of the little rooms. The question had been nagging at me. Two weeks apart. Normally I wouldn't have freaked, but the last time we were in L.A. together we didn't do so well.

"I'll be in L.A. for the first few days for the holidays," Landon said, wrapping his arm around my shoulder. "I'm hoping you'll come by and meet my parents, though."

I paused. "We're meeting parents?"

"Well, I already know yours," he said with a mock smile.

"Yeah, they kind of hate you." I cringed. "Was that a little harsh?"

"Nope, you nailed it. They do hate me."

"Everything is easier here." I looked over the water, taking in the exquisite beauty that was like nowhere else on earth. It was hard to believe that we'd seen so many amazing places and people, yet there was still so much more to go. But eventually, it would end. Panic crept in at the edges of my serenity. "I mean, when this is over, we'll be back in L.A. Well, you will. I still have a year at Dartmouth. And you have competitions and tours. Even if we make it through this program intact, how are we — ?"

His mouth covered mine in a deep kiss as his hands framed my face. "We'll figure it out."

"But what if we don't?" I asked, needing a certainty he couldn't provide me.

He picked me up, carrying me with one of his arms tucked beneath my knees as the other supported my back. "Simple. We agree that we will. We decide not to let it fall apart."

He walked down the wooden platform without breaking a sweat. His breathing was even and steady, where mine was picking up the more my mind spun. "That's not how a relationship works."

"Sure it is."

Did he seriously think it was that easy?

"It's not," I argued. "You aren't just happy because you say you are. Shit happens, Landon. Look at what happened to us before."

He stopped at the end of the platform, where there was only one bungalow left. "We crashed and burned. We were hit with a set of circumstances that I wasn't mature enough to deal with. I made the best decision I could with what I knew at the time, and it was the wrong one. That's what happened last time."

"What stops it from happening again?" I asked, my heart thundering in my chest. I felt like I stood at the edge of a huge precipice, and I was asking if he had a parachute…or wings.

He set me on my feet. "We do."

I shook my head. "That's not good enough."

He cupped my face. "That's all I've got. When the problems arise, we'll take them one at a time."

"That's like saying, hey, I know this giant tsunami is headed this way, but don't worry, we'll devise a plan when it hits the shore!" The panic had moved from the edges of my mind to fully consuming any serenity I'd tried to keep ahold of.

"Rachel…" His eyes went soft, like he was trying to soothe a wild beast, and I realized *I* was the wild beast.

And my leg was caught in a trap.

"Why are we worrying about this now?" he asked, being all logical and shit.

"We're going home in a couple days!" I shouted.

"Yes?"

"I'm going to be in L.A., and you're going to be in Aspen! I'll be at home with my parents who hate you and will spend the whole break trying to convince me to leave you, and you'll be snowboarding and acting all Nova-like." My chest tightened, the pressure harsh and a little nauseating.

He tugged my hand and walked me into the bungalow.

"So you're worried that we'll be apart for two weeks."

"Yes, but it's more than that, and— Landon, you can't just walk into someone's room." My eyes swept over the bungalow, and I sucked in a reflexive breath. It looked like it had been stripped out of a vacation magazine—dark hardwood floors with mostly open walls and shades, and a giant four-poster bed sat in the center of the room with netting draped over it.

"It's not more than that. You and I can make this work anywhere in the world because we're both incredibly stubborn. We'll decide not to let the petty shit get to us. We'll work through the issues that come up, and we'll make the choice to stay together."

"Landon, the room. Someone's going to come back." Anxiety was reaching a critical level here, but I couldn't tell if it was from the knowledge that we were trespassing, the thought of spending two weeks without him, or that little unspoken *L* word in my heart. One thing I did know? I had ten thousand emotions all warring for supremacy.

He put one hand on my hip and cradled my face with the other. "Rachel, the room is ours. I know you're scared. I know this break is going to be a little test. But I also know that I love you—there's no one else I want in my life, my heart, my bed. We're going to be okay."

I blinked up at him, trying to quiet my slamming heart, to draw a breath through lungs that had forgotten how to work, to process everything he said, and went with the first item because the rest was just too much. "The room is ours?"

"Yes." He smiled and kissed me lightly. "I got it for us when I realized we'd have an overnight here. The ship doesn't leave until the morning."

All of those conflicting emotions felt like a rising tsunami in my chest—barely visible on the surface but powerfully deep and capable of so much damage if I didn't get myself under control. I took in the details surrounding us as a distraction. The pretty linens, sturdy furniture, the glass area of the floor to see into the water. "This must have cost you a fortune." He'd made plans for us...not just for tonight, but for a possible future. Even before, when we'd agreed to the apartment in L.A., I'd always been the one to push the plan.

"Yeah, I'm not exactly hurting for it," he said with a small laugh. "We've been with Pax, Leah, Penna, and an entire boat full of people for the last seven weeks. I just wanted to have you to myself for a night. Leah packed you a bag and everything."

That wave of emotion grew bigger, monstrous, until it threatened to swamp me. He'd had a bag packed. Another plan. He wanted me to meet his parents, to see myself in his future. Maybe...just maybe he wasn't going to walk away this time. Maybe we could really have everything we'd missed out on before. Maybe this was real.

My throat closed as the wave broke over me, washing away what puny defenses I had left against him. All of my emotions, the fear, the mistrust, the excitement, and even the love flowed over me and then stripped me raw—left me vulnerable in ways I hadn't been since the last time I'd given my heart to him.

It was too much and yet not enough all in the same moment, because I needed the very words, the promises I was terrified to depend upon again. I needed them with a force that terrified me—the same way I needed *him*.

The lump in my throat made it almost impossible to breathe, and my nose burned, like my body knew it couldn't contain this hot mess of emotion any longer without combusting.

Oh, hell no. Don't you do it. Don't you dare do it!

Then I started crying, and not just dainty, pretty tears. Oh, no, these were gut-wrenching sobs with the most unattractive noises *ever*.

"Rach. Baby..." Landon pulled me into his arms, holding

me against his chest as I sobbed.

"No," I said, pushing back to stand on my own. "Don't. Be. Nice. To me." Oh, great, now I was hyperventilating, too. "I'm like…psycho over here, petrified that we'll get home and you'll leave me, and then you go and do this super-sweet thing. And it's perfect!" I shouted, like he'd done something wrong.

"Oh God, Rach." He reached for me, and I retreated until I was standing on the perfect deck that overlooked the perfect water in perfect Fiji that my perfect boyfriend had set up for us.

"I'm so sorry," I cried, unable to stop. "It's so nice, and just…everything, and here I am losing my shit because I'm so scared of losing you."

"You're not going to lose me," he promised, grasping my upper arms. "We're never going down that road again."

"It's just that all of this… I've tried so hard to block you out, to keep my walls up, but it's like you Trojan horsed me, because you've always been there. I never stood a chance. I've hated you so much because it was the only thing to keep me from admitting how very much I loved you." Holy shit, why couldn't I stop crying? Every word was yelled, ungraceful and ugly, yet raw and so very real.

"Baby." His eyes went soft and filled with so much joy, so much love, that I started crying even harder.

"Because I am so in love with you, and I want us to work, Landon. I *need* us to work, because we're the only thing that makes sense to me."

And that sounded like a seal barking. Great.

He laughed. "God, I love you."

"And I love you!" I shouted. "Now, if I could just stop… crying!" I sucked in another stuttered breath that sounded something like a donkey braying. "Make it stop. Seriously!"

He kissed me, swinging me up into his arms. "I can make it stop."

Then he jumped off the deck into the water, carrying me with him. I took a deep breath just before the Pacific washed over us in a surprising wave of warmth. His lips were on mine as we sank to the bottom of the shallow lagoon.

My legs slid from his arms to wrap around his hips, my breath held in that perfect moment where the world stopped and there was only us.

Once my lungs burned, we kicked for the surface.

I sputtered with my first breath. "Seriously?"

He grinned, more beautiful than I had ever seen him. "Hey, it stopped."

I kicked back and splashed him, sending water all over his gorgeous face.

"You can't be mad," he said, swimming toward me.

"And why is that?" My sundress billowed around me, caught in the ebb and flow of the water.

"Because you love me." He pulled me to him as he treaded water.

"I do," I admitted, my voice steady and sure—like the storm had passed over me and all that remained was love and the freedom that came with it. "What are you going to do with it?"

"Everything," he answered, then kissed me. He tasted like salt water and Landon, and I gave myself over to him, trusting him to keep me afloat. His arms held me tenderly, but his mouth was open, carnal, and a hot contrast to the water around us.

My arms around his neck, I returned his kiss with abandon, letting go of every worry and fear that had held me back. As if the waters had baptized us, I forgave him of every past transgression and gave us a clean slate—a place to start over fresh.

We kissed hungrily, our bodies moving with each other until I was ready to challenge any public indecency laws Fiji might have. I wanted him—needed him—more than I needed air, more than I needed my next heartbeat.

His hand moved to my ass, my dress long having abandoned any pretense of cover, and he played with the edge of my bikini bottoms. As his fingers swept under the fabric, he skimmed my center, close enough to bring the barely banked fire of my constant craving for him to life, but too far for me to do anything but rock back into his hands and whimper for more.

"I need you," he said, his voice carrying a desperate edge.

"Then take me," I ordered, our breathing harsh.

Balancing me on his front, he moved the short distance to the ladder and then urged me forward. I scrambled up the ladder, the heat of the deck dissipated by the puddle of water I stood in. I undid the buttons on the front of my dress and had it peeled off by the time Landon reached the top. His shirt quickly joined it in a wet heap on the dark wood.

My stomach clenched at the sight of his honed, lean body as he raked his hair out of his eyes, water sluicing down the carved lines of his abs. His skin was as colorful as the setting around us, his tattoos rippling and moving with his motions as he stalked me across the deck.

I was more than willing to be caught.

How was this man mine? How could someone so perfectly built, so intelligent, so reckless and incredibly sexy only want me?

"You're so fucking beautiful," he said to me, as if he'd read my mind.

I braced myself against the railing of the deck, and then his mouth was on mine, his hands in my hair and his tongue in my mouth. He felt incredible against me, his stomach tensing as my fingers explored him, his breath slightly shaky as he left my lips in favor of my neck, licking and sucking the drops of salt water from my skin.

His hands ran a path from my shoulders, down the sides

of my breasts, over my hips and around, until he grasped my ass and lifted me against him. "As much as I'd love to fuck you out here, I'd rather make love to you in a bed, if you don't mind," he whispered against my jaw.

"I don't care where we are as long as I get you," I told him.

He groaned, and we were on the move before I could lock my legs around his waist.

I felt the shade of our room, but every other sense was consumed by Landon—his saltwater taste, slick skin, and incredible body were all I could register until my back hit the softness of our bed.

He loomed above me, looking down at me like I was something rare and precious. "I didn't plan this, you know. The room, yes, but the rest…"

My smile was instant. "I want you too badly to care if you did."

"I love you," he told me as he brought his lips to my neck. "I'm going to tell you a million times in a million ways."

"And I'll love every one of them," I said, my voice hitching as his thumb ran over my pebbled nipple.

I thanked God that I'd chosen a string bikini as he reached to untie the simple tie that held my top together in the back, and then again behind my neck. Once my breasts were bare, he instantly warmed them with his hands and mouth, sending my back off the bed. The water had chilled my skin but made me so very sensitive to his touch.

My fingers ran through his hair, holding him against me as he used his tongue and teeth to set me on the edge. "I'm going to kiss every inch of you," he promised, kissing a path down my stomach. His tongue swirled around my belly button, dipping in momentarily and then venturing farther south to the line of my bottoms.

He looked up at me with expectant eyes, and I loved him even more for it. Even though I'd said yes, told him I loved him, that I needed him, he always made a point to make sure I was comfortable.

"Take them off," I begged, shifting my legs. Instead of pulling them down my legs, he tugged at the string with his teeth, and I watched in fascination as they came undone, sliding free to bare me to him.

His outspread hands ran down my hips, ridding me of the last of my wet swimsuit. "Now you," I ordered.

He shook his head and instead placed hot kisses to the inside of my hips. "No. If those come off, I'll be inside you in a millisecond."

"I'm okay with that," I said, my hips arching for his mouth. I wanted him with a ferocity I'd never known, a desperation that bordered on insanity.

"I'm not," he said with a grin. His tongue licked the seam where the front of my thigh met my belly. "I need to see you come apart first, to have you so hot that you're burning."

"I'm already burning," I protested, impatient.

"Not even close." He laughed darkly, then separated my thighs with his hands and set his mouth on me.

"Landon!" I cried his name, uncaring that it was still late afternoon and there could be people in the nearby bungalows.

"See? I want you on fire," he said just before his fingers separated me for his tongue.

Oh. My. God. Every nerve ending in my body came alive, and every sensation centered in the aching of my core, the streaks of heat he sent spiraling through me with each stroke of his tongue against my clit.

He circled, sucked, jabbed, laved, brought me to the edge and then held me there while I panted, my hands gripping at his hair, the covers, anything that might hold me to the earth.

"Are you on fire yet, baby?" he asked, his voice the perfect semblance of control and calm.

I moaned in answer, shamelessly rocking my hips against

him for more.

The pressure in my belly was tight, coiled, and I rode the edge of my orgasm as he held it back, controlling my pleasure with his hands—his mouth.

"God, you taste incredible," he said against my flesh.

My inner muscles fluttered, needing him, and I no more than lifted my hips for him than he slid one of his fingers, then two inside me. "So wet. Are you ready for me? Do you need me, Rachel? Because I'm dying for you."

"Yes!" I cried.

With a crook of his fingers and the sweet suction of his lips, I came apart, my orgasm tearing through me like lightning. I screamed his name as my back bowed, unbelievable pleasure consuming every thought, feeling, and sense.

He brought me down, kicking back the waves with his kisses, until I was sure he'd killed me in the best way possible. "That was amazing," I said, stretching under him, my body feeling languid, deliciously warmed.

Just when I thought I couldn't possibly be more aroused, he rose above me, licking his lower lip like he had to savor even the slightest taste of me. The hot, possessive look in his eyes was even more of a turn-on than his hands had been. *Boom.* That ache returned, another need clawing at me, not just for my pleasure—but for his.

I sat up, pushing my wet hair away from my face, and kissed him. My hands tucked into the waistband of his swim trunks and I pulled. The wet fabric protested, but with his help, I got them off, revealing wet, hot, nude Landon.

His abs cut in serious fuck-me lines down to his hips, and my fingers trailed them until my right hand reached—

"You still have it," I whispered, grazing the small infinity symbol on his left hip that was normally hidden under his waistband.

"Of course I do," he said with a smile. "You're still my

infinity. Even when you were gone, you were still here."

I leaned forward and kissed him sweetly, hoping my lips could convey what my voice simply couldn't. Maybe it was only one tattoo among so many, but it was mine, and he'd kept it. Kept a piece of *me*. I hadn't done the same for him.

He was the perfect model of a man, his muscles tight and firm—powerful without heavy bulk, carved like a master sculptor had chiseled him from stone, which was exactly how hard he was as I pushed him to sit in the center of our bed.

Sliding one knee on either side of his hips, I straddled him. His erection slid through my core until it rested between us, and Landon moaned. "You're going to be the death of me."

"Happily," I said, then blinked. "Please tell me you brought condoms."

The corner of his mouth lifted. "I learned my lesson the last time you yelled at me. They're in my bag."

I sighed in relief, then kissed him like my life depended on it. The rub of my breasts against his chest was exquisite, and I moved my hips restlessly against him as our tongues intertwined. His fingers grew impatient, digging into my hips with a wonderful bite. I loved the feel of him losing control—of being mine.

His breathing grew ragged as I sucked on his lower lip, then caught completely as I reached between us to stroke his length. He was hot and heavy in my hands, and I ran my thumb over the soft head that contrasted to the hardness of the rest of him.

"Rachel," he gasped. "God, baby. Yes." His hand stroked up my spine to grasp my neck, pulling me in for a hungry kiss.

As he rocked within my hand, I felt him grow even thicker, and my core clenched in response.

"Are you on fire for *me*?" I asked, turning his words on him.

Maintaining his grip on my neck, he pulled back to look

at me, his eyes burning an intense shade of green. "I have always burned for you. I will always burn for you. You own me like no one ever has, or ever will. Only you, Rachel."

I knew why he said my name, because he'd been unable to for so long, but instead of reminding me of how many women there had been in the past, it only made me feel needed, powerful. No matter what had happened in the years we hadn't been together, there was one simple truth: we had always belonged to each other.

After one more kiss, I leaned over the edge of the bed, thankful his bag was nearby. A quick search and a rip of foil later, I rolled on the condom, savoring his intake of breath.

"How do you want me?" I asked, rising above him.

"However you'll take me. I'm yours."

His hand reached between us, and his thumb brushed over my hypersensitive clit, the light movement enough to send a jolt of need soaring through my belly.

On my knees, I moved until he was positioned at my entrance, and my breath caught at the enormity of our actions. "I love you," I told him, not because I needed to hear it back, but because I needed him to understand what this meant to me.

"I have always loved you," he promised.

He captured my mouth in a scorching kiss as I slid down, taking him inside inch by perfect inch.

"Look at me," he said, breaking our kiss. My eyes popped open to watch his as I sank farther, stretching to accommodate his size. "I have only ever loved you," he whispered, his words invading my soul as he took over my body, consuming every spare inch I had to give.

He felt like home.

Our breaths mingled in stuttered pants, our eyes locked, our bodies fused. I rocked, sliding until I completely sheathed him. Once I started, I couldn't stop, setting a rhythm that he met, his jaw locked in restraint, his eyes dancing with fire.

I kissed him, savoring the way he had completely taken over. "I love the way you fill me," I whispered. "You feel so damn good."

As if I'd broken the string of his control, he growled and flipped us until my back hit the bed. Then he grasped my hands, holding them above my head. "That's because you were always meant for me. Mine."

"Yours," I admitted, arching against his measured thrusts.

Each movement brought a higher level of pleasure, and it kept getting better. I wrapped my legs around his hips, and he hit deeper, harder, until I was writhing beneath him, my moans in time with his thrusts.

It was the same as it had been between us, the sweet fire, the desperate need, but it was also different—even better than what I thought had been the best sex of my life.

His muscles were rigid as he kissed me deeply, and I could almost taste the restraint he was using, how tightly he held himself in check.

I swirled my hips, and he groaned. "Fuck, Rachel," he drew out my name.

Releasing my hands, he sent one to my hip and then lifted one knee so he could take me even deeper. I cried out as he used his hand between us to bring me back to the edge, my body on overload from every sensation.

That tight spiral of need took over, and my orgasm hit me, ripping his name from my lips. I shuddered around him as I came, and his thrusts sent me soaring even higher, until I separated from my body and saw stars.

The minute I fell apart, he snapped, his thrusts even deeper, harder, his rhythm abandoned in favor of the primal need we both felt as he took me over and over again.

His kiss broke into a guttural moan of my name as he came, his body shuddering and then tensing above mine—lust, love, and wonder etched on his face as he looked down at me.

God, I loved this man.

My heart swelled, flooding me with euphoria as he collapsed, then rolled us to his side so I could breathe. We didn't speak; our eyes did that for us. It was everything I'd been starved for and so much more, a union that didn't just slake my body's needs, but my soul's.

He kissed me softly as our breathing calmed.

"Is it just me, or have we gotten even better at that?" I asked, feeling slightly drunk on pleasure.

His smile was lazy, and all the more gorgeous for it. "Just imagine how good we're going to get."

I stroked his face, letting his day's worth of stubble rasp the skin of my palm. "I'm not sure I can take anything better."

His forehead puckered. "Are you sure? Because I've been dreaming of this for the last two and a half years. I have quite a few ideas."

"Oh, really?" I teased, my fingers tracing the raven tattoo that flew down his right pec.

"Really," he promised in a low, sultry voice that already had my exhausted nerve endings waking back up.

The things this man did to my body with just his voice were criminal.

"Like what?" I asked.

"I thought for starters, we'd try out the huge Jacuzzi tub in there," he said, motioning behind him. "Then I figured it would be night, and I could take you back on that deck and watch you come under the moonlight. But, I mean…only if you're up for it." His eyes took on a wicked, sexy gleam.

"Oh, I'm up for the challenge," I promised.

One bath and an orgasm later, I found out that he could balance me on a railing and take me at the same time.

Given how loudly I screamed his name, I was certain that our neighbors heard us. I was also certain that I didn't care.

Chapter Twenty-Five

MIDAIR

"Mind if I sit?" Pax asked as he stood next to my empty seat.

I took off my headphones and let them drape over my neck.

"Since my girlfriend just stole your seat, I feel like I have to say yes," I told him and moved over.

We were thirty thousand feet over the Pacific and only a half hour from LAX and reality. At least we were in the Wilder Enterprises private jet. With twenty of us on board, it was crowded enough. One good thing about having two weeks off from the cruise would be the luxury of space.

"You look happy," he said, clasping the seat belt as I did the same. We'd hit some wicked turbulence an hour ago that I had no wish to repeat.

"Is this where we have the epic man talk?" I asked.

"Nawh," he said. "I'm just glad you two worked your shit

out."

I looked ahead and over to where Leah and Rachel sat, deep in conversation. The past two days had been perfect— not just the sex, but the feeling of commitment, the idea that we just might make it…if I didn't fuck it up.

"That remains to be seen," I said quietly.

"What do you mean?" he asked.

I swallowed the fear that had been knocking at my door since the moment she told me she loved me back on Fiji. "I meant to tell her…before."

"Before what?" he asked, his eyes narrowing.

"Don't be stupid," I snapped.

His hands went up to his shoulders like he was under arrest. "Okay. For fuck's sake, you're testy for someone who finally got laid."

"Seriously?"

"Come on. She's all mellow, and you're looking at her like she's a cake you can't get enough of. You two fucked."

I cringed. "Don't…" I shook my head. "Unless you want me talking about Leah like that, just don't."

His mouth opened, then closed, then opened again. "Fair enough. I've just never known you to be sensitive on that shit."

"Yeah, well, it's Rachel."

"Understood. Now what has you freaked out? What the hell didn't you tell her?"

"Why I left."

His eyes widened. "What? She knew it was for the competition, right?"

"Right. But she doesn't know *why*."

"Oh, for fuck's sake," he said, sliding his hand over his face. "You fought with that girl for the better part of two months and you never told her?"

I shook my head. "She was so pissed. If I told her to start

with, I never would have gotten within a hundred yards of her. She might have left…and taken Leah with her."

"Oh no, you do not tie Leah to this. I made that mistake and it almost cost me her in the first place. As a matter of fact, you saw what me keeping shit from her almost cost me. How the hell can you be so stupid as to repeat my mistake? You're the smarter of us."

"It's not exactly easy," I hissed. "All I've ever wanted is a second chance with her. She's the only woman I've ever loved—the only woman I *will* ever love. So I figured I'd tell her when she started talking to me again. But then she did, and I didn't want to chance losing her. So then I figured I'd do it when we were in Fiji. That was why I rented that bungalow. I figured if I told her there, we could work it out away from everyone else, and then carry on."

"But instead you decided to…" He opened up his hands like he was asking me what the fuck I was thinking…because that's exactly what he was doing.

"Then she told me she loved me, and well…" I opened my hands in the same fashion.

He shook his head. "You know what? I got nothing. How the fuck are you going to clear this up? She's about to be home in a few hours, and you know how much her parents hate you."

"I don't know. I keep trying to open my mouth and just tell her, but…" I raked my hands over my baseball hat. "But I'm terrified of losing her. I know without a doubt that she's it for me. She's the only woman I'm meant to be with. What the fuck do I do if she leaves me?"

Pax's eyes drifted to where Leah sat. "Beg. You get on your goddamned knees and beg. You apologize, and you explain. At this point, it's not even that it happened, it's that you hid it from her. That *they* hid it from her."

"She's everything to me," I said quietly.

"Yeah. I know just how you feel. Grab on tight, because knowing Rachel, you're not in for an easy time of it once she knows. You'd better just pray that she loves you enough not to cut your ass off."

I watched her laugh with Leah and cursed myself. Why hadn't I told her? Found a second to lay it all out? *Because you knew it would destroy her, one way or another.*

"It's not fair. No matter what I do, she's going to hate us both. She's never felt like she was enough, you know? The way I left her…I don't know how to mend that tear I put there, and this will just rip her further apart."

"You've got her cornered here, but I'm not sure I want to see her go ballistic in a contained environment. She's liable to take down the plane."

The captain's voice came over the intercom. "We've begun our initial descent into Los Angeles. Flight attendants, please ready the cabin for landing."

"Or I guess now you just pray," Pax said. He must have seen my general look of dismay, because his shoulders slumped. "Look, man, she loves you. It's written all over her damn face. You two are a force of nature, and anyone or anything who steps between you gets crushed—believe me, I know. What happened was over two years ago. It's in the past. You just show her that you are there for every day of her future, and she'll forgive you. She might not forgive them, but that's between her and them."

"Yeah. Thanks, man." I sat back and watched LAX approach, so lost in my own thoughts that I barely noticed when Rachel took Pax's seat. Her small hand slipped into mine, and she squeezed.

As the plane touched down, she kissed my cheek. "Welcome home," she said with a smile.

I turned and held her face, wishing I could pour all of my love into her, that I could somehow make everything perfect.

Then I kissed her, praying that she remembered everything I'd told her in Fiji, that we were stubborn enough to see this through—that it was always our decision to make us work.

"I was already home," I said against her lips. "My home is wherever you are."

She smiled, and I felt like the biggest bastard on the planet.

We deplaned on the tarmac, where there were cars waiting to take us to our homes. "Want to share?" I asked.

"I know you need to get home. It's okay. You go, and I'll see you tomorrow for dinner, right?"

"Right," I told her, kissing her again because I could— because I was terrified that it might be the last time. "I love you, Rachel. I know we're home, and that things back here are...different, but no matter what your parents say, or me leaving for Aspen, that doesn't change."

"I know," she said. "Stop stressing. You're acting like me."

I laughed. "Maybe I just hate thinking about sleeping in an empty bed."

She wound her arms around my neck as her bags were loaded into the car behind her. "Well, it's only for a couple weeks. Then maybe when we're back on board you can sleep in my bed."

"Or you can sleep in mine," I offered.

"After you burn the sheets, ban the camera crew from the suite, and get a new mattress," she said with a quick grin and a kiss. "I love you."

"Done deal."

I gathered her to me, kissing her like my life depended on it, memorizing the feel of her lips, her lavender-and-peppermint scent, her gentle sigh in my ears. I'd tell her tomorrow at dinner.

As long as they didn't tell her first.

Chapter Twenty-Six

RACHEL

"You sure you don't need help with these, miss?" the driver asked as he handed me my suitcase.

I handed him twenty dollars in return, the feel of American money almost foreign in my hand. "I've got it. Thank you for bringing me home."

A minute later I walked up the landscaped steps to my front door. The lawn was still manicured, but something was off about it, same as the drooping flowers. Wait…where was the Christmas wreath?

I fumbled with my keys but got them into the lock, turned, and opened the door. "Hey, guys! I'm home!" I called as I hauled my suitcase into the foyer.

"Rachel?" Mom called out before she came skidding around the corner in her socks. "You're home!" She engulfed me in a hug and her chocolate-chip-cookie scent. "I'm so glad you're here! How are you? How was your flight?"

I laughed and hugged her back. As amazing as the trip was, I'd really missed her. "I'm glad, too. I'm fantastic, even better than that, and it was good."

She pulled back, examining me like she was going to find a pod person under my skin. "You're smiling. Everything is good with the boy?"

"Landon, Mom, and yeah, he's…" I sighed. "He's absolutely wonderful."

Her lips pursed, but she didn't dig in. "Okay. Well, your dad isn't home yet."

I blinked. "It's eleven p.m."

She forced a smile. "You know how things are at work right before the X Games, and since they're sponsoring again this year…"

I nodded. "It gets nuts. Right." Ever since Landon and I had split, they'd kept any reference to the sport in general under wraps. It was nice to be able to discuss it in the open again, freeing. "Okay, well, I really want to wait up for him, but I'm exhausted. It's only seven p.m. my time, but it's tomorrow, or some craziness."

Jet lag was a bitch.

She nodded, petting my hair. "You must be exhausted. I baked for you, but of course those can wait for tomorrow."

"Chocolate chip cookies?" I guessed.

She nodded, the hopeful look in her eyes giving me a renewed energy.

"We can't let them go to waste," I said, dropping my backpack next to my suitcase. "How about we have a couple and I tell you about Nepal?"

Her eyes went wide. "I'd love to hear all about it."

An hour later, she was filled in on that aspect of the trip—the good and the bad, and though she cringed, she stayed with me. It had to be hard for her, overpowering her nearly insane overprotectiveness, but she did it for me, and I loved her all the more for it.

I nearly jumped out of my skin when I heard a key in the lock.

"Rachel, baby?" Dad called.

"Daddy!" I squealed, running into his arms like I was five years old. He caught me up easily, swinging me around.

"You've lost weight. Have they been feeding you?" he questioned in an overly serious tone.

"Just lots of exercise," I told him. "Don't worry, Mom's already stuffed me full of cookies. I'll be round again in no time."

He glanced up at Mom and nodded. "I'm glad to see you home, sweetheart. You must be exhausted."

I swallowed back a perfectly timed yawn. "I am. But I'm glad to see you, too. I've missed you guys."

He forced a smile. "Why don't you get some sleep? We should talk about some stuff tomorrow."

I leaned up and kissed his cheek, breathing in the comforting scent of the same aftershave he'd used the last twenty years. "I love you, Daddy. And I know where this is going, but Landon isn't up for discussion. I love him. He loves me."

"Rachel…"

"We can talk tomorrow, but you both need to know that there's nothing you can say about him that's going to change my mind." Before they could start in on me tonight about my inability to steer clear of reckless boys, I waved. "Good night!" Hoisting my backpack onto my shoulder, I wheeled my suitcase to the back bedroom of our ranch-style house.

I didn't bother unpacking, just grabbed a set of pajamas out of my dresser and got into bed, dragging my iPad with me. *Ah, sweet wifi.*

I wanted to text Landon, but my parents had put my

number on hold while I was gone, and it wasn't like I had Landon's number anymore, anyway. But I knew exactly where I could find him. I logged into Facebook for the first time since I left and smiled like a loon as I clicked on settings. It felt symbolic, unblocking him. His entire life unfolded to me on the computer—pictures, updates, statuses he'd been tagged in.

I stayed off the pics—I didn't need to see the parade of women he'd been with in the last couple of years. Instead I sent him a quick PM.

Rachel: LOOK WHO I FOUND.

A couple minutes and flashing dots later, he responded.

Landon: HOLY SHIT. SHE EXISTS ONLINE.

Rachel: HA-HA. MISS ME YET?

Landon: YOU HAVE NO IDEA. MY BED IS COLD AND LONELY.

I smiled, loving the rush of sweet emotion even his typed voice brought to me.

Rachel: MAYBE I CAN SEE IT TOMORROW NIGHT?

Landon: HELL YES.

I MEAN, IF THAT'S YOUR WISH.

Rachel: I THINK WE CAN WORK SOMETHING OUT.

Landon: I MISS YOU ALREADY.

Rachel: I MISS YOU, TOO.

Oddly enough, it was true. We'd only been apart a couple of hours, and I already hated the twenty minutes of distance between us. I liked that he was a few suites away back on the boat, that I had nearly instant access to him twenty-four hours a day. I'd been spoiled.

We typed out our good nights, but before I fell asleep, I heard my notifications ring. I accepted his request with a giant, goofy grin on my face.

He'd just changed his relationship status.

He was mine in the eyes of the world.

I turned off my light and rolled over, trying to settle into bed, but although everything was perfect, something nagged at me that I couldn't put my finger on.

I woke up from a dead sleep three hours later, realizing what it was.

There was no Christmas tree in our living room.

Something was up.

• • •

The smell of bacon greeted me with the morning, and I donned my proverbial armor as I made the short walk to the kitchen.

"Good morning," Mom said with a smile as she flipped bacon in the pan.

"Hey, sleepyhead," Dad said from the other side of the kitchen where he worked with the mixer.

I slid onto the bar stool at the counter that separated our living room from the kitchen and watched my parents carefully. At first glance, everything seemed fine. But there were little things, like the way they hadn't immediately grilled me about Landon or the safety of what we'd been doing in Nepal.

There was no Christmas tree, no lights, no wreath, and the holiday was only a week away.

"So, I'm thinking about going to Aspen for the last few days of break," I said casually, watching for any reaction. "Landon and Wilder will be up there practicing for the X Games before we head back, and I'd love to get some time on the slopes."

Mom tensed. She hated when I went snowboarding or did anything that didn't come with a seat belt and air bags. "Oh?" she asked, flipping the bacon again.

My eyes narrowed.

"Well, I mean, if that's something you're interested in, I

could definitely see if we could open up the company's house there," Dad offered. "I mean, we'll be up there all of January for the Games, so why not?"

My mouth hit the floor. Dad hated me anywhere near extreme sports—or Landon, for that matter.

What the hell?

"And I was thinking maybe I'd get a tattoo in the next couple of days, too."

Mom's grip tightened on the spatula, and Dad turned around, swallowing with force. "Okay…well, you're a grown woman and whatever you choose—"

"Cut the crap!" I snapped. "What the hell is going on? You two are acting weird and there's no Christmas tree, or any of the usual overkill that Mom likes to deck the halls with— sorry, Mom, but you do. Are we doing something insane like going to Disney for Christmas or something? Are you pulling a John Grisham and Kranking me? Because I love you guys, but I've seriously been traveling the last two months and all I want to do is hang here at home."

Dad switched off the mixer and came to stand next to Mom.

They locked eyes, and she moved a few feet away toward the sink.

A sick feeling settled in the pit of my stomach. "What's going on?" I asked in a voice I barely recognized as my own.

"Rachel, there's something your mother and I need to tell you."

"Is someone dead? Did something happen while I was gone and you didn't tell me?"

Mom came around the island bar and took my hand. "Nothing like that, baby. It's just that your dad and I…well…" She looked up at my dad, but he wouldn't meet her eyes.

"We're getting a divorce," Dad said.

The ground shifted beneath my feet, and even though I

sat on the stool, immobile, it felt like I was falling, like they'd just demagnetized the poles and now my compass spun without direction. "I don't understand."

"Oh, honey. We didn't want to tell you while you were gone. That's so much stress on you, and we figured it was best to let you be happy," Mom said softly.

"How long?" I asked Dad, who still wouldn't look up. He took the bacon off the stove, like that was going to help us in any way.

"We've known since before you left," she whispered. "Your dad moved out the week after you called from Dubai."

I shook my head, trying to make it all fit. "You've known for months? But you were here when Mom called me," I said to Dad.

"She asked if I would come over, and of course I wanted to talk to you," he said, glancing up.

"But…but you were happy. You loved each other. You… I just don't understand! You guys are like the poster children for marriage. Hell, you're like the inspiration for perfect people. It doesn't make sense. I know you used to be unhappy, but that was like twenty years ago…"

You adopted me. I fixed everything. You said I glued you back together.

"Rachel, just because people fall in love when they're twenty doesn't mean that it lasts. Sometimes people grow apart," Mom told me.

"Or sometimes people simply decide that you're not what they want anymore and forget to tell you," Dad said quietly, looking over at Mom.

Her eyes dropped to her hands.

That sick feeling spread from my stomach to my heart. "What happened, Mom?"

She gave me a pained smile but only met my eyes for a flash. "It's not important."

Not only had my parents' marriage disintegrated while I was gone, but I didn't even get to know why.

Suddenly the home I was raised in, with so many birthdays, holidays, and family movie nights, felt more foreign than the countries I'd been in the last two months.

"Dad? You don't live here anymore?"

He shook his head. "No. I bought a place closer to the office. But I have a room set up for you."

"She's not going with you," Mom spat.

"Oh, she's going to stay here with you? After what you've done?"

"This is her home. You can leave it, but she's not going to."

"What the hell would you know about home? After you brought *him* here? In our house? Our bed?" Dad's accusation echoed in my brain, reverberating until it was all I could hear even though their fight continued around me.

"Never around."

"Unfaithful!"

"Lonely!"

The words wrapped around me in a cacophony of ugliness. How did this happen so quickly? How could something I'd always seen as unshakable crumble without me noticing?

Was all love doomed to end up here?

Why didn't I see it? Why didn't they tell me? Why was I enough to bring them back as a baby, but not now?

"She's not going with you!"

"Well, she's sure as hell not staying with you!"

The world came back into sharp focus.

"Enough!" I shouted as I stood. The bar stool crashed to the hardwood floor behind me.

They stared at me in startled silence as I tried to force the words out. "I'm not a child anymore. Maybe that's why this is all happening. I don't know. But I do know that I'm capable of making my own decisions, and right now, I don't want to be around either of you."

I turned and made it to the living room before they spoke.

"Rachel, we're sorry. We wanted to do this better. Gentler," Mom said.

"Did you cheat on him?" I asked her quietly, needing to know.

She looked down at her hands.

"And you just moved out? Gave up? Just like that? You couldn't even tell me?" I asked Dad.

"I couldn't stay here. There's a lot you don't know," he replied quietly.

"Yeah. I see that now." I sucked in a breath. "I think I'm going to leave. You two figure out your stuff, because you're acting more childish than I ever could. If you want to dissolve our family, that's your choice. I don't get a say. But I also don't have to sit here while you hurl poison at each other."

Twenty minutes later I pulled out of the driveway in my car, everything I brought home in my backseat. I'd never even unpacked.

It had taken less than twelve hours to upend everything I thought I knew.

I wasn't sure how long it took to get there, mostly because I didn't really remember most of the drive. I only hoped I hadn't run any red lights, and I wished for the millionth time that my cell phone had been turned on. But once my parents informed me that true love doesn't last forever, there was only one person I wanted to see.

I needed his arms around me, his voice in my ear promising that we'd make it. I needed Landon.

The giant gate at the front of his house never failed to intimidate me.

My parents were comfortable. Hell, my dad had a high-level job at Gremlin. It wasn't like we were struggling, but this place was insane.

The dressed-in-all-black guard came up to my car and knocked on my window.

"Hi?" I said as rolled it down.

"Is that a question or a statement?" he asked with a smile.

"Both, I guess. I'm looking for Landon?"

The guard raised his eyebrows at me.

"That was a statement," I clarified, tapping my steering wheel.

"Name?" he asked.

"Rachel Dawson." For the love of God, I wanted my cell phone. God, what if he wasn't home? What if he was just generally busy? Was I intruding? It was shades of John Hughes over here with the lack of communication.

The guard pressed the radio at his shoulder. "I have Rachel Dawson here to see Landon?"

The response was garbled, but the guard smiled at me patiently while we sat in the most awkward silence known to man. The radio sounded again, and the guard nodded. "You're clear. Head on up to the front door."

"Thank you," I said and followed his instructions once the gate separated to let me through.

After making my way up the winding drive, I put the car in park just in time to see Landon jump the bottom steps to get to me.

I threw the emergency brake and killed the ignition but didn't bother to pull the keys out.

"Hey, Rach, what's going—*umpf*." He grunted as I hit him nearly head-on, diving into his arms. They instantly closed around me, cradling my head to his chest in his safe, secure embrace.

I sagged, all the adrenaline and energy that got me here suddenly gone. For a moment, I simply stood there and breathed him in, pretending we were back in Fiji, or even

Nepal. Anything but where we were, and he let me, not questioning my need or pushing me.

"I'm sorry I barged in," I finally said, looking up at him.

"You're never barging in. You're always welcome," he promised, kissing my forehead. "But maybe you'll tell me what's got you upset?"

"My dad moved out. They're getting a divorce." Saying it aloud made it feel so real.

"Oh, baby." He brushed my hair back from my face, stroking my skin. "I'm so sorry."

"I never caught on that they were unhappy. I was home all summer, and the months up until I left for Madagascar. It all happened right under my nose. How did I miss it?"

"Because they didn't want you to know. Parents do their best to protect their kids, and they probably thought they were doing what was best for you. I'm not saying it was right, but you can't blame yourself for not knowing."

"How does that happen? You choose your person, and then one day decide that they're not your person anymore? I don't understand how that happens." Or why I couldn't stop it—why I couldn't see it.

"I wish I could tell you," he said. "I don't have all the answers."

"Just tell me that won't happen with us," I begged. "Tell me that it doesn't always end like that."

He sucked in his breath and gazed at me intensely, like he could see into my soul. "I promise you that I will never cheat on you. I will never lie to you again—I learned my lesson when I lost you. I will be yours for as long as you want me, Rachel Dawson, because you're the only woman I will ever love. Do you understand me?"

I nodded, and he clutched me to him, tucking my head under his chin as he rubbed circles on my back. "Remember, we are what we decide to be—you and me."

"You and me," I repeated, closing my eyes.

"Do you want to come in?" he asked.

I'd already started to nod when a guard leaned over the stone fence that separated the driveway from the house. "Sir, her father is here."

Landon tensed. "Do you want to see him? The beauty of having security is that I can say no."

"It's okay. I was a little harsh on him."

Landon waved him in, and a minute later, my dad parked on the other side of me. He climbed out of his immaculate convertible and ran his hand over his silvered hair. "Rachel."

"Dad," I said, keeping Landon's hand firmly in mine as I turned to face him.

He looked back at Landon and grimaced. "Can we talk alone?"

"I'm just going to tell him what we say anyway."

He sighed and walked toward us, a manila envelope in his hands. "I'm sorry about what happened this morning," he said.

"Me, too. And I'm sorry for what Mom did. You don't deserve that."

He swallowed, pain flashing across his eyes. "Yeah, well, sometimes it's the people we love most who hurt us the deepest." His gaze flickered to Landon, and I knew he was thinking about what had happened years ago. "You need to know that I tried. I won't say anything more, and I don't want you to take this out on your mother, but…I tried to make it work, Rachel. We just can't. I can't. I had to go."

I dropped Landon's hand and went to my dad, hugging him tight. "I'm so sorry, Dad. I shouldn't have been such a wreck. I was just in shock. It's always been the three of us, and now…now I don't know."

"I know. And we both love you very much. That's not something you should ever doubt, okay?"

"I don't," I told him, giving a tighter squeeze before pulling back.

"And I know this is important to you," he said, fidgeting with the envelope. "The other papers, I'm not sure where they are. Once your birth certificate was in after your adoption, nothing else ever mattered. We shut the door on how you came to us and concentrated on being the family you were always meant to have. There's not a lot of information in here, but maybe it will help you feel like you've found whatever it is you're missing."

I took the envelope from him with a slightly shaky hand. "Thanks, Dad."

He nodded and looked back at Landon. "I'd really like you to come home with me, Rachel. If not me, then your mother. Anything but here...with him."

My stomach sank. "Dad, not today. I know you and Landon have some harsh feelings between you, but I seriously don't think I can take anything else today."

"He's not good for you, Rachel."

"He loves me," I countered. With everything else that had gone to shit today, it was the one thing I was certain of.

"Not enough," he said softly, sadly.

"What do you mean?" That sick, nauseating feeling was back in my belly.

"Today has been hard enough on you. Why don't you just come home with me and we'll have a good, long talk about it?" he offered.

After this morning, I'd had quite enough of being managed.

"No. You tell me now."

"Rachel," Landon said, coming up behind me.

I turned toward him. "What is he talking about?"

Landon looked straight over me to my father. "You really want to hurt her like this?"

"You were the one who didn't stay away," Dad snapped. "Someone that willing to walk away in the first place isn't deserving of my daughter. She's worth a hundred of you."

"On that, we agree," Landon said.

"Dad, Landon and I talked about what happened, and if I can forgive him, then I need you to try." I got it, he was on overprotective mode, especially with what was going on with him and Mom, but he couldn't take out his insecurities on Landon.

"So he told you why he left?" Dad challenged, his blue eyes going hard.

"Please don't," Landon pleaded quietly. "For both our sakes."

Dad's eyes narrowed. "You'd like that, wouldn't you? The difference between us, *Nova*, is that I'm firmly ready for my daughter to hate me, if it's what keeps her out of harm's way and away from you. Can you say the same?"

My grip tightened on the envelope. "Dad?"

"What did he tell you, sweetheart?"

I didn't look at Landon. I wasn't sure I could. "That he had to rejoin the team or they couldn't put on the competition. It was an all-or-nothing deal."

"Did he tell you why?"

"Rachel," Landon whispered.

"Because he left."

"You're just going to hurt her more," Landon said, his voice breaking.

Dad looked over my head at him. "I'd rather hurt her now than her think she can spend her life with someone who can be bought from her side."

"Bought?" I asked, finally looking up at Landon.

There was so much pain in his eyes, and my first thought was to take it away. How ridiculous was that? "How were you bought?"

He reached for me, but I stepped backward.

"Gremlin pulled the sponsorship of the event, but it wasn't because I'd left. It was because I was with you."

I spun and then backed away from them both, moving toward my car. Pieces clicked in my head, the puzzle anything but pretty. "You pulled their funding," I said to Dad.

He nodded. "I did."

"And you dumped me to get it back?" I asked Landon, hoping there was another answer, any other way this had gone down.

"Yes."

"That and more," Dad added. "Gremlin signed the Renegades for thirty months as a team once Landon returned. With a sizable advance to get them going."

"You've been his paycheck."

"Yes, and his is a great deal bigger than the others'. That was the deal when he gave you up."

My heart shattered, the pieces sharp enough to cut through my soul. I shook my head and backed up, but Landon followed. How stupid could I be? I knew Gremlin sponsored their events—I should have logically realized they'd sponsor the individual athletes as well. Or maybe I'd just assumed that Dad hated Landon so much he wouldn't do business with him. But he'd paid Landon even more to dump me, and Landon had taken it.

How could I have been so wrong about Dad? About them both?

"You have to let me explain. My parents were pissed about what had happened between me and Pax. They didn't support my career choice, and you were that final straw. They cut off my money."

My head snapped up. "Money. Are you fucking kidding me? Leaving me for friendship, I forgave. Pax and Penna are basically family to you, and even though you destroyed me, there was still this honor about your choice. But *money*? What the hell am I supposed to do with that?"

Panic was etched across his features. "I didn't have a job. Without the competition, I couldn't even afford to rent that apartment with you. What the hell kind of life did that leave us?"

"One that we made together! You could have come to me. We could have figured it out together."

"With everything you'd already given up for me? Your dad showed up and told me that if I walked away from you, he'd have Gremlin restore the funding and sponsor us individually. The competition would go on, and he'd pull every string he had to get you back into Dartmouth, even though you'd just turned them down for me. All I had to do was walk away from you and you'd have the life you were meant to have without me fucking it up for you."

"You took money for me?" I shouted, uncaring about the rest. "I didn't care about Dartmouth! I would have lived anywhere with you. I would have left L.A. I didn't need the money, the fame, the sport—*you* did. How much was our love worth to you, Landon? Six figures? Seven?"

"It wasn't like that. Yeah, it was more than the other Renegades, but I'd gotten us in way over our heads, and it was the only way to put it all back to the way it was—to fix the mistakes we'd made."

"I'm not a goddamned mistake!" I screamed. Jesus, didn't *anyone* want me for what I was? Just me. Only me.

"No, you're the best choice I've ever made," Landon swore fervently. "But I wasn't *your* best choice."

"Don't believe him, Rachel," Dad added.

My head snapped toward him. "Oh, no. I'm done listening to you. You bought me—" A self-deprecating laugh took hold, racking my shoulders. "Twice, I guess."

"If you want to accuse someone of that, look at your

boyfriend," Dad snapped.

For fuck's sake, I had whiplash.

"What are you talking about?" Landon asked.

"Oh, come on. You didn't think I'd realize what you'd done? Wormed your way back in with my daughter while we've been in negotiations for our sponsorship of the Renegades for the X Games? Now that your thirty months are ending? How much is it going to cost me this time, Nova?"

"What?" Landon balked.

I laughed. "Of course." I shrugged. "Of course this is what happens." I looked at Dad. "You needed me to fix your marriage, and apparently I didn't do that well enough." Then I turned to Landon. "You needed me to secure your funding. When were you going to dump me, Landon? Tonight? Closer to the X Games? I'm so damned stupid."

At that moment, I had the strangest longing for my broken wrist—for the pain that had semidistracted me from this heartbreak the first time. But this was a hundred times worse. This time I didn't only feel like I'd been rejected, I felt like an utter fool who'd been played.

And everyone knew Nova was the ultimate player.

"Rachel—"

"Sweetheart—"

I threw out my hand and warded them both off.

"Fuck you both."

Chapter Twenty-Seven

LANDON

LOS ANGELES

My chest lost the ability to process oxygen, no matter how badly my brain willed it to breathe.

She looked at me from the other side of her car, and it took every ounce of restraint I had not to jump the hood of the car and force her to stay—force her to listen.

"Rachel, please," I begged.

Everything that had softened about her hardened, from her posture to the now stone-cold set of her brown eyes. Fire, I could fight. Fire, I could arouse, ensnare, draw her out and fight back.

But apathy? I had no chance.

"You told me that we would always be what we decided. That our relationship wasn't in anyone else's hands."

"I remember." Memories of Fiji hit me, holding her, loving her, finally letting myself believe that we could be together what we'd never managed to be apart: happy. But the woman before me had changed. In seconds she had rebuilt her walls that had taken me months to break down, and once again it was me who'd sliced her to the quick.

She nodded once, businesslike. "Well, I've decided that we're done. You obviously got what you wanted. You have your funding." She looked over to her dad. "And I went to Dartmouth. And now I'm done being controlled by both of you."

She slid into her car, her head held high, the perfect example of class and elegance, but the way she gunned it out of my driveway told me that under that cold exterior, my Rachel lurked.

"I hope you're satisfied," her dad said to me.

I clenched both my fists and reminded myself that I couldn't afford an assault charge at the moment. "Me? Look what you did to her!"

"Rachel will bounce back, and she'll be safe. Away from you and your reckless, girl-destroying ways. You don't think I know your reputation, *Casanova*? You picked the wrong daughter to go after. I've spent my entire career around selfish assholes like you, and she's entirely too good for you."

"You're right. She is, but I love her. If you don't believe me, then that's not my problem, it's yours. I will get through to her. I will get her back. I might not be the best man for her, but there's no one in this world who loves her like I do."

"It will be interesting to see you try. But you need to realize that there's nothing I won't do to protect my daughter. You go near her, and I'll withdraw your sponsorships. And maybe you can do without mine, but what about when the other sponsorships fall? All it takes is a simple phone call and a hint at scandal. Are you telling me there's not one skeleton, one girl, that would come out of your closet?"

I stared at him in stunned silence. Gremlin was our biggest

sponsor, but not our only one. If they pulled out, the others would question it, and us.

He sighed and rubbed his hand over his forehead. "You're not good enough for her. You never were. Just let her go. She'll learn to be happy, and she deserves it. There will never be a day on your circuit where she'd not be confronted with some woman you've slept with, some mistake you made. Give her a chance to find a future with someone who didn't ruin his with his past. Let her go, and I'll make sure your sponsorships remain intact."

Without another word, he turned and got into his car, taking the driveway out.

Ten minutes ago, I'd held her in my arms. She'd trusted me to hold her together when the rest of her world came apart. Ten minutes ago, my lips had brushed her forehead, and she'd clung to me, knowing that I would keep her safe.

Ten minutes ago, she'd loved me.

Just like the mudslide, the avalanche, the moments she'd broken down crying in Fiji, it happened so fast and altered everything.

Ten. Fucking. Minutes.

• • •

"Where is he?" I shouted as I walked in the front door of Paxton's house in Aspen the next day. It had taken me all evening to explain to my parents why I was leaving, and when they wouldn't stop arguing about how to stop me, I finally decided not to give a fuck and packed a bag.

"Who?" Alex asked, coming out of the kitchen, his mouth full of pizza.

"Wilder," I snapped.

Alex's eyes widened, and he pointed toward the rec room. I took the steps at a near run, finding the rec room inhabited by at least six of the Renegades. Pax put up his pool cue and turned to me with a giant smile.

The rage I'd kept carefully bottled exploded.

"Landon! To what do we owe this—"

I swung my fist and laid my best friend out on the ground.

Paxton rotated his jaw and looked up at me like I'd lost my mind.

Three of the guys rushed me, but Little John put up his hand and they all backed down, putting us in the center of a makeshift ring. Not that I cared. I was pissed off enough to kick all of their asses.

How could he do it? Hell, he'd gotten her there in the first place.

"What the fuck was that about?" Pax asked, getting to his feet.

"Did you know?" I asked. God help him if he did.

"You're going to have to be a little bit clearer than that."

"When you sat next to me on that airplane, telling me to come clean to her, to get everything in the open, did you know that the only way for me to secure our sponsors would be to give her up? Did you?"

"Landon, I have no clue what you're asking me."

"When you orchestrated everything, from getting her on board to doing everything you could to get us back together, did you do it for leverage?"

Pax put up his hands. "No. I don't even know what the fuck you're talking about."

"Rachel's dad, Paxton. He's pulling the strings at Gremlin, and not only did he out what happened two years ago, he's going to cut all of our funding if I don't walk away from her again. Why the fuck would you go back to Gremlin for sponsorship knowing he was there?"

Pax shook his head. "I didn't."

"What?" I barked.

"I did," a voice called from the other side of the pool table. Nick wheeled around the table in his chair until he was right in front of me. "You're not going to hit a guy in a wheelchair, are you?" he tried to joke.

"Don't tempt me. I love you like a brother, but what the hell?"

"Pax put me in charge of the X Games shit while you guys are tooling around the globe," he explained. "Gremlin was the natural choice—they've been our biggest sponsor. I had no clue you were back with Rachel. None. You never told me, even when you called to start arranging the Nepal shit. I get that you like to keep your personal life personal, but in this case, you bit yourself in the ass. In fact, when I checked in for info on how that was going, I was assured that you two didn't have a chance in hell and weren't even speaking."

I blinked. "What?"

"Oops," Zoe said, hopping down off the bar.

Every Renegade turned to look at her. "What the fuck do you mean, *oops*?" I snapped.

She shrugged. "You weren't speaking at that time. Besides, Gremlin has sponsored us every year since you left Rachel. How was I supposed to know you'd actually get back together with her? By the time you two were…whatever it is that you are, I wasn't about to call up Nick and let a piece of ass ruin our sponsorships. Team first, right?"

I ignored her, because if I didn't she was going to find her ass out in the cold.

"Why didn't you tell me?" Pax asked Nick.

"We were still in negotiations. I didn't want to fuck up and count my chickens before they hatched. I'm so sorry, man."

"Clear the room," Pax ordered before turning to Nick and me. "You two stay."

"But—" Zoe protested.

"Get the hell out, Zoe."

She left with the others, but not without throwing a serious pout.

"What are we going to do about her?" I asked Pax.

"We? We're not doing anything. You can figure out how to deal with Zoe, since we still have another five months on the *Athena* once we get back."

"Are you shitting me?"

Pax shook his head. "Nope. She didn't set out to sink the team, she pulled the move of a jealous ex-girlfriend. If she's a monster, then she's one that *you* created because you couldn't keep your dick in your pants the last two years. Zoe isn't our problem: Gremlin is."

For fuck's sake, my head hurt. I tried to compartmentalize and put Zoe way in the back of my priorities. "Fine. What are we going to do?"

Nick ran his hand over his short, buzzed hair. "I can make some calls, but if you pissed off Mr. Dawson, I don't know. He'll do the same thing he did a couple years ago and block us."

My head spun. How the fuck was I going to get us out of this? Sure, my parents had money, but they'd never agreed with this lifestyle, and the minute I went pro, they stopped supporting me. All of my income now came from prizes at competitions and sponsorships. I couldn't even touch my trust fund until I graduated college.

"Yeah, well, we're not the newbie kids we were a couple years ago," Pax argued. "Our name has some pull."

"It does, but you haven't been at a single competition this year. When it was time for your sponsors to re-up, you weren't looking too pretty," Nick replied. "I don't want to ask, but I have to. Is Gremlin an op—"

"Fuck, no," I spat. "I'm sorry, guys. I'll quit the Renegades before I bow down to her father. I'm not walking that same path twice. She means too much to me for that shit."

Paxton squeezed my shoulder. "Don't worry. We've got your back. We'll figure it out. I have no fucking clue how, but we'll think of something."

"We'll think of something," I repeated.

Paxton rubbed his forehead. "I miss Penna. We need to see what she thinks before we make any decisions."

"She answering her phone?"

Paxton shook his head. "She's been off the radar since yesterday. I figured she needed some space to get her shit straight. She's been a mess since—" Pax cut himself off.

"Since my ex tried to kill you? Yeah. I know," Nick bit out.

"So, I have almost no chance of getting Rachel to speak to me, we've almost certainly lost all of our sponsors for the year, and our fourth Original is in hiding from us," I said.

"We're fucking rocking it." Paxton groaned. "What are we going to do?"

Maybe it was only eleven thousand feet—nowhere near twenty-one, but I needed all the practice I could get before leaving for Nepal in a few weeks. More importantly, I needed something, *anything*, to distract me from the way my heart was breaking, even if it was just for a few hours.

I took a deep breath. "Same thing we always do when life sucks. Strap up and ride."

Chapter Twenty-Eight

TAHOE

"You sure you don't mind?" I asked Penna as we sat in front of her giant fireplace in her giant house with my giant broken heart. It had been two days since I walked out on Landon. The first night I'd spent at Leah's—the most logical place to go, but I knew if I stayed with her, Paxton would find out and tell Landon.

So we came up to the one place the other Renegades would never look for me—Penna's lake house in Tahoe.

"Not as long as you pass me one of those," she said, motioning to the bag of marshmallows in my pajama-clad lap. Best part of no boys? No makeup, hair up in knots, pajamas and slippers all around.

Leah passed the bag to her, taking one for herself, and we all roasted our fluffy white treats over the fire. It toasted, turning brown the longer I held it over the flames. Its once soft exterior hardened, forming a protective shell around what was becoming an overly tender center.

I dipped it lower with my skewer until the flames caught, catching the marshmallow on fire, then brought it out to watch the flames consume it. That was what happened when you got too close to the fire. It didn't matter that you'd already hardened—if you touched the flames, you got burned.

"Rachel?" Leah prompted.

I quickly blew out the marshmallow the way I wished someone could do for me—I still felt like my heart was on fucking fire. I spun my skewer, looking at the marshmallow from every angle. Sure, the flames were gone, but all that was left was a charred mess. The weight became too much for the blackened mess, and it slid down the skewer toward my hand, leaving its gooey insides a sloppy mess along the metal rod.

I wondered when I'd get to that stage—when I'd no longer be able to keep my emotions safely locked away.

"So, are you going to eat that, or…?" Penna asked.

I glanced over and saw both of them staring at me with faces like they expected a psychotic break at any moment.

"Nope," I said, wiping the marshmallow off with a paper towel. "It's ruined."

"Do you want to talk about it?" Leah asked softly. "You've been a locked box since you showed up at my door two days ago."

"Nope," I answered, reaching for another marshmallow.

"Oh, no, we're not going to help you torture harmless tasty treats," Leah said, snatching the bag away. "It's comfort food only."

I sighed and stretched my legs out to the side, close enough to the fire to feel the intense heat, but not close enough to burn myself.

That's what I should have done with Landon. Kept him just far enough away to keep the singe off me.

"Are you sure?" Penna asked, licking her fingers clean. "I'm a really good listener."

"I'm good," I promised.

"And I'll never tell them—the boys," she added.

"Seriously, I'm fine," I lied. "I don't need to talk about it. I just want to forget it all happened."

"The stuff with your dad? Or Landon?" Leah asked, knowing the barest basics of why I'd run.

"I don't want to talk about them," I reiterated.

"Okay," she said slowly.

I didn't even want to think about it. That just stirred up the feelings—the ones that felt like they were choking me in their need to be expressed, while my brain was shoving them back inside to stay sane. Sanity was good. It was safe.

"I mean, what good is talking about it going to do?" I asked, staring into the fire. "It's not going to take us back two years. It's not going to stop Landon from taking money from my dad to walk away from me. It's not going to change the fact that no matter what I do, I will never compare to the Renegades. I'll never be enough to be his number-one priority. Talking about it won't change the way it feels—like my soul is being shredded by a cheese grater."

"So you don't want to talk?" Penna asked.

"No!" I snapped, feeling the tightly reined tethers of my control slipping. "He took money for me! And what's worse—my father *paid* him. Is this the Middle Ages? Am I worth more than a cow and two pigs?"

"Technically, those went to the husband for taking you—" Penna said.

"He threw me away—us away—so that he could have his sponsorship, his dream. But he was *my* dream. He was all I wanted, and I'd given up everything for him. And Dad watched me cry. He held me together and helped me pack up what I'd unboxed in the apartment. He helped me take care of breaking the lease and getting into Dartmouth. He saw how heartbroken I was and said nothing. Nothing! Just assumed he knew what was best for me and then manipulated Landon out of my life."

"So you're more mad at your dad," Leah said, scooting close enough that our hips and shoulders touched.

"Yes!" I shook my head. "No. Dad offered Landon everything he wanted, so yeah, that fucking sucks, but it was Landon who took it, who walked away without so much as a backward glance."

"He looked backward," Penna said softly.

My narrowed gaze snapped to hers. "You're defending him?"

"What happened was shitty, and I can't defend what he did to you, but I know the pressure he was under. Our parents..." She sighed. "Our parents aren't all the Waltons. We are each other's family. Landon chose to protect his family."

"Just when I was starting to like you," I grumbled.

"He's my brother."

"I know. Sometimes I just wish that he'd let me in that close, to put us on that same level, and I don't think he ever will." I sucked in a breath as my chest tightened and closed my eyes against the prickle of tears. I could not cry over Landon. Never again.

"I have to go home tomorrow," Leah said after a few moments of silence. "It's Christmas Eve, and my parents will kill me if I don't show up."

"Of course," I told her, missing her already.

"Do you want to come with? There's plenty of room. Or you, Penna?" Leah offered.

Penna shook her head. "My parents are with Brooke, and I'm honestly okay with it. She needs them more than I do, and I kind of like the silence. It's perfect for not talking about the things you need to." She shot me a pointed look.

"I'm not talking about it."

She just nodded.

I looked at Leah's pleading eyes and nearly gave in. "No. I'm staying here with Penna like we planned. I can't see either of my parents right now. The phone call to tell them that I was safe was hard enough, let alone the dozen calls I've sent to voicemail from both of them. I mean, for fuck's sake, does everyone lie and cheat? Do any of us have a shot at a normal relationship?"

Leah bit her lip, and I wished I could take the words back.

"I mean, other than you and Wilder."

"No, totally. I knew what you meant. Just…you know, if you need to talk, you can call me at any point."

I shifted my gaze back to the fire, watching the flames dance and crackle. "No. I don't need to expose how fucking stupid I am—what an utter moron I must be to have fallen for him again."

"Rachel," Leah said softly.

I drew my knees to my chest and wrapped my arms around them to hold myself together. "I let him in. I knew I shouldn't, and I did anyway. Being with him felt so stupidly right, and I let myself get carried away by the trip, and the way he's always been able to *get* me, and the sex…God, the sex. And I let everything fool me into believing that maybe we had a shot, that we could make it."

"I still think you can," Penna said, picking at her cast.

"Seriously?"

"I think he's changed. Losing you…it altered him, and I think the Landon you love now wouldn't make that same choice."

"He hasn't changed." My voice broke, and the grief I'd tucked away reared its ugly head, consuming me in one swift wave. God, it hurt. Everything hurt.

"What do you mean?"

"Your contracts are up next month, so one call to my dad and there's even more money on the table if he'll just walk away again."

"You're shitting me," Penna said, sitting up straight.

"Nope, it's the truth. Dad outed him. The Renegades have been in negotiations for the sponsorship for months. What convenient timing, getting me to fall back in love with him just in time to play his trump card with my father."

"I didn't know," she promised softly, reaching over Leah to rest her hand on my arm. "I swear to God, I didn't know. I never would have let that happen."

"Oh my God, is that…is that why Pax brought you—us—on board?" Leah whispered in horror.

"I don't know. No matter what happens with Landon, I know that Wilder loves you, Leah. That is something I would bet my life on, so no matter what, you can't let this affect what you have. One of us deserves a happy ending."

"I'm going to fucking kill him," Penna seethed.

"Please…just…I don't want to talk about it. I don't want you to talk about it *with* him. Can we just have a quiet couple of weeks before we have to go back?"

"I'm glad you're still going," Leah said.

"He's taken everything from me…twice, and I can't let him take any more. I want to finish the trip, and now with all the shit going on with my parents, going to Korea feels more important than ever. So I can deal with the ship as long as Landon stays the hell away from me."

"We'll help you," Penna promised. "After I kill him. Sorry, I know you love him—"

"I don't love Landon now," I bristled. My heart screamed at the lie, and a sharp, physical pain ran through me. My eyes fluttered shut, and I leaned my forehead on my arms as I subtly rocked. How was I going to face him? "Losing him that first time nearly killed off my heart. I still don't know how I was able to fall for him again… How am I going to get through this?"

Leah wrapped her arm around my shoulder. "Just like we did before."

I rolled my head onto her shoulder as the first tears fell, streaking down my face to land on her shirt. "I need to hate him, and I do."

"I know." She rested her temple against the top of my head.

"It hurts so much more this time," I admitted on a sob.

"I know." She took my hand with hers. "It's going to be okay. All of it."

"Why can't I be enough for him?" I cried.

"You are. You are always enough. Once this passes, you'll see it, you just need to get through the worst of it, and there's no timeline for heartbreak. You of all people know that."

"This wasn't what I pictured, or how I planned. This wasn't how things were supposed to happen. Why did I let him in again?"

She tightened her arms around me. "Because love makes us do things we swear we'll never do."

I dragged another stuttered breath through my lungs, shaking my chest. "I don't want to love him."

"I know."

We left the rest unspoken, because uttering the words would have made me even more of an idiot. No matter how he'd hurt me, how obvious it was that I could never trust him, it didn't change the fact that even broken, bleeding, pretty damn pulverized, my heart still belonged to him. Traitorous bitch.

Chapter Twenty-Nine

RACHEL

AT SEA

I slammed my laptop shut. Another hour and we'd be out of internet range. I wouldn't have to worry about how to reply to Dad's emails, because it wouldn't be an option.

I thought I was protecting you. You shattered me.

I knew when he took the money that he'd never be good enough for you. Fair point, but would Dad have ever grown to like Landon if he'd turned it down? I'd never know.

I love you. You manipulated me.

You're the most important person in my life. Shit, he didn't even have Mom anymore, and that wasn't his fault.

I never should have interfered. But you did, and now I'm broken.

Please forgive me. Maybe one day. Just not now.

Now I was back aboard the *Athena*.

Two weeks and three days and two hours. That was

how long it had been since I'd set eyes on Landon. I was exceptionally proud of those two hours since we'd been back on board. I'd barred him from our room, which I knew could only last temporarily with all the Renegades running around.

"See Leah yet?" Penna asked, flipping through my adoption file and glancing at her laptop screen.

"No, she flew back with Wilder," I said, fidgeting with my highlighter. I hadn't talked to my best friend since that night in Tahoe, which was killing me. "See any of the others yet?"

Penna shook her head and chewed on her pen for a moment. "Nope. I needed the time away, and they understood that."

"As evidenced by the ten bajillion missed calls."

"Hey, I didn't see you answering any of Leah's once she got to Aspen."

"I didn't want to talk about Landon," I said with a shrug. *Or hear his voice in the background, or chance that he'd use Leah's phone to call me.*

"I didn't want to talk about stunts or the documentary."

Touché. I knew that Penna missed her Renegade family. Her self-imposed exile was taking a toll on her, but just like talking about Landon was off-limits for me, her distance from her team was where she drew the line.

There was a knock at the door, and I looked over from where Penna and I sat at the dining room table.

"I'll get it." Hugo sighed, having just restocked our coffee machine. "Hey, man," he said after he opened it. "Uh, any change on the status of letting Landon in?" he asked carefully.

Penna raised her eyebrows at me in question.

"Nope," I answered. "Not since he asked an hour ago."

"Are you sure?" Penna asked, looking up from her notes.

"Yes!" I snapped. "There will always be an excuse. Always some reason. I was stupid for listening in the first place."

She gave me that look—the one that told me she

thought I was being a moron—but I didn't care. I was in self-preservation mode, and if that meant I looked like an idiot to everyone because I wouldn't give him a chance to talk himself out of another bullshit lie, then fine. At least I was still breathing, still functioning.

"Sorry, dude," Hugo said, then shut the door. "Are you ever going to—?"

"Don't fucking start with me, Hugo." I waved a finger in his direction.

"Fine, but tomorrow's class is hands-on, so you can't get out of seeing him."

I shrugged. "Then at least I have today."

That was my motto since he'd crashed my world. I would handle everything one moment at a time. I could get through the next four days with Landon. Then we'd be in Hong Kong, and then I'd be leaving for Korea, and he'd be on his way to Nepal for a week. One whole week without trying to dodge him or constantly having to talk myself into staying put.

The problem with loving Landon was that it didn't stop just because I realized he'd never really loved me—that I'd always been a tool for him. No, I was that sad, sorry girl I always swore I would never be, itching to see him, desperate to hear his voice.

I wasn't avoiding him because I was pissed…well, partly. The main reason I couldn't see him was because I was terrified that I would melt with his first excuse and I'd find myself right back where I started—madly in love with the guy who only used me.

I was a lot of things, but a masochist wasn't on that list.

The sliding door opened, and my heart stuttered until I saw that it was Leah. Her hair was a little windblown and her cheeks pink beside a wide smile. For the slightest second I resented that she was so fucking happy, but then I shoved those evil little feelings far away. Out of all of us, Leah deserved a happy ending the most.

"There you are!" she said, running over to hug me.

"I missed you," I said as I squeezed her extra tight, wishing I didn't always have to share her with the enemy camp.

"Well, you wouldn't have if you would have picked up the phone any time in the last few days." She took the chair next to me and leaned back, folding her arms across her chest.

"Yeah, well…" I struggled for a moment and finally shook my head. "You know what, I don't have a good excuse. I just didn't want to hear his voice, or his excuses."

"Speaking of which, you don't have the whole story. You need to talk to Landon."

"Good luck on that," Penna muttered while typing something.

"Not interested," I said.

"He didn't know that they were renegotiating the Gremlin contract. Nick was handling it all, and Zoe told him that you weren't together, so Nick never thought it would be a conflict of interest."

I scoffed. "Yeah, and if you believe that, I have a gorgeous bridge to sell you."

"I'm serious, Rachel. Landon is devastated."

"Yeah, okay," I said sarcastically. "Landon is a master of lies when he needs to be."

"Paxton even told me—"

"Wilder lied to even get us on this ship, Leah. He's not at the top of my trustworthy list, either." My hand tightened around my highlighter, and I flipped the page of the textbook I was currently studying.

"Okay, well, he even called your dad."

My attention darted toward her. "Wilder?"

"Landon," she said with an exasperated hand flail.

"Oh, yeah? Did they discuss how much I was worth this time? I mean, I loved him more, so I should be worth more, right?"

"Holy shit, it's like trying to talk to a brick wall," Leah muttered.

I slammed my hands on the tabletop. "Landon lies! When will you realize that? That's all he's ever done to me. Lie and leave. It's what he's good at. I know you love Wilder, but you've known him for all of five months. I've known them for *years*."

"That's not entirely fair—" Penna interjected.

"He turned down the Gremlin offer!" Leah shouted.

A tiny kernel of hope flickered in my stomach. I squashed it mercilessly. "Right. If he actually did that, I'm sure he's just holding out for more money."

"Can't you believe me?" she asked.

"You, I will always believe. But no, I don't believe anything he says."

"Can't or won't?"

"Both. If I even open myself to the possibility, give him any benefit of the doubt..." I shook my head. "Look, I'm holding myself together by a thread. It's killing me to know that he's just down the damned hallway. Hell, I can't even sleep without him creeping into my dreams, and I can feel the madness, the heartbreak, the utter destruction hovering, waiting for me to break down and let it in. All I have is this tiny thread, and I'm not giving him the scissors. Or you—as much as I love you."

Her eyes and posture softened. "We can't talk about this, can we?"

"No," I said quietly, knowing I was drawing a line in our friendship that had never been there before.

She dropped her gaze to her lap, her eyes darting back and forth, which I knew meant she was weighing her options. Leah was nothing if not logical. Finally she looked up and forced a smile, but it was sad. "Okay. If that's what you need."

"It is."

She drew in a shaky breath. "Talk to your parents lately?" She forced out in an obvious change of subject.

Tension drained from my shoulders, but guilt quickly took its place. I hated shutting her out. She didn't deserve it.

"I saw my mom right before I flew out. It was…" Sad. Horrible. Frustrating. "…heartbreaking." She'd begged me to understand, but I couldn't. All I saw when I thought about either of them were a pair of liars. "Dad has sent a bunch of emails apologizing, but I can't get past my anger long enough to write him back. I understand his reasons—getting me back to Dartmouth and away from a guy he thought would break my heart—but all he did was break it that much faster."

"I'm sorry."

"Thanks. I'm so angry at them both, which is kind of ironic since I was adopted to save them from divorce the first time they thought about filing. Man, everything is just shit right now. Is there anything happy to talk about?"

"Maybe," Penna said, resting her air-casted leg on the chair in front of her. She'd lost the cast over Christmas break, but when the doc told her she should be okay to walk on it, she didn't believe him. She'd requested additional support, hence the air cast.

I hadn't said a single word to her about it. If she wanted to hide behind her injury, then who the hell was I to stop her? I'd blatantly hidden behind her all Christmas, knowing that her house was the one place they'd never look for me.

Funny how the one Renegade who had hated me ended up being my saving grace when shit went south.

"Please, fill my heart with sunshine," I said with more than a hint of sarcasm.

"Good. I think I may have found something. But don't get excited until I check it out. We don't exactly have a lot to go on."

By not a lot, she meant next to nothing. The only papers Dad had given me were the ones from the court at my adoption. The ones that didn't mention my name at birth, just that my birth mother's name was Seo-yun Jhang, which turned out to be one of the most popular names in Korea.

Not so helpful.

But it did have the one thing I needed: the name of her birthplace.

"Do you think you found it?" I asked.

She grimaced. "There's an orphanage there that did a heavy number of adoptions back when you were placed, but there's no guaranteeing that's it. It would be like assuming you lived your whole life in L.A., when in fact you live in New Hampshire most of the year while you go to Dartmouth."

"Right," I said, dropping my head into my hands.

"I'm not saying it's not possible," Penna reassured me.

I sighed. "It's a long shot, but I have to take it. It's the closest I'll ever be, and even if it's not where I was adopted from, then…"

"Then what?" Leah asked, squeezing my hand. "Will you feel like you did everything? Because that's what this is for, you feeling whole. Not the result."

I nodded. "I think so?"

She looked at me, watching for whatever sign she always used to see right through me. "Okay. Then I'll go with you."

"No. You have the Great Wall thing," I protested.

She shrugged. "Pax is always going to be jumping off something, revving some engine, or generally trying to get himself killed. You'll only have this happen to you once."

"Hell, maybe I'll go, too," Penna muttered.

"You're supposed to go with Landon," I countered.

"I thought you didn't care," Penna said, looking at me from over her laptop.

I played with the pen on the table in front of me. "I

don't want him to die. I want him to get his ridgeline. It's complicated."

"Love is weird," Penna said, her fingers furious on her keyboard.

"It generally sucks," I said.

"I've never been in love, so I'm not really qualified here," Penna said with a shrug.

"Never?" Leah questioned, her eyebrows nearly to her hairline.

"Nope. Never really had the opportunity," Penna clarified.

"Bullshit." I laughed. "I've never seen a woman who is surrounded by more beautiful men or more uninhibited opportunities to hook up with them."

She closed the laptop and leveled me with a single glance. "First, I worked my ass off to get where I am. I'm at the top of a men-only division, and I'm respected for my abilities and not just my ass. There's zero chance I'm going to give it up to any Renegade, or anyone who could open his mouth on the circuit and ruin my badassery. None."

"And second?" Leah asked, her eyes wide.

Penna sighed. "I've never met someone willing to fight past the anti-testosterone barrier Pax and Landon have around me. The guys are all too busy trying to impress them or beat them. That isn't exactly conducive to relationships."

"I'd never really thought about it that way," I told her. "I'm so sorry. As much as I hate what he's done to me, as much as it hurts, I wouldn't change it."

Penna gave me sad smile. "That's because you still love him."

"I do." There was no point lying to her or myself. "But that doesn't mean I'll ever give him the chance to do it again. This time is worse than the first, which is something I didn't think I was capable of surviving. And the funny thing is that it doesn't hurt. I'm just…numb. It's like I'm in shock, and my body isn't willing to admit that it's somehow breathing without a heartbeat. If I just keep moving then it will be okay, but eventually the rest of me is going to catch on."

"I know the evidence is damning, but the whole thing with sponsorships is so complicated—" Penna stopped midsentence when my glare cut her off. "Got it."

"Let's talk about something else, anything else," I suggested. It didn't matter how much I loved these girls—I wasn't up for spilling my guts any more than I already had.

"Want to pick out a new teapot in Hong Kong?" Leah offered.

"Those are for when we get through the shit in our lives. Not while we're in the middle of it."

She squeezed my hand. "I have the utmost faith that you will."

I was glad one of us did.

• • •

"Rachel." Landon sighed my name like he'd seen a ghost or something.

"Don't," I said as I slid into my seat in Civ.

"Please," he begged quietly.

Be strong. I looked over at him and did my best to mask any physical reaction I had to seeing him. He'd lost a little weight, but nothing to be concerned about. After all, his first priority was his sport, not my broken heart. But his eyes, those gorgeous hazel orbs that I had lost myself in too many times, were haunted. They reflected every ounce of pain I hadn't let myself feel.

"I'm stuck here in this class with you for the next month, and there's nothing I can do about that. But the least you can do is not make it hard on me to pull good grades. If you want to talk to me, fine, we'll talk later. But please don't make me feel like I have to skip class and avoid you. That's not fair, considering I did nothing wrong."

His shoulders slumped, and he nodded. "That's fair."

"Thank you."

Dr. Messina took the podium and began our lecture, saving me from the potential disaster of communicating any more with Landon. Maybe he had it right the first time—it was easier to walk away when you didn't have to see the person every day.

One by one we stood, presenting our small papers comparing and contrasting two of the cultures we'd been studying. I took copious notes, doing my best to concentrate anywhere but on Landon sitting next to me. On his eyes that watched every time I flipped the page in my notebook. On his hands that flexed on the desk like he had to keep himself from reaching for me.

Good job not noticing.

I presented and managed to keep my eyes locked on our professor, who sat in the back of the room. That effort alone deserved an A. When Landon spoke, I focused on my notepad and definitely did *not* listen to his comparison involving the Dani tribe and their courting rituals.

I did not think about the way I'd started to feel like he was my forever.

I did not remember his hands on my body.

Slamming my notebook closed, I got the hell out of there as soon as she dismissed class.

"Rachel!" Landon called down the hallway.

"You okay?" Hugo asked.

"I'm fine," I assured him as I stopped. "Go ahead."

He looked skeptical but left me in the hallway like I'd asked. Students walked around me, all headed to their various classes as I stood like a rock in a rushing stream, blocking the flow.

"Hey, can we talk?" Landon asked.

"Sure." I hardened every single defense I could muster against him and followed him into an empty classroom. He shut the door behind us, and I held my books in front of me like they could shield my heart from whatever he was going to throw at me next.

He put his on the desk. *Probably because he knows he has nothing to fear from me.*

I'd never been the one to dish out the deathblows in our relationship.

"What can I do for you?" I asked.

He leaned back against the desk closest to the door. "Talk to me."

"Okay, well, how is the Nepal trip coming? Do you have it all mapped out? Weather check? I've heard it's snow season, so I'm a little skeptical, but hey, it's your dream, so I'm all for it."

"Seriously? You want to talk about Nepal?"

"I don't really want to talk. But you do, so I'm obliging you. Talk away."

"Look. I didn't know about the sponsorship deals. As far as I knew, we'd already killed the Gremlin contract, but Nick didn't know. He was the one negotiating on our behalf. I would *never* agree to take any amount of sponsorship money to keep me away from you—"

"But you did," I interrupted softly. My voice was flat, the byproduct of the blessed numbness that still gripped my heart. "That's exactly what you agreed to the first time we tried this."

His eyes closed in pain, like I'd just wounded him. "I know. You have no idea how sorry I am—how much I regret that decision."

"I don't."

"You what?" He leaned forward.

"You leaving me like that led me to Leah, which in turn led her to Wilder. I can't regret any role I had in that, no matter how badly it hurt. I can't regret seeing your true colors."

"Rachel."

"I only regret that I didn't pay close enough attention, that I let my guard down again when I already knew what you were. Everything that happened the first time—that's on you. And we've been through it so many times that I'm just sick of thinking about it. The fact that you did it for money..." I shrugged. "I could have gotten over it if you'd just told me."

"I was so scared of losing you." His voice strained, emotion bleeding from him in a way I couldn't let myself feel.

"Ironic, since you lost me by not telling me," I replied.

"Did I? Did I lose you?"

"You sold me to my father, Landon." The reality of it struck me as I said it, and I felt the first crack in the ice around my heart. *Keep it together.*

"Not this time. I didn't. The first time I fucked up, but I didn't make the same mistake. I promise. You have to believe me." He stood and crossed the distance between us. I flinched when he took my face between his palms but didn't protest.

That simple contact broke through my numbness, and as though someone had melted the ice with a flamethrower, my heart burned, and it *hurt*.

My eyes fluttered shut against the onslaught of agony, my body reaching for his, unable to recognize that he was the cause of the pain.

"Rachel, please. I know this is bad, but we are so good together. Fate, destiny, whatever you want to call it—you're my infinity, my always. Tell me what I have to say to make this right. Tell me what to—"

"There's nothing," I said quietly, opening my eyes to see his locked on me. "Maybe that's why this hurts so damn much now, seeing you and knowing that we'll never be *us* again. I love you. I think there's a huge possibility that I will always love you. And that doesn't make me feel good. I don't feel cherished, or respected, or loved. I feel stupid. You make me feel small and insignificant, and that's not something I'm okay with."

"No. God, no," he said, shaking his head. "You are—"

"Stop," I begged in a harsh whisper as my eyes prickled. "Just stop. I can't hear another word out of your beautiful mouth. Or maybe I can. Maybe the problem is that I can stand here and talk to you because I've already come to the conclusion that it doesn't matter what you want to tell me. There's nothing you can say that will *ever* make me trust you again."

He sucked in his breath, his eyes watering just like mine were.

"So let's just agree to stop this. Stop hurting each other. Because there can always be love—it's foolishly blind—but one thing I've learned from my parents is that relationships can't exist without trust."

I stepped out of his hands, the separation feeling more than physical.

"I love you," he argued.

I smiled sadly as a single tear escaped down my cheek. "That's what makes this so much harder, Casanova. I almost believe you."

For the first time since I'd met him, he let me walk away without a fight.

Chapter Thirty

Well, this plan was better in conception than execution.

How did I not think to bring a book? I'd already been trapped in here the last half hour, and I was going to go out of my mind if I had to stay here much longer with only my thoughts for company.

I checked my watch. She would board any minute now.

Pray she doesn't have to use the bathroom.

I looked in the bathroom mirror, noting my bloodshot eyes and pale complexion. Good thing I'd managed to ditch the cameras. That had been the hardest part about arranging this whole damn thing—getting Bobby off my back.

This had to work. I was out of fucking options if it didn't.

"Holy shit, a private plane?" I heard Rachel's voice and tensed.

She's here. My breath suddenly came in harsh bursts, and

I grabbed the soft hand towel off the rack, covering my nose and mouth to muffle the sounds. I was always shit at hide-and-go-seek.

"I just asked Pax to get us there," Leah said, her voice slightly nervous.

"I'm not sure I'll ever get used to the amount of money those guys drop."

"They're insane, right?" Leah asked.

"If you ladies will take your seats, we'll begin takeoff procedures," the flight attendant told them, his voice calm. At least he knew I was hidden in the damn bathroom.

Of every way I'd ever tried to talk to Rachel, this had to be the most insane. She was also the only woman worth going to this length for. I refused to lose her. Not after everything that we'd been through. If I couldn't make her listen, I'd make her see.

If she didn't beat the shit out of me first.

Which is feasible considering it's Rachel.

"We're almost ready for you," the flight attendant whispered through the door.

"Thank you," I whispered back.

My heart jumped as I heard rustling in the cabin. I pressed my ear against the door and listened. This was by far the stupidest shit I'd ever pulled, or the most epic. Only Rachel could decide.

"You in good and tight?" Leah asked.

"Yep, I'm good," Rachel answered.

"Good! So, I know this feels totally out of the blue, but you'll understand in a minute."

"What—?"

"When I was on Mykonos with Pax, his mom said something to me. She told me that even love couldn't stitch together two souls that were too stubborn to bend."

"I'm sorry? What the hell are you talking about?"

"Okay. Um. I'm saying *bend*. Remember that I love you, and that anything I do is always with your best interest at heart."

"Leah…"

I almost laughed at the slight growl I heard in Rachel's voice.

"Remember when I didn't want to come on this to start with? And you told me that I had to step outside my comfort zone?"

"Seriously. What's going on?"

I heard the sound of a buckle coming undone. "Consider this me telling you the same. And you know…if it doesn't work out right, then I can just hop the next flight."

"What? Where are you going? Why are you leaving? Leah, I'm going to Korea, not the freaking grocery store! You can't just hop over—"

"I love you!" Leah called out. "Bend!"

"What?" Rachel shrieked. "How am I stuck? What the hell?"

I heard the sound of the door closing, sealing the fuselage.

"You can't close that door! We're not leaving without her!"

"I'm sorry, miss. I'm under direct orders."

Then there was silence as the plane rumbled down the runway.

"Are you fucking kidding me?" Rachel screamed.

That was my cue.

As the plane increased speed for takeoff, I passed the small couch in the back of the private plane and made it to the groupings of single seats that faced each other, using the seat backs as leverage. Fuck, we were going fast.

"Landon!" Rachel hissed as I took the seat opposite hers and buckled in. "What are you doing? We're taking off!"

"If walking down the center aisle of a plane while it's

taking off was the most dangerous thing I did, I'd be out of a job," I told her calmly.

Her eyes flashed fire at me. "You'd better explain. Fast. I'm not in favor of being kidnapped, and if you think I'm headed to Nepal with you, you're out of your goddamned mind."

I smiled. "God, I missed angry you. You're so beautiful when you're pissed."

"Oh, then I'm about to be fucking gorgeous," she promised as we lifted off. "I can't believe you would do something as low as this."

"We're not going to Nepal," I told her softly.

Her eyes swung toward mine, wide and cautious. "I'm sorry?"

"We're not going to Nepal," I repeated.

She swallowed, and her hands finally stopped fidgeting with her buckle. Then she sat back in her seat and raised an eyebrow.

My Rachel was back.

"We're going to Korea. I have the itinerary; the arrangements are all made."

"You hijacked Wilder's private plane to take me to Korea?"

My hackles bristled. "It's not Pax's plane. I chartered it for you, since I don't like him taking care of what's mine."

"How very alpha of you. Do you turn at the full moon, too?" She crossed her arms in front of her chest.

"Maybe. When it comes to you, all bets are off, and I wouldn't put it past you to bring out any sort of tendency in me."

She cracked a begrudging smile, and I almost fist pumped.

"You told me that nothing I could say would ever make you trust me again," I started, and my heart jumped into my suddenly dry throat.

"I did."

"You also told me that you still love me."

Her eyes dropped before they slowly returned to mine. "I did," she repeated in a softer voice.

"You're correct. There's nothing I can say to you that's going to make you trust me. I lost that right years ago. I realize that now, that while you've loved me these last couple of months, while we've been together, you've never fully trusted me, otherwise you would have listened to me when your dad dropped his little funding bombshell."

She remained silent, but she didn't scream at me, so I counted that as a point scored.

"I did that. I lost your trust, and though I won your heart back, I never worked on the trust factor. So I'm done telling you to trust me. I'm done telling you that I love you, that I need you, that you're the only priority in my life. I'm going to show you instead."

Her eyes widened slowly. "It's too late."

"No, it's not. For a love like ours, too late is when we're dead. It doesn't matter how many years pass, you and I will always be drawn to each other, we'll always find our way back. We'll always have this between us. I'm not sure about you, but I'm not prepared to live my life like that, always wanting you, craving you, and not having you. That kind of life is bullshit."

"What do you recommend?" she asked, not giving away a damn thing. Just once, I wished that she'd wear her emotions instead of hiding them away like a weakness. But then she wouldn't be Rachel.

And I loved Rachel just how she was—stubborn and hard-shelled with a soft-as-caramel center.

"I can tell you that I called your dad from Aspen and told him to fuck off—that he could stick his sponsorship deal up his ass. That there's no amount of money that can buy you from me."

"Landon," she whispered, her body sinking farther into the seat.

"But I knew when we talked on the ship, that wouldn't be enough. It wouldn't be enough for me to tell you that I liquidated most of my savings with Wilder to finance the rest of the year, since we lost every sponsor that we had."

Her mouth dropped slightly.

"It wouldn't be enough for me to tell you that I was sorry, that I was a stupid kid when I took the deal the first time. You think you weren't enough to hold me, that I needed more—that I needed the Renegades. But that wasn't the full reason. I'm sorry I made choices for you that I had no right to, but it was because I felt that I wasn't good enough for you. You, who risked everything for me—turning down Dartmouth, walking away from the Renegades, your parents, everything you knew. I couldn't let you walk away from an Ivy League education, from the life I knew you deserved—not when I had just lost my sponsorship and had no way to even take care of you. Your dad offered me a way to fix everything that I'd broken. All I saw was a way to give everyone back what they lost…except me. I put my heart in a box and became a shell until I found you again."

She looked away, and I forged ahead, knowing I had to drive it home, that I couldn't go halfway with Rachel. She demanded everything, because that's what she gave.

"I knew it wouldn't be enough to tell you these things, that I will walk away from this life if it's what you need to believe that there's nothing more important to me than you."

Her eyes jerked back to mine, widening with each word I spoke.

"So I'm showing you. I canceled Nepal."

"Landon, no." She shook her head softly, just enough to move her hair.

"Yes. There is nowhere else on this earth that I'd rather

be than here with you, and this is the only way I could think to prove it to you."

Watching her walls crumble was beautiful. Her mouth softened along with her eyes. But with the fortress down, I saw the pain there, how much I'd put her through.

"I don't…" She shook her head and then rested her forehead in her palm for a moment while she composed herself. "This is all…amazing, Landon. But I don't know if I can trust you again."

I ignored the stabbing pain in the vicinity of my heart and nodded. "I get that. And I'm going to spend every moment of the rest of my life proving that you can. From now on you are my only priority. Everything else comes second. I'd rather have one of your kisses than win any competition, free ride any mountain, or even have a Renegade name. I'm yours to do with what you will."

Her teeth sank into her lower lip, and I would have given everything else I had to kiss it free, to show her with my body how perfect we were for each other, how nothing else would ever compare.

"And you're not kidnapped," I told her with a small laugh. "The pilot is under your command. Wherever you want to go, we'll go, which includes turning the plane around and leaving me in Hong Kong while you head to Seoul."

She tilted her head like she was considering it, and I almost regretted those words. But I was done making decisions for her. I needed her to choose me just as badly as she needed to be able to trust me.

"But I'd really like to do this with you," I requested softly.

It felt like eons while she weighed her options, but I sat there quietly and waited. I'd learned my lesson when it came to pushing Rachel.

Finally, she looked at me and lifted her chin slightly.

"Okay. You can come."

Every muscle in my body relaxed as I sank back against the seat. "Okay."

She gave me a tentative smile. "And thank you. For the plane. For arranging it all when you didn't have to."

Of course I'd arranged it. I wanted to see where my future wife had been born, the place she'd spent her earliest months. But I also knew she wasn't ready for that future, not now... maybe not for years. I knew it with the same certainty that told me she was the only woman I would ever love, ever need enough to give up everything—even the Renegades—for.

So I swallowed back the giant ball of emotions too numerous to be named and nodded. "Anything for you."

I just prayed she knew that I meant it.

Chapter Thirty-One

RACHEL

KOREA

"Are you sure this is right?" I asked, the giant map taking over most of my view of the rural road. We were about an hour outside Seoul, which meant we were close. Supposedly.

"Nope." His answer was way too chipper. "Penna supplied the directions, and she could be getting back at me for any myriad of transgressions."

I snorted. "Great. You just watch out for mudslides, and I'll try to figure out where we're at."

He leaned over the steering wheel of the little SUV. "Blue skies, bright sun, no rain, no mud. We're in the clear."

"You forget," I said, trailing my finger down the skinny line of the road on the map. "You're traveling with the curse."

He swerved onto the shoulder and hit the brakes.

"For fuck's sake, Landon!" I shouted, catching myself on the dash even though my seat belt locked me into place.

He ripped the map down, more furious than I'd ever seen him. "Enough! You're not a damned curse."

I rolled my eyes at his bluster. "Maybe *we're* the curse."

His hands flexed on the wheel, and he took a deep breath, his eyes showing an unspoken battle.

Then he lurched across the console, grasped the back of my head, and pulled me into his kiss. His mouth opened over mine, his tongue demanding entrance, and in my surprise, I gave it to him.

Two seconds later, I melted, unable to resist the effect he had on my body, my heart. He kissed me breathless, until my tongue was as wild in his mouth as his was in mine, until I clutched the fabric of his shirt in my fists.

Then he let me go.

I blinked at him, dazed and more than a little turned on.

"Does that feel cursed?" he asked.

I touched my fingers to my lips. "Sometimes."

He sighed in exasperation.

"Sometimes I hate the control you have over my body, the way I melt for no one else but you. But no, it's not a curse."

He relaxed in his seat, checked the mirrors, and pulled back onto the empty road. "Well, okay then."

I hid my smile with the map and shook my head. As much as I hated loving him, it was pretty much a foregone conclusion in my life. And as much as I didn't trust him, I also couldn't ignore that he'd given up Nepal for me.

He'd been right—showing me was the only way he could earn that trust back.

And he was doing a damn good job of it.

"Left up there," I told him after I figured out just where we were on the map.

He made the turn, and we were on an even more rural road, had that been possible. The hills rose up across the fields from us, but I saw the outline of a town ahead.

"You ready for this?" he asked.

"No," I answered truthfully. "But it seems like it would be a shame to turn around and go home at this point."

"Truth."

My stomach tied itself in knots as we crossed the river and entered the small town. Everything was gray, but I didn't know if that was normal or a consequence of the cold January weather.

We passed through a small, thriving part of town, Landon's head moving constantly as he drove—taking everything in. "There's a hotel there," he said.

"How can you tell?" I asked, unable to see where he was gesturing to.

"It says 'Hotel.'"

"Smart-ass," I muttered, but it brought a much-needed smile to my face.

A few more turns, and I was genuinely ready to puke. What the hell was I thinking? What was I going to do? Walk up to the door and assume they spoke English? That they'd have any idea what I was talking about? That this was the one-in-a-hundred chance that the same orphanage in the town my biological mother was born in would be the same orphanage I was adopted from?

"You've gone silent. That's never a good sign," Landon commented.

We came upon a large, gray building on the right-hand side. "That should be it," I said, matching it to the picture Penna had printed out for us.

Landon pulled the SUV over and parked but didn't shut off the engine. I cranked the heat, my hands suddenly cold.

He reached for them and warmed the digits between his palms. "What do you need?"

"I don't have the first clue."

"You don't have to do this today. We can fly back

tomorrow afternoon and still make the boat. If you need time, I can give you that."

I shook my head. "I didn't come this far to chicken out." My hand sought the door handle, and I pulled, a rush of frigid air hitting my face.

"Do you want me to wait here?" Landon asked.

My booted feet hit the pavement, and I looked at him watching me with no expectation, just overwhelming support. "Come with me?"

He immediately shut off the engine and got out of the car, locking it as he made his way over to me. I took the hand he offered and squeezed, needing something solid.

He opened a metal gate that was the only opening in a three-foot-tall stone wall, and we walked inside the small yard. There were no toys that would mark this as an orphanage, but there were two uniformed teenage girls sitting on a bench toward the back, their heads bent over a book.

One of the girls looked up as we approached the door, and I had the weirdest chill slide down my back—like I was looking at an alternate timeline where I'd never left. A timeline where I spoke Korean and grew up surrounded by girls exactly like me. A timeline where I'd never met Landon.

In every timeline. His comment from the courting ritual hit me, and I squeezed his hand a little harder as we ascended the half dozen stone steps that would bring us to the door.

He lifted my hand and kissed the back.

My breath caught, my heartbeats slowed, and the world around me paused as I crossed the last foot to the door. I lifted my hand to knock on the door but lowered it, looking at Landon. "Do I look okay?"

He smiled and tucked a strand of my purple highlights behind my ear. "You look perfect. You are perfect. And no matter what happens here, I know exactly where you belong—with me."

I sucked in a full breath of air, turned to the door, and knocked three times.

My heart raced, slamming against my ribs as the door opened a few seconds later.

An older woman with graying hair answered. She was a little shorter than I was, but not by much, but that didn't affect the authoritarian way she held herself. She looked at us expectantly.

"Um. Hi. Do you speak English?" I asked.

She scoffed. "Do you speak Korean?"

My mouth snapped shut. "If I spoke Korean, I would have," I said softly.

"You look Korean."

"I'm American." The moment it left my mouth, I realized the significance—the difference. Though I might physically resemble this woman and those girls, my culture, my language, my habits were from a world away.

Her sigh was loud and exasperated. "Then it is a good thing I speak English."

I nodded, and Landon wrapped his arm around my waist. It was only then that I realized I'd been shaking. "I know this sounds crazy, but is this an orphanage?"

She shook her head. "No."

My stomach sank, and a bitter taste filled my mouth. All of this effort, and now...nothing. "Oh." Landon's grip on me tightened, and I leaned on him. I forced a smile to my lips. "Well, thank you. I'm sorry to have bothered you."

We turned and heard her shift behind us.

"But it used to be. It was converted into a girls' school in late 2000."

I spun back to her. "Were you here when it was an orphanage?"

She nodded. "I am headmistress now, but I have been here through every incarnation."

I smiled, a laugh bubbling up with the hope that filled me. "I know this is a long shot, but my mother was born in this town, and I was adopted. I was hoping maybe you could tell me if it was from here."

Her eyes narrowed, darting from Landon to me. "What is your name?"

"I don't know the name I had when I was here."

She sighed again with the same exasperation. I would have bet a million dollars that she was tough as nails as a headmistress. "What is it now, American girl?"

"Rachel. Rachel Dawson."

Her eyes widened, and she reached for the doorframe to steady herself. "Rachel?"

"Yes, ma'am." A feeling bigger than myself crept in, invading every cell until I knew I stood on the edge of something I could not yet comprehend.

"You should come in," she said softly.

I looked up at Landon, and he nodded.

"You know who I am," I said to the older woman.

She nodded. "You're Seo-yun's girl."

The tea in front of me was cooling quickly.

Landon sat across from me at the small kitchen table. It was scratched from years of use but still in usable condition and well cared for, which accurately described everything in the building around us.

He watched me carefully but didn't push. He knew me well enough to leave me alone with my thoughts. I knew *him* well enough to know he needed to be let in.

"I can't believe she lived here," I said quietly. Had she done dishes at that sink? Sat at this table? In this chair? Had she worn the same uniforms as the girls outside?

"You lived here," he added, sipping his tea from a handleless cup.

"I lived here."

"You did," Mrs. Rhee said as she came in the door with a file box in her arms. Landon rushed to take the box from her, and she nodded her thanks as he put it on the small table next to the door. "That's all I have left of Seo-yun's things," she told me as she took the seat next to me. "She would want you to have them."

"Thank you," I told her, prying my eyes away from the box. "It's more than I ever could have asked for."

She nodded, openly studying me. "You have her eyes, the set of her chin. Do you have her sharp tongue?"

A smile played at my lips. "Yes. I think I do."

"Good. I don't remember every baby, you know. Not from those days."

"How did you know I was her daughter?" I asked, trying my best to be patient. I felt like I'd found a well of information, but I didn't want it a bucket at a time—I wanted to drink from the waterfall.

"Your mother," she said, looking out the window at the girls who still sat on the bench outside. "She was an orphan. Never adopted, though. She came when I began working here. I was only twenty-five." She smiled, lost in her memory. "She was a bright child, hated rules—hated anyone smothering her spirit. By the time she was eighteen, she had moved to Seoul. I was happy for her, to see her success. But she came home less than a year later, in labor with you."

Mrs. Rhee tilted her head, and her forehead puckered as she remembered. "It was raining, and her time was so close that we could not get her to the hospital. We called for a doctor and delivered you in a bedroom upstairs. It was…long. Difficult." She looked back at me like she was searching my face for signs of my mother. "You were small for a baby. Early,

I think."

"And then she went back to Seoul?" I asked, then cursed myself silently. Maybe it was best that I didn't know. But I was here. I had to ask every question I could think of, because I would never get this chance again.

Mrs. Rhee shook her head sadly. "She died two weeks later. Blood poisoning, they said."

"Sepsis," Landon said softly.

Mrs. Rhee nodded. "Yes. But she loved you."

My gaze went back to the box on the floor. She was dead. Not that I'd ever been on a mission to find her, but now that mission would never be possible. It felt as though someone had opened a window in a room I thought previously solid, only to find the view was of a brick wall.

The conflicting emotions gave me whiplash.

My mother hadn't given me up because she was too young, or unwed—though she'd been both. It hadn't been a cultural dictate, or a personal choice. She'd never been given the option to raise me.

Something about that both killed me—knowing that I would never know more—and yet gave me a sense of peace. I wasn't unwanted. I'd been loved from the moment I was born, and when my mother could no longer love me, Mom and Dad stepped in and carried through.

"Did she ever mention my father?" I asked.

Mrs. Rhee's eyebrows rose. "She described him as someone who was never meant to stay."

My hands cupped the now chilly teacup. "And then my parents came? Adopted me? I know I was really young."

"You were. It was the fastest I have ever handed a child over—yet another reason I remembered you. But I placed a call the day after your mother died, and you were gone soon after."

"And now you're a girls' school, not an orphanage?"

"Now we educate young women, some of whom are orphans, but we no longer care for babies here." She glanced up at the clock and gave me a tight smile. Our time was limited.

My brain scrambled, trying to think of anything to ask. A thousand questions went through my mind, but they all seemed trivial, and everything about this woman told me she didn't have time for trivial.

"How is your funding?" Landon asked.

Her brows lifted in surprise. "We can always use more."

"I'll see that you get it," he promised.

She inclined her head but made no other response.

"What was she like, my mother?" I couldn't help but ask.

Her features softened, and she reached for my hand. "A lot like you. But something tells me you are a lot stronger. She would be proud of your courage in coming here, happy that your parents have cared for you so well." Her eyes dropped to the table and then back to mine. "Your mother—your American mother—was so overjoyed to hold you. Scared, but I remember thinking that you would be okay."

I swallowed, emotion clogging my throat. "I am. I'm okay. I have a wonderful family." *That's currently falling apart.*

"Good. She never would have done that to her hair, though." She motioned to my highlights, and I smiled.

A young girl came through the door speaking rapid-fire Korean, which Mrs. Rhee answered.

"I'm so sorry," Mrs. Rhee told us. "I am needed with the girls. Have you gotten what you came for?"

"Yes," I said, my eyes flickering back to the box. "More, really."

We said our good-byes, and I tried to memorize every detail about the house, the yard, even the street as Landon loaded the box into the back of the SUV. I grabbed my camera from the front seat and started snapping dozens of pictures.

"Do you want to stay for the night?" he offered as I

photographed the house.

"No," I said quietly, lowering the camera. "I don't think there's anything more here for me. Do you think we can make it back to the *Athena*?"

He glanced at his watch. "It will be late, but we can make it."

"Let's go," I said, taking one last look at my birthplace. He kissed my forehead and helped me into my seat. With my nerves scraped raw, it made me feel cared for, cherished.

I was quiet on the drive, and Landon filled the silence with music, occasionally lifting my hand to kiss the back of it. He gave me the quiet and the space I needed while my mind spun in circles.

He took care of everything—made every arrangement as we returned the SUV and headed to the plane. No security. No TSA. Just Landon, me, and the box that carried the ghost of the woman who gave me life but whom I would never know.

I buckled my belt and held his hand as we took off, the plane lurching into the sky to carry us back to the *Athena*.

"How do you feel?" he asked, finally breaking the silence once we'd reached cruising altitude.

"Like me," I said, meeting his worried gaze. "Like me, but somehow more."

He brushed my hair back and kissed my forehead tenderly. "What can I do?"

"Can you grab the box?" I asked. "I kind of want to go through it now. If not, it might sit there until I think I'm brave enough to open it, and that will have made the trip feel like a waste."

"Sure thing," he said, unbuckling. "Why don't you come back here? There's more room."

I unbuckled and followed him, sitting on the floor in front of the small couch.

"Ready?" he asked.

I nodded and rose up on my knees to undo the folded sides that kept the box closed. A quick pull and it was open.

I filled my lungs with a deep breath and dived in. There were a handful of CDs, mostly Korean pop that I didn't recognize, but some American Top 40, too. A few items of clothing that told me my mother had been shorter than I was, a bracelet and a colorful blanket laid on top of two smaller boxes. I took out one of the boxes and removed the stuffing to reveal its ceramic treasure.

My throat closed, and my hands shook as I examined the small, smooth porcelain.

"It's beautiful," Landon said.

"It's a teapot." I laughed. It couldn't have been more perfect in its simplicity, with its long, straight handle and light green shine.

"I guess you're more alike than Mrs. Rhee realized." He took it from me, and I reached for the last box.

It held only a small envelope with a handful of pictures. My birth mother stared back at me with a smile and my eyes, happiness emanating from her as she leaned against a bridge that overlooked what I assumed was Seoul. She couldn't have been more than seventeen.

By my age, she'd already died.

There were a few more just like it in different places in the city, and she looked equally happy in all of them. "She was beautiful," I whispered.

"Just like her daughter," Landon answered, sitting closer to look at the pictures with me.

I flipped to the last one and my breath abandoned me.

She was held in the arms of a soldier—an American soldier. *He wasn't meant to stay.* Mrs. Rhee's words were on repeat in my head as I stared at her face—and his. They looked so happy, wrapped in each other—it was so right and so wrong all in the same picture.

"Rach…" Landon said, peering closer. "Oh my God. Isn't that…?"

Eyes I knew as well as my own stared back at me, and I was immediately thankful we'd skipped dinner, because I knew it all would have come back up. My finger brushed across the DAWSON name tag just above my birth mother's hand on the army uniform.

"My dad."

Chapter Thirty-Two

LANDON

LOS ANGELES

I rubbed my scratchy eyes. Jet lag was fucking killing me. I glanced at my watch and then blinked. I'd forgotten to set it back to L.A. time, and it was still reading like we were in Japan. We'd only been gone three weeks — just long enough to finish out the term and all but one final a week early. Our Civ papers were turned in, but we had to do a Skype presentation for our final grade.

It was the only way the Study at Sea faculty would agree to the time off we needed for the X Games. We'd asked for ten days. They'd agreed to seven. Like I was in any shape for the Games. I'd counted on the Nepal trip to keep my physical edge, but I would never regret the trip I'd taken with Rachel in its place.

It had been the last time I'd seen her seminormal.

The moment she'd put the pieces together — that her dad was hers biologically — she'd withdrawn. She wasn't sad, or angry, or sarcastic—she was simply gone. Even sitting in the car next to her now as we drove toward her parents' house, she was lost in her own thoughts.

I couldn't blame or push her. It wasn't like I knew the appropriate time to let her process a bombshell that big, but two weeks seemed about right. And since I knew she'd asked for both of her parents to meet her at their house, I figured the shit was about to hit the fan.

So I did what had become my usual these last two weeks—picked up her hand and kissed the inside of her wrist. "Want to talk about anything before we get there?"

She shook her head.

"I wish you would. It's killing me to watch you go through this and not lean on anyone. Leah says you haven't talked to her, and Penna says the same. I feel like you're this bottled-up stick of dynamite that's going to blow at any minute, and I wish you would talk to me."

Even if she blew up on me, it was better than the silence, than being locked out of her head. I had zero clue of what she was thinking. Was she still pissed at me? Still doubting me? Was she just biding her time so she could walk away from me for good? Was all the progress we'd made just in my own head?

She looked over and forced a flat smile, but her eyes softened. How was it possible to miss someone so much when they sat right next to you? Fear ran down my spine, cold and unwelcome. What if this was her way of walking away?

"I don't know what to say to them," she said with a shrug. "I've gone over so many options, and none of them seem to fit. I'm not mad. Okay, maybe a little mad about the lie, but I'm mostly sad that there's this whole history that I didn't know, that they didn't think I was capable of hearing."

"Have you ever kept a secret?" I asked as we turned into her neighborhood.

"Sure," she answered. "More than my fair share of secrets

involved you," she added with an arched eyebrow.

My heart leaped at the show of spirit—of *my* Rachel shining through. "Okay, we're a great example. At first, we kept us a secret because it would hurt Pax, right?"

"Right."

My gaze dropped to her lips as I remembered those days, the stolen moments, the times I kissed her while my best friend was waiting for her in the next room. Now I had her, but it felt like she had one foot out the door…as usual, and that fucking terrified me. Add that to the fact that I was delivering her to the lion's den, where her father had successfully ripped us apart not just once, but twice, and I was ready to vomit.

"Eventually the biggest problem with keeping the secret was that we'd kept it for so long. It was no longer about the fact that we were in love, that I'd craved you since the first time I saw you standing with your dad at the Gremlin booth at the Tahoe Open. The issue was that every day we didn't tell added to our sins until they compounded and gained interest."

"You think they didn't tell me because they'd kept the secret for too long already?"

"I think that it's worth the thought." We pulled into her driveway, and the car rocked to a stop. *Too soon. I haven't had enough time with her.* I wanted to pull her into my arms and kiss away the confusion on her face, the uncertainty that clouded her eyes, but we hadn't crossed any sexual lines since Fiji, and I knew she had to be the one to make the first move.

Maybe it was wrong, or selfish, but I needed her to need me, too. Needed her to depend on me, rely on me, to trust that I would be her safe place if the world went to shit. *Trust. Ha. That's funny.* I even sounded sarcastic to myself.

"When does your flight leave for Aspen?" she asked.

"When you're ready," I answered.

"What? You can't wait on me. I have no idea how long it will take to feel like I can leave."

I shrugged. "I'm not going without you."

She downright glared at me, and I wanted to sing with the joy of it. "And what happens when you miss your events? When you don't win the prize money you need because you turned down Gremlin's terms?"

Unable to stop my hand, I brushed my knuckles against the soft skin of her cheek, savoring the contact. "You're not a term."

"Landon, I'm being serious."

"I am, too. What happens if you need me and I'm not here? I promised you that you are my priority, and I meant it. I'm here while you deal with this. I'll be here when you need me, and I'll be standing here when you swear you don't, anyway. If you're ready to go, we'll go. If not, then I won't."

She glanced to the open door, where both of her parents stood, looking just as nervous as they should.

"What time is the flight?" she repeated.

"I have tickets on a commercial flight at noon tomorrow," I answered.

"Commercial?" She quirked an eyebrow. "Slumming it with us normal people?"

I laughed. "All my extra money went to a private plane overseas. Now I'm on a budget until we figure out how to swing the circuit, since Pax's dad confirmed that he's only funding the documentary. You're worth it," I promised softly.

She looked away, and I wondered how long I had before she tried to bolt again. Heaviness settled in my stomach. Was there any way I would ever actually earn back her trust, or was I always going to be watching for her to run?

"Don't wait on me," she instructed, and I prayed she only meant for the X Games. "You can't afford it, and I won't be the reason you miss your medals. Not that you'd actually miss them."

I breathed through the spark of anger her words sent through my veins. What the hell did I have to do to prove to her that she was more important?

"I'm not leaving without you. I mean it," I said in the most serious tone I could muster without letting my absolute rage seep through. "Didn't Nepal prove that to you?" I'd given more than my pound of flesh, and I wasn't asking the same from her—just the tiniest glimmer of trust. How much more could I fucking take before I snapped on her and set us back when our relationship status was already so delicate?

"You did," she admitted. "But this is different. You won't let Wilder down. With Penna out, they need you."

"Well, I need *you*!" I put my hands over my face and took a deep breath. Then I tried to rein in the anger, the frustration, the terror that she'd walk into that house and her dad would somehow turn her against me permanently. "I love you, Rachel. You know that. And I'll wait for as long as you need me to, but I'm begging you to start giving me the benefit of the doubt. I can love you with everything I have in me, but I can't love you enough for the both of us. At some point you have got to stop taking hits at me just to see how far you can push before I'll leave. I'm not leaving, but I'm not sure you can say the same, and that scares the shit out of me."

She glanced away and then back to me, but after a minute of silence, I realized she wasn't going to respond.

"Your parents are waiting," I told her.

"Thank you for bringing me home," she said. "Why don't you just check us in for the flight. If I make it, then we'll go. If I'm not there, go without me."

My jaw flexed.

Before I could say something that would put us on the downward spiral, she kissed my cheek. "See you later."

I nodded as the love of my life stepped out of the hired car and took her bag from the driver. She didn't look back, not that I expected her to.

She still didn't believe that I'd be standing there if she did.

Chapter Thirty-Three

Los Angeles

The grandfather clock ticked its rhythmic beat behind me as I squared off against my parents in our living room. Scratch that—Mom's living room. Dad hadn't lived here for three months now.

"We're happy to see you, sweetheart," Mom said, crossing her legs and uncrossing them. "We've missed you so much."

I took the small envelope out of the back pocket of my backpack and put it on my lap. Then I looked at my father.

"When I was thirteen and I had to have a blood transfusion after that skiing accident where I cut open my leg, you told me that it was okay because it would be your blood, that it was a miracle we were the same blood type."

Dad shifted in his seat. "Yes. You recovered."

"It wasn't a miracle, was it?" I asked softly.

Mom's eyes widened to saucers. "Rachel, what are you

asking?"

I put the picture of my dad and Seo-yun on the coffee table between us and pushed it in his direction, never breaking our stare.

Mom gasped and covered her mouth.

Dad sagged in his chair, like I'd popped the balloon that kept him upright. Then he smiled. "It wasn't a miracle."

"Because you're my biological father," I said.

Mom whimpered while Dad's eyes watered. "Because I'm your biological father."

I'd already known that, but hearing him admit it felt like the last piece of the puzzle I'd been looking for fell into place. In that moment, it was Landon's voice in my head, telling me that maybe they'd kept the secret for so long because it had simply been *that* long.

"I have two questions."

"Of course," he said, his voice tight.

"Why the lie?"

My parents locked eyes, and I saw it then, the years of partnership, friendship, love, and parenthood that all passed within a glance. Dad nodded, and Mom took a deep breath.

"Because I was embarrassed. Not of you, Rachel. Never you…"

"Because you were married when it happened," I guessed. "I did the math. It happened right after Dad left Dartmouth and did his three years to appease his father. Right?"

Mom nodded, the movement causing a small cascade of tears down her cheeks. "We were on the rocks. We'd been married three years, and we'd just learned that I was infertile. Your dad went to Korea for a year, and I didn't know if we'd make it through."

"I didn't know about you," he told me. "Not until Mrs. Rhee called me from the orphanage saying that Seo-yun had died. At that point, your mom and I were falling apart—

I'd told her about the affair, and we were in the process of consulting lawyers about divorcing."

"But you didn't," I said, knowing that I had been what kept their marriage together. I looked at Mom. "You forgave him? With me?"

Her lip trembled. "Not at first. I yelled, I screamed, I cursed God that he could have a child when I couldn't, that his affair had given him the one thing I never would be able to. But…" She looked over at my dad.

"I couldn't raise you on my own, and she knew it," he continued. "I never stopped loving your mom. I can't regret what happened in Korea because we have you, but I begged her take me back—to take us—and she did."

Mom smiled at Dad and laughed a little. "I took him back because I loved him, and because more than anything, I wanted to be your mother."

My chest tightened, and I blinked back the tears that prickled at my eyes. "You are," I told her.

"I know, sweetheart. We agreed to work on our marriage and to bring you home. We didn't want rumors swirling around you…or, selfishly, us, so we said we'd adopted you, and as soon as we had your dad's papers in order, I officially adopted you." Her face crumpled for a second before she regained her composure. "I have loved you from the moment I held you. I have never wanted to hurt you. Not like this. I just…" Tears broke free, and she crossed her arms over her stomach. "I just didn't want you to look at me differently. To see Dad as yours, but me as a glorified stand-in."

I flew across the small space, hitting my knees and hugging her. "Never. You're my mom. Where I come from doesn't change that, and I didn't go on this search trying to replace you, because that would be impossible. Maybe I wanted to add another layer to my history, but Mom, you're the core. If anything, I love you more because you loved me when you didn't have to. You forgave something I'm not sure I could have and then loved me like I wasn't the evidence that it happened."

She held me tight, enveloping me in the scent of chocolate chip cookies and home—love. "We should have told you. I'm so sorry, Rachel."

"Don't be," I told her. "The benefits of finding this out while I was gone is that it gave me time to get over the shock and the anger of the lie. I just needed to understand it."

She pulled back, cupping my face and smiling through her tears. "The reason is that three people loved you more than anything, and we made some mistakes trying to protect you." She looked over to my dad. "And maybe the *we* part didn't turn out like we'd hoped, but you"—she looked back at me—"your strength, and your beauty, and your stubbornness... well, you're the best thing we've ever done. So don't be sad that we're over, or think that you failed to keep us together."

My mouth dropped open, and she just shook her head at me.

"I know how your mind works—I'm your mother. I need you to realize that you weren't the glue that kept us together, as much as our purpose. And now you're raised. You're a gorgeous, self-assured woman, and now we need to find what else we're meant for."

I nodded and hugged her, pulling her tight. Then I stood to find Dad already standing next to me and embraced him just as deep. I couldn't imagine the strength it had taken him to go back to her with me, for such a proud man to humble himself.

I couldn't equate this man with the same one who had torn me from Landon not just once, but twice.

"I love you, Rachel. You are what I'm most proud of in my life," he told me.

I nodded and pulled back. "And I love you. You've been

the driving force of my life, Dad. But I haven't forgiven you for Landon, and I don't know if I can. You protected me, did what you had to when I was a baby, but I'm a grown woman, and just as I'm not standing here judging you for an affair you had when you were twenty-four, you can't judge me for loving the kind of man you raised me around. If you didn't want me near extreme sports, then you should have chosen a different career. You don't get a say in who I love, and you don't get to sabotage the best thing that's ever happened to me because you don't approve."

"Rachel—" he started.

"I'm not done. You didn't just go after Landon; you went after the entire Renegade team. You blackballed them, killed every sponsorship opportunity, and potentially ruined careers and lives because I wouldn't follow your rules, because I dared to fall in love. What does that say about you? I don't know how to reconcile that the man who did that is the same man I've always looked up to."

"It was a business decision based on personal reasons."

"It was wrong."

Silence stretched between us, until he finally sighed. "I'll make some calls in the morning."

"That's a start."

"He turned down the Gremlin funding."

My heart skipped a beat, then swelled with the love that had never died when it came to Landon. "Yeah, I know. You were wrong about him."

He grimaced. "That remains to be seen..." He took a deep breath. "But if you insist, I will attempt to give him a second chance."

"Since you were the reason he screwed us up the first time."

He sighed.

"Dad, he's not the one in need of a second chance—you

are. And as much as I love you and understand that you were trying to protect me, if you ever try to come between us again, I will walk away from you without a backward glance."

He paled, swallowing hard. "I won't. I'll trust you to make your own choices."

"I'll believe it when I see it," I said softly.

"You will," he promised.

"I have one more question," I told him.

"Anything."

"Why can't you forgive Mom for doing the same exact thing you did?"

• • •

Mom handed me a cup of coffee as I sat up, blinking the sleep from my eyes. I was so tired I felt nauseous, thanks to a five a.m. bedtime.

Last night had turned into one epically long episode of *Dr. Phil*.

"You look like you need this."

"Thanks," I muttered, taking the cup from her and sipping carefully, praying the caffeine would hit straight to my veins. I needed to get to the airport early enough to not worry Landon.

One thing last night had taught me—forgiveness was earned and given. Maybe Dad hadn't earned it yet, but Landon more than had, and I'd yet to give it. It was time for me to step up and let him love me.

"We okay?" she asked, balancing on the edge of my bed.

"Yeah," I told her. We weren't fixed, and I wasn't sure we ever would be, but after a long night of talking, I felt like maybe we were on the right path. And if she and Dad figured their shit out, well, that was just a bonus.

"Good. Did you want to shop today? I know you're on a

tight schedule to get to Aspen tomorrow, but I'd love to sneak in some time with you," she said, her swollen eyes hopeful.

"Tomorrow? Mom, I'm leaving today…" The clock blinked at me. Eleven thirty a.m. *Holy shit.* "Mom, I'm so sorry. But I'm late. Oh my God. Landon."

"Today?" she asked.

"My alarm!" I shouted as I flung myself from the bed, tripping on the covers and falling headfirst onto the floor. My coffee spilled all over the comforter. *Great.*

"Oh, I turned it off. We were up so late, and you need your rest."

I gawked at her from the floor. "I'm going to miss the flight!"

"Oh," she said.

"Not *oh*, Mom. This is bad. So bad." My head swam. He was going to think that I stood him up—hadn't I basically challenged him last night? I'd already been so distant the last month. Hell, I hadn't been remotely nice since freaking Dubai, and now this.

I scurried into my clothes. "Phone. Is my phone on?"

"No, but you can use mine."

"I don't know his number!"

"Well, that's what these new cell phones do to you. When everything is in memory—"

"Mom! Not the time!" I said, firing up my iPad.

He was tagged at LAX but didn't show as online.

And I was still an hour away.

I sent a message to him and held my breath, nausea turning my stomach, but he didn't reply and the status showed *unseen.*

I sank to the floor. "I missed it. I can't possibly make it in time." I closed out the iPad. "I need to get to Aspen."

"Well, you're not going to get there by sitting on your butt and moping," she said, taking my now empty cup and standing. "Get your stuff together and let's figure something out."

An hour later, my phone had been turned on and I paced the floor while Mom looked at flights into Colorado.

I'd tried Landon at least three times, but he wasn't answering. Probably because he was in the air. Finally, I took a deep breath and called the one number I'd never thought I would again.

"Rachel?" I'd never been so relieved to hear Wilder's voice.

"Is he there yet?" I asked.

"What? Who?"

"Landon? Who else would I be calling you about?" I snapped.

"Someone's got her shitty attitude back."

"Wilder!"

He sighed. "No. He's not here. He called from LAX when you didn't bother to fucking show up for him and canceled his ticket. Now, thanks to you, he's missing the qualifications for the Big Air competition, which was the one he *didn't* medal in last year, so he doesn't get the automatic in."

Okay, now I felt like an even bigger shithead.

"I'm sorry. I slept through my alarm."

Wilder was silent.

"Wilder? Did you hear me?"

"Seriously?" he asked. "This isn't some test to see if he loves you? If he'll put you above everything? Because I'm pretty sure he just fucking proved it, and if that's the kind of shit you're going to put him through—"

"Will you stop fucking talking? How the hell does Leah put up with you? No, it's not some test. My mom turned off my alarm because we had a huge family thing last night and she didn't know I needed to catch a flight. That's it."

"Well, he's not here. Thanks to you."

"Can we move past that and discuss where he *is*?"

"Did you try his place?" Wilder asked.

I rubbed my forehead. "No, I thought the guards might laugh at me if I showed up asking about his whereabouts."

"Guards?"

"Yeah, those scary, armed dudes who stand outside the gates?"

Wilder laughed. "That's his parents' place. Not his."

Why hadn't I thought of that? "Okay, where is *his* place?"

"Oh, this is rich."

"Wilder! For fuck's sake!"

"Rachel!" Mom snapped at me as she came back into the room. "Language!"

I tried to inhale some patience with that breath. "What's his address, Wilder?"

He told me, and I blinked, then opened and shut my mouth. "Are you sure?"

"Yeah, that's not something I could forget. And apparently it wasn't something he could forget, either."

I hung up the phone, kissed my mom on the cheek. "I think I found him!"

"Good. I think I may have found the way to get you to Aspen."

"What?"

She told me her plan, and I was all smiles as I ran out the door. This might work! My chest tightened and threatened to explode with how much I loved that man. All the hell I'd put him through, every test, every snarky comment—he'd taken them all and waited for me.

And as I pulled up to his place, I realized he hadn't been waiting overnight for me to show up—he'd been waiting two and a half years.

Chapter Thirty-Four

LOS ANGELES

I threw a tennis ball at the wall and caught it repeatedly while the first qualifying round of the Big Air event played on the big screen in my living room.

I could still make my spot for the third round tonight if I left soon, but it would cost me the one thing I wasn't willing to give up: Rachel.

She'd missed the fucking plane.

What was I supposed to do with that? Was it her way of telling me we were over? That we had no chance? Did she think I'd go without her and prove her right?

My jaw tightened, and I threw the ball harder, catching it as it snapped back. Better the ball than the cell phone I'd pulverized an hour ago when our plane had taken off without us. She hadn't shown, her phone had gone straight to voicemail, and mine had gone straight into the arrival lane of traffic, where it had been unceremoniously run over by a taxi.

What if this was it? What if there really was no way to get through to her? No way to show her what she meant to me? What if everything had been in vain?

Questions fired through my brain faster than I could answer myself. I felt like I was on pause, waiting for the next time she'd hit play. I couldn't even settle on an emotion—they were all over the place. I was frustrated that she couldn't just fucking talk to me like every other girl on the planet. *She's not like any other girl on the planet—that's one of the reasons why you love her. Touché, brain.*

I was hurt that she hadn't shown, confused as to why. If I had to be honest, I was completely fucking pissed off that I hadn't warranted a phone call.

But none of that compared to the stark, empty feeling that immediately preceded the terror I tried to keep at bay. Rachel was my center, my gravity, the perfect balance to me in every way. She was the only woman I would ever love, and I couldn't picture my life without her now that I finally had her back.

I wanted our future.

What the fuck was I going to do if she didn't?

I couldn't live without her—couldn't go back to the empty shell I'd been before she'd shown up. My breaths came so quickly that I nearly looked for a paper bag to keep from hyperventilating.

Calm the fuck down.

It took a few minutes, but my breathing and heart rate came back to normal. I wished I could have said the same for my brain. It was on overdrive, trying to think of every possible scenario as to where Rachel could be.

Was she testing me? Just the thought of that sent another wave of anger through me.

The clock read a little after two p.m. The pizza I ordered

would be here any minute and then, after I'd gotten rid of the hangries, I'd go over to her house and make her see that I loved her. I'd hold a goddamned boom box over my head if that was what it took.

Yeah. That's what I'd do. I'd blare "Skinny Love" and let her be blown away that I still remembered her favorite movie and our favorite song…as soon as I figured out where the fuck to get a boom box.

The doorbell rang, rescuing me from my lame romantic plans, and I headed for the pizza that would save me from any more hunger-based dementia.

I grabbed a pen on my way so I could sign the receipt and opened the door. "Hey, there…" My mouth dropped to the floor. "Rachel?"

She looked edible in her jeans that were slightly ripped at the knee and vintage tee. "You live here?"

"Yeah," I said quietly, more stunned that she'd shown up to find me than the fact that she'd discovered the last secret I'd kept from her. "How did you know?"

"Wilder," she said, tucking her thumbs in her jeans.

"Right."

She looked at me expectantly. "Are you going to invite me in?"

I shook the cobwebs from my brain. "Yeah, of course." I opened the door to its full width, and she stepped inside, her eyes sweeping over the space and no doubt cataloging the changes I'd made in the last couple of years.

"They told me I had to find someone to take over the lease or pay the full year," she said, her voice quiet.

"Your dad called me. I told him I'd take care of it."

"He assumed you'd paid the lease fee."

"He assumed a lot of things about me. Most of them were wrong."

"Yeah, I'm picking up on that now," she said as she walked

into my kitchen—her kitchen—and ran her hand along the island counter. "These were Formica. And the apartment ended at that wall." She pointed to the wall my flat screen hung on.

"I bought the building. It's what I used that extra money for. Then I knocked a couple of the other units out."

Her eyes were wide, but she simply nodded. "I like the granite."

"You said you always wanted dark granite and white cabinets. But I remembered how much you loved the layout, so I didn't change it."

She leaned back against the island and looked up at me as I assumed the same position against the opposite counter. "I didn't stand you up."

"Didn't you?"

"I didn't mean to," she clarified. "We had this thing last night, and Mom turned off my alarm. I made the mistake of launching into them before I clarified my plans for the morning."

"That happens when you're confronting your parents about the secrets they keep."

"Familiar with that, are you?" she teased.

"I watch a lot of *Dr. Phil*," I admitted.

She outright laughed, and then her smile faded. "You missed the Big Air qualifications."

I shook my head and pointed to the TV. "I didn't miss them. I'm watching them right now." Hell, I'd miss the actual round I was slated for if it meant I got to keep her.

She swallowed, her eyes softening. God, that look…it gave me all kinds of hope, and that felt more dangerous than any trick I'd ever pulled. "That's not what I meant," she said.

"I know."

"Wilder's pissed."

"Wilder's pissed when anything doesn't go his way."

But my anger was diminishing with every breath I took, just knowing she was here.

She bit into her lower lip, and I crossed the distance between us. I gently pressed my thumb to her chin, urging her teeth to let go of the tender flesh.

"You stayed," she whispered.

"I did."

"You chose me."

"I always will."

She smiled, and my heart pounded, demanding things I was slightly scared to go for. I wanted her in my arms, her mouth on mine, her love and heart mine to claim. But more than that—I wanted her to want the same thing.

"Because you love me," she said.

"Because I love you," I promised.

"Good," she said. "Because I'm so in love with you that it hurts."

She leaned up for a kiss, and I moved away, even though it almost killed me to do it. "But do you trust me?" That was what it would always come down to between us, and as much as I wanted Rachel—needed her—I needed her trust more.

She met my gaze head-on, her eyes clear and steady. "With my life." She swallowed. "Enough that I had Dad extend a sponsorship offer to the Renegades."

Goddamn, I loved this girl. "You're not scared that I'm just using you for it? That I'll leave the minute he offers me more money?"

She shook her head. "I'm not. And I had him make the offer before I knew you hadn't left." She looked up at the light I knew she'd broken her arm trying to change. "Before I realized that you'd always loved me."

"I have," I promised her. "There was never a moment that I didn't love you. There will never be a moment that I don't love you. You can love me or not, but that will never change the way I belong to you."

This time when she launched at me, I caught her, filling my hands with her curves as her mouth met mine.

Hell yes.

Her tongue swept inside my mouth, and I gave her control for all of thirty seconds before I took it back, kissing her until she rocked against me, her legs wrapped around my waist.

"We don't have time," she gasped.

"We have all the time we want," I told her as I kissed a path down her neck. Two seconds with her ass in my hands and I was already hard—my body demanding hers.

"No, really," she said on a breathless sigh as I bit that place where her shoulder met her neck.

"What I have planned can't wait."

"But I can get us to Aspen."

"But I can get us to our bedroom," I told her as I carried her up the steps to the lofted area of the apartment. Fuck the qualifications. At that moment I needed her under me more than I needed another X Games medal.

"We don't have—"

I kissed her quiet and walked into the space I'd designed with her in mind. A few steps later I put her in the middle of our bed, then worked her out of her shoes, jeans, and shirt until she lay there in only her underwear.

"Did you know I've never had a woman here?" I asked.

"What?" she responded, leaning up on her elbows as I stripped.

"Never. Not once. Only on circuit or at parties, or at their place. I never brought anyone here, because it was ours. And maybe you wouldn't come back, but if there was even the slightest chance, I wanted to be able to say that I kept this for us. Only us."

I palmed my dick, stroking up and down the hard length while she watched, her eyes hazing with desire. If she licked her lips like that one more time, it was going to be over before I touched her.

She flipped around and crawled toward me on the bed, the very fantasy I'd always imagined while sleeping here. "And what did you want to do in here?" she asked, like she'd read my mind.

"This," I said, my only word of warning before I lifted her from the bed and kissed her, filling my hands with her ass, filling her mouth with my tongue.

My fingers found her wet and wanting, already slippery, and I groaned with the feeling of her. "God, Rachel, I don't know if I can wait."

"Then don't," she said, kissing my ear.

"Fuck, I don't have condoms," I growled.

"Didn't we already have this discussion?" she asked.

"I wasn't exactly expecting you to show up," I said, cursing my stupidity.

"Well, I did," she said. "Check my jeans."

I balanced her on the bed and picked up her jeans, finding a foil packet in her back pocket. "That might be the sexiest fucking thing I've ever heard," I said, ripping it open and rolling the condom on.

"I'm glad you approve."

I swept my fingers through her wetness and then pressed and swirled on her clit. Her knees buckled, and I caught her. "I approve of everything you do."

"More," she begged, and I willingly gave, beating back every instinct to bury myself inside her.

Instead I used my fingers to pump in and out of her as I stood her back up, teasing and tonguing the rigid peaks of her nipples. I wanted to do this for the rest of my life, and for the first time in forever, I felt like I might have a shot at that dream.

"Landon," she moaned, rocking against me, the sound of

her cry revving me even higher.

Her breaths came faster, her muscles tightened, and I knew she was close. God, I wanted to be there with her—needed to be inside her when she flew.

"I need you now," I warned her.

"Yes," she said.

It was all the permission I needed. Lifting her slightly, I slipped her thighs around my hips and held her ass as I slid inside her tight, welcoming warmth.

Fuck, she was so hot it felt like I was being branded in the best way possible.

Her ankles locked behind my back, and her arms looped around my neck as she met me in a ravenous kiss. I lifted her up and down, using my body to stroke hers to completion.

She cried out every time I dropped her slightly, letting gravity help me take her deeper, and when it wasn't deep enough, I leaned her against the wall next to my bed and began a rhythmic pounding that had her keening in my ear for more. Harder. Deeper.

Of course I was ecstatic to oblige.

But I held back just enough to keep her on edge, and even though she arched against me, knowing how to take her own pleasure, I denied her that tiny bit of friction she needed.

"Landon!" she cried out in frustration.

"Tell me you love me," I demanded.

"I love you," she told me in pants of her breath against my lips, our foreheads pressed together.

"Tell me this is forever. You and me. Always."

"Forever." She gasped as I swirled inside her, hitting her clit. "Always."

I kissed her with stark relief and passion, then changed our angle to give her everything she needed, thrusting until she came apart in my arms. She clamped down on me as she came, squeezing me like a vise, her head thrown back in the most gorgeous display of ecstasy I'd ever seen.

She pulled me over with her, and I came with a shout, her name a prayer on my lips.

Our breathing was ragged as I backed up to the bed, collapsing until she lay against my chest.

"We. Really. Have. To. Go," she said, every word between a breath.

"I had more fun when you were coming," I teased.

She smacked my chest. "Get up and let me show you how much I love *you*."

That was an offer I couldn't refuse, and within twenty minutes we'd dressed and headed out the door. I paid the pizza guy on our way out, and she fed me bites of a slice as we headed toward the airport, my hangries long forgotten.

"There's not another flight out today," I told her.

"Trust me," she said sweetly, using my words against me. As we got closer, she changed her orders. "Turn here."

"This is the private airport," I said.

"Yep," she answered.

I followed her directions until we pulled onto the landing strip. "Is that…?"

"My dad," she answered.

Fuck. My. Life.

I parked the car where she directed and pulled both of our bags from the trunk. "Mr. Dawson," I said as we approached him.

He'd ditched the stiff suit in favor of jeans and a Patagonia vest.

"Mr. Rhodes. My daughter tells me I've misjudged you."

I wrapped my arm around Rachel, who tucked into my side like she'd always been there. "In some ways, sir. In others, I was exactly what you thought."

He nodded. "That's fair. She tells me that you need to get to Aspen, and I happen to be headed to the X Games for the company. Want a lift?"

I stood dumbstruck for a second until Rachel poked me in the ribs. "What do you say? Want to take your curse for a little spin in Aspen?" she asked, wiggling her eyebrows.

I shook my head and kissed her, uncaring that her dad watched us. I was never going to hide my love for this woman again. Ever.

"No. But I sure as hell want to take my lucky charm."

She grinned, and I lost my heart all over again when her nose crinkled. "Then I guess we'd better get going. You've got medals to win."

I agreed with her, but only so she'd get her butt on the plane.

I'd always felt like there were two sides of me when it came to this sport, and I still couldn't figure out how I'd found a woman who could love both.

As Nova, I'd win those medals, hit the ridgelines, smile for the cameras, and win the glory. I was unstoppable with her next to me.

But as Landon, I knew the truth: medals were nice, but I'd already won something so much more precious than gold—Rachel's love.

Can't get enough of The Renegades?

Turn the page to read an excerpt from *Rebel*.

The woman I can't get out of my head is the one I can never have.

I'm the youngest professor on this campus,

And that woman just walked into my class.

Chapter One

LAS VEGAS

That kid was still staring.

I stood in the lobby of the Bellagio, scanning through my text messages, blatantly ignoring most of them, but when I looked up, the gangly, mid-teenage boy was still gawking. The kid was wearing a Fox Motocross hat and a shirt from the Nitro Circus World Games, and judging by the way he was glancing from me to his phone and back again, he knew who I was.

Luckily, my phone went off, making it easy to ignore the fact that he was probably tweeting out my location right now.

Great.

Little John: ARRANGEMENTS ARE MADE.

Penna: THANK YOU. OUT FRONT IN FIFTEEN?

Little John: I STILL THINK THIS IS A SHIT IDEA.

Penna: I'LL BE SURE TO NOTE THAT.

I slid my phone into the back pocket of my jeans as the kid headed in my direction, glancing to see where his parents were in the check-in process.

"Excuse me?" His voice cracked.

"What's up?" I asked with a smile.

"I know this is probably stupid, but are you…Rebel?"

Busted.

"Sure am." I forced the muscles in my face to maintain the curve to my lips.

The kid's eyes went wide, and my smile turned genuine. "I love you." He turned ten shades of red. "I mean, I love watching you. Oh crap. I'm not a stalker or anything."

Laughter gently shook my shoulders. "Don't worry. I absolutely knew what you meant."

A couple selfies later, the kid was on cloud nine.

"Do me a favor?" I asked him as I signed his hat.

"Anything."

"Can you wait a couple hours until you post that on social media? It's really important." I knew the kid might do it anyway, but I felt better having a promise.

"Yeah. Sure. No problem!" He gave me an enthusiastic head nod.

"Thanks." I handed him back the hat as his parents approached.

I had already turned to walk toward the bar when he called out.

"Rebel, does this mean you're back?"

"We're about to find out," I told him just before I slipped out of view.

It always floored me when I was recognized in public, that we'd somehow gotten famous enough for that stuff, but this time felt different. Maybe it was because I was off on my own for the first time—without Pax, or Landon, or Nick… or Brooke. Maybe it was because I hadn't participated in a Renegade stunt in the last three months.

No. That wasn't it. It was because the kid managed to know me when I was having trouble recognizing myself anymore.

Rebel. I'd earned the nickname early, seeing as I never conformed to the societal norms my parents expected for a little girl. Motocross bikes, snowboards, parachutes, bungee lines, those became my dollhouses. The X Games took the place of cotillion. I bucked every trend, and gold-medaled in the Whip, which, up until me, had been a guy-only event. Instead of joining the Junior League, I gave in to my addiction for adrenaline and extreme sports, founding the Renegades with three of my closest friends who became my brothers. The number one way to get me to do something was to tell me that I couldn't. I rebelled.

But this time was different.

This time, I was rebelling against my friends—going off book.

The noise from the casino assaulted my ears as I headed toward the bar where Patrick said he'd meet me. My flowy tank top and skinny jeans paired with black Vans weren't exactly the norm in the bar, but I was used to sticking out.

A quick scan of the room told me Patrick wasn't here

yet, so I headed toward the bar, leaning against its granite top.

"Can I help you?" the bartender asked.

"Ice water with lemon, please," I ordered, sliding into the chair.

"Coming right up," she said and left to fill the order.

"Living dangerously?" A deep, slightly accented voice asked from next to me.

I turned toward him and nearly sucked in my breath reflexively. *What a killer smile.* The guy was gorgeous in a can't-help-but-stare kind of way, with thick black hair cut military short, deep, chocolate-brown eyes, tanned skin, and a grin that had me leaning against the bar in hope that it would catch the drool no doubt pouring from my mouth. Dimples and… *Oh my fucking arm porn.* The sleeves of his dress shirt were rolled up, hinting at the tantalizing lines of his bicep. My stomach clenched, the first physical reaction I'd had to spotting a hot guy in *years.*

He cocked an eyebrow at me, that smile turning sexy, deadly—he was more than aware of his impact on me, but it came across as playful instead of the cocky, sleazy way I was used to. I let loose a grin of my own and shook my head at myself. I was constantly surrounded by hot, scrumptious, defined men, and here I was losing my shit over a stranger in a bar.

A stranger who didn't know me, what I did, or what had happened to me in the last three months.

"I'm Cruz," he said, turning on his barstool to face me fully.

"I'm Pen—Penelope." My full name sounded odd, since I always went by Penna. But I wasn't Penna tonight. Or

Rebel. Hell, I didn't know who I was.

"Penelope," he repeated, caressing my name with his accent.

Never mind, it sounds delicious when he says it. What was that? Spanish? Not quite, but it was just as sexy.

"You're not drinking tonight?" he asked, running his thumb down his still-full glass. No wedding ring.

I thanked the bartender and put a five on the bar as she handed me my lemon water, then turned back to Cruz. "Nope. Need a clear head."

One of his black eyebrows rose. "Underage?"

"Wouldn't you like to know?" *Are you flirting?* I didn't flirt. Ever. Maybe for the cameras and the crowds, but never on a personal level.

"I would," he said, leaning forward.

Acknowledgments

First and foremost, my undying gratitude goes to my Heavenly Father, who blesses me beyond measure with more than I could ever deserve.

Thank you, Jason, for not just pushing me toward my dream when things are going right, but for pulling me from the darkness when things go so unbelievably wrong. Your unwavering faith in me is what makes this possible on every level. Thank you for every time you get up before me... okay, okay...*every* day...to make the boys' lunches, for every folded load of laundry, for every time you get them to hockey practice so I can squeeze in another hour. I couldn't imagine a better partner for my life. Also, you seem to only get hotter with age.

Thank you to our kids—you guys have such gorgeous souls and you don't even know it. Thank you for every time you've been patient with me when my office door is closed, and thank you for every time you barge in and remind me that what matters in life isn't what happens in this office but what goes on outside. You are my world, my reason, and my everything.

Thank you, Mom and Dad, for understanding when I'm a grouch on deadline and not rolling your eyes at my constant procrastination. Thank you, Kate, for simply being you. Everyone should be as lucky to have a sister as close as we are. Thank you, Emily, for the last twenty years of being my best friend. Here's to another twenty.

Thank you to my amazing editor, Karen. This one, more than any other book we've worked on together, is here because you are always so incredibly patient with me. Plus, you have an amazing talent for digging out what I really meant to say. Thank you for always demanding the best—you truly make me a better writer, and I couldn't imagine doing this without you. Huge thanks to the entire Entangled team, Liz, Melanie, Jessica, Brittany, Candy, and Curtis—you guys are simply amazing. To my incredible publicist, Melissa, thank you for guarding my sanity and being there no matter what. Now if you only killed the spiders in my house, life would be absolutely perfect.

Thank you, Allison, for running my group with such joy and enthusiasm. Thank you, Linda, for chasing every squirrel that comes your way. Best signing partner ever…just don't tell Jason. Huge thanks to my phenomenal agent, Louise Fury—I can't think of anything more comforting than when you tell me, "I've got you," and I know that you do. Thank you for never sleeping so that I can…but seriously, you should sleep at some point.

Thank you to the incredible authors who are also some of my closest friends. Molly Lee, there are no words, but I know that you know. Gina-freaking-Maxwell and Cindi Madsen, thank you for making "fetch" happen and reminding me when to wear pink. Jay Crownover, you might be the best neighbor ever. Sorry there's no beach—ahem—scene in this one, but I'll hook you up on the next one. Lisa, Michelle V.,

Kristy, Lauren, Laurelin, Alessandra, Christine, Claire, and Rose, thank you for always being there when I have ludicrous questions. Mandi, Heidi, Isabelle, and the rest of the TBR group, thank you for amazing chat sessions that constantly allow me to procrastinate. Katrina, you are a goddess. Lizzy, Jenn, Kennedy, you gals are such class acts. The bloggers who work so hard to promote, review, and support authors. You guys are my rock stars: Aestas, Natasha T., Natasha M., Wolfel, Kimberly, my love—Jillian Stein, Jen, Reanell, Lisa and Milasy, Angie, Beth and Ashley, and the countless others I can't fit here. If I've forgotten you, please forgive me and my sleep-deprived brain. Liz Berry, thank you for taking a chance on me and always making me feel extraordinary.

My Flygirls…you guys…you're everything.

Lastly, thank you again to my husband. You fill our lives with such amazing moments, such joy and love in every ordinary minute that our life has become something truly extraordinary. No matter what happens in this life, my favorite title will always be Mrs. Yarros.

**Love a Rebecca Yarros book boyfriend?
Come and meet Xaden Riorson.**

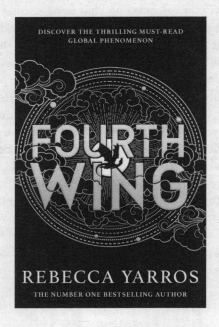

**Dive into the global phenomenon,
Fourth Wing, today.**

'This book contains an addictive, drug like essence
that will make you relinquish all responsibility until
the very last word. Do not say I didn't warn you'
GLAMOUR

Available now

PIATKUS

JOIN OUR SQUAD

CADETS, SIGN UP TO OUR
NEWSLETTER AND KEEP AN EYE
ON OUR SOCIAL CHANNELS FOR
OFFICIAL CORRESPONDENCE
FROM THE EMPYREAN